THE VIRGIN'S GUIDE
TO *Misbehaving*

JESSICA CLARE

BERKLEY SENSATION, NEW YORK

THE BERKLEY PUBLISHING GROUP
Published by the Penguin Group
Penguin Group (USA) LLC
375 Hudson Street, New York, New York 10014

USA • Canada • UK • Ireland • Australia • New Zealand • India • South Africa • China

penguin.com

A Penguin Random House Company

THE VIRGIN'S GUIDE TO MISBEHAVING

A Berkley Sensation Book / published by arrangement with the author

Berkley Sensation Books are published by The Berkley Publishing Group.
BERKLEY SENSATION® is a registered trademark of Penguin Group (USA) LLC.
The "B" design is a trademark of Penguin Group (USA) LLC.

For information, address: The Berkley Publishing Group,
a division of Penguin Group (USA) LLC,
375 Hudson Street, New York, New York 10014.

ISBN: 978-0-425-26237-5

PUBLISHING HISTORY
Berkley Sensation mass-market edition / June 2014

PRINTED IN THE UNITED STATES OF AMERICA

10 9 8 7 6 5 4 3 2 1

Cover photo by Lóránd Gelner/Getty Images.
Cover design by Lesley Worrell.
Interior text design by Tiffany Estreicher.

For my mom, who had the thankless task of strapping a sulky child into a Boston brace every morning and was at my side every moment of my "fun" scoliosis journey, right on through surgery. I think we ended up all right.

ONE

There were days, Elise Markham decided, when the world seemed to be hideously unfair.

If the world was fair, she wouldn't have been born with that awful port-wine stain on her entire left cheek. It didn't matter that she'd had it lasered away in her teen years. When she looked in the mirror, she could swear she still saw traces of it there, discoloring her from jaw to brow. And if she saw it, so did everyone else. If the world was fair, karma wouldn't have then turned around and slapped her with scoliosis during puberty that involved wearing a bulky back brace and made her even more of a social misfit.

If the world was fair, that would have been enough and she wouldn't have had to go through the other awful things teenage girls did, like pudgy thighs and pimples and braces. But she had. She'd endured those things and then some.

All of which had told Elise by the age of thirteen that the world wasn't fair, and she needed to stop wishing it was.

Because, if the world was fair? Her new friends would not be trying to set her up on a blind date.

"What about that really quiet, tall officer?" Miranda asked, raising her margarita glass and licking the salt from the rim. "The one who's the sheriff's son. He's not bad looking. He gave me a ticket last month for speeding and I thought he was kind of cute. In a law-officer sort of way."

Miranda and Brenna sat across from Elise in a cozy booth at Maya Loco, the only restaurant in tiny Bluebonnet. Beth Ann was at the bar, getting a refill on her drink and chatting with a friend. It was busy in the restaurant, the noisy hum of voices and clinking forks making it difficult to hold a quiet conversation.

Not that it stopped the women she was seated with. At her side in the booth, Brenna shook her head. She twirled her short red mixing straw in her drink as she spoke. "He hooked up with that weird blogger chick. Emily's sister. You're a few months too late."

"Oh. Rats." Miranda screwed up her face. "I know this is a small town, but Jesus. There have to be some hot, eligible men around here."

"It's really okay," Elise said, but her voice was so quiet beneath the din of the restaurant happy hour that she wasn't sure anyone heard her. "I don't need to date."

"I stole the last hottie," Brenna said with a sly grin. She winked at Elise and adjusted her purple bangs on her forehead. "Lucky for me he's into tattoos and kinky sex."

Elise made a face at the same time Miranda did. "Um."

"That's her brother, you sicko," Miranda said. "Gross."

"Doesn't matter. He's hot. Those uptight clothes and frumpy glasses? Mmm." Brenna fanned her face. "Great big cock—"

"Still her brother," Miranda said.

Elise nodded. Brenna was weird. Sweet, but weird. No one could predict the things that came out of her mouth, so it was best for Elise to just sit back and let someone else correct Brenna when she spouted off. Not that Elise would ever say something to hurt Brenna's feelings—her brother's fiancée was strange, but Elise thought she was great. Brenna marched to the beat of her own drum—she wore old T-shirts and ill-fitting clothing more often than not. Actually, most of the time it was Grant's clothing, which was odd to see. But her uptight, once-lonely workaholic brother worshipped Brenna, and for that, Elise adored her as well.

"There's got to be someone," Miranda muttered.

"Someone for what?" Beth Ann slid into the booth next to Elise.

Self-conscious at the appearance of the statuesque blonde, Elise straightened, careful to raise one shoulder above the other so it wouldn't look like she was slumping. Adolescent scoliosis had made her incredibly aware of her posture, and she was constantly self-correcting and hoping no one else noticed. Of her three new friends, Beth Ann was the most intimidating. Miranda was pretty but scholarly. Brenna was cheery and strange, and dressed like a slob. But Beth Ann? Beth Ann was completely perfect, from her delicately mani-cured nails to her faint tan in November and her immaculate blond hair. She was also dressed in a dainty gingham dress topped with a matching cardigan and slingbacks.

She was intimidating, all right. But Beth Ann was also the sweetest person that Elise knew, and she was going to be her partner in a new business venture, provided Elise decided to stay in Bluebonnet. But . . . she hadn't decided yet.

"A man for Elise to date," Miranda offered, delicately licking a large grain of margarita salt off of one finger. "Since we're all paired up, we thought it might be a good idea to find Elise a man, too."

Elise shook her head and whispered, "I really don't—"

Miranda snapped her fingers, cutting off Elise's thoughts. "I know! What about one of Colt's brothers?"

"Oh, honey, no," Beth Ann said in her sweet drawl. "Berry's the only one close to her age and he's not right for her. At all."

Brenna leaned across the table toward Elise and gave her a mock-conspiratorial whisper. "Colt's brothers are all named after guns. Berry's short for Beretta. It's all very redneck."

"Honey," Beth Ann said again. "She knows that. She grew up here, remember?" Of the four women at the table, only Brenna wasn't originally from Bluebonnet.

"Actually, I don't know them all that well," Elise said in a small voice. "I went to boarding school as soon as I was old enough." And she'd never left the house much before that, too ashamed of the gigantic purple mark that had disfigured her cheek. Even now, she had to fight the urge to drag her long hair over that side of her face to hide it. "But it's okay." She did remember hearing Grant's stories about Colt's poor-as-dirt family while she was growing up. Not that she was a snob, but when even Colt didn't want to associate with his family, it was bad.

Beth Ann patted Elise's hand. "We'll find you a good guy, honey. Don't you worry. I have a few single clients. Let me think."

God, she didn't want anyone. Or rather, no one would want her. But her friends seemed determined to find her someone to date, which made her want to cringe and hide. She felt like a charity case, which only made things worse. *Our poor ugly, shy friend can't find a man? We'll just have to find one for her.*

The worst part was that she knew they meant well; but it still hurt. It hurt that she was ungainly and unattractive enough to have to resort to charity. Being single and alone was so much easier. No hopes to get up. "I don't really want to date right now, Beth Ann," Elise said in a low, soft voice. "I just don't think—"

"Nonsense," Brenna interrupted. "You just sit in your room every night over at the bed-and-breakfast unless we drag you out. That's not healthy."

"That's not true," Elise protested, then bit her lip. Okay, so it was a little true. "Sometimes I go out and take photos." But only at times when she wouldn't risk running into too many of the nosy, well-meaning people of Bluebonnet. People who would stop and try to have a *conversation* with her.

Elise wasn't good with conversations. Actually, she wasn't good with small talk, period.

"You don't want to date?" Miranda looked crestfallen. "Really?"

It wasn't that Elise didn't, exactly. She wasn't the type that guys dated. And she was getting up toward the age that it was starting to become weird. Never dated by twenty-four? You're clearly a freak. She didn't know how to date, how to make out, anything. It was easier to just eschew it entirely. "I'm concentrating on business right now," she said. "And besides, like Beth Ann said, I grew up here. There's no one in town who interests me. No one here is my type."

"So what's your type?" Brenna wanted to know.

Her tongue felt glued to the roof of her mouth. Should she lie? She was a terrible liar. Really, the only thing she was excellent at was taking photos and avoiding people. But admitting her type would make it pretty obvious who she liked. More than liked, really. She had a schoolgirl crush on a man who was sexy, covered in tattoos and piercings, and rode a motorcycle.

But only one man in Bluebonnet matched that description. So Elise said nothing, because speaking would have betrayed her thoughts, and she had no desire to be humiliated like that. She simply shrugged her shoulders.

"Do you like tall men?" Brenna prompted. "Short men with a coke-can dick?"

"Let it go," Beth Ann said, coming to Elise's defense with a laugh. "If Elise doesn't want someone in town, I can't say I blame her."

"We could always get her an out-of-towner," Miranda said with a sly glance in her direction. At her side, Brenna gave a chortle and elbowed her, then nodded in the distance.

Beth Ann and Elise turned.

Coming across the crowded restaurant, beer in hand, was

none other than the object of Elise's crush, Rome Lozada. *Oh no.* Elise immediately turned away, feeling her face turn a bright, beet red that would make the remains of the old stain darken on her face. *Please, no.*

Oblivious to Elise's distress, Brenna waved a hand. "Rome! Hey! Come sit with us!"

Elise whimpered in her throat. Luckily, the restaurant was too noisy for it to be overheard. She stared down at her iced tea, unable to work up the courage to lift it to her mouth, lest someone notice her movements. Maybe Rome was meeting friends and wouldn't be sitting with them.

To her dismay, he came and stood at the end of their table. "Ladies." He gave them a gorgeous smile, and Elise felt her pulse flutter. No man should be that pretty. "Am I interrupting girls' night out?" He glanced at their group, and his gaze seemed to linger on Elise. "Hey, Bo Peep."

She averted her gaze, staring at her drink. With a quick shift of her chin, her hair fell forward. "Hi." His nickname was so embarrassing. He called her that because he said she looked lost. She was pretty sure that was supposed to be an insult, wasn't it?

"We're just trying to find Elise a man," Miranda said, a hint of slurring in her voice. Too many margaritas for her. "You know of any good pieces of man-meat?"

"Other than yourself," Brenna said, and gave him a wicked, lascivious look. "You're the best man-meat we have in town. Other than all the ones that are taken, of course."

"Am I?" Rome laughed at Brenna's outrageous comments. "Maybe I should volunteer to be Elise's man-meat, then."

Elise wanted to crawl under the table. She shrank down, just a little, and kept staring at her glass. Was he really volunteering to date her? Or just humoring a tipsy Brenna? Was this a suggestion born out of pity? That would be just awful. Elise's throat felt knotted in embarrassment. No one as gorgeous as Rome Lozada would even look in her direction, except for the fact that her well-meaning friends were trying to coerce him into asking her out. Ugh.

"Brenna," Beth Ann said in a chiding voice. "Be nice." Elise felt Beth Ann shift in the booth, turning toward Rome. "What these two drunks aren't telling you is that Elise isn't interested in dating anyone in town. There's no one who's Elise's type. She's already said so, but these ladies won't take no for an answer."

Oh god! Now Beth Ann had just told Rome that he wasn't her type and she didn't like him. That was either a blessing or the worst thing ever.

"That so?" Rome gave a hard-sounding chuckle. "Guess Elise is too picky for the likes of me, then."

She wanted to protest, or apologize, but the words wouldn't form.

"Now, now," Brenna called, and Elise glanced over at her long enough to see her reaching out and patting Rome's tattooed arm. "Don't be sad. I'm sure you're other women's type. Just not Elise's." She leaned in and whispered loudly, "You probably talk too much."

Miranda snorted and drank again.

"You ladies sound like you're enjoying your drinks," Rome said, voice cool. "I take it you have a designated driver?"

That was her. Elise raised her hand, not looking up.

Rome made a noise of approval. "Well, I'll leave you be, then. Enjoy your drinks. See you at work tomorrow, Brenna."

"Bye, man-meat," Brenna called after him. Miranda dissolved into giggles. Beth Ann only sighed at their antics.

Elise had been nursing a crush on Rome for a few weeks now. She'd stayed overnight at the Daughtry Ranch when she'd first come in to town, visiting her brother, Grant. Her brother and two of his friends from high school, Dane and Colt, had started a survival expedition business where they took businessmen and school groups out in the wild and showed them how to survive. They ran it all out of a big ranch on the outskirts of town, and there was a big lodge that doubled as a rec room and office for the business.

Elise had crashed on one of the couches one night and woken up to see Rome Lozada staring down at her. She'd immediately become flustered because the man was utterly, insanely delicious, and he'd simply laughed and called her Bo Peep. She'd been totally tongue-tied around him.

That hadn't changed in the last two weeks, unfortunately. She was still tongue-tied around him.

Elise watched a droplet of condensation slide down the front of her glass, wishing she were back in her nice, safe room at the bed-and-breakfast. Rome Lozada, the hottest man that Elise had ever seen, thought she was a snob and too good for the men in Bluebonnet.

Yep. That clinched it. The world was definitely not fair.

Elise stared at the email rejection in her inbox, wondering if it was possible to have your heart broken through a message. If so, hers had just been pounded into smithereens.

While it's a great idea, Crissy had written, *I'm afraid that I'm not a big fan of the photographs. There's something missing in them. There's no life, no energy. I hate to say it, but they read like they were taken by a teenager, not a grown woman. I know you've been working hard at finding the right thing for the magazine, but this isn't it, either. I keep coming back to the feeling that your pictures are a little too safe and unmemorable. It's like . . . there's not enough life experience and it shows in the photos. I'd love to have you take a year off, go out and live a little, and then come back with a fresh, bolder perspective.*

Professionally, Elise knew it was great feedback and an encouraging response.

Personally . . . it hurt.

She'd been friends with Crissy since college, when they'd both taken journalism classes. Elise had steered toward photojournalism while Crissy had gone more toward the editorial side, but they'd remained friends even after graduation, and had vowed to work together on a future project. Crissy had been working for a popular women's magazine for the last few years, and Elise had submitted a few concepts for photo spreads, but each time they were rejected with the same sort of commentary.

Lifeless.

Something missing.

Not quite what we're looking for.

Unmemorable.

Not enough life experience.

How the heck did something like that show in her photographs? Elise didn't understand. Her photos were gorgeous—not that she was biased, of course. They were crisp, the colors were good, but when she looked at them again, she had to agree: something was missing.

She just didn't know what that something was.

Frustrated, Elise opened up Photoshop and stared at the pictures she'd sent to Crissy, trying to determine what was wrong. They were photos she'd taken a week or so ago of Rome Lozada, he of the gorgeous body and even more gorgeous face. He looked delectable, of course. Nothing could make that man look bad. In the photo, he was covered in mud and his skin was gleaming with beaded droplets of water. He looked insanely good and her heart ached just gazing at him.

But like Crissy said, there was something off in the photo. It wasn't Rome. It wasn't the scene. It was just . . . Elise didn't know. Heck, if she knew, she'd be able to fix the issue.

Unable to come to a conclusion, she flicked her mouse and Photoshopped a crayon-like smile on Rome Lozada's face.

Take that.

Considering the picture, she played with a couple of editing filters and ended up elongating his crotch to a ridiculous length, just because it made her laugh. *The things we go through to feel better about our work,* she mused to herself.

She set the modified picture as her computer desktop background just to amuse herself, and then sighed in frustration. She'd been hoping that photo shoot would lead to a layout, and that layout would be her big break. It would have also given her yet another chance to see Rome Lozada, shirtless and sexy.

More than anything, it would have been her chance to prove herself.

Unfortunately, Elise was getting nowhere fast. She had a backup business in mind with Beth Ann—pinup photography. But Beth Ann wouldn't be back for several weeks, as she'd gone to Alaska on her honeymoon with Colt just yesterday. So while the pinup photography would be fun, it was on hold at the moment. She needed Beth Ann for hair and make-up and for dealing with people. She couldn't do it on her own.

So Elise was more or less at odds and ends until she had a new project. She could return home with her parents, but the thought of doing that made her unhappy. She wanted to make something of herself.

She was tired of living at home. She was twenty-four years old. She'd been out of college for two years now, and she was still only freelancing for the occasional family photo.

Her parents wanted her to relax and take a break, since the photography was stressful. That was the problem with her parents. They sheltered her and thought she was fragile. Maybe she had been at one point, but she was an adult now, and she was tired of being protected from the world.

She needed to see things with new eyes.

How, she had no idea. Elise wasn't good at jumping out of the box.

But . . . Brenna was. Elise considered this and then grabbed the keys to her rental car. Brenna would have ideas. Sure, they'd be insane ideas, but maybe she could sift through the crazy stuff and find a decent one that would be a start.

To Elise's chagrin, the tiny parking lot at Wilderness Survival Expeditions was nearly full. She squeezed her rental into one of the back parking spaces in the gravel lot and then cautiously made her way toward the main cabin. Out on the front lawn, Dane Croft stood with a pack looped over one shoulder. Four men were lined up in front of him, all dressed in wilderness gear. They had no packs, and one had painted his face with camouflage and seemed to be devouring every word that Dane said.

They glanced over at her as she headed for the doorstep, and Elise self-consciously shrank back a bit.

Dane gave her a quick wave. "Hey there. We were just heading out." He nodded at the men in front of him. "You guys ready?"

"Ready," they chorused.

Dane nodded at her and then gestured for the men to follow him, and they took off across the grass in quick, eager footsteps.

Elise watched them leave, then headed into the main log cabin. Wilderness Survival Expeditions used to be a ranch, she had been told by her brother, Grant. An emu ranch, of all things. The main "house" of the business looked like an enormous log cabin, complete with rustic kitchen and enormous stone fireplace. Scattered around the parking lot were a handful of personal cabins where the instructors lived. They were all childhood friends of her brother . . . well, except for the newest one, Rome.

The hottest, most delicious, newest one, she thought. Elise sighed as she entered the cabin, biting her lip. Part of her wanted to open the door and see Rome, and part of her dreaded running into him.

But when she went in, only Brenna was seated at her

desk, and Elise felt a pang of disappointment. No hot, vaguely scary guy to gawk at.

"Hey," Brenna said, waving cheerily at Elise. She had her new puppy in her hands and forced the puppy to wave a paw. "What brings you here this morning? You come to hang out?"

Elise smiled at her brother's fiancée and sat down in the chair across from her desk. "I was a little bored and thought I'd come and see about taking some photos. The light is great today."

"Working? Barf." Brenna nuzzled her puppy. "No one's really working today. Isn't that right, Gollum?"

Elise tactfully refrained from pointing out that Brenna was, in fact, at work, and seated at her work desk. "Where's Grant?"

"Sleeping in. I wore him out." She gave Elise a wickedly smug smile. "I wouldn't ask questions if I were you."

"Um. Okay. I don't think I want to know more."

"So how goes the man hunt?" Brenna looked excited. "It's been a week. You score yet?"

"Man hunt?" Elise shook her head, feeling the hot flush creep up her cheeks. "I'm not looking for a man." But even as she said it, a flurry of images flashed through her mind. Rome Lozada, shirtless and muddy. Crissy's email. Not enough life in her pictures.

"What about those beefcakes that Dane just took into the woods? We could always call them back for a minor emergency and send you off with them." Brenna gave her an encouraging look and wagged her eyebrows. "That's how Miranda met Dane, remember?"

"Um, I don't think any of them were my type," Elise said in a soft voice. One had camo on his face and looked as if he'd want to skip the camping phase and go right to the skinning of animals.

"You're so picky. No one's your type, according to you." Brenna kissed her puppy's wrinkly forehead.

Elise gave her a faint smile. She wanted to ask Brenna

how she could get more life experience—Brenna would know more than anyone.

But there was something that held her back. Maybe because Brenna was distracted this morning by the puppy? Maybe because she'd run into a few men on the way in and that had set her on edge?

She realized that anything she asked Brenna would be innocently blurted back out to her brother, Grant, and right now she didn't want to have to deal with it. She could just imagine the pitying looks that Grant would send her way. His poor, fragile baby sister.

She was so tired of being the delicate flower everyone had to protect.

Mentally, she squashed her idea of asking Brenna about ways to get life experience. She'd simply have to think of something on her own.

"So whatcha working on?" Brenna asked. "More pinups?"

She shook her head. "Not until Beth Ann gets back. I have the keys to her salon, but no appointments set up. We still don't even have a website." And if she wanted to be honest, the pinups were fun if Beth Ann was there. By herself, she couldn't really do hair and makeup. She didn't have the skill. "I thought I'd see if you guys needed pictures for the paintball brochures."

"Probably," Brenna said, cuddling her puppy against her chest. "Sounds kind of boring to me."

"I don't mind it," Elise said, watching Brenna play with the puppy's ears. It was like trying to keep the attention of a two-year-old. How on earth did she not drive ever-so proper, work-oriented Grant insane? "Is it okay if I go ahead and head out to look at the grounds?"

"Sure," Brenna said. "I'll stay here in case Grant wakes up and wants me to work. Or did you want company?"

"No, I'm fine. I know where it is. Thank you, though."

"Have fun."

Chickening out, Elise shouldered her camera bag and headed out of the lodge.

The day was a great one for photos. The skies were bright but overcast, ensuring that any photos she took wouldn't be a mess of shadows. There was a hint of a chill in the air, but Elise tugged the sleeves of her old sweatshirt down over her bare hands to warm them. The breeze scattered the leaves, and she watched it for a minute, then decided that it would be good for the picture. She could always take new ones in the spring if she was still in Bluebonnet.

Not that she had a reason to be. She was just drifting, in between everything, at home nowhere.

She hated that. But if she set down roots in Bluebonnet, she'd need a reason to keep hanging around. The Wilderness Survival Expeditions business was too small to need a photographer on hand at all times. Beth Ann already had her hands full with her salon. Elise didn't have a home here, or a car. Or anyone that she could say she was staying for.

There was Grant, but Grant had Brenna. The last thing he needed was his pathologically shy sister lurking around in shadowy corners, cringing at the thought of someone talking to her.

Elise headed up the trail to the area that had been fenced off for the paintball course. They'd set aside a few acres, enclosed it with a rail fence that was already getting covered with multiple colors of paint, and were working on adding obstacles and scenery for game scenarios. Rome and Colt's pop had actually built a rather neat castle construct, and she wanted to get a photo of that for the brochure, since it would likely be the focus of a multitude of games.

She pulled her camera out and selected a lens, then did a few test shots, reviewing them on the screen on the back of the camera. As a hobbyist, she loved "real" film and developing her own photos in a darkroom, but practicality meant that digital won out almost every time. There was never an issue with too many chemicals, not enough chemicals, and underdeveloped photos when all you had to do was import your file.

Elise tucked her bag near the fence post, out of the way, and began to trek through the rolling hills and bushy growth of the paintball course. She snapped a few photos here and there, testing shots, playing with angles, and trying to mentally picture what would look good in the brochures. In several spots, mini barricades made of stacked logs had been set up at corner angles for defensible positions. Someone was putting a lot of work and thought into the paintball course, and Elise was impressed by it. Heck, she didn't play paintball and it even looked like fun to her.

Over a ridge, she made out the edges of the castle. Constructed entirely of wood, the castle was about twenty feet tall at its highest, and had walls about ten feet high angling over to the side of a cliff. It was defensible, but the back end was open so no team could dig in and corner themselves. The tops of the castle walls were crenellated, and an orange flag was flapping at the top of the castle itself. The side of the wall facing her was painted gray with black lines denoting a brick pattern. It was rather cool, she admitted to herself, and snapped a photo of it from afar, then moved closer to get additional shots.

As soon as she stepped around the wall, she nearly ran into a shirtless Rome.

Elise gasped in shock and stumbled backward, only to have Rome reach out and grab her arm before she could topple over.

"Careful," he told her. "Wet paint."

Her eyes widened and she stiffened in surprise. She hadn't been expecting anyone out here, and she hadn't heard him working. The shock of seeing another person was bad enough; the fact that it was Rome, the object of her crush, had her speechless.

As always, Rome was mouth-wateringly beautiful. If she'd come up with a dream of what the ideal dangerous man would be, Rome fit the description to a tee. He was big and muscular, his torso thick and rock-hard, and his arms enormous, as if he worked out on a regular basis solely for the purpose of packing on muscle. In contrast to his dangerous body, he had a near-perfect face—beautiful blue eyes with thick, black lashes, a chiseled jaw, and a firm, unbroken nose. And he was pierced—through the nose, in both ears, in his lip. It only added to his wicked look.

Every time she saw him, she was struck by two things: how utterly pretty those blue, thickly lashed eyes were, and how completely covered in tattoos he was. Rome looked as if he'd never said no to someone wielding a needle, and his chest was covered from neck to navel with designs; both arms were colorful sleeves of tattoos. Tanned skin peeked out between the designs, along with the gleam of sweat on his body. He was shirtless despite the chill of the day, dressed only in a pair of sweatpants and combat boots.

Just the sight of him made her entire body lock up due to a mixture of longing and fear. Longing because he'd never want someone like her, and fear that he'd mock her or be cruel, as cocky men so often were when they came across a shy woman. His hand felt like a brand on her arm, scorching hot. She looked down at his tanned hand on her pale arm and noticed that even his long, strong fingers had tattoos.

Elise gulped and twisted her arm out of his.

"Sorry," he said. "Didn't mean to scare you." He gestured with his other hand, which held a dripping paint roller. "I just didn't want you to trip and ruin your clothes."

She blinked at him, her mind racing. She should say something, she decided. She'd seen Rome about a half dozen times now, and she'd seen him without his shirt before. Every time he'd been nothing but polite. And it was just the two of them outside. This would be the perfect chance for her to smile and say something polite, like Beth Ann would, or crack a joke like Brenna.

But she wasn't Beth Ann, and she wasn't Brenna. She was Elise Markham, and she was tongue-tied. So her mind raced through a list of things to say, discarded each one, and ended up remaining mute.

"You taking pictures?" Rome asked her. "You want me to move out of the shot?"

She clutched her camera closer to her breast, letting her hair swing over her cheek to cover it. Oh god, she was outside in natural light. That was when the stain on her cheek was most visible. What if he noticed it? What if he saw that one of her shoulders slumped lower than the other? What if he asked about her posture? She'd be humiliated.

Hunching her shoulders, Elise skittered away a foot or two and popped on her lens cap. She stared at the ground. *Say something*, she chided herself. *Anything! He's going to think you hate him worse than he already thinks you do!*

But she thought back to the other day, when she'd seen him at the restaurant.

Maybe I should volunteer to be Elise's man-meat . . .

Oh god. What had he thought about their drunken suggestion? Had he been revolted? He probably was. He could get any girl he wanted—

"You okay?" Rome asked as she remained silent. She could feel his gaze on her.

She could tell him she was fine. That she wouldn't have fallen over, and so it wasn't necessary for him to grab her. She'd liked that grab, though. Even now, her skin throbbed where he'd touched her. She brushed her fingers over her arm, struggling to think of something to say that would sound strong. That would come out right.

But when nothing came to mind, she turned and bolted, hurrying away back to where she'd abandoned her camera bag.

She was *such* a coward.

TWO

Rome watched Elise Markham run away from him as if the hounds of hell were nipping at her feet and tried not to feel annoyed at the sight.

He'd never met a girl so completely wigged out at the sight of tattoos and a few piercings. He knew he wasn't the most clean-cut guy, but hell. He wasn't that grotesque, was he? Elise Markham had probably grown up with a silver spoon in her mouth and a Porsche in the driveway. She probably thought guys like him were just the help. That thought soured him on her, fast.

Sure, she was pretty. Damn pretty. Sweet and innocent-seeming, two things that cranked his chain. But she flinched and ran every time she saw him. It was either hate or fear. He couldn't decide which one, and it was downright puzzling, considering that he was polite to her at all times.

But he remembered the words of her pretty friends in the restaurant. *There's no one in town who's Elise's type.*

No one good enough for Little Miss Blueblood. That was the story of his life, Rome mused. Never good enough for the right kind of girls. He slapped the roller down into the gray paint and then ran it back over the wall, glad for the diversion of painting.

Work was always a good distraction, and this was clean, honest labor. He'd gladly do this until the sun went down. By then, he'd have pretty, snobby Elise Markham out of his head.

Six hours later, Rome had the base coat of the last castle wall painted, and he'd cut down some more logs to make another mini bunker to hide behind. He was rather pleased with how the paintball course was turning out. Pop was too old to help with the grunt work, and Dane was picking up all the training classes while Colt was on his honeymoon. Grant was doing whatever the boss did. Probably fucking his cute, crazy little secretary again, Rome figured.

That left Rome in charge of getting everything ready for the paintball course to open up next month. He didn't mind. At this point, all it required was a little imagination and brute strength, and those were two things Rome had in spades. Plus, no one had fired him for lying about his credentials yet, so he still had a paycheck coming in and a roof over his head.

Things were looking up, really.

He put the paint and rollers away in the storage shed at the back of the main lodge and swiped at his brow again. He was sweating like a pig, and his muscles ached, but it was a good ache. The ache of a day spent in hard, honest labor. He liked that. It was, however, time for a shower and some food. Food first, he decided, and headed into the main lodge through the back door.

Once he went inside, he heard voices in the kitchen. Old habits sprang up and he slowed his steps, pausing to listen.

"I don't know that you should feed that thing Cheetos, Brenna." That was Grant's voice.

"Gollum likes Cheetos, doesn't he?" Brenna made kissy noises at what Rome assumed was her puppy. "And you're just being pissy and taking it out on us right now. Just spit it out already, baby."

There was a long sigh from the kitchen. "You saw the way Elise ran out of here. Do you think *he* was harassing her?"

"He? I don't seem to recall anyone that we hired who was named *He*."

"You know who I mean. Rome. He's a rough sort, Brenna. I still can't believe you hired him. I— Hey. Don't make that face at me. I'm just looking out for my sister."

Rome tensed. Either this was perfect fucking timing or shit timing. Either way, it was good to know what his employer thought about him. He waited, listening in on the conversation.

"You're being a snob," Brenna said. "Just because he has some tattoos and piercings, it doesn't mean that he's a criminal."

"It doesn't mean that he's not," Grant countered. "I'm just worried about Elise and our clients. I don't want him to give anyone the wrong impression, and I certainly don't want him scaring my sister."

"If your sister is scared of a few tattoos, she must be terrified of me. Just imagine what she'd think of my piercing."

There was a long pause. "Please tell me you didn't show my sister your piercing."

"Of course not. That's your property." There was a sultry note in Brenna's voice.

"Good. I was about to get a little bizarred out. And quit distracting me with thoughts of piercings."

"But I like distracting you." Brenna's voice lowered to a purr. "In fact, if you're good, I might just distract you as soon as dinner is ready."

"I guess that's my cue to go home and make it."

"I do believe it is," Brenna teased.

Things were quiet for a long moment, punctuated by a few pornographic groans and a puppy bark. Then it got quiet. Rome waited, body tense with anger.

"You can come out, now," Brenna called to him. "Grant's gone."

Rome frowned to himself, then stepped out of the shadowy hallway and into the kitchen. Brenna stood near the counter, wearing a pair of jean cutoffs that were two sizes too big and a T-shirt that read TULANE. Her new puppy was on the counter, licking an orange Cheeto.

She gave him an appraising look, as if he'd been stripping purely for her pleasure. "Well, hello there."

He ignored her playfulness. Brenna was obnoxious to everyone. It was harmless. "How'd you know I was there?"

"Gollum tried to go into the hall to greet you, and he's normally a scaredy-cat, so I figured someone familiar was there. And Pop's in town and Dane's in the woods, so I thought it was you." She wiggled her eyebrows at him. "So I distracted Grant. You're welcome."

He felt the sour burn of anger in his stomach. "Your fiancé hates me."

"He does," Brenna admitted, fishing another Cheeto out of the bag and offering it to her puppy. "But I wouldn't take it personally. Grant doesn't like anyone until he gets to know them. Just look at how long it took for us to get together despite him practically vibrating with sexual tension whenever he was around me." She looked over at him and winked.

Rome went to the sink, washed his hands, then headed to the icebox and grabbed some lunch meat. He made himself a quick sandwich and took a bite out of it. Brenna didn't seem to be leaving, so he asked, "Am I in danger of losing my job?"

She sighed and gave him an annoyed look. "Not you, too. Look, you're fine. Grant doesn't like you, but he didn't like me, either, and I'm still working here. Just stay busy and low-key and he'll relax. He's got his panties in a bunch because his sister is here and his entire weird family seems to think that Elise is fragile and will break if someone looks at her wrong."

He wasn't sure he believed her. He'd let down his guard too many times and gotten dicked over in the past. He pulled a bit of meat off of his sandwich and offered it to her puppy. "I need this job, Brenna."

"I know you do, Rome. And you've got me on your side. Don't worry. Grant's just a freak." She patted his shoulder and then wrinkled her nose at her now sweat-and-grime-covered palm. "He'll calm down once Elise is back home and he realizes you aren't a serial killer or something."

She sounded so confident that he couldn't help but hope she was right. "I did see Elise today," Rome admitted. "She came out to the paintball course while I was working on it. Saw me and turned and ran."

"That girl's kinda strange, no doubt about it. Nice kid, but strange."

Rome took another bite of his sandwich, determined not to smirk at Brenna calling Elise a kid. He figured they were the same age, but there was a worldliness to Brenna that Elise was lacking. He swallowed, and then said, "Her brother doesn't have to worry about her where I'm concerned. She's scared shitless of me."

"That's weird."

"How is that weird? Her brother is convinced that I'm a convict just because I have a few tats." He might not have been wrong about that, but Rome wasn't going to bring that up unless absolutely necessary.

"Yeah, but Elise actually talks to me about stuff, and I wasn't getting a fear vibe from her when it comes to you, if you know what I'm saying." She wiggled her eyebrows at him.

Rome rolled his eyes. Brenna thought everyone was as horny as she was. There was no mistaking Elise's terror when she'd fled earlier today, though. That wasn't sexual tension. That was the opposite.

"Probably to be on the safe side, you should avoid her, though." Brenna shrugged. "If she makes Grant all freaked out, you don't want him coming down on you."

"I have no intention of bothering her, trust me. I like this job and want to keep it."

She winked at him and scooped her puppy up off of the counter. "I hear you. Now if you'll excuse me, I have a fiancé to go molest."

Brenna left and Rome finished his sandwich, made another, devoured it, and then headed off to his own cabin. His mood was black as he played through the day in his head over and over again. Elise's fear of him. Grant's perpetual dislike. Brenna's careless words.

By the time he got back to his own cabin, he was fuming. He looked around at his place. It was threadbare but clean. The roof over his head didn't leak, the bed had blankets on it, and he had his own bathroom. It was private, and best of all, it was his.

It had been a long time since he'd had a place of his own. He didn't want to lose it because some rich bitch thought he was scary.

He calmed down a bit after a long, hot shower. Then he toweled off with his one threadbare towel—as soon as he got his next paycheck, he'd have to get himself some linens—and headed back into his room. He dressed and then lay on the bed, staring at the ceiling.

Rome didn't have a TV in his small cabin. The main lodge had one, and it served as a rec room for the employees most nights. He'd spent several evenings having a beer with the guys and playing Xbox, but tonight he didn't feel social. He was still pissed. Plus, Dane—who got along with everyone—was out in the woods, so his fiancée, Miranda, would be by herself. Seeing as how one female was scared of him, he didn't need to alarm another. And since Colt and Beth Ann were in Alaska, that meant it'd be Pop, Grant, and Brenna.

No thanks.

Maybe he'd ride into town, have a beer at the bar. He picked up his phone to check the weather. It had started looking nasty earlier, and riding a Harley through a rainstorm wasn't his favorite thing to do. Before he could check his weather app, though, a new text message flashed on the screen.

It's J. You should know Dad's out of prison and wants to catch up with us. I'm on the road but should be heading to Texas soon. Just a heads-up if you want to meet.

His brother, Jericho. Damn it. Rome deleted the message. The last thing he needed was his family hanging around and ruining what he had here.

That evening, Elise decided to stay in. It wasn't that she couldn't drive out to the main lodge and hang out. She'd be welcome.

It was that she was feeling a little weird about catching Rome shirtless and then running away like an idiot. Better to stay away for a few days until everyone forgot. Grant and Brenna wouldn't miss her—they'd be too wrapped up in each other—and the sight of them flirting just made her feel even more like a third wheel.

Everyone she knew in Bluebonnet was paired off and living their own lives. It was Elise who was floating around, aimless. She couldn't expect everyone to entertain her forever.

So tonight she'd be staying in at the Peppermint House.

The bed-and-breakfast was the only thing close to a hotel near tiny Bluebonnet, Texas. It was in the process of being renovated, but what was done so far was charming and adorably Victorian. Elise's room was full of pinks and mauves, and the four-poster bed made her feel like a princess. The owner of the bed-and-breakfast, Emily Allard-Smith, was also as friendly and relaxed as they came, and Elise liked her a lot.

She headed downstairs and nearly ran into Emily, who was heading out the door, a food container and her keys in hand. She looked surprised to see Elise. "Oh. Are you staying in tonight?"

Elise gave her a sheepish smile and let her hair swing in front of her face. "I was considering it."

"Oh! I thought you'd be going out." Emily immediately

turned around and headed toward the kitchen. "Let me whip you up some dinner."

"It's okay," Elise said, trailing behind her. "Really. I can order a pizza or something."

"Nonsense," Emily fussed, putting her keys down on the counter and opening the fridge. "This is a bed-and-breakfast, and I feed my guests. Is a sandwich okay?"

"A sandwich is fine." Elise sat on one of the barstools in the kitchen and admired the container of cookies Emily had placed on the fridge. "You heading to the police station?" It was no secret that Emily loved to cook, and when she didn't have many guests, she ended up baking for the police station and the fire department. Elise was constantly being stuffed with delicious pastries every morning, thanks to Emily's obsessive baking.

"No, heading over to visit Luanne." She pulled a ton of ingredients onto the counter and began to construct an enormous sandwich for Elise, layering vegetables and condiments with all kinds of meat. "Hank's working the late shift, so Luanne's working on my webpage. She wants me to go over some of it with her, and I thought I'd bring some cookies as a thank-you to Hank."

"That's your sister who's dating the police officer, right?" Elise hadn't met her, but Emily mentioned her once or twice.

"That's right. Hank has a real weakness for cookies. Actually, so does Luanne." She topped the sandwich with a thick slice of freshly made bread and shoved two colorful toothpicks through it, then sawed it in half. "Voilà. How's that for dinner?"

"Impressive," Elise said with a shy smile. "Thank you so much."

Emily waved a hand. "It's nothing. You sure you want to stay in? I'm guessing you could hang out with me. Luanne wouldn't mind. My sister's a bit of a string bean and obnoxious at times, but she has a good heart."

"No, I'm fine. Thank you."

"You sure? You need to get out more often! You're young and single."

Elise tensed. She rather hoped that Emily wasn't going to start trying to set her up with someone. "You're young and single, too."

"Actually I'm older than you, and I'm divorced." She shrugged. "Old before my time, I guess. And I'm the one going out. You sure you don't want to go?"

"I'm sure." Elise took a big bite of her sandwich so she wouldn't have to talk.

"Okay. If it storms, I might stay at Luanne's a bit later. The weather looks kind of foul at the moment." She gestured at one of the cabinets in the kitchen. "There's candles in there if the power goes out." Emily looked uncomfortable and hesitated. "You're not scared of ghosts, are you?"

Elise nearly choked on the mouthful of sandwich. Coughing, she shook her head.

"Just making sure." She bit her lip. "You sure you don't want to come with me? I hate the thought of you sitting here in the dark if the power goes out. With, you know . . . my visitor."

Elise swallowed, her throat burning as she gulped the food down. She placed a hand in front of her mouth as she spoke. "I . . . don't really think this place is haunted, Emily." She'd been warned by Em that there were rumors of a haunting, but no one ever seemed to hear anything but Emily herself. Elise had been here a few weeks now and hadn't heard a peep. She wasn't scared.

"Are you sure? You're my only guest at the moment. I'd hate for you to leave."

"I'm sure." She picked up her sandwich again, indicating she would continue eating. "I'm just going to finish this and then work on my photos some more. It's all very boring."

"All right," Emily said after a long moment. Then she picked up the cookies and her keys again. "There's beer and wine in the fridge if you want anything. Help yourself. I'll be home later."

Elise waved her off.

The evening was quiet enough for several hours. Elise went back to her room, fired up her laptop, and poked around on Photoshop, cleaning up a few photos and adjusting the coloring. When it began to thunder, she shut down her computer and went downstairs to the living room to watch the weather on TV. She curled up on the couch with a beer and flipped between local channels.

Sure enough, there was a crack of lightning and the lights went out.

Elise sat in the dark for a moment, then headed to the kitchen to light some candles. While she was in the kitchen, her phone rang.

It was Emily. "Power dead over there?"

"Yep, all dead," Elise told her. "I'm lighting candles."

"Okay. I'm going to stay here for a bit. I think I saw some hail, so I'm going to wait for it to pass. Luanne says Hank doesn't want anyone on the roads in this, so I'll be home in a few hours."

"No worries," Elise said softly. "Thank you for checking on me."

She got off the phone with Emily and took a few candles into the main living room. The big Victorian wasn't that creepy with the lights off, not really. It was just great mood lighting. She wished she had something to do, though.

So much for getting more life experience. Even tonight, she was all alone and rather enjoying it. What did that say about her?

Candle in hand, she peered out the front window at the driving rain. A moment later, it began to hail.

THREE

When it began to rain, Rome cursed his luck and paid his tab, then headed out for his bike. There was nothing worse than riding a motorcycle in a downpour, but he didn't have any other transportation. He put on his helmet and straddled his bike. It'd be a shitty ride home.

A moment later, he'd barely gone a block before it began to hail, and hard, pebble-sized pellets began to thump against his jacket, stinging with every connection. Okay, so there were worse things than driving home in a downpour.

Cursing to himself, he saw the sign for the bed-and-breakfast and pulled in there. The yard of the garish Peppermint House was thickly treed and would provide some safety for his bike, at least. He parked it under the nearest tree and pulled off his helmet. Waiting out the storm under a tree would be fine for his bike, but it would suck for him.

Rome glanced up at the house as hail poured down. The place was dark, but there was a candle in the window. Someone was there, at least. He tugged his jacket over his head to protect it, then jogged up to the front door of the bed-and-breakfast.

He knocked on the door, then rang the doorbell. The sound of the hail pounding on the roof was so loud that he wasn't sure anyone would hear him. "Hello?" he called out.

After a long pause, the front door of the bed-and-breakfast opened a crack. A face peeked around the corner, holding a candle.

It was Elise.

Rome was stunned. She was the last person he expected to see. "Hey, Bo Peep . . . can I come in?"

She opened the door a little wider, and he went inside.

When the door shut behind him, the roar of the rain and hail muted, and he was left staring at her shadowed face as she held the candle. Her eyes were wide, but he didn't see fear in them.

And that made him feel a little better. "Hi," Rome said quietly. "Is it going to bother you if I hang out here for a bit? The weather's kind of shit."

She shook her head and he wondered if she planned on speaking to him.

But after a moment of quiet staring, Elise gave him a faint smile and turned and headed deeper into the house. Intrigued, Rome stuffed his hands into his leather jacket and followed her. With the candle flickering as she walked, Elise was forced to cup a hand close to the wick, and he saw she had slim, pretty fingers. The rest of her figure was barely illuminated in the soft light, and he caught sight of a fuzzy sweater and tight jeans or leggings. Her long, silky hair spilled over her shoulders, and he wondered if it was as soft as it looked.

And he stiffened at the thought of how this would go down. Would she return to Grant and say Rome was harassing her? Would he get canned simply because he'd picked the wrong place to show up during a hailstorm? Fuck. He didn't know what to do. Rome hesitated, but when Elise didn't turn around, he sighed to himself and followed her. She wasn't speaking, and that made him uneasy. He hated the silence between them, because it was impossible to tell what she was thinking.

"Anyone else here?"

She shook her head.

Oh great. "Listen, I'll just stay until the hail lets up, and then I'll head back to the ranch. I won't be here for long."

She didn't speak.

Damn it, couldn't she say something? She was probably terrified of him at the moment, and he couldn't think of a single thing to say to relax her. He was here in this big, empty house with her and the lights were off. It was the perfect scenario for a guy to take advantage of a girl, and he was sure the idea went through her head, too. Rome groaned and scrubbed a hand over his face, trying to think of how to extract himself. Maybe the hail would be the better option.

But he didn't leave. Instead, he watched as Elise lit a few other candles on the table, and then sat down next to it.

He considered heading back out into the storm. Just bolting before she could accuse him of anything. He wasn't going to touch her, but he didn't know what she'd say to dear old brother, and he was already on edge around Grant. Grant was just waiting for him to fuck up so he could fire him.

"You sure you're okay with me being here?"

She nodded, but she didn't look at him, and that made Rome feel worse. Just then, it began to hail harder, and he groaned. He was stuck. Fuck.

Well, if nothing else, it'd be a good time to clear the air with Elise Markham and get it out in the open that he didn't mean her any harm. "Could you please say something?"

Rome watched those big eyes raise, shining in the candlelight, and he watched her tug on her long, silky hair again. She seemed to be pulling it over one cheek. Then she straightened. "Sorry." The word was whisper soft.

That was progress, at least.

He moved and sat across from her on one of the couches, leaning in to the candlelight so she could see his face. "I'm not entirely sure what I did to you to make you so scared of me, but I just want you to know that you're safe with me."

She stilled.

Ah fuck, he'd scared her now, hadn't he. Maybe just saying she was safe made her think of bad things, and now he'd gone and fucked up. He sighed and scrubbed his face again.

"I'm not scared," she whispered, her voice so low he could barely hear it.

Rome looked up, surprised. That was the longest sentence she'd ever said to him. "Then what's with the silent treatment?"

She twisted her hands in her long hair again, pulling it over one shoulder and stroking it in a way that almost seemed agitated. After a moment, she blurted, "I'm . . . shy."

That . . . hadn't been what he'd expected to hear. Of course, watching her anxiously stroke her hair over her shoulder, over and over again, her gaze cast on the ground, made him wonder how he'd missed it.

Elise Markham wasn't an ice princess who hated his guts. She wasn't scared of him because he looked dangerous.

She was really shy.

A stab of pity rose in his chest. "How do you do, Shy. I'm Rome." And he stuck his hand out for her to shake.

It was a silly gesture, of course. They'd met several times already. But it kind of felt good to start fresh.

She looked up at him, startled, and then gazed at his hand. A small smile curved her mouth and she delicately put her hand in his. She pulled away again a moment later, but the connection had been made.

"At any rate, I promise not to bite," Rome teased. He was so relieved to find out that Elise was just *shy* that it felt like a weight had been lifted off his shoulders. Grant's wrath wouldn't fall on him tonight. Thank fucking god.

Elise gave a small giggle and he was fascinated. The candlelight filled her face with shadows, but her smile was pretty and soft. She was a gorgeous girl, really. Why on earth was someone like her so shy?

He took off his jacket, since it was warm in the house. "So what do we need to do to get you past this shyness so you'll actually speak to me?"

She blinked at him a few times, and her hands pulled on her hair again. Her mouth worked, as if she were trying to spit out words, but nothing came for a long moment. Then, she finally admitted, "I . . . just need to get comfortable. That's all."

"And you're not comfortable around me because you don't know me?"

She paused for a moment, then nodded.

"But Elise, I'm hurt. You've seen me shirtless." His tone was teasing, almost flirty. "I'd ask to see the photos of the shoot, but we don't seem to have power at the moment."

A flicker of emotion crossed her face, and she seemed to hug herself a little closer. "The photos aren't any good." Her voice seemed a little braver, stronger.

"Oh. Huh." He wondered why, but she didn't seem like she was volunteering the information. "That's a shame. If you ever need me to get shirtless again, though, you just let me know."

Her eyes widened and she went silent again. As he watched her face, her throat worked, and he wondered if she was blushing.

For some reason, he found that charming. Hell, he was fascinated by her shyness. It didn't seem like an act, and she was far too pretty for it to rule her life. Did she go around with downcast eyes all the time? How did she even date?

Did she date? He suddenly found himself curious about that. She had a sweet body, all soft curves, and that long hair was making him nuts. Her face was lovely, too, but if she hid it and stared at the ground, no one would ever see it.

He wondered if Elise got by in life by blending into the wallpaper.

She jerked to her feet, surprising him. "Um." She hesitated, and clasped her hands, then unclasped them, all anxious motion. "You want a beer?"

"A beer would be great."

She nodded and disappeared off into the darkness. For a moment, he wondered if she'd come back, but she returned a minute later with two beers and offered him one, then turned and sat back down across from him. A girl who drank beer. He liked that. Rome popped the cap off his and watched as she did the same, then took a swig. She had a long, graceful throat, he noticed.

He also noticed she'd gone silent again. Her gaze had moved to the beer in her hands, and she stared at it. That wasn't good.

Rome tried a different tactic. "I'm not really good with small talk," he admitted. "I never know what to say."

She flashed him a grateful smile, her eyes meeting his again, and he felt like he'd just been somehow rewarded. "Me too."

He took another swig of his beer. "I suppose we could talk about the weather, but I guess it's pretty obvious that it's shitty."

She bit her lip and nodded, her gaze flicking down again.

Damn it, he wanted her to look at him. To see him. Not stare at her beer all night.

"You want to play a game? I can ask a question, and then you can ask a question. It'll help break the ice until the power comes on or the storm leaves and I'll be on my way."

She gave him another one of those small smiles. "That's not really a game."

She was right. "All right then, sassy pants, if you don't answer the question the other person asks, you have to chug the rest of your beer. Sound fair?"

Her head tilted, that long, glossy hair sliding over her shoulder in a waterfall. "You're driving."

"I'm also gonna answer everything you ask." He winked at her.

She ducked her head again. Oh, damn it. He'd made her shy. But after a moment, she straightened her shoulders and nodded. "Fair enough."

"Okay, then." He pursed his lips, then took a swig of his beer, thinking. No yes-or-no questions, since that would allow her to be quiet and he wanted her to actually talk to him. "How long are you in Bluebonnet?"

She shrugged.

"Oh, come on. That's not a real answer." He pointed at her with his beer. "Unless you want to chug that, body gestures are not considered an answer. That's cheating."

"It's not cheating," she protested.

"It is. I can't believe we're on the first question and you're already cheating."

"Fine, then. Here's a body gesture," she retorted, and flipped him the bird.

He threw his head back and laughed, utterly surprised—and delighted—by that spark in her. She watched him, her eyes gleaming with her own amusement, and she lowered her finger. "Now come on," Rome coaxed. "Gimme a real answer."

"I don't know how long I'm in Bluebonnet," she murmured. "Until I'm tired of being here, I suppose. I don't have a firm deadline or a job to get back to."

Interesting. He thought being a photographer was her job. Was it not? But he couldn't ask more questions. Not right now. "All right. Your turn."

Elise gave him a startled look, then thought for a moment. "How many tattoos do you have?"

He was surprised by that question, too, and the way she ducked her face, almost bringing a shoulder up to her cheek as if she could hide it. Strange. "Sixteen, if the sleeves both count as one apiece. I've got three on my stomach, the two sleeves, four on my back, one on my neck, one on each hand, and two on each leg."

She nodded.

It was interesting that she'd asked about his tattoos, not about him or why he was in town. He wanted to pursue that a bit more. "Do you like my tattoos?"

Her eyes widened and she stared at him again, her mouth silently working. She didn't speak for a long moment, and he wondered if she was going to answer. Then, she dropped her gaze and began to chug her beer, her throat working.

He couldn't help it; he laughed again. "You are a trip, Elise. You wouldn't hurt my feelings if you said no."

She didn't reply, simply finished her beer and primly wiped her mouth with long fingers. He was fascinated by that dainty movement, and the grace in her step when she stood up. "I'll get another beer."

He watched her head off, amused. It had been a while since he'd been that interested in another girl, but Elise Markham was fascinating. She seemed shy and sweet, but she drank beer like a pro and knew when to bite back. And she was interested in his tattoos. That added up to a rather interesting puzzle, and Rome liked puzzles.

Elise returned a few minutes later and carried two beers again. She handed him one. "For just in case."

"Why, Elise," he teased. "You going to try and find something I won't answer?"

She simply gave him a challenging smile and sat back down across from him. For a moment, he wished she'd sat next to him. Maybe that was too much to hope for too fast. At least she was talking to him.

"My turn," she said, and popped the top off her new beer. "Where are you from?"

"That's a pussy question," he teased. "And I'm from Houston originally."

"Pussy questions are allowed," she said in that prim, small voice.

"Fair enough. Where are *you* from?"

"Here." She smiled. "Bluebonnet."

"Then why are you staying at a bed-and-breakfast?"

She raised an eyebrow at him. "I thought it was my turn?"

He chuckled. "Yes, ma'am. Sorry if I spoke out of turn." Sassy little thing. He rather liked Elise Markham when she was peeking her head out of her shell.

"Where did you go to college?" she asked.

"No college," he told her bluntly. "High school dropout." Might as well get that out of the way, too. "So now it's my turn. Why are you staying at a bed-and-breakfast if you live in Bluebonnet?"

"I used to live here," she corrected in that soft voice. "My family moved to a lake resort up in Tahoe a few years ago. I'm just here visiting my brother."

It seemed like they were both a little uncomfortable with the direction of the questions. Time for something light-hearted, then, when it was his turn again.

She thought for a moment. "Why did you come to Bluebonnet?"

"Mostly because I hadn't been here yet. Wanted a small town to relax in." To hide in. "Kick back, see what it had to offer. And I stayed because I got a job." He shrugged. "I would have moved on if I didn't." When she simply nodded, he smiled at her and took another swig of his beer. "Now me. Let's see. How old are you?"

If it wasn't all dark and shadowy, he could have sworn she was blushing. "Twenty-four. How old are you?"

"Twenty-eight. How come a twenty-four-year-old still lives with her parents?"

She hefted her beer as if she were going to drink it, and then narrowed her eyes at him. "None of your business."

"That's not an answer. No boyfriend or roommates?"

"Those are new questions."

"Well, seeing as how you didn't answer the last one, I thought I'd try again."

She considered her beer, then made a face at him. "I live at home because it's . . . safe. No one bothers me there. And I haven't had a good reason to move out." She seemed a little disgusted with her answer, as if she were disappointed in herself.

"Fair enough." He noticed that she didn't admit to a boyfriend, though.

"What about you? Family or friends here in Bluebonnet?"

He noticed she didn't say "girlfriend." "Just me. I try to avoid family whenever possible."

Her smile peeked out again at that, and he found himself smiling back. "Mine's not so bad," she admitted. "Just a bit overbearing."

"Mine's bad," he said bluntly. He didn't want to think about them right now. He cast around for something to ask her. "Any tattoos or piercings?"

"Nope," she said. "So what do you think of working with Brenna?"

He eyed her and the charming little smirk she had on her mouth. "You trying to set me up?"

"That's a question and it's not your turn," she replied lightly.

He gave her a sour look and then chugged his beer, declining to answer what he really thought of Brenna, since Elise was friends with her. Brenna was a good girl, but she was a nut.

Elise giggled, and damn, he rather liked hearing that sound. "We going to play like that, huh?"

"Like what?" she asked, all innocence.

"All right, my turn, then. How come I can't see the photos you took?"

She gave him a frown and began to chug her beer.

"That bad, eh?" he asked, watching her throat work with something akin to fascination.

She shook her head and finished drinking, then gave a tiny, ladylike belch and clapped a hand over her mouth in horror.

He laughed.

"That's not funny," she told him, but she was laughing, too.

"It's kinda funny. I had no idea you were such a rude chick."

"My turn to ask a question," she said in a lofty voice. "So how come you're avoiding your family?"

Rome wagged a finger at her. "Tricky girl." He raised his fresh beer and downed it in a few gulps. No way was he talking about those fucktards, especially to a girl like Elise. She wouldn't even begin to understand the Lozada family. He finished his beer and placed the empty bottle on the table.

"I thought you were going to answer everything," she said, and he could have sworn that was a teasing note in her voice.

"I thought you were going to play nice," he rebutted.

"I'm nice," she said, but her face broke into a mischievous grin that delighted him to see. "And I should go get some more beer."

She returned a minute later with several more beers, placing half of them in front of him. "This is a bed-and-breakfast," she declared. "It won't kill you to stay the night, or you can stop drinking now."

"But we're just getting started," he teased. "No way I'm stopping now." Especially not now that he was making a few cracks in that shell of hers. "And I just thought up a terrific question."

"Uh oh," she said, sitting down again. Still across the table from him. Well, Rome—the city—wasn't built in a day.

"It's a doozy," he warned her, popping the cap off of another beer. "You ready?"

She picked up a new beer and popped the cap off. "Hit me with it."

"Where did you lose your virginity?"

She stared at him for so long that he almost thought she'd

answer. But then she picked up her beer and began to chug it, and he was a little disappointed.

When Elise finished her beer, she made a face and considered him for a long moment. "That was a terrible question."

He shrugged. "Hey, I figured if we're going for the jugular, might as well make it a good one."

"I'd ask you about your virginity but I suspect you'll be more than happy to share the details of that experience with me."

"I would. You asking?"

"No." She thought for a minute, then asked, "How many women have you slept with?"

"Enough to know what I'm doing." He grinned to take the light rebuke out of his words, enjoying the fact that she had that weird look on her face that he was pretty sure was a flush. "You want details or something?"

"I'm trying to think of things you won't answer."

"Oh, I'll answer that."

"Figures."

He thought back to prior girlfriends and replied. "Five."

"Five?"

"What, you don't like that number?"

"It just seems low."

"Well, that's either flattering or insulting. Why would it seem low?"

She thought for a moment, and then said, "I decline to answer that," and drank another beer.

He laughed. Elise Markham was definitely not boring.

For the next while, the game became more edgy and intense. It had gone from a friendly "get to know one another" game to a challenge to make the other person drink by not answering. Elise was a smart cookie; she figured out quickly that he'd answer anything personal . . . except for when it came to his family. And he learned rather fast that Elise absolutely refused to answer anything sexual.

By the time they figured out each other's weaknesses and

exploited them, empty beer bottles littered the living room and the candles had turned into little puddles of wax on the table. Elise had passed out on the couch in a drunken stupor, and Rome thought that looked pretty good to him. He blew out the candles, lay down on the sofa, and fell asleep.

He woke up a short time later to the sound of keys in the front door, and sat up, rubbing his face. A woman walked in, shrugging off her jacket, and she smiled at the sight of him. "That must be your motorcycle up front," she whispered, giving the sleeping Elise and the scatter of beer bottles an amused look.

"That's me," he said. "Still raining?"

"Still raining," she agreed. "I have extra beds, though. You're welcome to one."

"Thanks." He got to his feet and looked down at Elise. That long, silky hair was trailing over her face, and her arm was flung off the edge of the couch. "Where's her bed? I'll take her up there. This doesn't look all that comfortable."

"Oh, you don't have to," the woman said. "Maybe we can wake her up."

Just then, Elise snored, and Rome chuckled. "Not with all the beer she drank."

"I see that." The woman's mouth twitched with amusement. "Good for her. I hate that she stays home every night. She needs to get out and have fun while she's young."

Rome bent over Elise and scooped her up into his arms. "She doesn't get out much, huh?"

"Not at all," the woman said, clicking on a flashlight and pointing it at the stairs. "Her room's this way. And thank you. I'm Emily, by the way."

"Rome," he told her, and hugged Elise a little closer in his arms. She fit rather perfectly there.

FOUR

The next morning, Elise woke up with her head pounding and feeling muzzy, and her body tucked into her bed. Surprised, she sat up and rubbed her forehead, trying to figure out how she'd gotten into her room. Her memories of last night's candlelit beer party were vague at best, but she remembered Rome's gorgeous smile and his teasing laugh.

God, last night had been wonderful. It had been the best night of her life, really.

She'd been astonished to see the object of her crush show up on the doorstep of the bed-and-breakfast, but she couldn't turn him away, not with the nasty storm. And she'd been even more shocked to hear that he thought she hated him. That was startling to hear, considering it was the opposite.

She *lusted* after him. Apparently she was doing a good job of hiding that. Too good, maybe.

When he tried to apologize for somehow offending her, Elise had taken a chance. Just a teeny one. And she'd chatted with Rome. He'd broken the ice with conversation, and she'd brought the beer. And talking to him? Playing that silly drinking game? That had been so much fun. She hated that she'd gotten so drunk that she'd fallen asleep, though. Had he been disappointed in that? Or was he relieved? Elise suddenly felt awkward and tense. What if she'd been too drunk to realize that he wasn't having as good a time as she was?

She was suddenly filled with doubt. She'd thought they'd had a lot of fun last night, but maybe it was purely one-sided? She got out of bed and realized she was still in her jeans and sweatshirt from last night. Huh. She never slept with her clothes on, and she didn't recall coming upstairs.

Elise headed downstairs for a drink of water, and met Emily in the kitchen.

The other woman gave her a knowing smirk, and stirred a bowl of batter. "Well hello, there, sleepyhead. How are you feeling?"

"Okay," Elise murmured. She rubbed her eyes and glanced back at the living room. It was sparkling clean, no hint of last night's bacchanal remaining. "Did I—"

"Drink all my beer and then some? Yes, yes, you did."

"Oh." She could feel the flush heating her cheeks. "I'm so sorry."

"Don't be. You two looked like you had fun." Emily gave her a knowing look. "How'd you manage to score such a hot date on such short notice?"

Oh jeez. "It wasn't a date. He got stuck in the rain and came in to stay dry."

"And so you two had a beer party?"

"Something like that." She was never going to stop blushing, was she? "Did he drive home last night?"

"Nope. He carried you up to bed and then stayed in one of the other rooms. Left this morning."

"Carried . . . me . . . up?"

"Yup." Emily's smug smile was full of pleasure. "Made me all weak in the knees to see a guy do that. Lifted you like you were nothing."

Elise definitely wasn't "nothing." She would be politely referred to as "sturdy." "I hope he didn't hurt himself."

"Not at all. Now . . . tell me the deets."

"There's nothing to tell."

Emily snorted. "Bullcrap. A man doesn't hang around and carry a girl up to bed if there aren't deets."

"He was just being nice."

Emily waved her spoon at Elise. "I've seen nice, and I've seen interested, and he's the latter."

That surprised Elise to hear, and she felt her cheeks flush even redder. Could that be true? Could someone as sexy as Rome be even remotely interested in someone as unattractive as herself? She touched her cheek, thinking. "I really like him, Emily," she said wistfully. "He's so gorgeous and nice."

"It's a dangerous combination," Emily agreed, putting down her bowl and getting out an ice cream scooper. She dug it into the batter and plopped a scoop of cookie dough onto a baking sheet. "You should tell him. Ask him out. Make the first move. I bet he'd like that."

Would he? Elise tugged on her hair, dragging it across the bad side of her face. She didn't know how to tell if a guy was flirting, but it seemed like he'd been flirting with her last night. Heck, they'd shot sexual question after sexual question at each other—too bad she didn't remember any of the answers. But it had been poorly lit last night. What if she approached him in daylight and he got a really good look at her discolored cheek? He'd seen her a few times before, but things always looked harsh under bright sunlight. What about the scars on her back, or her hips and shoulder that didn't exactly align, thanks to the scoliosis and subsequent back surgery?

She was filled with doubt. The thought of asking a guy out—especially one as smoking hot as Rome—seemed like a pipe dream.

"Well?" Emily prompted.

"I . . . don't even know where to begin," Elise confessed in a small voice.

"I do," Emily said. "You take a shower, fix your hair and makeup real nice, wear a sexy shirt and some tight jeans, and show up with some cookies for him. Tell him you had fun talking and would he want to go get a beer sometime? Voilà." She plopped another scoop of dough onto the sheet. "In fact, you can take him these cookies."

"You make it sound so easy."

"Oh, it's not easy. But a guy like him? You'll be kicking yourself if you don't at least try to get into his pants."

Emily had a point. "I'll go shower," Elise said.

"Do it fast before you can talk yourself out of it," Emily suggested.

That was not a bad idea.

An hour later, Elise was driving out to the Daughtry Ranch with a container of fresh-baked oatmeal raisin cookies on the car seat next to her. Her heart was knocking a mile a minute in her chest, and she kept checking her reflection in the rearview mirror. She was wearing a good deal of makeup, a larger amount than she probably should have on her bad cheek, but there was nothing to be done for that. Better to look like she was heavy on the powder than to have him question why one of her cheeks was slightly discolored. The rest of her makeup looked great, though, and she was wearing a tight black sweater that was supposed to be worn with an undershirt that she'd strategically neglected to put on. The low cut of it played up her cleavage, and Emily had tried to press high heels on her, but she'd declined. After all, if she had to find Rome out on the grounds, that was going to be really hard to do if her heels were constantly sinking into the earth.

She parked at the far end of the parking lot, hoping that no one would come out and say hello to her. Grant or Brenna would notice her makeup and her tight sweater, and the last thing she wanted to do was field questions from them. Elise grabbed the plate of cookies, pocketed her keys, and hesitated.

God, was she crazy for doing this? What if he was just being polite? What if he was totally being nice to her just because she was Grant's "fragile" sister? She'd die of embarrassment if that was the case.

Elise wavered, suddenly full of doubt.

There's not enough life experience and it shows in the photos . . .

Damn it. She'd never get anywhere being afraid. What was the worst that could happen? Her hands trembled as she brushed a lock of hair out of her face, and she tried to calm down. Maybe he would laugh in her face. Maybe he would call her terrible names and stomp on her feelings. She could lick her wounds and return home to Tahoe and never see him again. It would hurt, but at least she could say she tried.

And really, if she was going to pursue a guy, it might as well be one as delicious looking as Rome Lozada. Aim for the top, she figured.

Steeling herself for the worst, Elise took a deep breath and stepped away from the car.

She avoided the main lodge. Yesterday he'd been painting the wooden castle, and she hoped he was out there again. If not, well, she'd cross that bridge when she got there. It was early afternoon, since she'd slept through the morning, but the ground was still wet from the prior night's storms and a little soft and muddy. She was rather glad she'd skipped the heels. She headed down the path into the woods, clutching the plate of cookies in front of her like it was a shield.

A few moments later, she found the edges of the paintball course and stepped inside the gate. There was no sign of anyone, but she wasn't quite at the castle yet. She continued farther in, swallowing hard and hoping she didn't hyperventilate before she found Rome.

This is a mistake, her mind chanted. *Turn around. Turn around.*

She ignored that little voice for now, heading down into the small valley that housed the newly built fort. The painting had been completed sometime since yesterday, and there was no sign of Rome. Frowning to herself, Elise circled to the back of the fortress and peered around the edge. No one.

Drat.

This is a mistake. Take this as a sign and just get out of here before your feelings get hurt.

That probably wasn't a bad idea. With a small sigh, Elise turned and headed back into the trees, heading for the main lodge.

A figure jumped out of the trees and headed right for her. She barely caught sight of tattoos and blue eyes before Rome's large body pushed hers up against a nearby tree.

"Duck," he commanded.

His voice was so urgent that she did, and she felt his big hand move over the top of her head. She was pressed against his chest, and the plate of cookies she'd brought with her were crushed against her breasts. His big body pinned hers against the tree, and Elise was so startled that the breath escaped right out of her lungs.

Immediately she heard a loud *thwack* and Rome groaned. "God damn it, Pop, you got me right in the kidney."

"Ha!" called a voice nearby. "You'd better hustle before Dane and his group show up and nail you again."

"You're not supposed to shoot me, Pop," Rome said in a dry voice, and his hand slipped from her hair. "I'm on your damn team."

Elise looked up and was shocked to see Rome's gorgeous face was mere inches from her own. She was close enough that she could see the stubble edging his jaw and the gleam of his lip ring. And what a beautiful jaw it was.

Then he looked down at her, and those impossibly blue eyes focused on her.

"Hey," he murmured, and she watched, fascinated, as the lip ring moved.

Her throat worked and she fought hard to speak. "Hi." It came out as a breathless whisper, but it was a start.

"What are you doing here on the course? We're running a few guys through and you're going to get pegged if you're not careful. Pop almost shot you."

She blinked. "Oh. I . . . um. Never mind." It would sound totally stupid to tell him she'd brought cookies now, wouldn't it?

He tugged at the plastic-wrap-covered plate currently smushed to her front. "What's this?"

"I . . . uh . . . cookies."

"For me?" He grinned, and the look was so roguish it made her legs feel like jelly.

"Um . . ." God, why couldn't she think of anything to say? But being so close to him, with his big body pressed up against hers? All the words went right out of her head. She just stared at him like a dopey, lovesick fool.

"Thanks," he said, and glanced around as the bushes rustled nearby. "You'd better leave before someone ruins that pretty sweater of yours." He glanced down, and she could have sworn he was looking at her cleavage.

"'Kay," she breathed.

"I'll distract them. You run out of here unless you want to be splattered in yellow. And thanks for the cookies. You can drop them at my cabin." He grinned at her again, and to her surprise, he leaned in and brushed a kiss on her parted lips, the lip ring skimming over her mouth. Then he hefted his paintball rifle and darted away, crashing into the underbrush.

Elise stared after him in shock, then darted back the way she came, running toward the cabins.

Holy crap. Rome had kissed her.

Her.

She wandered toward the cabins in a daze, clutching the

cookies. He had said to leave them at his cabin. She knew which one was his, since Pop had given her a tour of the place a few days ago. Should she just walk right in and put them down? Leave a note? She wished she'd had the chance to talk to him.

Of course, if she was a ballsy sort of girl, she'd wait for him to come back and talk with him then. Elise bit her lip and thought of that kiss. It had been brief but utterly distracting. She touched her mouth and thought of the scrape of his lip ring against her mouth.

All right, then. If she was going to do this, she was going to go all in. Sucking in a deep breath and steeling her courage, Elise went to Rome's cabin to wait for him.

Rome headed in from the paintball course, rather pleased with himself.

Today, he decided, was a good fuckin' day. He'd woken up in a nice plush bed, had breakfast courtesy of the nice lady who ran the bed-and-breakfast—who hadn't charged him a dime—and rode his bike back to the Daughtry Ranch for a day of work. He, Brenna, Pop, and a few other people they'd rounded up had run a crash course on the paintball grounds to see how things played out, and everyone had been impressed at the work he'd put in, even Grant.

They'd be opening the paintball course in a few weeks, and Grant had mentioned that it would be Rome's baby to handle. He was fine with that. In fact, he was looking forward to it. He'd run the best damn paintball course and keep his job secure.

The icing on the cake had been pretty, soft Elise Markham showing up to see him. With cookies. He didn't give a shit about the cookies, really, but he was pleased with what they represented. She'd shown up bearing gifts as an excuse to see him, and that made him grin. She'd looked so soft and sweet when he'd pressed her up against the tree that he couldn't help but kiss her, and he had enjoyed the wide-eyed look on her face in return.

It was a shame he'd had to run her off, but maybe he'd head into town tonight to see if she was at the bed-and-breakfast. Maybe she'd want to get a drink.

Of course, maybe he was thinking with his dick. He should stay away from Elise if he wanted to avoid riling up her brother—and his boss—Grant Markham. The man had already shown that he was a bit sensitive when it came to his sister.

But damn, there was something about Elise Markham that fired Rome up on all cylinders. It wasn't just that soft, innocent expression on her face—though he had to admit that it did incredible things to his libido. It was the fact that underneath all that shyness there was a fiery, smart, sassy girl just waiting to come out. And he wanted to be the one she showed up for. Maybe that was rather Neanderthal of him, but he didn't care.

Her brother would care, though.

Rome sighed and scrubbed a hand through his short, sweaty hair. Best to just stay away from her until things were more secure with his job and Grant wasn't looking for any excuse to can his ass.

Fine, then. He'd stay in tonight. Take a nice hot shower, relax, and maybe break out the Xbox in the main lodge. Shower first, though. He was sweaty as hell, and dirty, and he ached from repeated smacks from the paintball gun that seemed to have left a mark despite the protective jumpsuit he'd worn that day. Stripping his shirt over his head, he rubbed it on his chest and stepped inside his cabin.

And stopped.

Elise Markham was sitting there on his bed, her hands on her knees. She stood up at the sight of him, her eyes wide and anxious.

Oh shit. He glanced around but no one was nearby. No one had seen her in his cabin. He shut the door behind him. "Uh, hi?"

"Sorry if I startled you," she murmured.

"Nah, it's okay. I'm just not used to coming home and finding a girl on my bed." He grinned to take the sting out of his words. "Not that it's a bad thing to come home to, mind you."

She ducked her head, letting that hair swing in front of her face, and he realized she was blushing. She wasn't speaking, though, and he realized that shyness was getting away from her again. If he wanted her to talk, he was going to have to prompt her.

"So what brings you by?" *And why are you sitting in my cabin, waiting for me?*

Elise stroked a hand over her hair, dragging it against her cheek again in that nervous habit he'd noticed last night. "I'm not . . . interrupting, am I?"

He rubbed his sweaty chest, watching as her gaze flicked there, then skittered away again. "Was just going to take a shower, but it can wait a bit. What's up?"

"I . . . uh." She swallowed audibly.

Hell, he was making her nervous. He needed to calm her down. Rome walked past her, trying to make it seem like he had shy girls in his cabin all the time, and headed to the small bureau where he kept his even smaller stash of clothes and pulled out a new shirt, tugging it over his head. It felt like a crime to toss a clean shirt over his dirty body, but if she was nervous at the sight of him, he wanted to do what he could to help her stay.

Curiosity was going to kill him at this rate.

"So . . . you remember last night?" The words came out in a rush.

He turned to look at her and grinned. "It was fun. Beer and good company. Can't complain."

A hint of a smile curved her full mouth and he was entranced by that. "Me either." She blinked rapidly a moment later, and her nervousness returned. "You know the game we played?"

"Yep, I remember."

Her hand stroked her hair again, pushing it against her cheek in that odd motion. It was almost like she was trying to hide her face behind it, which was bizarre. "I didn't answer some of the questions."

"I didn't, either. That's why we got so loaded." He grinned at her to take the sting out of his words.

"I didn't answer any of the sexual questions," she said in a small voice, and her gaze dropped again. "You might have noticed that."

"I might have," he said slowly. She looked like she wanted to crawl through the floorboards and disappear into the ground. "Why?"

"I didn't answer them because . . ." She swallowed hard again. "I don't have any experience. None."

Rome stilled.

He'd suspected as much, but hearing her admit it, her body tense with anxiety, was an entirely different thing. Why was she confessing this, and confessing it now?

"I guess . . ." She paused, thinking. "So. I haven't told anyone, but my photos for the shoot were rejected. Everyone says the same thing every time. Not enough life experience."

She looked so frustrated and unhappy that he felt a twinge of pity. "That seems unfair."

"They're right." Her eyes focused on him, and for a moment, gone was the shyness. "They're all right. I'm twenty-four years old and I've been sheltered and protected all my life. I've been missing out on everything. I was home-schooled and then I went to a girls' school. I attended a small, private women's college and graduated as fast as I could. I've never had a boyfriend. I've never had sex. I've never spent the night with a man. I'm missing out on everything, and I'm so sick and tired of it. And I want to change. I want to experience things." Elise's voice took on a soft, wistful note. "I want to go to parties and stay out all night. I want to do crazy things. I want to have sex under the stars. I want to do everything. I want to go wild and experience life."

During her impassioned speech, Rome went from surprised to angry. At first, he'd been flattered that soft, sweet Elise was coming on to him, but then she started talking about "going wild" and "doing crazy things" and he realized she was approaching him because he was tatted and pierced and rode a bike. It wasn't him she was interested in, he realized, but what he represented. And he'd been hit on like this before. Some sheltered woman figured she'd find herself a biker to slum with, and he'd leap at the chance to nail her.

And Rome was disappointed. He'd thought Elise would be different than that. Didn't seem like that was the case. He crossed his arms over his chest. "So why are you telling me this?"

That flash of surprise crossed her pretty face and she began to fuss with her hair again, dragging it over her cheek. "I . . . uh, thought it was obvious."

"That you want to go slumming?" His voice was cold.

"What?" She looked genuinely surprised.

"That's what this is about, right? You want to live on the wild side a little, so you picked me to hit on because I look just dangerous enough to appease your sensibilities?" He let his tone show just how disgusted he was with the thought.

"No," she said softly. "I picked you b-b-because you kissed me." She looked utterly crushed, blinking rapidly as if fighting back tears. She grabbed the cookie plate and moved toward the door.

Ah, hell. Rome stopped her, putting an arm against the doorjamb and preventing her from skittering away. "You telling me you've never been kissed?"

"I have," she mumbled, but she wouldn't look at him.

"You have," he repeated. He wasn't sure he believed that.

"A guy kissed me once," she said, and her voice was so low he could barely hear it. "On a dare. It was at a dog party."

A dog party? What the fuck? He knew what dog parties were. They were little shindigs thrown by bored, asshole kids who recruited the worst date they could find to parade in front of their friends. They were cruel, shitty things. Why was someone as sweet and vulnerable—and hell, gorgeous—as Elise invited to a dog party? Because she was shy? It didn't make sense. "I think I'm missing a piece of the puzzle here."

She pushed at his arm, indicating she wanted to leave.

He ignored it. In fact, he leaned against the doorjamb, blocking the door entirely. "Why were you at a dog party?"

"Isn't it obvious? I was the dog." Her voice held a note of bitterness.

"Actually, no," he drawled. "It's not obvious. You're not a dog, Elise. That's why I'm so confused about this whole mess. I get that you're shy. I don't get why someone as pretty as you would get invited to something like that."

She swallowed hard, and her face was tilted away from him. "You think I'm pretty?"

"I have eyes, don't I?"

She looked at him, then, and her eyes were shining with tears, even though her mouth was curved into a faint smile. "Thank you," she whispered.

"Don't thank me," he said gruffly. "Just explain."

She licked her lips, and he hated that he was fascinated by that little flick of pink tongue. "After the party, I had laser treatments. On my face." Her hands brushed over her cheek. "I had a really large port-wine stain. From here"—she touched the tip of her eyebrow—"to here."

And she touched her chin.

Rome frowned. She was looking away from him again—looking anywhere but at him, actually. He touched her chin and tilted her head toward him, and she closed her eyes but let him examine her face.

There. Just barely there was a faint staining of her skin. He'd never noticed it before, but now that she'd mentioned it, he could see a faint, too-pink shadow covering one side of her face. It was the cheek she always dragged her hair over, and he realized this must be what she was trying to hide from him. The skin was smooth—almost too smooth, he realized, and the discoloration was faint, like a tan that had occurred on only one cheek.

He wondered how much of it had been lasered away. "This is what makes you think you're ugly?" His thumb brushed over her jaw.

She shuddered against his touch, a tremble racking through her. A tear spilled down her cheek, dripping onto his fingers. "Most of it is gone, but I still see it every time I look in the mirror." Elise straightened her shoulders and reluctantly pulled away from his touch.

That small confession went a long way toward helping him understand her, though. What, he wondered, was this costing her? She agonized over speaking to him. Confessing about her scar must be killing her, he realized.

And he hated that.

Rome reached up and brushed his fingers over her cheek again. She jerked away, startled, her eyes wide, as if shocked that he'd touch her. Did she always think like that? Like she was a hideous beast that no one would want to touch?

Fuck. No wonder she was so shy.

"Is that why you've only had the one kiss?"

"Two, now," she said softly. Her gaze dropped to the floor again.

Ah, yes. That quick little peck he'd given her in the woods. If that counted as a kiss, then damn, the girl needed a real one. "So that's why you picked me? Not because you want to go slumming with someone from the wrong side of the tracks, but because I kissed you?"

She looked up at him, startled, and he realized the thought had never crossed her mind. "I like your eyes, too," she blurted, and then her face lit up a bright red, the stain on her cheek becoming more obvious with her blush.

He couldn't help it; he laughed.

Elise made a soft whimpering noise and pushed at him, trying to get him away from the door.

He didn't budge. Oh no. This girl was not going anywhere.

"So," he murmured. "What exactly did you have in mind?"

FIVE

What did she have in mind? Was he going to make her say it? She thought it was obvious. Hadn't she made it clear what she wanted from him?

Elise stared up at him. It was hard to look at him directly; every instinct in her body told her to flee, to run away before he hurt her feelings.

But the look in Rome's eyes was soft, and she remembered his light touch on her cheek that had sent shivers through her body and awakened things she thought she'd never get the chance to feel with a man. Things that usually happened only under the covers, late at night when she touched herself.

When she was silent, he raised an eyebrow at her. A pierced eyebrow.

Okay, so he was going to make her say it.

"Well," she began softly. "Um . . . I'd really like to have sex."

"Right now?"

She could feel her cheeks heating. "It doesn't have to be right now, no."

His mouth twitched. "Tomorrow, then?"

Oh god, would she be ready tomorrow? What did she need to do to prepare? She hadn't given much thought to talking to him beyond handing him cookies and hoping for the best. "I suppose tomorrow works? What time is best for you?"

He laughed.

Her heart stuttered in her chest out of fear, and she flinched backward, hurt.

Immediately, his hands were smoothing down her hair, holding her in place. "I'm not laughing at you, Elise," he soothed, gazing into her eyes. His hand brushed over her cheek again, and she wanted to lean into that soft touch. "I'm laughing at the thought of making an appointment to have sex with a virgin. Don't you think we should start smaller? Maybe with kissing?"

"Oh." She smiled and let out a long breath. "Yes, that sounds good." Kissing. They could start with kissing.

"And did you want to kiss me? Or shall I kiss you?"

"You really want to go through with this? With me?" The words erupted out of her before she could stop them.

Rome smiled again, and his hands slid from her hair to cup her face gently. "Let's see. A gorgeous, smart, funny girl is asking me to have sex with her and is surprised that I'm interested? Is this a joke?"

She shook her head, even though it was trapped by his hands. It wasn't a joke. "You think I'm gorgeous?"

"When you're around, I have a hard time looking away from you," he said, and she watched his lips form the words, fascinated. "But," he said, continuing, "I tell myself it's a bad idea and I should stay away."

That broke her out of the soft, delicious bubble created by his voice. "What? Why?"

"Your brother is my boss and he's very protective of you," Rome said, and he dropped his hands. "And I'm just the tatted-up hoodlum he's looking for any excuse to fire."

"He wouldn't fire you for having sex with me."

"Wouldn't he?"

Well, okay, so Grant might. He was just as overprotective as her parents. Everyone was determined to smother her, weren't they? God, that was so frustrating. A surge of anger shot through her, burning away any lingering shyness. She was her own person, wasn't she? If she wanted to kiss and date a man covered in tattoos and piercings, she could.

So she steeled her courage, looked up at Rome, and put her hands on his chest. "What if I'm the one kissing you?"

"What do you mean?"

"I mean, if I'm the one kissing you, he can't fire you for kissing me back, can he?"

Rome's mouth twisted into a wry smile. "That's not how it works, sugar."

"So you're telling me no?"

He sighed. "I should, shouldn't I? I'm probably the wrong guy for this. I'm not good with this sort of thing, and your brother will kill me if he finds out, and I really need this job." But then he placed his hand over hers on his chest and rubbed it, clearly trying to soothe her.

Those hands touching her were like magic. She felt each brush of his callused thumb over her skin as if it were sweeping over her entire body. "We just won't tell him," Elise offered.

"Your car's out front, isn't it?"

Elise sighed in frustration. It was. That meant anyone who pulled into the parking lot would see it and know she was here. The ranch wasn't busy enough that she could hide her car and hope no one would see it. "Then we meet somewhere else," she suggested, thinking. She scratched at his skin through the thin material of his shirt, idly fascinated by the hard, warm muscle underneath. "Maybe the bed-and-breakfast?"

"Too public," Rome told her, and his voice had dropped to a husky whisper that made her skin prickle. Oh god, she loved the sound of his voice when he was speaking low and private like that.

"What about Beth Ann's salon?" she asked breathlessly. "I have the keys and she's gone for the next few weeks."

"Has potential. Tomorrow, then?"

"Tomorrow?" She stared at him, dazed. Her gaze slid back to his mouth, that beautiful, firm mouth with the ring on the side of his lower lip. "What's tomorrow?"

He chuckled. "You said you weren't ready for sex today."

"Oh. Right." She felt her face heat again. "I need to get ready."

"Ready how?"

"I honestly have no idea," she admitted.

He chuckled and put a finger underneath her chin. "I'll bring condoms if you want. We can meet after work, at six. How's that."

Oh god. They were meeting after work. She was going to have sex tomorrow. Elise swallowed hard around the knot in her throat, and she nodded. "Good. Sounds good. And I'll get the condoms. Don't worry about that. No problem."

She didn't want to seem like a total ninny in front of him, after all.

His finger tilted her chin up. "Look at me."

She blinked, looking up. She hadn't realized, but she'd been staring—and talking—to his chest for most of the conversation.

"Do you want a kiss?"

Oh. Oh god. Did she ever. But worry shot through her and she dropped her gaze again. What if she messed it up? What if she was a terrible kisser and he decided to call things off? What if he—

"Elise," Rome murmured, and his thumb held her chin firmly, angling her back up. "Look at me. Quit panicking. You're not going to do it wrong. It's just a kiss. If you're not good at it at first, you'll get better. I'll show you how. Understand?"

She blinked rapidly and looked up at him again, her breath coming in shallow, nervous little pants. Then, she nodded. "Okay. Kiss. Yes. I mean, yes, I would like a kiss." Her face hurt from all the blushing she was doing.

"Good. Because you're not leaving here without one." He continued to hold her chin and his face leaned in toward hers, mouth parted.

And Elise realized he was going to kiss her right *now*. She gave a nervous squeak, only to have it smothered by his mouth.

Her entire body tensed and her eyes closed. He was kissing her! She should relax and enjoy it, but the shock of it made her mouth firm into a thin line, and she began to breathe faster through her nose—and then stopped, because she didn't want him to think she was snorting like a bull. She didn't know what to do. The stubble on his face rasped against her cheeks—not an unpleasant feeling, really, just a different one—and she could feel he was still sweaty from his time on the paintball course. His mouth moved gently over hers, though, and his lips felt curiously hard and soft at the same time. She could feel that ring, too, and—

"Elise," he murmured against her mouth. "Relax."

"Okay—" she began to say, but his tongue swept into her mouth instead. She made a sound of surprise, but it was swallowed by him. His tongue brushed against hers, and then her entire body lit up in response.

Oh . . . oh wow. So that was a kiss. His mouth, wet and hot on her own, the flick of his tongue brushing against her own, his lips melding to hers. He was insistent, his mouth working against hers in an almost reflexive, sweeping motion that made her want to open wider. So she did, and his tongue slid deep, so deep that she practically felt it between her legs.

Elise moaned as his tongue thrust into her mouth again, and he kept the kiss deep and wet and slick, working over her mouth. Eventually, he pulled away, and she mewed a protest. But he didn't go far; instead, he began to press small, soft kisses on her lips. First her upper lip, then her lower. He ran his tongue over her lower lip, tracing it with the tip, and then bit gently on it and sucked.

And she felt all of that, every ounce, between her legs. Her knees went weak. It wasn't just a kiss. It felt like he was making love to her mouth.

Elise realized that this was what he was offering. This sensual feasting upon each other. His mouth on her, making her nipples ache and her pulse beat between her legs. She wanted his touch everywhere. Had she said she'd wait until tomorrow? She wanted him now, and she wanted to experience everything right at that moment. If he'd have led her to the bed, she'd have gone gladly without a second thought.

Rome pulled away and Elise felt bereft. Her eyes opened and she looked into his face. His eyes were such a gorgeous, dark blue, his lashes thick. And his expression was as if he wanted to devour her whole, a mixture of hunger and possession. It made her weak in the knees to see it.

"Not bad," he said softly, and leaned in to kiss her mouth lightly again. "But next time, hopefully you won't be so tense." And he grinned at her.

Tense? She felt like his hands on her neck were the only thing holding her up. Her knees felt like jello. How on earth was she tense? But she agreed. "Okay."

He chuckled. "So you want to meet tomorrow still?"

"God, yes," she blurted, and then wanted to hide her face in embarrassment.

But Rome only grinned. "Tomorrow, then. At the salon."

She nodded. "Tomorrow."

He let her go, and she turned to the door. Her first step was wobbly, but she managed to grasp the doorknob and turn it. She glanced back to look at him, but he was already heading toward his bathroom, stripping his shirt off, and so Elise shut the door and walked calmly out to her car, swallowing hard.

She got into her car and stared at her dashboard for a long, long time.

Holy shit.

That kiss had been . . . amazing. If that was what she was in store for, dear god . . . She was terrified and beyond excited, all at once. She shifted in her seat and felt the flesh between her legs throb.

She was incredibly wet, just from that small touch. Elise moaned to herself, pressing a hand between her legs. Sure enough, the crotch of her jeans was damp. Just kissing Rome had made her that turned on?

God.

Tomorrow seemed so far away.

The next day, Elise was pretty sure she was going to have a nervous breakdown. Her palms were damp, and she changed her shirt twice because she kept anxiously sweating through-out the day. Emily gave her strange looks when she showered twice in the same afternoon, but she was too polite to ask about that sort of thing.

Elise spent all day prepping. She wasn't exactly sure how she should prepare for sex. Shaving legs and such seemed like a given, and she lotioned up her limbs, then painted her nails and toenails. She could have gone somewhere to get a pedicure, but Beth Ann's salon was closed while she was on her honeymoon, and it felt like a betrayal to go anywhere else. She curled the ends of her long hair, put on light makeup, and dug through her lingerie drawer for her pret-tiest underwear and bra. Sadly, having sex wasn't something she normally considered, and her "prettiest" bra was plain white. Her panties were pretty unexciting, too; a pair of cotton briefs with a cute heart pattern was about the best she could do. She hated the sight of it and wondered if there was enough time to head out to the city and go shopping for something like that. The closest mall was at least forty-five minutes away, and she pushed the thought out of her head. She'd dress sexy for the next time.

Then she swallowed a hysterical giggle at the thought of "next time" and hoped that Rome wasn't so disappointed that there wouldn't be a next time. She critically studied her body in the full-length mirror in her room. One shoulder was slightly higher than the other, and the same with her hips. She twisted around, looking at her back. One shoulder blade was more prominent than the other, and a long, thin scar stretched from her neck to her tailbone, along with a matching six-inch one on her hip, remnants of back surgery to correct her scoliosis. It had been done when she was a teenager, and it wasn't completely aligned; the doctors couldn't perfect her back, only correct the worst of the curve. As a result, she looked like a doll that had been built slightly "off." Self-consciously, she turned and tried to stand in a way that would make her hips look straight. Then she sighed, uneasy. She'd ask Rome to have sex with the lights off. It'd be a little disappointing because she wanted to look at all of him, but with the lights on it would mean that he'd look at all of her, too, and she didn't want that. Maybe they could have sex with her clothes on.

Elise would suggest that.

She dug through her closet for her favorite pair of skinny jeans and slid them on, and considered her shoes. God, why didn't she have something sexy or cute? All she had were sneakers. It wasn't like this was a date, though, so she wasn't sure why she was freaking out so much. But it felt important that he thought she was pretty today. She considered . . . and then dug out the box of retro wear that they'd put together for the photo shoots. No one would see it but Rome, so she could borrow from it, right? She'd bought the stuff, after all.

There was a pair of shoes in her size that were cherry red platform heels with a peep toe. Okay, so she hadn't been looking for something quite that bold, but nothing else seemed right. After a moment's hesitation, she slipped them on. They were tall—really tall—but they made her legs look great. Okay, they'd stay. Now she needed some clothing to match them. She dug through the box for a bit longer and eventually came up with a red tank top and a tiny black sweater-shrug that fastened just over her breasts. It definitely wasn't her normal wear but she needed the extra bravado today, and a college sweatshirt wasn't going to do it.

Finally prepared for her date, Elise stared into the mirror at her reflection. Not bad. Not bad, really. She let her hair swing over her cheek and put one hand on her hip so it would seem like the tilt was deliberate. If she could just stand like that, she'd be almost pretty.

Then she sighed at her reflection. If she stood like that the entire time, he'd think she was mental.

She grabbed her purse and keys and headed down the stairs. She could hear Emily talking on the phone in the kitchen, and the clatter of pots and pans. Perfect time to creep out. Of course, she didn't know why she was sneaking out; Emily wasn't her mother. But she was heading for a rendezvous with a man for sex. That didn't feel like something you boldly strolled out the front door for.

Elise climbed into the rental car and immediately headed to the next town. She needed to bring condoms, and there was no way she was going to buy those in tiny Bluebonnet, where someone was sure to ask questions. Oh, the fun of a small town. At the pharmacy, she grabbed a box of the first condoms she saw, then raided a few other aisles so it wouldn't look like she was trucking for dick and only dick. She grabbed tampons, blush, nail polish, and socks, and then headed to the counter, her face burning as she paid for everything.

Then, she could delay no longer, so she drove back to Bluebonnet.

Beth Ann's small salon was a tiny cube of windows along the charming Main Street shops of Bluebonnet. Down the street was the city hall and library, and a few windows away, she knew Miranda's mother ran an antiques shop. She cruised past the row of empty parking spaces in front of the salon, and then drove around to the back of the strip so she could park—okay, hide—her car.

Luckily for her, Beth Ann's salon had a back door, and she snuck in through there, unlocking the door and practically running inside in her haste not to be seen. She turned on the lights, and they flickered for a moment, then came on. Elise stepped into the small salon and surveyed her surroundings.

Everything was still set up for the photo shoots. They'd had their first pinup shoot last weekend, just before Beth Ann had left for Alaska, and nothing had been moved since. Beige sheets of fabric covered the mini blinds over the windows to create a basic background, and more of the fabric was draped on the floor. A white stool sat amidst the fabric, the only seat in the room, the barber chair still in the front waiting room next to a row of seats. Heck, even her tripod was still in place. All she needed to do was set her camera on there and go to work. It was thoughtful of Beth Ann to leave everything in place in case she needed to utilize the studio.

She crossed her arms and studied the setup, eyeing her tripod. Too bad she couldn't get the right pictures of Rome. He'd make such a great subject. She thought of all those tanned muscles covered in tattoos, that delicious ring in his lip, and shivered. She wished she could shoot him again, at the moment when his eyes got all sleepy and long lashed because he was aroused.

But . . . she was assuming she could arouse him, right? Here she was, dressed in borrowed heels and a top that wasn't even hers because her own clothes were too frumpy. And it was just lipstick on a pig, because the moment those cute trappings came off, she'd just be a freak with crooked hips and scars and granny panties. She pictured Rome's beautiful eyes widening at the sight of her, and his disappointment when he saw what she really looked like.

She covered her face in her hands and groaned.

What the hell was she doing? Rome Lozada was gorgeous. Utter perfection. She was one step away from being the Hunchback of Notre Dame. There was no way he'd be interested in someone like her if she hadn't come on so strong.

Hey, wanna have sex? Yes? Sure, let's meet and hook up.

What guy in his right mind would say no? And then he'd go back to his buddies and tell them all about how he'd nailed the local dog.

She flinched at the thought, her arms tightening, and she stumbled back to the light. She was crazy for doing this. She couldn't go through with it. No way was she setting herself up for another ego bruising like that. This was a mistake and she had to leave before he got here. She'd just text him later tonight and tell him she'd changed her mind, and just avoid him until she left town. No harm, no foul.

Elise grabbed her keys and opened the back door of the salon to leave . . .

. . . just as a motorcycle pulled up next to her car, the helmeted driver raising a hand to wave at her.

Flustered, Elise froze on the doorstep. What did she do now? She'd have to tell him to his face that she was having second thoughts. That was so much harder than a text. Oh damn.

Rome swung a leg over the motorcycle and pulled his helmet off. He grinned at her. "I'm not too late, am I?"

She stared at him. Her mouth worked, but no words came out. God, she must look so stupid, all dressed up so he could fuck her. And he was being so nice and friendly about it, too. That would change as soon as she told him she didn't want to do this, that she was chickening out—

"You okay?" He approached her, a frown on his face. "You look a little on edge."

"I, um . . ." She swallowed hard.

"You're having second thoughts," he guessed.

She dropped her gaze, unable to look him in the eye.

"You want to go get a drink instead?"

Elise lifted her head, a hint of a frown on her face. "What?"

He shrugged, those blue eyes capturing her and making it impossible to look away. "You're all pretty tonight and I'm here, and you're freaking out. You want to get a drink? Take things slow?" A hint of a smile tugged at his face. "That's how most relationships go, you know. Couple of dates, couple of kisses, one thing leads to another, et cetera."

She blinked at him.

"You not a drinker suddenly? I know you like beer."

"No, that's not it," she said hastily. "It's just, um . . . relationships?"

He tilted his head, eyes narrowing. "You got a problem with going on a date with me?"

She shook her head. "Sounds nice," she said shyly. She just wasn't sure why he'd want to date someone like her. A quick secret bang was one thing, but a date was . . . well, it felt like more.

"So you want to go get a drink?" he asked again, and offered her the bike helmet tucked under his arm.

"I do. Just not Maya Loco," she said quickly. That was the only place in Bluebonnet to get a drink.

His mouth twisted. "You worried someone will see you dating the trashy biker?"

Trashy biker? She blinked in surprise. "Actually, I was worried it'd get back to my brother, and you said you wanted to stay off his radar."

He inhaled. "Ah. Right. Okay. I know a place a few towns over. You want to go?"

She nodded. "Do you have another helmet?"

"Nah, you can use mine." He winked. "Not much of a loss if *I* bite it, but people would be sad if you died."

Before she could comment on that grim explanation, he tugged the helmet out of her hands and put it over her head. As he tied the strap under her chin, he murmured, "You look hot tonight, by the way."

And she was glad he couldn't see her blush under the visor.

They drove for a good while down the highway, and just when Elise was going to ask him where they were headed, he exited and took her down a few side streets until they parked in front of a rather rough-looking building with a bunch of bikes in front of it. Neon signs in the windows advertised a million different kinds of beer, and several people were loitering around the corner of the building, dressed in more leather than she'd ever seen.

Okay, he'd taken her to a biker bar.

Elise sat, frozen, until he reached backward and patted her thigh as an indication that she should move. She did, swinging a leg over the bike and nearly stumbling, thanks to her ridiculous shoes. Rome caught her arm, grinning, and then he got off the bike, too. He reached for the helmet and unbuckled it under her chin, then pulled it off and set it on the seat. When she didn't speak, he glanced over at her.

"You okay?"

She leaned in, sidling as close to him as she dared, her gaze darting around. "Is this a biker bar?"

"It might be. That a problem?"

She bit her lip. "I've never been." Heck, she hadn't been to a real bar, much less a biker one. She'd always avoided that sort of thing before.

"You said you wanted to live a little, right?" He grinned at her, all piercings and boyish smile. "Besides, I know the owner. He's a good guy." He tugged an arm around her waist

and looped his thumb into one of the belt loops of her jeans
and nudged her forward.

She moved with him, her own fingers sliding to his belt
loops. For balance, she told herself. That was all.

The inside of the place looked just like she'd imagined
it would from the outside. More neon signs lit the place up,
the only decor other than the mirrors behind the counter
and a dart board on the wall. There was a jukebox in the
corner, and the music coming out of it was classic rock. Such
a cliché. The bar was long and the seats nearly full—and
almost all men. There were a few tables in the back, and
Rome dragged her toward one, for which she was eternally
grateful.

He let go of her and pulled her chair out, grinning as she
sat down. As soon as she thumped into the seat, he leaned
in, resting his hands against the back of her chair, his mouth
moving so close to her ear that her nipples got hard. "What
do you normally drink?"

She swallowed hard. "Light beer?"

"I think you need something stronger. Okay if I get you
something different?" At her nod, he chuckled, and his
breath tickled her ear. "One shot of Jäger, coming up."

A shot? Oh jeez. Elise wanted something that would go
down easy, that she could ease into getting a little tipsy with.
Not much, just enough to loosen up. When she had mixed
drinks, she normally went for something with an umbrella.
Most of the time, there wasn't much of a point of drinking
other than the occasional beer; she usually only drank
around family, and getting plastered in front of your parents
wasn't exactly something she planned on doing.

When Rome left her side to go to the bar and get drinks,
she gave his back a panicked look and surveyed her surroundings. The interior was slightly smoky, thanks to the
cigarettes that everyone at the bar seemed to be having.
Weren't there no-smoking laws? Everyone she could see was
male, wearing leather, and drinking beer. Was she the only

girl in here? That made her terribly uncomfortable. She shrank lower in her seat, avoiding eye contact and wishing Rome would return in a hurry.

He returned a few minutes later with a couple of dark-looking shots. To her dismay, he put both of them in front of her. "Bottoms up."

"What's this?" she asked.

"Told you. Jäger."

She stared at it. "You not going to drink one?"

"I'll get new drinks in a minute. Wanted to make sure you were okay over here. You looked a little scared." He nudged a shot glass toward her. "That'll help."

Elise nodded and picked it up, slowly raising it to her pursed lips.

"Don't sip it," he advised. "Trust me. Just chug it."

All right, then. She sucked in a breath, then tipped her head back and downed the shot. The peculiar taste of the shot touched her tongue—something between cough syrup and licorice—and then it burned its way down her throat. She coughed, putting down the shot glass and raising a hand to her mouth.

Rome laughed and slapped her on the back. "You okay?"

She nodded, her eyes threatening to stream tears. "Strong," she wheezed, waving a hand in front of her mouth as if that would take away some of the burn.

"The next one will go down easier. Trust me."

Elise swallowed hard. She had to drink another? She shook her head even as he nudged the shot toward her.

"Come on," he coaxed. "After that, we'll go to the easy stuff."

"What about you?" she coughed.

"I don't need loosening up," he told her with a grin. "I'm not the one who looks like she's about to be attacked at any moment."

He had a point. She braced herself, grimaced, and chugged the second shot. Nope, he was wrong—it burned just as bad as the first one. Coughing, she covered her mouth and grimaced. This time, tears did stream down her face.

Rome chuckled. "I'll get you something to sip, how's that?" He took the shot glasses away and stood, then pressed a kiss to the top of her head before heading back to the bar.

She wanted to tell him to stop with the drinks, that she didn't want to drink any more, that she wasn't having fun . . . but that kiss on top of her head had silenced her. It had been so easy and affectionate and utterly spontaneous, and it made her wish she hadn't been such a chicken about the whole thing. So what if he thought her body was ugly? She would get to have great sex with him, right?

She was so stupid for pushing him away, really.

Her belly burned with the shots of alcohol, and she felt warm all over. A little more relaxed, too, if she was going to be honest with herself. Just a little looser. She glanced over at the bar, looking for Rome, and noticed he was leaning over it, his butt sticking out as he chatted with the bartender. Man, he sure did have a nice butt. She sighed, thinking of it. Was it bad that she wondered what it'd look like, naked? Would it be small and tight, or would he have nice big muscular buttocks? She tried to picture it in her mind. How pinchable would it be? Elise raised her fingers and squinted, pretending to pinch it from afar.

Which meant, of course, that Rome chose that moment to turn around with two new drinks.

She dropped her hand, feeling guilty and obvious as he returned to their table.

"You okay?"

She nodded, face hot, and looked for a change of subject. When he set a glass in front of her, that seemed like the perfect opportunity. "So what's this drink?"

"I got you a Crown and Coke. It's a little easier than a shot and it'll keep your nice buzz going."

"How do you know I have a buzz?" She picked up the glass and sniffed it.

Rome grinned at her, that piercing on his lip catching her attention. "Because your eyes are all soft and you're smiling at me instead of looking like you want to crawl under the table."

"Oh." Yep, that'd do it.

"You feeling better?"

She nodded and lifted the drink to her lips, taking a small taste. It was strong, but smoother than the shots she'd done. "So are you trying to get me drunk so you can have your way with me?"

He laughed, taking a healthy swig of his own drink. "Nope. Just wanted you to relax a little. You looked pretty tense earlier."

She was.

"You regretting things?"

"I kinda figured *you* would be," she admitted.

He frowned as if she'd said something strange. "Me? Why?"

Elise pulled her hair forward, dragging it across her bad cheek. "Obvious reasons."

He lifted his pierced eyebrow. "Obvious reasons like . . . what?"

She snorted. "Obvious reasons usually don't need explaining."

"I think this one does," he said slowly. When she went to lift her drink again, he put a hand over her wrist. "Maybe you slow it down on the alcohol a little. You don't have to drink it all at once. I want you to have a nice, friendly buzz, not get sloppy drunk. That wasn't my goal here."

Oh. She put her drink back down.

"Now, tell me why I wouldn't want to have sex with you."

For some reason, the knot that usually formed in her stomach was relaxed, and she shrugged and gestured at herself. "This. All this."

Rome leaned back in his chair. "What's wrong with all this? I thought it looked pretty damn good tonight, myself."

He did. Rome always looked good, but tonight he looked dangerously so. She couldn't stop staring at the piercings on his face that seemed to only make him more attractive, the black inkwork that peeked out from under the collar of his long-sleeved tight black T-shirt, and the jeans that hugged his ass just right. Even his beat-up combat boots looked rugged and masculine and totally, completely Rome. But herself? Dressed up in totteringly high heels and a shirt she'd have never left the store with? "This isn't me."

"How is it not you?"

She sighed heavily, leaning forward to prop an elbow on the table and place her chin on her hand. Her hair draped over her shoulder, and Rome leaned in and brushed it back. "I borrowed this stuff from the photo shoot because I wanted to be pretty," she admitted in a low voice.

"You're always pretty." His blue eyes held her captive.

She snorted, feeling loose enough to argue with him. "Bullshit, Rome."

He raised an eyebrow. "Why is that bullshit?"

She glanced around to see if anyone was paying attention to them. When she was satisfied nobody was, she leaned in and drew a circle in the air, focusing on her cheek. "This. And other stuff."

"Other stuff?" he asked, and he reached out to touch her, brushing his hand over her cheek where the port-wine stain used to be. "Such as?"

She lowered her voice and leaned in. "My body."

"What's wrong with your body?"

"It's crooked. Scoliosis. And I have a scar." She nodded slowly and gestured. "Great big one."

His lips twitched with amusement and he leaned in, gesturing that she should move closer. "I don't know if you noticed," he said in a low voice, "but I have a lot of tattoos."

"I noticed."

"So I think I can handle a scar or two."

"And I didn't have any pretty underwear," she told him sadly. "No girly cute stuff. Never had a reason to buy it before."

"So . . . you didn't want to have sex with me because of your scar and because you didn't have cute underwear?"

Why did it look like he was trying hard not to laugh? She was having a serious conversation with him, darn it. She nodded, trying to give him a haughty look. "These things are important."

"You know what I think?"

"What?"

"I think two shots of Jäger was too much." He reached for her Crown and Coke. "Maybe I should drink that."

She held it away from him, and when he raised an eyebrow, she took another sip, giving him a challenging look. "I like how I feel."

"Oh, I bet you do."

Gosh, he was so cute when he smiled. He was smiling at her right now, all blue eyes and long lashes and piercings. The septum piercing in his nose gave him a dangerous look, but it was the lip piercing that she found so fascinating. She wanted to touch it, suddenly, and reached forward to graze her thumb over his lower lip. It was so soft, so wonderfully in contrast with the hard metal of the ring. She ran her fingers over it, fascinated.

He took the tip of her thumb between his lips and brushed against it with his tongue.

She sucked in a breath, heat flooding through her body. Oh wow.

"So were those the only reasons you didn't want to have sex, Elise?" He pulled her hand away from his lip and held her wrist, and began to slowly press nibbling kisses on her palm.

She stared at the sight, fascinated by the tickling motions, and feeling that sexy heat climb through her body again. His mouth on her skin was incredible to watch. "I don't want to be in another dog party," she admitted in a low voice. "It hurts too much."

His fingers tightened on her wrist, just a bit. "I would never do that to you, Elise. I think you're gorgeous. Incredibly shy, but sexy as hell. And I want you to not be shy around me, because I'm no better or worse than you. I'm just me and you're just you, understand?"

"It's hard," she admitted in a low voice. "No one's ever wanted me for me before."

"I know the same feeling." He pressed another kiss to her palm, his tongue swiping against the heel in a way that made her tingle. "And they're idiots."

She smiled.

"That's better," he said, nipping at her palm again and then stroking over it with his tongue. "And if you're not ready for sex quite yet, I'm fine with that. Most people don't jump right in, you know."

"I'm ready for sex," Elise admitted, "I bought condoms at the pharmacy. Ribbed for my pleasure. I'm just a big chicken."

Rome chuckled. "Fair enough."

"I don't want to be chicken, though."

"You don't have to be chicken forever," he said with a grin that made her knees weak. "We'll work through that."

"Okay," she breathed, entranced by his smile.

"So." He studied her palm, holding it in one hand and tracing a finger down it with the other. It kept her neatly trapped close to him, and stopped her from drinking. Not that she was objecting to any of that. She was fascinated by his small touches. No one ever touched her because they just wanted to touch her.

She almost wept with the sheer delight of it.

"If you want life experience, Elise, I'm here to help you in whatever you need."

"Thank you," she told him, unable to take her eyes off his finger on her hand as it traced the lines of her palm.

"What did you have in mind?"

"I honestly have no clue," she admitted.

"You can't think of anything you'd like to do?" He seemed surprised by that.

She thought for a minute, her mind circling. What could she do in Bluebonnet? She was here to take photos . . . Her mind suddenly flashed on Beth Ann's salon, still set up like a photo studio. "Would you let me take more pictures of you?"

"Of course," he said, and kissed her fingertip. It made her nipples harden in response.

"Nude?"

He paused. "What?"

"Too much?" She was disappointed. "Maybe just topless?"

He looked surprised. "You want to take nude pictures of me?"

She slid her chair closer, pulling her hand from his, and then she was practically squeezing next to him on his side of the table. Her hand slid over his arm, pushing up the short sleeve of his black shirt, and she stared at his tattoos and the lines of his muscles. "This is beautiful, you know. You're beautiful to me. I'd love to photograph this. All ink and muscle and skin and light and shadow." Her fingers slid under the shirt and she kept touching all that skin, so warm and delicious. "Mmm."

"God damn, Elise," he murmured hoarsely, leaning in to press a kiss on her jaw as she cuddled closer. "You sure you're a virgin? Because you're making my dick hard as fuck."

She nodded and slid her hands out of his shirt, tilting her mouth toward his for a kiss. "All virgin." And his mouth was so close to hers that she wanted to lick that little ring on his lip, just a bit of a tease with her mouth. So she did.

And he gave a small groan low in his throat that was gorgeous to hear.

"So can I do more photos of you?" she whispered against his mouth, barely audible through the music blaring in the background. "Sexy, gorgeous photos of all this skin?"

"I don't know if I'll do nude," he told her softly, and his tongue snaked out to graze against her lips in a way that made her whimper. "But we'll start with shirtless and take it from there. Sound good?"

"I can't wait," she breathed. And she really couldn't. "I want to see what you look like under all this. I want to see every one of your tattoos. I want to touch them."

His mouth slid over hers again in the barest approximation of a kiss. "For a virgin, you sure do talk sexy."

"Do I?" She seemed pleased at that. "It's too bad we can't do the photo shoot tonight, but all my equipment is back at the Peppermint House."

"We're not doing anything tonight," he told her in a firm voice, and pulled away from her. "You're a little more tipsy than I'd prefer."

Well, poop. He was abandoning her? She draped her arms around his shoulders and pressed her chest against him, enjoying his low groan of frustration. "But what if I want to do all kinds of things tonight? All kinds of naughty things?"

"Elise," he murmured. "Damn it. I didn't know you'd be a cuddly drunk if I got a few shots in you."

She trailed her fingers along the collar of his shirt and then dipped one in to touch the dip at the base of his collarbone. "I can do more than cuddle if you want. I'm feeling pretty good right now—"

"No—" He pried her hand out of his shirt.

" —but we'd have to have the lights off."

"I . . . Huh?" He gave her an odd look. "You want the lights off? For the photo shoot?"

"No, for sex."

He rolled his eyes. "There's nothing wrong with your body, Elise. And I intend to show you that. As for tonight, we're not doing anything more intimate than, say . . . playing darts." He gestured at the nearby dartboard.

"We're not?" She stuck her lower lip out at him.

"We're not," he said, and got up from the table. He returned a moment later with darts in hand and gave her the blue ones. "Come on. I need a distraction and I'm betting you've never played darts in a biker bar."

He needed a distraction, did he? Just when she was feeling cuddly and a bit, dare she say it, horny? "But what if I want to make out?"

"Not tonight," he told her firmly. "You're too drunk and it's my fault. Now, darts."

She picked up one of the darts and then gave him another pouting look. "But I wanted to kiss you again."

"Darts."

"But—"

"Darts," he repeated.

She gave the darts in her hand a long look, and then lifted one to her mouth and licked the length of it suggestively.

He groaned and took it away from her. "You know what? No darts after all. I don't think I'm going to be able to stand for much longer."

Elise giggled.

SIX

An hour later, they'd paid the bar tab and driven back to Bluebonnet. Elise was surprised to find the bike pulling up to the Peppermint House. She frowned as Rome helped her off the bike. "I left my car behind the salon."

"Give me your phone."

Her eyes widened and she handed it to him. "Are you going to text me dirty pictures?"

"No, I'm going to give you my number. Call me tomorrow and I'll drive you to get your car."

"You're no fun," she told him, wrapping her arms around his neck as he put his number into her phone. He put an arm around her waist to balance her, since she was a little tipsy, and she liked that. He was so warm and so big. Her mouth was also rather close to his ear, and one of those fascinating gauges was inches away from her lips. She wondered if she could stick the tip of her tongue through the hole, and licked his ear experimentally.

Rome groaned again. "God damn, Elise. I'm not getting

you drunk again until after we have sex, because you are one frisky girl when you get a bit of alcohol in you."

She giggled and sucked on his earlobe. "I like touching you," she murmured.

"Christ, I like touching you, too, and I wish to hell you weren't drunk," he told her, dragging her away. "Now," he said, handing back her phone. "Call me tomorrow, okay?"

She bit her lip and nodded, giving him a wide-eyed stare. "Tomorrow."

"That's right." He stared at her for a long moment, and then grabbed her by the face and gave her a long, hot, tongue-filled kiss that made her knees all weak again. Then he released her just as fast. "Fuck, I'm going to regret not screwing you in the morning."

"Me too," she said with a sigh.

"Call me," he demanded, pointing at the phone.

"I will," she said, smiling drunkenly.

Oh god, she was never going to live this down.

Elise pulled the blankets over her head, wishing her memories would go away.

Call him? Not in this lifetime.

Seriously, how drunk was she last night? Elise rolled over in bed, blanching at the weird taste in her mouth and squinting at the daylight seeping through the blankets. She'd only had two shots and a mixed drink, right? Well, okay, she vaguely remembered stealing a couple of sips from Rome's drink when he wasn't drinking it fast enough. That had been enough for a hangover, apparently.

And enough for her to lose all control of her ever-loving mind. She recalled tonguing his ear, and running her fingers under his shirt . . . and asking him to pose nude for her.

She also recalled him fending her off, which was pretty damn humiliating. And licking a dart. A dart! Who knew where that thing had been? Dear lord.

Definitely too much alcohol, too fast.

She pulled the blankets off of her head and fumbled for her phone to check the time. There was a text message on her screen.

Hope you're not too hung over this morning. Had no idea you were such a lightweight.

She groaned again and rolled back into her bed, texting a response. You're still talking to me?

Well, yeah. Why wouldn't I?

Because I made a fool out of myself last night?

Nah, you were cute. You're a v. cuddly drunk.

She didn't even know what to say. Was he flirting via text or was he just informing her that she was a gropey drunk? She thought for a minute and then sent, Yeah, sorry about that.

It's ok. So when did you want to go get your car?

Oh god. She didn't want to see him right now. Not when she was still feeling weird about everything. That's okay. I'll walk there and get it.

I don't mind. I'm off today.

No, really, it's okay.

There was a long pause, and she thought maybe he wasn't going to answer her. Then, finally, he replied. You blowing me off, Elise?

Oh no. Were his feelings hurt? For some reason, the thought of that bothered her. I just feel weird about things. I acted like an idiot last night.

Actually, I thought it was cute. I thought you were cute, though you probably regret telling me about your panties.

Yes, yes, I do. She put a hand to her cheek, hating the flush there. It was more than just the mention of the panties, though. He thought she was cute? She couldn't stop smiling. You . . . sure you still want to hang out with me?

You bet. I won't even make you drink Jäger this time.

A wild giggle erupted in her throat. So I guess you didn't like me THAT grabby, she texted back.

Oh, I did. This time, I just don't want to feel like an ass if I get grabby back. So what are you doing later?

Her heart pounded, just a bit. I don't know, she sent back. Did you have something in mind?

Was thinking about picking up wings and a movie and staying in my cabin. You wanna come with?

You're just inviting me because you secretly want pizza and can't balance a pizza on the back of that bike.

Tell you what. I'll get the beer and the movie and the cabin. You get a pizza. :)

She laughed. I knew it!

My secret is out. :)

There's a flaw in this plan.

What's that?

My car's still over at the salon. You'd have to come get me, take me there, and then I'd have to go get a pizza.

And this is a problem . . . ?

Well, if I'm doing all the work, I have to consider this proposition very carefully. What kind of movie?

Ummm. Something with lots of explosions and car chases. Or are you into stuff with subtitles and weeping?

Let's go with explosions.

You're a girl after my own heart.

She was still blushing. You're forgetting something else.

What's that?

If I park my car in the ranch parking lot, my brother will see it and start looking for me.

This is indeed a dilemma. Let me think this one over.

Don't hurt yourself.

Why, Elise, that was rather sassy of you. I approve. I should send you more text messages.

She was feeling rather sassy, darn it. Dirty ones?

Depends on if you're good or not.

Quantify "good" for me.

Damn, did you just text me "quantify"? That's kinda hot. You a nerd?

Nope. Don't get your hopes up too much.

Damn. Well, how about we skip the food and I just come pick you up instead?

I can bring sandwiches if you like?

Now you're talking. So what time should I come get you?

After dark. If my brother sees me . . .

Gotcha, gotcha. After dark. Meanwhile, I'll be spending my day in the main cabin, suggesting that Grant take Brenna out for a nice dinner, just the two of them.

Sneak.

Pretty much. I'll call you when I head over & we'll get your car later. Wear something comfortable. Be you. Not those crazy shoes you wore last night . . . even though those were pretty damn hot.

Sneakers it is. When he didn't text her back, she grabbed her pillow and squealed into it like a teenage girl. Rome wanted to see her again and he was picking her up for a date tonight. Oh my god. The man of her dreams was interested in her. This couldn't be real, could it? She scrolled back through the flirty series of text messages they'd exchanged. It seemed legit. *Please, please don't let him be messing with me,* she prayed.

If this was all an elaborate hoax of some kind, she didn't think she could take it. She liked Rome far too much, and the devastation would be too sharp.

Elise fixed two brown bag lunches, stuffed with enormous sandwiches and bags of chips. She stole a few of the fresh-baked cookies Emily had on the counter while she was in the kitchen, too, and packed them all into one large grocery sack.

Emily had baked three kinds of cookies that day, since she was agitated over her attic. She always baked more when she needed favors from someone. "I swear I heard something up there last night. It sounded like footsteps. You didn't hear it?"

Elise shook her head. "I didn't hear anything." She didn't mention the fact that she'd been drunk and probably would have slept through a tornado.

"I'm going to see if one of the officers can come over and check things out this morning," Emily told her as she put another pan of treats into the oven. "Hank's a fan of the peanut butter chocolate cookies."

Elise hesitated. "Do you want me to go take a look?"

"Nah, you seem busy and my sister said she'd send Hank over anyhow." Emily pulled off her oven mitts and gave her a scrutinizing look. "You going somewhere tonight?"

She considered telling Emily where she was going; on one hand, she was excited—and okay, a bit proud—that she had a date tonight. On the other hand, Bluebonnet was a small town and if one person found out she was seeing Rome, it'd be all over in a matter of days. "Um."

"I won't say anything," Emily said. "Especially not if it's Mr. Tall, Pierced, and Tattooed."

She felt her face flush with color, a sure giveaway, and pretended to concentrate on folding down the top of the paper bag in her hand. "How did you know?"

"He's the only person I've seen around you other than family. Given that he's sexy and carried you up to bed oh so tenderly the other night? I had a hunch."

"Have you . . . Does my brother . . ."

"Does your brother know? Why would he? It's none of my business who you see." Emily winked at her and put a few extra cookies onto a square of foil and folded them up, then handed it to her. "Tell Rome I said hello, and have a good time."

"You rock."

"Hey, someone around here needs to get laid," Emily said with a cheeky grin. "If it's not me, I hope it's you."

Okay, that was embarrassing. She wanted to correct Emily, to tell her she was only going to have dinner and a movie with Rome. That it wasn't that kind of date . . . except it *was*, wasn't it? He was going to help her get some life experience, and she was going to lose her virginity.

So yeah, it was pretty much exactly that. So why was she so embarrassed at the thought? Elise scooped up the bagged sandwiches and gave Emily an awkward smile. "Thank you for everything. You don't know how much I appreciate it."

"Hey, you're a customer and a friend. It's my job to make you happy." Emily grinned. "I'll leave the front door unlocked as usual. And I won't wait up."

Elise's phone buzzed with an incoming text, saving her from stammering a few more excuses. She grabbed the bagged sandwiches in one arm and pulled her phone out with her free hand, thumbing on the screen. Sure enough, there was a text from Rome.

I'm out front. Want me to come in and wait?

She smoothed a hand over her hair and rushed for the front door, shoving her phone in her pocket on the way out. She hoped she looked okay tonight. She'd skipped all makeup except for a little lip gloss and a bit of eyeliner and mascara. The remains of her port-wine stain were more visible this way, but she figured if it was going to freak him out, it was better to get it out of the way before someone got too attached. Her hair was in a long, loose braid over one shoulder and she'd pulled out an old cable-knit sweater and her favorite comfy jeans and slip-on sneakers. Definitely not going for sexy tonight. Even her panties were still granny, sadly. If the man said he didn't care about her appearance, she'd definitely be testing that, wouldn't she?

Elise slipped out the front door and glanced around. Parked in front of the bed-and-breakfast, his bike parallel and taking up two spaces, was Rome. He held the motorcycle helmet in one hand and grinned at her in the twilight. He wore jeans, too, and heavy, beat-up combat boots and a wifebeater under a plaid shirt. It was very casual clothing, but it only made her notice the tattoos and piercings more, especially when he grinned at her in greeting.

"Howdy, neighbor," he mock-drawled. "You ready to get your movie on?"

She nodded and held up the oversized brown bag that she'd packed both of their sandwiches in. "Got food."

"Perfection." He held the helmet out to her. "Your brother took Brenna out for dinner, so we'll be able to sneak into my cabin without being seen."

"Oh good," she breathed, and stepped closer to take the helmet from him. But he didn't give it to her. Instead, he fitted it on her head and buckled the strap for her, his fingers brushing under her chin. It was an intimate gesture, and it made her heart pound with excitement and anticipation.

He offered her a hand and she tucked hers into his, holding his fingers as she slid a leg over the back of the bike and then moved to sit behind him. She tucked the bag of food between their bodies and wrapped one arm around him, the other around the food.

"Nu-uh," he told her. "Both arms around me or we're not going anywhere. I want you to be safe."

"But . . . the food."

"I can eat a flattened sandwich," he told her. "Just press your body against my back and it'll trap the bag between us."

She did, trying not to blush since it meant her breasts were pushing against his back. The sandwiches were, too, of course, but who cared about those?

Rome slid a hand down her arm, then patted her clasped hands over his front, as if approving. Then he started the bike. "Hold on tight, baby."

And they were off.

The Daughtry Ranch was about fifteen minutes outside of Bluebonnet, off one of the side roads and in the middle of nowhere, the land heavily treed. Elise knew they'd chosen this location because they needed the rugged land for the business, but fifteen minutes outside of town meant she spent fifteen minutes with her breasts pressed against Rome's strong, broad back, playing his words in her head over and over again.

He'd called her "baby." Was that just a casual endearment? Did he call all women "baby" like some guys called them "doll" or "sweet cheeks"? Or did it mean something else? Was she obsessing?

Probably.

When they exited the highway to the ranch, Elise held her breath and bit her lip, anticipating the worst. What if they pulled into the parking lot just as Brenna and Grant pulled out? What if Miranda and Dane saw them? What if Pop did?

But all her fears were for nothing—they pulled into the parking lot and it was empty. Rome parked in the last space at the far end and grinned back at her as he turned his bike off. "Saturday night. Everyone's out but us."

Good, she thought.

He helped her off the bike, handed her the now-flattened bag of sandwiches, and then undid the chin strap on the helmet for her, removing it and placing the helmet back on the bike. Then it was just her and him, and she stared up at him mutely, unsure what to do next.

Rome solved that problem for her. He took the bag from her hands and leaned in to give her the barest brush of a kiss over her mouth. "I'll get that for you."

She let him take it from her numb hands, thinking about that quick, easy kiss as they walked one of the small trails to his cabin.

He had one of the smaller ones, she'd noticed before, and it was set squarely in the midst of the others, between Pop's cabin and Grant's larger cabin-slash-house. It was the sight of Grant's cabin that made her hurry to walk a little faster, just in case someone emerged from there, even though she knew no one was home. She was still a chicken, really, when it came down to things.

He opened the door to the cabin and let her go in first, and Elise studied his small home anew as she stepped inside. There was a single lamp lit by the bedside table, and his bed—a full—only had one pillow. A quilt that she'd seen tossed over the back of one of the lodge couches covered his bed, and nothing hung on the walls. No pictures, no posters, nothing. He had a small counter in the back of his cabin, and next to a sink was a mini fridge.There were two doors in the cabin—one to a closet and one to a bathroom. Directly across from the bed there was a small nightstand, and a tiny TV-DVD combo sat on top of it.

There were no chairs. How had she forgotten that? Where were they going to sit when they watched the movie and ate? She glanced at the bed and blushed, realizing that they'd probably both have to sit there.

"You want a beer?" Rome headed to the back of the cabin and placed the bag of food on the counter, then reached into the mini fridge to pull out a cold beer. He turned and held it out to her, and she saw that he'd picked her favorite brand, the kind she drank that night during the storm.

"Thanks," she murmured, twisting the lid off and taking a sip. She only tasted it, though. It seemed like she was constantly getting drunk around him, wasn't she? If this kept up, she'd be an alcoholic before she lost her virginity.

He opened a beer for himself, took a long pull, and then set it down on one of the nightstands. "You want to eat now or watch the movie now?"

"We could do both at once, I guess?"

"Sounds like a plan." He popped open a DVD case and slid a disc into the TV, then flicked it on. "Sorry the TV's so small. I didn't have one, so I borrowed this one from Pop."

"It's fine." She didn't care about the screen size.

He glanced over his shoulder at her, a grin on his face. "I hope you're in the mood for a classic."

"Classic?"

"*Lethal Weapon*. I thought it'd be fun. You like it?"

"Never seen it."

His eyes widened as if she'd said something shocking. "Well, consider this part of your education."

They got sandwiches and chips to go with the beer, and Elise deliberately trailed a step or two behind Rome, waiting to see where he sat. When he sat down on the left side of the bed and leaned back against the headboard, his legs stretched out in front of him, she did the same, but on the right side. The pillow lay sandwiched between them like an armrest, but she didn't touch it. She was too nervous.

This was the first time she'd ever sat on a guy's bed and watched a movie. Again, she felt like an awkward teenager. She took slow, methodical bites of her sandwich, her gaze glued to the tiny screen as she ate. She was barely paying attention to the movie. Instead, she was attuned to everything Rome did. His body was relaxed and casual on his side of the bed, legs stretched out. He ate with gusto, devouring his sandwich and chips in a matter of minutes, whereas she picked at her food and barely sipped her beer. He chuckled at the movie now and then, which inspired her to make a token attempt at laughing, as well, so he wouldn't realize she was paying more attention to the way his foot twitched when he laughed than what was going on on-screen.

"You not going to eat your chips?" he asked at some point, when she was only halfway through her sandwich.

She shook her head and mutely offered him the bag, which he took with a smile of gratitude that made her heart flutter in her chest. She'd have passed him her sandwich, too, if he'd simply smile at her again.

But eventually the food was gone and Elise wiped her hands with a napkin, unsure of what to do with herself now.

Rome kept watching the screen, but he pulled one leg in and leaned forward, unlacing his shoes and then dropping them on the ground next to the bed. Then, he glanced over at her. "You want to take your shoes off? Get a little more comfy?"

"Okay." She kicked her sneakers off, wiggling her bare toes as she put her legs back on the bed.

He glanced over at her feet. "Cute toes."

She blushed and looked over at his feet. His socks looked worn and a bit threadbare, and she was pretty sure one toe was about to pop through the fabric. "Cute socks."

He snorted. "They're on my list of things to buy on pay-day." And he slid an arm around her shoulder and dragged her against him, ever so casually.

Elise stiffened in surprise, her cheek resting on his shoulder. The pillow was still sandwiched between them, pressing against her stomach, but the rest of her was cuddled against him and his arm lay over her shoulders like a blanket. She felt his fingers twitch against her sweater, and then his hand pulled on her long braid. As she watched, his fingers tugged at the band holding the end and then he pulled it off. Her hair immediately cascaded free, and he began to stroke and drag his fingers through the length.

"That's better," he murmured, "don't you think?"

She didn't respond; she couldn't. All the words—and air—had been sucked out of her body. Instead, she was acutely aware of the feel of his body against hers, the scent of him, the heat of his skin. She didn't know where to put her hands. One was trapped against the pillow, but the other was in no-man's-land. After a moment of indecision, she placed it against his stomach.

That was a mistake. Oh, sweet lord, the man didn't have an ounce of fat on him, did he? She could practically feel lines of muscle under her fingertips, and she wanted to jerk her hand away, because her body was responding to that small touch as if it were starving. Her breasts ached and felt tight, and her pulse felt as if it were throbbing right between her legs.

And his hand kept right on stroking through her hair, his fingers tangling and dragging through in a repetitive, almost soothing motion.

Something exploded on screen and she jumped a little, surprised at the sound.

He turned toward her, ever so slightly, and his mouth seemed inches away from hers. "You okay?" he murmured.

She nodded against his shoulder. "Just startled me."

"You enjoying the movie?"

She couldn't tell him a thing about the movie, but she was enjoying being here in the bed with him. It was terrifying and wonderful all at once, and yet she couldn't stop wishing for a lightning storm that would short out the TV and make him pay attention to her.

So she only nodded.

Rome's hand tugged on her hair again, then released it slowly, and it slid through his fingers. "I love this."

Her breath caught in her throat. "You do?"

"I do. It's like silk." His thumb rubbed on her hair, and she wished, oh she wished that it was rubbing on her body instead. "I keep imagining this falling all over me when we have sex."

Elise sucked in a breath. She pictured it, her leaning over him, her hair spilling over her shoulder and brushing against his tattooed skin. Her pulse thrummed in response.

His face tilted toward hers again, and their mouths were close. "I keep picturing us having sex a lot, you know. Do you?"

No words formed in her mouth. She wasn't sure what to say —or even if there was a breath of air left in her body. She'd been picturing sex the entire time they'd been sitting here on this bed, but she wasn't brave enough to tell him that. A small whimper escaped her throat instead, and her face colored with embarrassment at the sound.

"Is that a yes, baby?" His big body shifted, and he turned toward her, his focus suddenly on her like she'd been hoping for all night. His hand cupped her cheek and his thumb stroked over the corner of her mouth. "Is that a yes that's too shy to come out of your mouth? You been thinking about sex with me?"

Her lips trembled, and her gaze flicked from his eyes to his mouth. *Words. I need words.* But there were no words in her throat. She felt curiously tense, like she'd shatter—or burst into tears—at the slightest movement, and that was silly. But her entire body was on edge.

So she just watched him, her heart in her throat, hope and fear and longing in her eyes.

Rome's hand smoothed down the side of her face, his gaze focused on her. "I think you do and you're too shy to admit it."

She closed her eyes and leaned into his touch, letting her body speak for her. Letting it show the aching need inside her.

The lightest brush of a kiss pressed against her mouth, and the sleek metal of his lip ring scraped along her lip.

Elise moaned in response, her mouth parting under his as he began to gently kiss her with soft, sweet presses of his lips against hers. His tongue flicked against her open mouth, and she whimpered again, this time the sound thick with need.

"Sweet Elise," he murmured, and his hand tangled in her hair, dragging her head back just a little. Then she felt his mouth press harder on her own, and his tongue slicked deep inside.

Then he was kissing her, wet and thorough, like she'd dreamed about, like she'd anticipated ever since she'd seen him pull up on his motorcycle in front of the Peppermint House earlier that day. Like he was devouring her with all the need and urgency that she felt beating a pace through her body. He tasted like beer and she should have been repulsed by it, but she was fascinated, instead. And when his tongue flicked against hers in a playful swipe, she responded with her own.

And this time, Rome groaned, his lips moving against hers as he spoke. "God damn. Kissing you is like falling into madness, isn't it? It's like you push away my brain with every little flick of that sweet tongue of yours, until I have nothing left in my head."

She didn't want talk, though; she wanted more kissing. More deep, wet, hot kisses that made her forget about everything in the world outside of Rome's mouth. Her tongue pressed experimentally against his lip, and she felt the metal of his piercing, so she licked at it, instead. She wanted to lick all of him, all over.

He shifted against her, and then she heard the click of a remote, and the TV went silent.

Elise's eyes opened in surprise. "M-m-movie?" she stammered against his mouth.

"Fuck the movie," he murmured, his beautiful face inches from her own. "I just put it on to relax you. I wanted to jump you as soon as I got you through this door."

He did? A gratified surge tore through her, and she reached for him, sliding her hand over his flat belly again. She really liked touching him.

Rome groaned again, and slid down slightly in the bed, and his mouth was kissing hers again, his hands pressing her down so she'd lie in the bed beside him, and she did. She felt him toss the pillow to the floor, the thump of it on the ground barely registering in her consciousness.

And then they were curled on the bed together, mouths locked, and nothing was between them any longer.

It was pure, delicious bliss. His mouth claimed hers, each kiss hungrier than the last. Rome's kisses were fierce and demanding, until she was gasping for breath and her body felt like liquid hunger. She wanted more, more, more. Her hands curled against his undershirt as they kissed, and she wanted to stroke them all over his body, but didn't know when—or if—he'd let her.

All she knew was that she never wanted this to end.

His fingers massaged her scalp, stroking and kneading as he kissed her. Then he paused, his forehead pressing to hers. "Can I touch you, Elise?"

She shuddered. "Please," she whispered. She wanted his touch so badly.

His fingers stroked down her face, her cheek, her jaw. Over and over, he touched her as she closed her eyes and willed herself to calmly breathe in and out, like a normal person would. Then he leaned in and gave her nose a small kiss. "Lie on your back for me."

She did, her gaze moving over him, his big body next to hers. His eyes were sleepy with desire, that blue turning a darker, smoky color, his lashes thick and gorgeous. She could drown in those eyes.

Rome sat up, and his hand moved from her shoulders down to her waist. He glanced up at her, and then back down, and his hand began to pull at the fabric of her sweater, easing it upward.

Elise tensed, thinking of her crooked hips and the way they didn't line up quite right. He'd notice it.

He glanced up at her, noticing her stiffness. "You want the light off for now?"

She relaxed a little, nodding. "Please."

He heaved his body over hers, reaching across to the lamp at the bedside. He clicked it off, and then they were in darkness. She blinked a few times, trying to adjust her eyes to the dimness. The only light that came in peeped in from the blinds, the starlight barely enough to let her make out Rome's shadow over hers.

Then his hand touched her bare stomach, under her sweater. "Can we take this off?"

She sucked in a breath and nodded, then realized he couldn't see that. Now she had no choice but to speak. "O-okay."

"Don't be afraid, Elise." His hand stroked her stomach again, the knuckles just barely brushing over her belly button. "I think you're beautiful."

Those words, soft and reverent, bolstered her confidence.

With a deep breath, she grabbed the edges of her sweater and pulled it over her head, tossing it aside.

His hands immediately began to stroke up and down her rib cage, half exploration, half soothing. "Breathe," he murmured.

She took in a long, deep breath, and was surprised when his mouth came down on hers again in a tender kiss. She opened her mouth to him, her hands going to his neck and clinging to him as he kissed her and his hand stroked her belly.

Ever so slowly, that stroking hand slid up to rest between her breasts, his knuckles brushing at her breastbone, back and forth, in a teasing, tantalizing motion that seemed more frustrating than exciting. She arched her back and made a sound of frustration.

In response, his hand moved to the side and gently cupped her breast.

All that pent-up excitement and frustration seemed to burst out of her at once. A sob escaped her throat.

"You okay, baby?" His whisper was soft, understanding. "I can stop at any time if you want."

She shook her head. She didn't want that. She wanted him to keep touching her. "I'm fine." And really, she was. It was just . . . utter relief that he'd touch her so intimately and not shy away. She'd longed to be touched for such a very long time, and the reality was almost more than she could bear.

But she'd bear it . . . because she wanted more. So she clung to him and lifted her mouth for another kiss, and this time Elise was the aggressor, her mouth capturing his and her tongue stroking to brush against his. Her nose brushed against the ring piercing his septum, and even that aroused her.

He groaned and his thumb stroked over her nipple, gently teasing the already tight peak.

The breath exploded out of her again and she cried out

against his mouth, her hips raising up in an involuntary gesture. She wanted more touch, needed more. She was desperate for it.

But all he did was gently rub that stiff, overstimulated little peak over and over again. "How does it feel, Elise?" he murmured against her mouth.

"G-g-good," she breathed.

"Just good?"

So, so good. More than good. But her mouth couldn't form the words. She mewed a protest when he lifted his hand, and tried to drag his mouth back down to hers, but he was shifting his big body.

Then she felt his warm hand cup her other breast, kneading it gently before he began to tease the tip with his fingers once more. She felt his other hand tug at the cup of her bra, pulling it down.

Then she felt his mouth close over her nipple.

She cried out. The sensation felt so overwhelming that she wanted to scream with everything she was feeling. It was too much. It wasn't enough. She wanted to push his mouth away, she wanted to drag him all over her skin. She wanted him to bite. Her breath came in sharp, rough pants, and his hand and mouth worked on her breasts, teasing both peaks. She could feel his tongue scrape over her nipple, felt him gently suck on the tip and then worry it with his teeth, just a little.

And god, she ached so much. She felt so, so empty inside. How was it that she could feel so full and supercharged, and yet ache with emptiness at the same time?

"You have the sweetest little breasts, Elise. God, these nipples. I could tongue them all night." His hands pushed her breasts together and he nuzzled in her cleavage, his lips grazing her breastbone. "You're so sexy. You sure you want some dirtbag like me touching you?"

She wanted all of him. "Please, please touch me, Rome," she panted. "I need it."

He groaned, and his thumbs flicked both of her nipples at the same time in a gesture that made her cry out with surprise and pleasure. "Unbutton your pants for me. I want to see if you're wet."

She sucked in a breath, but her hands went to her jeans, trembling. He continued to tease and play with her nipples with his hands, driving her wild as she tried to undo her jeans. Her fingers were having a hard time working, her concentration scattered as he continued to touch and tease her breasts.

Then her jeans were undone and she reached for him again, stroking a hand up one of his strong arms. She loved touching him. For a moment she hated that the lights were off; she wished she could see her hand grazing over his beautiful tattoos. "You're so warm," she murmured. So warm and delicious.

"And you're so soft," he murmured, and his hand left her breasts and skimmed down her belly. Then his fingers were grazing at the edge of her panties—her hideous granny panties—and teasing her skin. "Beautiful, soft Elise. Can I touch you anywhere?"

She thought she'd die if he didn't. "Please," she whispered again.

His fingers slipped deeper, moving under her clothing, past the waistband of her panties. She felt them graze the crinkle of her pubic curls, and then brush over her mound, cupping it under her clothing.

And Rome hissed. "Damn, you are so wet. Are you that turned on, Elise?"

She whimpered. Oh god, she was so turned on. "Touch me. Please, keep touching me."

"Baby, I don't think I could stop if I wanted to," he said, and she felt his fingers part her flesh, stroking the slick folds and sliding through them. He groaned. "So fucking wet. I want to just bury my face there and eat the hell out of you."

She gasped, stiffening at the thought.

"Not tonight," he promised. "Tonight we're just playing, all right?" And he leaned in and kissed her again, even as his fingers stroked through her wet folds and brushed over her clit. Elise cried out at the touch. That had been the most intense thing she'd ever felt.

But then he was still touching and exploring her, even as his mouth claimed hers. His fingers slid back and forth in her folds, rubbing her, circling in the slickness. One pushed deep, circling at her core and then sinking in.

She whimpered, her fists tightening on his shirt. That . . . had felt a little twingey with pain.

"Fuck, you're tight," he murmured against her mouth. "Relax, baby. I've got you. We're just exploring. Nothing more."

She nodded against his kisses, his tongue slicking over hers again, and when he thrust into her mouth, his finger mimicked the motion and she moaned. Oh, that had felt decadent. Her hips rose in response, wanting more of that touch.

Then, his thumb brushed through her folds again, and she felt it land on her clit. Her eyes opened wide with shock at the sensation, even as he thrust his finger deep into her once more.

Her nails dug into his shoulders. Oh god. That was . . . Her legs trembled, and she began to stiffen. She wanted him to pull away—no, wait, she wanted him to do that again, but harder—and all the while he continued to kiss and thrust into her mouth with his tongue and stroke his fingers deep inside her, his thumb grazing over her clit as he did. And it was overwhelming.

She'd touched herself to bring her body off before. Lots of times, actually. But this intensity? This intrusive, incredible touch? It was completely different. Her own touch was like a soft, soothing comfort. This was a raging inferno of desire, and she felt as if she were about to be engulfed. A sob tore at her throat again as he continued to stroke her higher, and her hips bucked against his hand, harder and more fiercely.

"That's it," he murmured against her mouth. "You going to come for me, Elise?"

"Oh," she sobbed, digging her fingers into his shirt. "Oh! Oh!" Her legs flailed a bit even as they locked up, and he continued to pump his hand in and out, his mouth teasing hers.

And it was too much. She came fiercely. She came so hard that a rush of wetness flooded through her panties and her entire body locked up, wracked with tremors, and another sob burst from her throat.

She'd never come so hard in her life.

She seemed to stay up forever, too, Rome's thumb brushing back and forth over her clit even as she came and came and came. But then she began to uncoil, ever so slowly. And as she did, she had the horrible realization that the thighs and crotch of her jeans were totally, completely soaked.

Oh my god, she'd *peed* on him. She'd come so hard she'd lost control of her bladder.

"God damn," Rome said in a low voice.

Horrified, she pushed his hands away, trying to squirm away from him. "Oh my god. Oh my god."

"What?" She felt his big body shift on the bed, and there was tension in his voice. "What's wrong?"

A hysterical laugh choked in her throat. How could he not know? She'd freaking *peed* on his hand. Humiliated could not even begin to describe how she felt at the moment. Tears of shame flooded her eyes and she swung her legs off the bed, then began to feel around for her sweater. Tonight had been so utterly perfect and . . . she couldn't believe it. He was probably just as horrified as she was at her reaction.

And where the hell was her sweater?

"Elise? What is it?" She felt the bed shift and then the light flicked on. He stared up at her, all soft, sexy eyes, gorgeous body, and an enormous tent in the front of his pants that she couldn't take her eyes off of.

She shook herself, then snatched her sweater off the ground after finding it in a nearby corner. Tears of humiliation were leaking down her face. "I'm so sorry."

"What? Why?" There was nothing on his face but confusion. No revulsion. Hadn't he realized what she'd done? He had to—the entire crotch of her jeans was sopping with her response.

She shook her head, unable to voice the words, and hastily dragged her sweater over her head, tugging it down as far as it would go. It only covered her to mid butt, though, leaving the rest of her jeans obviously wet. She wanted to cry. Well, cry harder. And escape.

Except he'd driven her here, and no one else was home.

Another sob escaped her throat. She'd figure something out. Hide in the main lodge—somewhere—until her pants dried and get someone to drive her home when they came back. Somehow.

She put a hand on the door, ready to leave.

Rome's body leaned against the door. "Elise, don't leave."

She shook her head, her entire body trembling from sheer humiliation. She couldn't look him in the eye.

"What did I do? Tell me what I did and I'll fix it. Did I go too fast for you?" Rome's eyes were filled with worry, and his handsome face was lined with frustration.

"What did *you* do?" Yup, her voice was hysterical. "It's what *I* did."

He shook his head at her. "Baby, you were amazing."

Was he being deliberately obtuse? "Up until the part where I peed on you," she said bitterly, and reached for the door again. "Please, just let me go."

"Wait, wait." His hands went to her shoulders and he dragged her away from the door, and began to nuzzle her neck again. "Holy fuck, Elise. Are you kidding me?"

"Let me go," she said softly, still avoiding his gaze but

trying to squirm away from his affectionate touches. "Please."

He didn't let her go. Instead, his arms wrapped around her and he continued to press kisses on every inch of her face and neck he could reach. "Baby, you squirted. You're a squirter."

"What?" She pulled away.

"It's a good thing, I promise. Not every girl's a squirter. And it sounds crude, I know, but I assure you, it's totally natural. You didn't pee on me, Elise. You came so hard that you ejaculated."

Her face burned so hot she was sure she'd never stop blushing, but she stopped struggling. "I've never . . . I mean . . . I never . . ."

"When touching yourself? Maybe I just made you come a bit harder than you're used to."

She glanced over at him, uncertain, and was surprised at the smug look of pleasure on his face. She relaxed a little, but god, she was still so embarrassed by her body's reaction. "You shouldn't look so happy about it."

"Are you kidding? I'm fucking stoked. You came so hard, and just for me." His hands ran over her body again, and he buried his face against her neck. "You were so goddamn wet I nearly came in my pants as soon as I touched you. Knowing I turned you on that much? How can I not love that?"

She struggled for something to say to burst his bubble of pleasure, but when she couldn't come up with anything, she said in a small voice, "My pants are all wet."

"Yeah, that's my fault," he said again, and his voice was all husky. "I didn't think you'd come so hard or I'd have stripped you naked. You can wear a pair of my boxers and we'll hang them to dry, okay?"

She nodded.

He released her with another satisfied little kiss to her mouth that would have been charming if she hadn't been so embarrassed, and went to dig a pair of boxers out of his clothing drawer. He presented them to her a moment later, and she scurried to the bathroom to change out of her pant- ies and jeans. She scrubbed her garments in his sink and hung them on the shower rod to dry, and then returned to the main room of the cabin.

Rome was lying on the bed, still fully dressed. He looked her up and down as she emerged. "That's a nice look."

She tugged on the hem of her sweater, feeling a little silly since it was currently paired up with boxers. "I hear it's the latest in Paris."

He chuckled and patted the bed, inviting her to sit next to him.

After a moment's hesitation, she did so, and he immedi- ately dragged her back against him, pulling her to his body for another long, lingering kiss. "I just want you to know that nothing about you is disappointing in the slightest. That was fucking amazing."

She snuggled against him, feeling a bit more relaxed now that the crisis was over. Really, her entire body was feeling pretty good right about now, though she ached a little between her legs, still, as if she were missing something. It was a good ache, though. "So what do we do now?"

Rome brushed a lock of hair out of her eyes. "What do you feel like doing?"

His eyes were still that sleepy blue of desire, she noticed, and she thought of that tent in his jeans from earlier. She glanced down at his lap and, sure enough, he was still hard. "Call me crazy, but isn't the goal of making out usually for both people to get off?"

He shrugged, and his finger traced her jaw. He just liked touching her, it seemed. "We're taking it slow, remember?"

"That seems . . . really slow for you."

He laughed. "I'm a patient man."

"My jeans won't be dry for a while."

He curled a lock of her hair around his fingers and gave her another soft smile that made her heart thud. "I don't mind if you stick around."

Rome Lozada seemed too good to be true, Elise suspected. He was a gorgeous man with wild piercings, even wilder tattoos, and a killer body. And he didn't mind when she acted all virginal and silly. So had she scored the jackpot here, or was there more to him that she didn't know? How could she tell?

He tilted his head, trying to keep eye contact with her. "What are you thinking?"

"Just wondering about you."

His eyes lit up. "Wondering about touching me?"

Well, no, she hadn't been, but . . . now that he mentioned it, it wasn't a bad idea. "Do you want me to?"

"Only if you want to. This is all about you tonight."

She thought about that earth-shattering orgasm he'd given her earlier, and how unfair it seemed that he didn't get one in return. But was she ready to just stick her hand in his pants and do to him what he did to her?

Elise wasn't so sure about that. "I'm feeling a little shy," she admitted.

"Just do what you like. There's no pressure."

"What if I just want to kiss you?"

"That's fine." He waggled his eyebrows at her suggestively, the hoop dancing, and she laughed.

"Maybe just a few kisses," she said, and leaned in to put her arms around his neck. But instead, he pulled her by the waist and dragged her to straddle his lap.

"That's better," he said, and his voice held a note of strain.

Elise tensed. Her current position was a vulnerable one. Spread over his lap, she had no choice but to face him, and her sex was spread open wide right over his straining groin.

But . . . gosh, he looked so gorgeous. She couldn't help

but reach out and brush her fingertips down the front of his shirt, then pull it gently open because she wanted to unwrap him like a package.

"Want me to help you with that?" His voice was husky, soft, and delicious.

She nodded.

He sat forward, and his face pressed almost into her breasts as he shrugged off the plaid shirt. She giggled, surprised, and the giggle turned into a gasp when he arched his hips . . . and his cock pressed up against her sex through the fabric.

Then he peeled off the undershirt and tossed it to the side. He sat back against the wall again, and all that tattooed, bare flesh was hers to explore.

Oh. "You look so . . ." Her fingers lightly touched the wing of a bird that curved across his pectorals. It was a hawk, but stylized in a way that looked like Southwestern influences mixed with Maori. It was all geometric lines and angles and suggestions of patterns.

"Busy?" he asked, and there was a wry smile on his face.

"Beautiful." Her fingers swept down the length of the bird's wing, then followed the symmetrical feathers down to the extended claws. She touched another tattoo on his shoulder blade, this one of a rather vicious-looking eagle. "Why birds?"

He shrugged. "I like them. They seem free."

Intriguing answer. She touched her tongue to one tattoo. "I was going to say your tattoos are 'lovely,' but that's the wrong word to use for a man, isn't it?"

"Any time you're touching me, Elise, you can call me whatever you want," Rome said softly, and that hoarse note was back in his throat. His hips bucked against hers again, and she felt that slow, languid throb in her sex once more.

This time, when he raised his hips, though, she rolled hers with him, and was rewarded with his groan of pleasure and the way he threw his head back, as if it was too much for him to take in.

He was stunning. She forgot all about learning him and decided she wanted to touch him very much, instead. Elise leaned forward and her mouth went to his neck, kissing at the Adam's apple that bobbed and swallowed with every roll of her hips. She was doing it automatically now, riding him with small flexes of her hips and thighs, and feeling him strain against her in return. It was erotic . . . but totally safe because there were all these clothes between them. But Rome's eyes were closed and she could watch him, fascinated, and kiss him to her heart's content.

She did, too. She pressed little kisses to his neck, and when she wanted to lick him, she licked him, tasting his warm, tanned skin. He had a tattoo of a raven on his neck, and she lightly bit at that, too, just because he seemed so utterly bite-able. Her breasts pressed against his chest and she continued to roll her hips, pressing down against his cock with every little movement and enjoying the way his breath seemed to hitch and relax in juxtaposition to her movements.

Her hands moved to his neck and she laced her fingers behind his head, feeling the soft buzz of the short hair at the base of his neck. She pressed a small kiss to his chin, then brushed her lips over his mouth . . . and took his lower lip between her teeth and tugged gently, mindful of the ring there.

He groaned, the sound rough, and then his hands were pressing to her thighs, her hips, and he began to push against her urgently, with more force. She followed his lead, returning his movements with a rolling of her hips. His eyes slid open, just a crack, and she was entranced by the hot desire she saw there, the raw need on his face. And she kissed him again, her tongue sliding into his mouth.

Rome sucked on it, even as he pushed her harder and harder, until she was bouncing on his jeans-covered cock, and the thin cotton boxers she wore didn't seem like much of a barrier, and she was getting excited all over again, the roll of her hips and the press of his need against her making her breathless.

But then his eyes squeezed shut, and his face contorted as if in agony, and she froze. His kiss became desperate, his breathing raspy, and she realized . . . he'd just come, too. Elise sucked in a breath, surprised.

Rome heaved a long, satisfied breath, holding her close against him. Then he kissed her mouth and said, "Now both of us have come in our pants tonight."

And what could she do but laugh?

SEVEN

Well, damn.

Rome held a sleeping Elise against his chest and stared up at the ceiling of his small log cabin. Despite the late hour, he was wide awake. His mind was whirling with all kinds of thoughts about that evening, and most of them were about the woman at his side.

There was no doubt in his mind that Elise was just as sheltered as she claimed—maybe even more so. The way she'd reacted when she'd come told him she wasn't as familiar with her body as she thought.

Of course, he'd been fucking elated. When she'd confessed that she was a virgin, he thought he'd have to go extra slow. Elise was skittish as hell, and when she got intimidated or scared—which was often—she shut down. But when he'd felt how wet she was, how totally turned on, the game had changed. This wasn't a woman terrified of sex who he'd have to gently ease into lovemaking. This was an erotic woman just waiting to be freed from her own restraints.

And she was completely into his touch; she couldn't fake

that kind of wetness coming from her pussy, nor could she fake the way she'd squirted when she came.

He'd never had a squirter before. Hell, he hated the term because it sounded disgusting, and he'd been as shocked as she was when it had happened . . . but damn if it hadn't been amazing. *He'd* made her squirt.

That did amazing things for his ego, he had to admit. And more than that, he wanted to see if he could get her to do it again. To see if she lost control so totally every time she had sex, or if that was just a lot of pent-up arousal breaking free. He was willing to bet that she went wild every time she was touched.

It was like Elise Markham was a gift, wrapped in a pretty, incredibly shy package.

He didn't get it, either. That cheek of hers was barely noticeable. Heck, he didn't think he'd have seen it at all if she hadn't pointed it out. He might have just attributed it to a trick of the light. He'd caught a glimpse of the long scar on her spine when she'd jumped from bed, and wondered about it, but he didn't ask. She was clearly sensitive about that sort of thing.

He hadn't teased her about the granny panties hanging on his shower bar, though he'd desperately wanted to. Elise wasn't quite ready for teasing, he suspected. She was still sensitive and fragile.

And yet . . . she slept in his arms like a baby. Even now her cheek rested on his shoulder, her arm thrown over his waist as if she'd slept next to men all her life. Her bare leg was tangled with his, and he loved the press of her body against his own. Just the feel of her was reminding him of the way she'd ridden his cock while sitting atop him, kissing him until he'd come in his pants.

That had been incredibly erotic, so erotic that his intentions on getting her off again had fallen to the wayside in lieu of his own pleasure. His hand stroked through her hair again, thinking about her. She deserved better than a guy like him.

Way better.

A girl like Elise was a treasure. She was smart, classy, and had wonderful sparks of humor under all that shyness. She was eager in bed, and starved for attention. Even now, she clung to him.

She'd make some guy a great girlfriend.

Unfortunately for him, it couldn't be Rome. It wasn't just the fact that her brother was just looking for an excuse to can his ass. Rome was pretty much living on borrowed time. It was a matter of days, maybe weeks, before someone got suspicious, ran a background check on him, and found out his past.

Then Grant wouldn't need an excuse to fire him.

Then Elise would stop looking at him with those soft, reverent eyes.

He'd be nothing but shit beneath their feet, and it'd be time to move on once again.

Rome dragged his hand through Elise's silky hair again, admiring the way it glided and fell through his fingers like water.

If he was a nice guy, he'd cut a nice girl like Elise loose before she got her feelings hurt. He'd tell her that it was wrong for him to fool around with her, and that she deserved someone better than him. She'd be wounded for a few days, but she'd get over it and they'd go their separate ways.

It was too bad he wasn't a nice guy, because he wasn't about to let her go. Right now, Elise Markham was the most fascinating thing in Rome's life, and he intended to pursue her and monopolize her until she blew him off. She would, eventually. It was just a matter of time.

But until then? Ah, being with her would be sweet.

He woke her up early, before the sun rose in the skies. She was lovely in her sleep, her dark hair all tumbled and mussed, her eyelids heavy, and he hated to rouse her. In sleep, her expression was so open, so peaceful, completely unguarded. But he knew she'd want to be out of his cabin before the day began, so he gently ran a knuckle along her jaw, pleased when she turned toward the gesture.

"Mmm," she said softly, smiling up at him, the shyness back in her face. "What time is it?"

"Before dawn. We should get you home before anyone notices you're missing."

"Oh." She sat up abruptly. "Yes, that's a good idea."

He watched her backside sashay as she headed to the bathroom. She filled out his boxers rather well, Rome thought, and made a mental note to take her someplace and get her some naughty underthings. After he got paid, of course.

Rome tugged on a shirt and a new pair of jeans, since he'd made a mess of his old ones last night while fooling around with Elise. Considering he only had two pairs of jeans, that meant today was laundry day.

Elise reappeared a few minutes later, her hair pulled into a messy knot atop her head that made her look even more well-fucked than before, and her hands smoothed down her wrinkled jeans. "They're a little wet still, but not too bad."

He finished pulling on his boots and laced them up. "You want to go get breakfast somewhere? My treat." He only had a few bucks in his bank account, but hey, he'd buy his girl some coffee if she asked for it.

She shook her head shyly. "I'm fine. I think I'll just go home and shower." Her cheeks pinked again.

"All right." He couldn't tell if she was blowing him off. Was she regretting last night? It was hard to tell with Elise—everything seemed to rattle her. He didn't like the thought of her pushing him away, though. "When did you want to get together again?"

She shrugged, silent.

That . . . definitely felt like a blowoff. Was it because she was embarrassed? Or because in the light of day she realized he was just some shitty loser with tats and she could do better?

He didn't like not knowing, so he couldn't resist pushing just a bit more. "You still want to do that photo shoot?"

This time, her eyes lit up. "You want to do it?"

"For you? Yeah."

The look she gave him was meltingly sweet. "I'd love to. When is good for you?"

He pocketed his keys, then looked over at her. "I'm off today and then work days until we open the paintball course. How about you?"

"Today might not be good," she said, nibbling on a long fingernail. "I haven't seen Grant in a few days, so I need to spend some time with him. Maybe tomorrow night?"

"Yeah, that's fine with me." He'd clear all the time in his schedule she needed.

She practically beamed. "Wonderful. You want to meet at the salon after work? I'll bring food again."

"I'm not one to turn down a free meal," he told her with a grin.

She ducked her head shyly.

"Hey," he said, touching her chin and forcing her to look up at him. "You're not feeling weird about last night, are you?"

Elise bit her lip and gave him a small, hesitant smile. "Just wondering why you'd spend your free time with me, is all, really. I can't be fun company."

"You're the best company I've had in a long time," he told her honestly. "And I'd spend every minute with you if I could."

At least until she started looking at him with loathing.

When he returned from dropping Elise off at the bed-and-breakfast, Rome's mood grew foul the moment he spotted the new motorcycle in the parking lot.

The owner of the bike was seated on it, arms crossed, enjoying a cigarette. He looked over at Rome as his bike pulled up.

His brother. God damn it.

Rome parked his bike next to Jericho's but didn't turn it off. "What are you doing here?"

Jericho tossed his cigarette on the ground and gave Rome a familiar smile. "Thought I'd come say hi. Check out the new digs." He nodded at the row of cozy cabins. "You camping or something?"

"I don't want to talk to you here, so either leave or let's go somewhere else."

"Breakfast? There's a Waffle House down the highway."

He gave a jerky nod and backed his bike out of the parking space, taking off and not bothering to see if Jericho was going to follow him. He was furious. If Jericho knew where he was, that meant his mother and father weren't far behind. They'd show up with all their issues, and he'd be drawn back in again.

And then his life would be fucked-up all over once more.

Rome seethed all the way to the Waffle House. He was still seething when he parked his bike and stomped into the diner, practically flinging himself at the first booth he saw. He knew the waitress was giving him odd looks, but he didn't much care. He didn't want to eat half as much as he just wanted to get this over with.

Jericho sauntered in, smiling at everyone. That was his brother—all easy grins designed to put people at ease despite his leather-clad, tattooed body. For some reason, Jericho never let anything bother him. Laid-back to a fault, that was J.

Rome couldn't act the same, though. Too much shit didn't roll off his back.

Jericho casually sat across from him and picked up a menu card. "So. Long time, no see."

"Not long enough," Rome said, arms crossed. "How'd you find me?"

"You made the mistake of picking a small town," Jericho said, shrugging. He smiled as the waitress brought him a coffee without him having ordered one, and Rome wondered if Jericho was here often. "I was passing through and some-one saw my bike and asked if I knew the new guy that worked at the wilderness school. You know people think that everyone who owns a Harley knows each other. Funny thing is, though, in this case, they were right."

It was his own fault. Damn it. He should have picked a bigger town than Bluebonnet, just kept on passing through until he found someplace he could be totally anonymous. He'd just have to up and leave again, like he always did.

For the first time, though, that bothered him. He thought of Elise's softly smiling face, the way she clung to him when she slept, and for the first time Rome didn't want to just pack up and skip town. Anger burned in his belly. "So what is it you want?"

Jericho raised an eyebrow, clearly surprised by Rome's cold tone. "Wanted to say hi to my brother. That so wrong?"

"I just know that wherever you go, Mom and Dad aren't far behind, and I want nothing to do with them."

Most parents, he imagined, would be concerned about their sons. Most parents would have a decent house, settle in the suburbs, and work normal jobs so their kids could go to school and have a nice, normal life.

Not the Lozadas. For as long as Rome could remember they had lived like hippies, skipping from town to town and going wherever the wind drove them . . . or the need for the next big score did. Edna and John had met during a drug-fueled bender and decided that they were perfect for each other. They didn't marry—no need—and lived the nomadic lifestyle of two bikers who had not a care in the world.

Their two boys, Rome and Jericho, weren't really

children to them as much as they were tools. Need to run a scam to pick up some money? Stick one of the boys on a street corner with a sign and watch the dollars roll in. Need someone to distract a cop while Edna and John raided a nearby house for stuff that was easy to pawn? Have Jericho cause a diversion a block away.

Hell, Rome and Jericho weren't even their real names. Jericho was John Lozada . . . and so was Rome. His father had given them the same name as him because he said he couldn't decide their names at the spur of the moment. As it turned out, having the same name as his father just made it easier for him to steal their identities and rack up thousands of dollars in debt. By the time Rome turned eighteen, his credit rating was shit, his juvie rap sheet was a mile long, and he was a high school dropout (hard to graduate when your toker parents are homeschooling you).

It was a shit lifestyle, but it was all Rome knew.

J was two years older, though, and even though J made it seem like he didn't care about a thing, it must have bothered him, because one day Rome woke up and J had left. Just up and left Rome with Edna and John. He'd expected his parents to be mad, but they didn't seem to care much at all. They just smoked a bit more weed, took J's share of the drug money, and leaned on Rome to pick up the slack.

And Rome found himself realizing that he could escape, too. That he didn't have to be locked into a lifestyle of crashing on people's couches and switching IDs until he found one that someone would take. A lifestyle of avoiding particular counties because of outstanding warrants for his arrest. Of taking off in the middle of the night and switching plates at the junkyard to avoid being caught.

So when he was old enough, Rome left, too. He got minimum-wage jobs, and he worked. He lived with a girlfriend, or a buddy, and paid rent, and planted roots in Houston. He was normal.

Of course, planting roots meant that people caught up

with you. It wasn't long before Edna and John showed up, wanting to borrow money. And when he felt guilty and gave them a few dollars, they'd come back from time to time, because they knew that he'd be good for it. Rome built himself a decent life, meanwhile. He worked at an auto-body shop, and when he broke up with his girlfriend, he got his own apartment. Bought his own bike.

Life was all right.

Then one day Edna showed up by herself. She needed bail money to get John out of jail. Or at least, that was her story. Turned out that what she really needed was a place to stash all the crack she was selling, and she hid it in Rome's bathroom, under the counter.

Two days later, the cops showed up at his place and he was off to jail.

Edna came to visit him, too. Begged for him to take the fall instead of her. It wouldn't be her first offense, and she was older and in poor health. If the hammer came down, she'd go to prison for years on end. But it would be adult Rome's first offense. They wouldn't throw the book at him, not for a first offense. Could he take the rap for his mother just this once?

And Rome wanted to say no, but looking at his mother shaking and trembling in front of him, weeping with fear, he hadn't had the heart to send her to prison.

He was always a fucking sucker for tears.

So he took the fall, and sure enough, they didn't throw the book at him. They took one look at him, at his tats, and at the amount of drugs, and his lawyer suggested they plead out. So he did.

He only got six years in prison.

Thanks to good behavior, though, Rome got out in four years. That was eighteen months ago, and he was learning that life was even harder after being a convict. No one wanted to hire an ex-con who was covered in tattoos, no matter how much he smiled or how hard he promised to work. If he did get a job, it was always for minimum wage, and they ended up letting him go for spurious reasons half the time. He went from job to job, unable to make decent money. And each time a job ended, he packed up his small bag of possessions, moved to a new town, and tried again. If he was on the move, John and Edna wouldn't be able to find him.

He did keep in contact with Jericho, though. Last he'd heard from his brother, J was working in west Texas. Plumbing or carpentry or some shit. Jericho wasn't a bad guy.

But wherever Jericho went, he suspected Edna and John wouldn't be far behind. If one Lozada was looking for him, the others would be, too.

Jericho was currently smiling at him over a cup of black coffee, like he was enjoying himself. Not Rome. He was pretty fucking miserable at the moment. He'd gone from a state of pleasure to misery in no time flat this morning, it seemed.

"So what do you want?" Rome asked again.

"Just wanted to see how my baby brother was doing." He shrugged. "And I'm actually in the area, myself. Had a job that was in this part of the state, and stuck around for a relationship. Neither one worked out, so I'm currently trying to find my feet again." He shrugged.

"And John?"

"Just got out of prison, I'm told. Sixteen months."

Disgust threatened to choke him. Sixteen damn months? Rome had done twice that for drugs that weren't even his. "Where are they at?"

"Last I heard, they were in Lufkin. But if they catch wind that you're over here and you've got a cushy little setup, don't think that they won't be heading over to say hello. The last thing you want is to find out that good old Mom and Dad parked their newest pot trailer in your neck of the woods."

And wouldn't Grant just fucking love that? Rome groaned and rubbed his face, trying to think. If John and Edna showed up, he'd have to get rid of them quietly without them raising a stink. The easiest way to do that was to pay them to leave, of course . . . but he was broke. Hell, he didn't have more than ten dollars to his name at the moment. If they showed up, Grant would be suspicious of what Rome was up to—with good reason.

And all he'd need to do was run a background check and see Rome's totally shot-to-shit credit, his prison record, and his felony rap sheet. Rome would get the boot, and he'd be on his way once more. No cozy little cabin in the woods, no job running a paintball course.

No beautiful Elise to cling to him while she slept. No soft, sweet, shy girl to look at him as if he'd hung the moon.

No one ever looked at Rome Lozada like that. He was addicted to it already.

"I like it here, J," Rome warned him. "I'm just getting back on track after doing time."

His brother sighed. "I know, man. That's why I'm here to warn you. Lie low. Get rid of the bike if you have to. People remember a guy like you driving something like that through."

He nodded, though there wasn't much he could do about the bike. He didn't have the money to rent a car. "They asking about me?"

"Of course. You're their baby boy." Jericho's mouth twisted ruefully. "And I'm guessing they need help with another scam of some kind. With our luck, Dad watched too much *Breaking Bad* in prison and now wants to set up a meth lab or something."

Rome snorted. That did sound like something John Lozada Senior would do. "I don't want them to find me."

"Then it's a good thing I told them I heard you were in Austin."

He looked at J in surprise. "You did?"

"Sure. You're my little brother, and despite things, we're family."

He gave Jericho a skeptical look. "Family doesn't have a lot of pull where I'm concerned."

"Can't say I blame you. It's your own fault, though. Mom uses those tears on everyone she knows will fall for 'em. If they show up again, you gotta be strong . . . and then check your shit thoroughly. And this time? Don't take the fall for them. Swear to god. That was fucking stupid of you last time."

"I know it. I know." He'd ruined his life for someone who didn't give two shits about the fact. It ate at him every damn day.

"Anyhow, I'm kicking around the area." J shrugged. "Wanted to make sure you were doing okay, was all. Ask if you needed anything."

Rome gave his brother a questioning look. "I'm good, thanks."

"But even if you weren't, you wouldn't tell me, right?"

Rome pointed, as if to say "bingo." "Learned my lesson already."

Jericho grinned and chugged his coffee, then put the mug down. "Well, I'll buy you breakfast at least. No strings attached. And you can tell me all about why you're so attached to this place. You working with a hot girl?"

"Even if I was, I wouldn't tell you," Rome told him. The last thing he wanted was anyone in his family finding out about Elise.

"Huh. Well, maybe I'll stick around for a bit. Was thinking about heading back out to Marfa, but this place is kinda growing on me. There's a bed-and-breakfast in town, too. I hear it's pretty reasonable." He flipped the menu over, studying it.

Rome stiffened, picturing Elise bounding down the steps of the Peppermint House once she saw a Harley pull up, assuming it was him. "Stay away from that place."

"Uh oh, the plot thickens." Jericho shook his head and waved the waitress over. "Sounds like I found out why my little brother's so interested in sticking around all of a sudden."

Rome glared at his brother as he ordered his food. He waved off the waitress when she looked to him for his order, and then she disappeared again.

J shook his head, as always, amused at Rome's bad attitude. "Don't be so angry. I'm not the one who turned you in last time."

Yeah, but he was family, and Rome had learned the hard way not to trust those. Behind Jericho's smiling, familiar eyes was the same con artist Rome had grown up to be.

"So what are your plans?" Grant flipped through Elise's photos as she toyed with layouts on her computer. She'd showered, taken a nap, and then woken up in time to go to lunch with her brother and Brenna that afternoon. They'd returned to the lodge and Grant had invited her to borrow Dane's desk so she could work on the brochure he wanted for the paintball course. So she'd set up her MacBook atop a mountain of papers on Dane's desk, between old chip bags and who knew what else, and tried not to watch the door in case Rome came in.

"Hmm?" Elise asked, glancing over at her brother.

"Once we have the brochures done, are you heading back home? Or are you going to stick around?" He picked through the printouts she'd made for him, casting one aside and then picking up another and scrutinizing it. "Do you think we should have some action shots?"

"We can do some action shots," she agreed, getting up from the borrowed desk to peek over his shoulder at the photos he was discarding. "And I'm not sure I'm ready to return home yet." Home was living with Mom and Dad like she was a twelve-year-old girl. It was past time for her to move out, but there'd been no hurry, really, and her mother panicked at the thought of Elise being on her own, as if she couldn't take care of herself for some reason.

"Well, if you're not going back anytime soon, you can go thrift store shopping with me," Brenna said from her desk. Elise looked over and Brenna was playing Mine-sweeper instead of working, her puppy on her lap. Typical. "I wanted to get some ideas for the wedding. I bet we could find some cute dresses at Goodwill."

"No," Grant said in a warning voice. "You are not having a Goodwill wedding."

"Why not?"

"Because my mother will die of a heart attack at the thought."

Brenna snorted. "Oh, she will not. Elise?"

Elise grimaced and raised her hands. She knew her mother's thoughts on used clothing, but she wasn't about to get in between these two. "I'm staying out of it."

"We could always get married in Bride and Groom T-shirts."

"Still no," Grant said, then pointed at one of Elise's photos. "I like this one. We should put it on the cover."

She picked up the photo. It was a long-distance shot from up the hill of the valley, showing the landscape and the built-up forts and the castle in the distance. "I like that one, too, but if you want an action shot, we should probably put it on the cover. It'll be more dynamic."

He nodded. "So how do we get action shots?"

"Invite some townspeople in for a dry run of the course?"

"Invite the Waggoners," Brenna advised. "Colt's brothers would probably love the chance to shoot some guns, and they won't care that it's nothing but paint coming out of them."

Grant chuckled. "You have a point there. I'll talk to Pop and see when he can get them over here."

"Not tomorrow night," Elise said quickly. "I'm meeting a friend in Houston." Her face blushed bright red, and she hoped Grant wouldn't notice.

He didn't, though. Instead, he turned back to his fiancée. "Why the thrift store clothing idea for the wedding?"

"It's brilliant," Brenna told him. "We can get some dresses on the cheap, and sell them back. Don't you think weddings are ridiculously overpriced anyhow?"

"It's supposed to be a special day," Grant argued, picking up his coffee mug.

Brenna rolled her eyes, adjusting her sleeping puppy on her lap. "If I want a special day, I'll bring home a big purple dildo."

Grant choked on the coffee he was raising to his lips.

Elise's eyes widened and she discreetly returned to her desk so she could clean up the photos on her computer. The good thing about Brenna was that she kept Grant distracted from what was going on with Elise.

For that, Elise loved her unconventional soon-to-be sister-in-law.

She opened up one of the paintball course photos in Photoshop, pretended to work, and daydreamed about Rome's blue eyes instead.

EIGHT

The next day, Elise went to Beth Ann's salon early so she could set up everything for the photo shoot. She toyed with the draping cloths, placed the stool and props, did sample shots, and then moved things over and over again until she was satisfied with the angles. Then she adjusted the lighting.

When there was nothing else left to fiddle with, she went out, grabbed a pizza and brought it back to the salon, got a six-pack of sodas—not beer this time—and waited for him to arrive.

Her body tensed when she heard the sound of his motorcycle purring behind the building. Excitement shot through her—and arousal. Just knowing that he was showing up for her was a turn-on, and she had been mentally picturing things for hours on end. How she'd set up the shot. What he'd wear in the shot. The expression on his face she wanted.

The last time they'd done photos together, Beth Ann, Miranda, and Brenna had all been standing around, watching and making comments. He'd been stiff and uncomfortable, and she saw that in his face when she looked at the photos now. That wasn't the Rome she knew—closed off, wary, and a little too alert. She wanted the carnal man who looked at her with melting blue eyes, whose long lashes made her think of sensual things, whose jaw seemed to be chiseled from marble. Whose abs were painted in symmetrical tattoos that couldn't mask the tight body underneath. The tanned skin mixed with the silver piercings. The look in his eyes when he was aroused.

That was what she wanted to capture on film.

And it wasn't so she could sell the photos or try pitching another layout to Crissy. This? This was for her. She wanted to see if she could capture Rome the way she saw him in her mind. She wanted to see that on film, and she wanted to prove that it wasn't in her imagination.

She just hoped he wouldn't chicken out on her or find things weird.

Elise headed to the back door and opened it to welcome him with a smile, just as he pulled off his helmet and swung his leg over his bike. "Hi."

"Hey, baby," he said, his voice so casual and sensual that it felt natural to hear the affectionate nickname come out of his mouth. "You look good."

She glanced down at her old, faded T-shirt and jeans, and gave him a wry look. "I dressed up just for you," she teased.

He chuckled and headed inside. "You always look good. I suppose I should have prefaced with that." And he leaned in and gave her a kiss of greeting, his hand moving to touch her neck in a possessive gesture, as if to pull her in closer.

She went happily, anticipating his kiss, and it was just as wonderful as she remembered. His mouth on hers was firm, delicious, and hinted of incredible things to come, and for a moment she wanted to be back in his cabin, back in his bed. But he'd agreed to come for photos, so she couldn't get distracted. With a small sigh, she eventually pulled away and gave him a little smile. "I brought pizza."

"You're always feeding me, aren't you?" He grinned and gave her another quick kiss. "Do I owe you anything for it?"

"Of course not," she said, shutting the door to the salon behind her and locking it. "Just consider it payment for the modeling job you're going to do for me."

He stepped into the main part of the salon, which was still draped with the neutral beige fabric, and examined it. She'd set up tables underneath the cloth in a few strategic spots and had added candles of varying heights and sizes. They were all the same bland color as the fabric, because she didn't want them to be the focus of the photo. Dozens of them sat on each table. Rome studied them, then looked back at her. "Should I be on the lookout for rose petals and a bubble bath?"

She bit her lip, feeling a little silly at what she was proposing. "If you don't want to do this—"

"No, I do." He moved back toward her and wrapped his arms around her waist, dragging her body against him. "I just thought we'd be doing more mud and dirt and tough guy stuff."

Her shyness was threatening to take over, and Elise stared at his chest, her fingertips resting on his pectorals. "I had an idea for something . . . softer. More sensual. Some candlelight, things like that. I want to see if I can get the light to play off your skin just right."

"Whatever you want," Rome murmured. "Do I need to get naked?"

She giggled, feeling a bit girlish and silly. "Actually, I don't need you totally naked. Just topless. And it can wait until after pizza."

"Sounds good to me." He leaned in and kissed her mouth gently again. "You lead, I'll follow."

Elise smiled and slid out of his grasp, then headed over to the far side of the salon, where the barber chair was pushed over to the side. The pizza box sat atop it, and the other chairs in the salon were covered with equipment that had been moved out of the way. She considered the seating. "Let me clear off one of these chairs."

"Don't bother," Rome told her. He sat down in the barber chair and dragged her toward him, pulling her into his lap. "Best seat in the house."

His thighs were hard underneath her butt, and she felt strange perching in his lap. "Am I going to be too heavy for you?"

"Don't be ridiculous." He wrapped an arm around her waist, anchoring her against him. "This way I get your sweet ass rubbing up against me while I eat. It's the best of both worlds."

She wanted to roll her eyes at his playful words, but she opened the box of pizza, balancing it in one hand and offering him a slice with the other. He took it, and she grabbed a slice for herself, and they ate in relative silence. Elise felt weird and awkward sitting on his lap and staring ahead while she ate.

He devoured another two slices while she picked at her one, and then downed a soda. When they'd both eaten, he wrapped both his arms around her and began to push her hair over one shoulder, lightly kissing her neck.

She squirmed against him, all eating forgotten.

"You miss me?" he whispered in a husky voice.

"It's only been two days," she said in a shaky voice. Thing was, she *had* missed him. Or at least daydreamed about him constantly. Maybe that was the same thing.

"Thinking about the other night when we were watching the movie?" His hands rubbed up and down her sides in a soft, teasing motion.

"I don't think we did much watching of the movie."

"I can't say I missed it."

She couldn't say that she did, either. Even now, she could feel the warmth of his body against hers, and her nipples were aching. She felt him growing erect against her ass, and pulled herself reluctantly out of his embrace. If she got all distracted, she'd never get this photoshoot done, and she wanted to concentrate. "Yes, well." She struggled to think of something to say, flustered. Eventually, she went back to work-related things. "You ready to get this started?"

"Ready if you are," he said, and got to his feet also. He pulled his black T-shirt off in a quick, fluid motion that took her breath away to watch, and then he was all bared skin and tattoos. "Where do you want me?"

On the floor, over me, her mind thought, and she swallowed the nervous giggle rising in her throat. God, she was just turning into the biggest horndog, wasn't she? "Come with me," she told him.

He shifted in place. "Will it be weird for you if I take off my jeans? I think I'm losing circulation."

This time, the laugh escaped. "Go right ahead."

He gave her a boyish grin and undid his pants, and, okay, she watched him move, his fingers dragging the zipper down and then pulling his pants to his thighs. Everything he did seemed full of sensuality, and when he stood in front of her in nothing but his cloth boxers, his cock making them stiff and tented in the front, she had to bite her lip to keep from moaning at the sight.

Was it bad that she really, really wanted to touch him at the moment? Forget all about the photo shoot and just touch him? But then she'd feel like she dragged him here under false pretenses.

"All right," she said, taking a deep breath to get control of herself. "Follow me."

She led him to the center of the floor, to the stool that sat amidst the draped fabric, and moved it, then gestured that he should stand where she indicated. "I wanted to do some of the shots seated, and some standing, but I think we'll start with standing." She'd wanted to do them seated to make him more at ease, but the thought of him seated and those boxers pulling taut over his cock was distracting her. Really, she was just changing her mind all over the place.

"All right," Rome said, and stood where she pointed, his hands on his hips. "What now?"

"Now we work on the lighting," she said. "You just stay there." She hurried over and picked up a long-handled lighter, and began to light the candles one by one.

As she leaned over, he brushed a hand on her ass, startling her. "This is pretty."

She jumped, startled, and gasped. "Don't do that when I have an open flame near all this fabric."

He laughed. "Sorry. Just in case, is there a fire extinguisher anywhere?"

She pointed primly at the opposite wall, where a red extinguisher was propped. "We'd better not need it."

"That's what I'm hoping," he said, but he didn't grab her again, and she was almost disappointed.

No, she *was* disappointed. But she'd pushed him away, so it was her own fault. She finished lighting the two dozen candles and reviewed her work, then nodded. "That looks good. I'm going to turn the lights off now."

"I'll stay right here," he said, pointing at his spot and grinning at her.

That grin made her nervous and all flustered again, but she smiled back at him, then hurried over to flick the lights off.

The effect of the candlelight was nice. She'd set up the candles so the light would flicker at different levels, and it gave a soft, shadowy glow to everything. She wanted that contrast of light and shadow to go with his muscles and his tattoos. But it wasn't quite perfect, so she wanted more.

"Don't think I'm weird for this next part, okay?"

Rome gave her a wary look. "You're not going to ask me to dress up like a unicorn or anything, are you?"

Elise laughed. "Nothing like that. But the entire concept I'm going for is light and shadow on skin, so I want to make sure it's noticeable." And she moved to the side of the room and picked up a tiny bottle of baby oil and demonstrated it to him.

He looked surprised. "You're going to grease me up?"

"Well, actually, I thought you could—"

He shook his head, interrupting her train of thought before she even finished it. "Oh no. If we're doing this, you're the one who's putting that stuff on me. Consider it payment for all this cheap modeling you're getting."

She shrugged, pretending nonchalance. "I can do that." She flicked the cap off and squirted a fair amount into her hand, and then began to rub her hands together to warm the oil.

His eyes gleamed as she held her hands out to him, and he stepped a bit closer to her. "Go ahead," he dared.

With his gaze bearing down on her, Elise suddenly felt shy. Hesitantly, she put her fingertips on his chest and marveled again at how warm he was.

He inhaled at her touch, long and slow. "That feels good."

It did, didn't it? She was fascinated by touching him. Instead of spreading the oil around in a brisk, businesslike manner, she traced her fingertips up and down his body, feeling the muscles under his skin and loving the way he felt.

Rome groaned, his breathing becoming ragged. "How is it that you're able to drive me so crazy with such a small touch, Elise?" His voice was a low murmur in her ear.

She didn't know; her own heart was pounding with desire, her pulse frantically thumping as she skimmed her hands over his pectorals, then pressed her palms to them, covering more skin. Touching him was an addiction, and she was so, so glad that he'd suggested she do this. She was getting aroused. Heck, she had already been aroused, but this just made it all the more evident, the heat pooling between her legs.

"How's it looking?" he whispered into her ear, and she shivered at the huskiness in his tone.

She smoothed her hands up and down his arms—big,

muscular arms—to spread the oil, and then tried to study him from an unbiased point of view. But all she saw was candlelight gleaming on big, tanned muscles and black lines of tattoos bisecting bronze skin.

As she watched, he adjusted himself, his cock tenting the front of his boxers. He looked huge and stiff, even through the clothing.

Elise looked up at Rome and her breath caught. There on his face, that was the look she was trying to capture. That sexy, "come hither and let me fuck you" expression. For a moment, excitement overwhelmed her desire and she grabbed a nearby towel to clean her hands off. "Hold that expression."

"What," he murmured. "The 'my cock is rock hard at the moment' expression?"

"That's the one," she agreed, heading back to pick up her camera. She pulled off the lens cap and focused, and groaned with how perfect the shot was. "Oh my god, Rome. You're so breathtaking."

"Yeah?" His voice was husky with need.

She pressed her thighs together as she began to take pictures, the shutter clicking and whirring a mile a minute as she took photo after photo. "Can you . . . can you pose for me? Maybe flex a little?" He did, and for the next few moments, she directed him in a variety of poses. He turned his back, he raised an arm over his head, anything she asked.

But after a few moments, she began to lose his expression again. She needed to see that soft, fuckable look in his eyes. She bit her lip, thinking. "Rome . . ."

"Hmm?" His hand slid down his oiled belly, creating a fascinating play of light and shadow that momentarily distracted her.

"Are you . . . are you still thinking dirty thoughts about me?"

His eyelids grew hooded again, immediately. "I am now."

She continued to snap photos, fascinated by his face, his eyes. "What did you have in mind?"

"Kinda thinking about dragging you down onto these sheets and eating the hell out of your pussy, just to see if I can make you squirt again."

Her breath caught, and her fingers shook on the camera for a moment. The man just licked his lips. A whimper escaped her throat as she visualized that. "Here?" she breathed.

"We're alone here, aren't we?"

"We are." They were so very alone.

"And you said you wanted some life experience."

She continued to take pictures, closing in on his beautiful mouth and that soft, sexy look in his eyes. The man was oozing sex at the moment. She couldn't wait to see how these pictures turned out.

"I think my eating your pussy would be a great experience for you," he murmured, his hand gliding over one oily arm, and she panned out to capture that motion. "Just bury my face in there and lick you for hours on end. You ever thought about that?"

His voice was so delicious and sensual that it was rolling over her like a wave. She was having a hard time concentrating. It wasn't just his voice or the mental image of him doing that to her; it was everything. And suddenly, she was tired of taking photos. She wanted to touch him again.

She *needed* to touch him. A mental image flashed through her mind and her breath caught. Did she have enough courage to do that?

God, she wanted to so badly. Steeling herself, Elise set the camera down on a nearby table and picked up the oil again. She bit her lip, and then looked over at him, all gleaming and beautiful in the candlelight. "I think we need a bit more oil."

"I think you're just using it as an excuse to put your hands on me," he said, even as she squirted more into her palms.

He wasn't wrong about that. "Maybe I like touching you."

Rome chuckled. "You don't hear me complaining."

She moved to his side again and stepped close, drinking in the sight and scent of him. Her hands stole to his stomach and she pressed them there, then glanced up at him.

His eyes were shadows in the candlelight, but she knew his gaze was completely, utterly fixed on her. Her breath catching in her throat again, Elise slid her slick, oily hands down into the waist of his boxers, her eyes locked on his.

Rome groaned, his entire body stiffening in response.

Startled, her first reaction was to jerk away and apologize. But his hands went to her shoulders, holding her in place, and she realized he didn't want to push her away; he was groaning from pleasure. Of course he was. She was just being a silly goose.

She could feel crisp hair against her fingers, and she wrapped her hands around the hard length of his cock. This was her first time to touch him there—to touch any man there. She was surprised at how hard he was, and how much heat he gave off. Her fingers curled around the circumference of his cock, and she gave it a light squeeze, testing his girth. "You're big."

"You're flattering," he said, strain in his voice. He leaned forward, and his mouth brushed against hers. "And god damn, but your hands feel amazing."

"Do they?" Her breath caught at his pleasure, and she ran her fingers up and down his length, wishing that his boxers weren't in the way. The head of his cock was wet with fluid—his pre-cum. She wanted to taste it, but her hands were oily. She'd taste it some other time, then. Her mouth brushed over his again, and she told him, "I want to stroke you off."

Rome groaned again. "Do you?"

"Can I?" Daring greatly, she curled her hands around his length again and pumped once.

His breath hissed. "Your hands feel amazing."

Did they? She stroked up and down his length again, testing. The angle she was standing at didn't make it easy, but that didn't matter. What mattered was his reaction to her touch, and Rome's eyes were near-closed in ecstasy.

And she loved that.

Elise stroked him again, letting her slippery palms do the work as she moved back and forth in a slow, gliding motion.

His mouth moved to capture hers, and the kiss he gave her was erratic and frantic, even as he bucked his hips against her, pushing her hands up and down his length. That excited her, and she moved faster, watching his reactions.

"Tighten your hand," he told her, his voice hoarse. His own hands went to her hair and he buried them there, his mouth moving against her jaw, her throat, as if he wanted to kiss and touch her, but her hands were distracting him too much.

She liked that.

Elise tightened her hand around him and stroked harder. "Like that?" She was rewarded with a groan and another pump of his hips.

His hand dragged down to cover hers, big and strong. To her surprise, he tightened her grip around him and then began to work himself, using her hand. Fascinated and turned on, Elise let him lead, watching his face as he closed his eyes, strain etched on every line of his face. Faster and harder, he worked her hand on his cock, and then with a low groan in his throat, he came. Hot, sticky threads of semen covered the inside of his boxers and got on her hands. Still, he continued to stroke her hand over him, wringing out every last bit of his orgasm.

Then, he slowly came to himself again, looked at her with those delicious, hooded eyes, and leaned in and kissed her.

"Did I do okay?" she asked shyly, dragging her hand

out of his. It was messy and covered in baby oil, but she was utterly entranced by what they'd just done.

"Hell, yes," he murmured, and his tongue swiped over her mouth. "And I'm going to eat your pussy as soon as we clean up."

Her breath caught in her throat. "I—I didn't— You don't have to—"

"I know," he told her. "But I want to. Are you wet for me?"

She nodded, entranced by the blue of his eyes.

"Did touching me turn you on?"

Oh god, yes, it had. "Yes."

"Then let me do the same for you. You think it won't give me pleasure?"

Her breath shuddered in her throat at the thought. "But . . ."

He stilled. "Or, wait. Did you need to take more pictures?"

She shook her head.

"No? Good. Because I can't wait to get between your legs." He pressed another hard kiss to her mouth and dragged his boxers off, then used them to wipe the come off of his cock, and then her hands.

And Elise couldn't help but stare.

It was the first time she'd been able to get a really good look at it. Last time, he'd kept his clothing on for her. But now, with the candlelight, she got to see everything.

His penis was big and thick, which didn't surprise her, since she'd felt that herself. The rounded head was a dusky, darker color, and a thick vein ran along the length of him. His balls hung underneath the shaft, and his groin was covered with a fine layer of dark hair, which was startling to see, as he only had the barest amount of chest hair and hair on his stomach, and most of that around his belly button.

He was beautiful, though. And raw with masculinity. And she couldn't stop staring. He'd come, but he was still erect, still big. Did that mean he could come again? She wanted to ask, but he was dragging her against him, his hands going to the waist of her jeans.

Rome pressed a kiss to her neck. "You going to undress for me?"

She thought about the candlelight, and how he'd see her hips, slightly off, her back a little rounded, and she stiffened, panic lacing through her. "I . . . I don't know . . ."

"Shhh," he murmured, and stroked an oily hand through her hair. He grabbed a handful of it and used it to drag her mouth toward his, then slowly, deliberately kissed her until she was breathless and distracted. "Maybe we just take these pants off, hmm? You can keep your top if it'll make you feel better, though I'd love to see those pretty breasts."

She bit her lip, putting a hand to his chest, and pulled away just as quickly, since he was still covered in oil.

"Yeah, I'm going to get you all greasy, aren't I? Ask me if I care." He gave her a roguish grin, and his fingers went to the button of her jeans and undid them. The fabric fell, loose, around her hips, and he shoved his hand into her panties.

And then Elise clung to him as his fingers slid against the slick folds of her sex and found her wet. "Ah, there's my girl," Rome murmured, and kissed her again. "All hot and ready for me. You like the thought of my mouth on you?"

The breath was sucked out of her lungs and she stared up at him, mute. "I . . . yes." The words squeaked out of her throat, almost forced. It had been hard to admit, and immediately, her face flushed in response.

"Lie down for me."

She glanced around, looking at the cloth-covered floor, then back at him, all naked and gleaming. "I . . . Be careful we don't knock over any candles."

He chuckled. "You don't have to lecture me about safety. I'm the one covered in oil at the moment."

Gingerly, she sat down on the floor, her legs extended in front of her awkwardly. She wasn't sure what to do. Lie back, flat as a board? The mental image of that was ridiculous. Sit cross-legged? She leaned back on her hands awkwardly, waiting for him.

Rome knelt in front of her, all gorgeous and oh so naked. He grinned, stealing her breath, and hooked one hand behind her knee, dragging her body toward him. The fabric bunched up under her, and Elise shifted awkwardly.

"Lift your hips," he commanded.

She did, and he immediately tugged on her jeans, dragging them down her thighs. Slowly, her panties—her horrible, embarrassing panties—were exposed. But he didn't tease her about them. He simply hooked a finger under the waistband and began to drag them down along with her jeans.

She was going to be totally naked from the waist down. Anxiety warred with excitement. She wanted to do this, but she was scared. What if he didn't like the way her sex looked? What if he noticed her hips didn't exactly line up to her shoulders? What if he saw that scar on her buttock and started asking about it? She bit her lip, uncertain if she should stop him or not.

But just then, he looked up at her and flashed a grin. "This is more fun than unwrapping gifts at Christmas."

It struck her as such an absurd thing to say that she snort-giggled. Pulling her pants off was nothing like opening gifts.

But he only grinned and winked at her, and then lifted one leg at a time to drag her clothes off them. Then he cast her jeans and panties to the side.

And she sat there, waiting, all anxiety, for him to say something.

His hand skimmed up her pale calf, then caressed her knee, leaving a gleam of baby oil behind on her skin. "Beautiful."

She flushed with pleasure. She didn't have great legs—they weren't toned, or tanned. They were actually a rather ghastly pale, but he made her feel pretty.

That hand continued to slide up her leg, and Rome's eyes met hers, so blue and intense. Then his hand pressed at the inside of her knee, a suggestion for her to part her legs.

Biting her lip, Elise did so.

The hand slid to her sex, covering her with his palm. He looked up at her, heat in his eyes. "Tell me if you get freaked out or scared, all right?"

She nodded slowly.

His hand moved, his thumb brushing over her curls. She was wet again, incredibly wet to the point that she would have been embarrassed were it not for the look of satisfaction on his face. His fingers slid between her folds and his gaze went back to hers.

It was hard to keep eye contact with him when his hand was touching her so intimately. She felt incredibly exposed, incredibly naked, and incredibly, terribly aroused. The urge to close her legs and push him away was real and strong, just as strong as the excitement burning in her, wondering what he'd do next.

"I'm going to put my mouth on you," he murmured. "I'm going to bury it in that sweet flesh and taste you. And I'm going to lick your pussy like it's my favorite dessert, and tease your clit with my tongue. And I'm not going to stop until you come."

Elise gasped at his words, her legs trembling. Knowing he was going to do it was one thing; having him kneeling between her spread legs and announcing how he was going to lick her was another entirely. But she couldn't break that intense blue-eyed gaze.

"You ready?" he asked her.

Oh god, she was supposed to say something? Like *yes, go ahead and start licking*? Couldn't he just start? Elise's mouth worked for a moment, and when no words came out of her locked throat, she gave him a wide-eyed nod.

Then Rome gave her that sexy, confident little grin that made her melt inside, and he leaned down, breaking their eye contact. She stared in wonder as he leaned over her spread legs and then shifted his big body.

And then his mouth was on her.

Elise froze, her body stiffening as she felt the first probe of his tongue against her flesh. It wasn't quite the fireworks and explosions she'd expected. Instead, it just felt like the gentle prod of an unfamiliar touch. She frowned to herself. Was he doing it wrong? Oh god, what if she was the one doing something wrong? What if there was a trick to this and she didn't know it—

"Elise," he murmured, not looking up. "You're tense as hell. Lie back, close your eyes, and relax, okay?"

"A-a-all right," she stammered, and lay back on the hard floor, trying not to feel embarrassed. "Do you need me to do anything—"

"Yeah. Relax."

"I'm trying to. It's difficult when you're sitting there between my legs," she retorted.

He chuckled, and a shiver broke out on her skin when she realized she could feel his laugh against her flesh. She wanted to look again, but she'd promised him she'd lie back and close her eyes, and she did.

"Why don't you try deep breathing or something?"

"Huh?" Why were they having a conversation about breathing when he was going to lick her between her legs?

"Yeah," he said. "It's a good way to relax. Breathe in, count to five, breathe out, count to five. Rinse and repeat. You're still tense as all fuck and it's making me antsy."

"Oh. Sorry." She obediently began to do as he'd suggested, breathing in slowly, counting, and then breathing out again. His mouth wasn't on her anymore, but she felt his hand slide up and down her thigh in a stroking, soothing motion. That was . . . rather nice, she had to admit. Almost nicer than when his mouth had been on her, but she wouldn't tell him that. It might hurt his feelings.

Maybe she just wasn't the kind of girl who liked oral sex.

She continued to breathe in and out slowly, her muscles slowly easing. Some of the tension was leaving her body, helped by his stroking hands. They were just stroking the insides of her thighs, now, sliding up and down her skin. His knuckles grazed where her thigh and hip met and she shivered, but it was a good shiver.

"You counting?" His voice was a low murmur.

"One, two, three, four, five," she chanted obediently as she exhaled, then began the count again in her head as she inhaled. This breathing thing was rather nice. She was definitely feeling relaxed.

Something pressed on top of her mound.

His mouth. Oh.

Her count was interrupted and she got distracted, then gave herself a mental shake and continued counting to herself.

"I'm going to touch you a little," he said in a low, husky voice that made her skin prickle all over again. "Keep counting."

"One," she said obediently. "Two, three—"

On four, his tongue flicked over her clitoris.

The breath whooshed out of her lungs.

"Count," he commanded, and his tongue flicked over it again.

She felt a little squirmy at the sensation of his mouth against her. Not tense like before, but, different. She wasn't sure if she liked it or not. "One," she began again, her voice sounding rather breathless even to her own ears.

He didn't wait for her to get to four that time. His tongue began to push and lick at her clit in slow, languid motions.

Oh. Oh. She wanted to push his face away. No, scratch that. She wanted to mash it against her clit and rub hard. Not soft and flicking like the touches of his tongue as they coaxed and teased her. She'd push hard, and rub to end the wonderful, awful tension he was creating with those small, flicking licks.

"You counting?" he asked between licks.

She'd forgotten her count. Her legs trembled and she fisted her hands, unsure what to do with them. "One," she began again. "Tw-uh-huh-huh," she sobbed as he changed tactics and began to suck on her clit. Oh god. Oh Jesus. Oh sweet heaven, that was good. Her hands found their way to his head and she tried to direct him to go back to licking. She could stand the licking. The sucking, though, that was going to make her crawl all the way out of her skin. "Th-th-threee," she exhaled in a wheezing gasp as he made a soft smacking noise, as if eating her was delicious.

"Mmm," he said in a low voice that made her shiver all over again. "This is some juicy pussy, Elise. Love how wet you get for me."

Of course, that made her get distracted all over again, especially when he groaned low in his throat and began to lick her all over again. Her hands on his head curled into fists, and she wished for a moment that his hair was long so she had something to hold on to. Instead, all she could do was press her knuckles to his scalp and try to hold on.

"Count," he growled between licks.

"One," she began again, and it ended on a bit of a sob when he did this incredible nuzzling thing with his lips against her clit. Then it stopped, and he went back to licking, which was frustrating and wonderful at the same time. Her hips rocked a little, trying to push against his mouth, and then she stilled, worried that she wasn't supposed to do that. "Sorry—"

"No, that's good, baby," he murmured between licks. "Show me that you like it."

"I like all of it," she wheezed, her hips rocking again.

"Yeah? Can I do more, then?" He nuzzled at her clit again, and she cried out. "Gonna take that as a yes," he told her.

She felt a finger press against the opening of her core. Her breath whistled out of her throat.

"Count," he demanded, and then nuzzled again.

Oh god, she was helpless against that nuzzle. "One—"

His finger pushed inside her.

She keened, her hips raising up. She felt his hand brace on her hip, forcing her back down on the floor, even as he continued to lick and suck at her clit. The finger inside her was joined by another, and then she was being stretched, fingers pumping in and out slowly, even as he continued to lick and suck at her clit.

And it was rapidly becoming too much. Her breath was coming in short, hard pants. "One," she gasped. "One. One. One. Oh god, one—"

He chuckled against her clit but she was beyond caring, because he did that nuzzle thing again and she pushed her knuckles against his scalp, her hips raising even as she tried to bear down against his fingers. Oh god, it was too much. "One," she cried out again.

"You gonna come?"

She nodded, her breath catching in her throat like a sob.

"Good," he said in a possessive, hungry voice, and then he began to lick and suck even harder, those fingers pounding into her.

Elise came with a keening cry that might have been "one" again. Her entire body locked up, and she felt the gush of wetness between her legs, felt his groan of pleasure, and heard the slick hammering of his fingers inside her, pushing in and out, and she just kept coming and coming and coming, her body arching like a bow.

And then she collapsed on the hard floor, panting and trying to catch the breath that couldn't quite seem to find its way back into her lungs again. Her hair clung to her forehead in sweaty tendrils; she hadn't even realized she was sweating.

Lord have mercy.

Okay, so she'd grossly underestimated what it was like to have a man eat her pussy. She'd been tense at the beginning and hadn't relaxed enough to enjoy herself. As soon as she had, though . . . holy crap.

"You," Rome said with a chuckle, crawling up over her with a pleased look on his face, "need a few counting lessons."

He looked rather satisfied with himself, his mouth damp and his lips a little red and swollen, as if he'd been thoroughly kissed. She supposed he had been kissing . . . it just wasn't her mouth.

Blushing, she ducked her head against his arm. "You were distracting me."

"I was," he agreed. "And you came beautifully once you relaxed." He leaned down and pressed a kiss to her mouth.

She opened her lips for him, pleased when his tongue skated against her own, and surprised to taste herself on his mouth. "Did I . . ."

"Oh yeah," he said, and sounded pleased as hell. "We're definitely two for two."

She ran a hand along the arm braced next to her head, and winced at the baby oil coating her palm. "I think we've made a mess of the staging sheets."

"Huge mess," he agreed. "We're probably lucky we haven't caught on fire, what with all the distractions and writhing we've been doing."

"You sure did look nice all oiled up, though," she said, sliding her hands up and down his front.

"Did I? I'm glad you liked it."

"Do you want to see the photos when they're done?"

He shrugged. "I only did it so you'd have to see me again."

Her eyes widened in surprise. "You didn't think I was going to come back?"

"I wasn't sure. You're awfully skittish at times."

Well, that was true enough. "But I'm still a virgin," she told him, pleased at the way his gaze seemed to grow hooded at the mere mention of the word. "That would defeat the purpose of our experiment."

"Experiment, huh?" Rome leaned in and kissed her again. "So what now?"

"Now I clean up the mess I made in here," she said, glancing at the flickering candles.

He tweaked her nipple through the fabric of her shirt, surprising her—and sending another bolt of lust through her body. "I meant you and me."

Elise wasn't sure what he was asking. "What's next . . . for you and me?"

He nodded, the look he gave her surprisingly intense. "You're still shy around me. I don't scare you, do I?" He tugged at her shirt thoughtfully.

She shook her head. "I'm not . . . I just . . . I'm not comfortable, I guess."

"I don't see why. You're sexy as hell." He brushed a lock of hair away from her face, the touch of his fingers tender. "I'm just shocked no one's scooped you up before me."

That didn't sound like the words of a man who was content to be used for de-virgining. Elise looked up into Rome's rugged face and gave a small, soft sigh. She touched his face gently. "Maybe I just got lucky."

To her surprise, a wry expression curved his mouth. "Yeah. Lucky."

He didn't sound like he believed her. Well, he wasn't the only one feeling like the other was going to have a harsh wake-up call sometime soon, was he? Why was Rome so down on himself? From what she knew, he was perfect. Strong, gorgeous, smart, funny, patient with someone as ridiculously silly as her . . .

Her fingers brushed against the lip ring. "So . . . when do you want to get together again?"

He nipped at her fingers, sending a skitter of excitement through her body. "I am at your beck and call." He thought for a moment, and then gave a small shrug. "Well, unless your beck and call is on a weekday, because your brother would have my head if I skipped out on work."

"We wouldn't want that," she said shyly. Should she suggest tomorrow night? Would that be too forward? Could you be too forward with a man who'd just licked you until you came? Who, even now, was sprawled between her legs, naked? Her fingers traced along a tattoo thoughtfully. "My schedule is more open than yours. Do you want to just text me when you're available?"

"I can do that." He leaned in and pressed another kiss on her mouth. "But for now, I suppose we should clean up this room, shouldn't we?"

She nodded, and tried not to think of him never calling her again. He would, wouldn't he?

NINE

A week later, Elise got the courage to drop the staging sheets off at the dry cleaner at the next town over. She tried not to blush when pointing out that the material was stained with baby oil and wax, and could they please get it out. Again, not something she wanted to take in to a Bluebonnet dry cleaner, since it was a small town and people talked. But all this subterfuge was getting a little ridiculous.

Would it really be so bad if people found out she and Rome were dating?

They *were* dating, weren't they? He'd taken her out a few times in the last week, and sure, they made out a bit—okay, a lot—but they also laughed and talked and did couple-type things. He wasn't pressuring her for sex just so he could bang her and get it over with.

That was dating, wasn't it?

And she hadn't expected it from him—she'd expected him to have sex with her, of course, but not more than that—and it was a pleasure to be around him. When he wasn't there, she found herself thinking about him. What was he doing that day? Did he think about her while he was at work?

She had it bad.

Of course, she was naive, but she was rather hoping she wasn't the only one. Just this morning, she'd gotten a text from Rome.

Woke up this morning and you weren't in my bed. Kinda sucked.

Which, of course, made her all giddy and giggly. She sent back: Did you check under the bed?

No sexy brunettes. Just a blonde, but I kicked her out.

Hey!

J/K. Maybe you should come check for yourself. :)

She thought about that smiley all morning. It matched the smile on her own face. Heck, she couldn't stop smiling. Okay, sometimes she thought about their interlude in the salon and how he'd buried his face against her sex, and then she blushed along with her smile. But mostly? Just smiling.

Her phone buzzed with another text while she was in the parking lot of the camera store, and she grabbed it eagerly. It was a picture this time, of Rome in one of the paintball jumpsuits, twin stripes of black face paint under his eyes. He had a paintball gun slung over his shoulders. As she admired the photo, another message from him popped up.

You liko?

Too much clothing, she sent back.

Oh man, he sent back a minute later. I should have known that I created a monster. You're asking for dick pics, aren't you?

No!!!

You sure?

I'm sure! Well . . . if you send one, I won't complain. But I'm not sending anything back!

Tease.

He continued to text her, distracting her from her

shopping. It was a good distraction, though, and she was humming as she purchased darkroom chemicals and paper. The candlelight photos she'd taken of Rome would be developed by hand. From start to finish, he'd be all hers. Maybe she'd put them in a scrapbook that she could pull out and look at from time to time.

Of course, that sounded horribly spinsterish, didn't it? Elise frowned to herself. Putting pictures of a guy in a scrapbook made it sound like she was planning for a future alone instead of enjoying what she had in the present. It seemed like mentally she still couldn't shake the fact that she was surprised someone wanted *her*.

It felt like there should be a catch somewhere. It wasn't supposed to be that easy in real life, was it? You didn't go up to a guy, ask him to sleep with you, and start dating instead. That sort of thing just didn't happen.

Her phone lit up with another text while she stared at it. You coming out to the ranch?

It took her a moment to realize that the text wasn't from Rome, but from her brother. I was. What's up?

We have some guys coming by this afternoon. Wanted to do some action shots for the paintball brochure if you can bring your equipment.

Can do. Her brother was being a little picky about the shots, but she didn't mind. It gave her an excuse to stay in Bluebonnet, and it made her feel wanted. That was better than taking pictures of trees and lake shots while hanging out with her parents.

Truth be told, she rather liked being on her own while in Bluebonnet. Maybe it was time to move out on her own after all . . . And then what? Sit at home in her apartment by herself? How would she pay the bills? Ask her parents? She and Beth Ann had toyed with the idea of doing pinup photo shoots, but that would only work if she stayed in Bluebonnet, and she wasn't sure the town was big enough to support a photography business. And was that what she really wanted to do? Hadn't she played with the idea of being a magazine photographer? There was a big difference between that and taking senior photos.

Elise hadn't figured out all the details yet.

Her phone buzzed again. Grant. And I need another favor. Oh?

I want you to go thrift shopping with Brenna. Make sure she doesn't buy anything hideous. Tell her you hate everything. You know Mother probably wants a big wedding.

Yes, but Brenna probably wants to dress up like Elvis.

Hence my problem. I'm stuck in the middle. Come help your brother out.

She chuckled. What are sisters for?

"I can't wait to start popping some tags!" Brenna bounded out of Elise's rental, her enormous purse slung over her shoulder as she headed for the sidewalk of the shopping strip and made a beeline for the ugly storefront that had "Thrift Store & Consignment" soaped onto the window.

Elise groaned and followed her in. Brenna was in high spirits, despite the fact that they'd driven for a half hour and Macklemore's "Thrift Shop" had played on endless repeat the entire time while Brenna's pug squatted and peed on the floorboards of the car and whined in fear. Elise wasn't very fond of that dog, and had suggested leaving it at home, to which Brenna had acted as if Elise had suggested they let the dog play in traffic.

Elise herself wasn't in a very good mood. She'd driven out to the ranch, but Brenna had tackled her before she'd been able to go in and sneak a peek at Rome to satisfy her eyes. That had put her in a funk. Combine that with the fact that he hadn't texted her in hours? Double funk.

Puppy pee on the floorboards? Triple funk.

But Brenna turned and gave her such an excited look, Elise's spirits lifted just a bit. "Isn't this fun?"

"It is," Elise lied, smiling and checking her phone one last time before sliding it into her pocket. "Where's your dog?"

Brenna winked and pointed at her oversized purse. "He's in here."

"Are you sure you're allowed to bring him in?" Elise glanced at the front door of the thrift store.

Brenna snorted. "Rich ladies do it all the time. Besides, Gollum's already peed, so he'll be fine for at least a half hour."

"Great," Elise murmured, and followed Brenna inside.

The interior of the shop was small and dirty, and immediately Elise wanted to leave. The smell of dust was overwhelming, and the woman behind the counter barely glanced at them before returning to texting on her phone. "You ladies let me know if you need help with anything," she called out.

"Oh wow," exclaimed Brenna, heading for a nearby rack. "Look at all this great stuff!" She pulled out a T-shirt with a panda on it and held it out to Elise. "You should get this."

Elise took it from her and glanced at it. "It's not my size."

"I know, but it's my size and then I can borrow it." Brenna gave Elise a beaming smile.

Oh yeah. Grant had warned her about Brenna's idiosyncrasies. That Brenna didn't like to actually own things . . . but she loved to borrow. Elise flipped the tag on the shirt and then sighed. It was cheap, at least. "All right. Is there anything else I want to get here?"

Brenna shrugged. "I was thinking about having the wedding colors be orange and pink. What do you think?"

"I think that sounds . . . hideous?"

"Me too." She grinned. "And it'll clash with my purple bangs. And then Grant won't hate on my idea of heading down to the courthouse."

"It's not Grant's idea as much as it is Mom's," Elise commented, following Brenna as she wandered through the store. "She's just really excited to have a new daughter-in-law."

"Your mom is sweet, but weddings are really a waste of money," Brenna said, then pulled another T-shirt off the rack and held it up skeptically to Elise. "Do you like this shirt?"

"I . . . guess?" It was cute enough—pink, with a ruffle across the neckline and spaghetti straps for sleeves. She'd never wear it, though. The scar on her back would be totally visible. "It's the wrong season for a tank top, isn't it?"

Brenna shrugged. "We could always add an orange skirt to this and voilà, wedding gear." She checked the tag. "Besides, it's dirt cheap." She handed it to Elise, who took it.

She should have guessed when Grant had tried to give her his credit card that she'd be the one buying everything today.

"Oooh, check that out." Brenna wandered over to a mannequin and fingered a fringed black vest with a deep vee-cut front and what looked like a lace-up corset on the waist. "You should buy that. It's totally slutty."

Elise stared at the article of clothing. "Um. What would you wear under that?"

"Nothing," Brenna said, and gestured at her boobs, pushing them up. "You just jiggle your shit under the nose of every man who comes by."

And what on earth made Brenna think that sounded a bit like Elise? "Um, I think I'll pass."

"You sure? It'd look hot on a date." And Brenna gave her a knowing look.

Elise felt a flush climbing her face. She tugged her hair over her cheek awkwardly. "Um."

"Oh, come on. Don't sit there and tell me you're not dating anyone. You totally have the 'I had a good fuck last night' look on your face."

Her eyes widened in shock. "What?"

"Yeah. I told Grant it's pretty clear you're getting some,

and that's why you're sticking around Bluebonnet. He blustered and huffed a little, but in the end, he's happy for you. That's one reason why we're out today, you know." Brenna gave Elise an incredibly obvious wink. "I'm supposed to dig out from you who you're seeing so Grant can do the whole 'big brother' thing."

"I'm not seeing anyone," Elise protested, but the argument sounded weak, even to herself.

"Oh please. You are a terrible liar. Look at how red your face is."

Elise ducked her head in embarrassment.

"And now you're staring at the floor. Typical avoidance reaction. You know what this means."

Elise looked up, forcing herself to make eye contact with Brenna even though it was killing her to do so. "What?"

"It means I'm going to have to start guessing." Brenna waggled her eyebrows at her.

"Please don't."

To Elise's relief, the puppy in Brenna's purse started whining, immediately distracting her. Brenna pulled him out and gave Elise a quick glance. "I think I'm going to take him outside to piddle. He might have the runs from breakfast."

It was strange to wish diarrhea on a puppy, but Elise was rather hoping for something like that so Brenna would remain distracted. "I think I'll just pay for these while you do that."

They separated and Elise headed to the register. The woman at the counter seemed to take an exceptionally long time with each. Elise paid for the shirts, pressing a hand to her cheeks to try and calm down a bit. Her face felt overheated and flushed. So Brenna knew she was seeing someone. That shouldn't be embarrassing, right? But Rome didn't want Grant to know, so she had to keep it a secret somehow.

She just needed to somehow misdirect Brenna. That wouldn't be easy, given that Elise's every emotion showed on her face. She thanked the clerk, took the bag, and slowly headed back outside to rejoin Brenna, determined to keep a poker-faced expression.

"All done?" Brenna asked, squatting next to the fat puppy currently toddling on the sidewalk.

"Yes," Elise said, and handed the bag to Brenna, since they both knew that was who the shirts were really for. "Think you can clean these for me?" She lied. "I don't have a washing machine at the bed-and-breakfast."

"I'll see what I can do," Brenna said cheerily, swiping up the shirts.

They got back into the car, Brenna fussing over her puppy, and Elise thought she was home free until she backed out of the space and Brenna spoke again.

"So, I've been giving some thought as to whom you might be seeing here in Bluebonnet."

"He's not in Bluebonnet," Elise said hastily, forcing herself to concentrate on the road. "Remember that I said I didn't like anyone in Bluebonnet."

"Yeah, but you're still staying in town, right?"

She shot a glance over at Brenna, who was distracted with her puppy, kissing its ugly face. "I'm staying at the bed-and-breakfast, yes."

"So . . . there're cheaper places down the highway."

"I like Emily's place."

"Yeah, but if you were seeing someone from outside, you'd probably spend more time out of town. But every time I call or Grant calls, you're in Bluebonnet. Which tells me something's keeping you here. And besides, you just admitted there is someone. You said he's not staying in Bluebonnet, which means there *is* a he."

Elise chewed on the inside of her cheek nervously.

"So that tells me that I'm on the right track," Brenna said. "Which leads me to about four different guys I can think of."

"Maybe I'm not dating anyone. Maybe I just got a . . . um . . ." Oh hell, she couldn't even say the word aloud.

"Vibrator?" Brenna giggled, the sound gleeful. "Yeah right. Besides, I don't see you walking into a sex store and buying one."

Elise's face felt hot again and she concentrated on the road. "Did you want to go to another thrift store? There's one the next town over, I think—"

"It's not a vibe," Brenna declared. "Though if you want to go by a sex shop while we're out, I'm game. I'd love to buy something that would blow Grant's mind. Maybe an anal wand."

Elise cringed. "Please don't mention 'anal wand' and my brother in the same sentence."

Brenna just giggled again. "I guess that's a no. Anyway. Four guys." She held her fingers up and wiggled them in the periphery of Elise's vision. "And Pop is one of them, but I'm guessing he's way too old for you."

Colt's father? Elise pictured him, all gut and whiskery chin and trucker cap. "He's nice, but no."

"That's what I thought. Which leads me to Berry, Colt's brother. And unless you've got a total hard-on for mullets paired with *Duck Dynasty* beards, I think we can rule out pretty much anyone in Colt's family after all."

"Um."

Brenna peered at her face, then sat back. "You're not all flushed. It's not one of them."

"It might be," Elise said, trying to deflect. Rome was going to kill her if she told Brenna. He was going to be furious. She bit her lip. "Please stop guessing."

"Nope. Just getting warmed up," Brenna said. "Now, there's Miguel that works behind the bar at Maya Loco, and he's a hot piece of prime meat, but I think he's got a girlfriend. Unless you chased her off." And Brenna stared at Elise's face. "Nope, no reaction. Not Miguel. Which leads me to my final guess."

"Oh?" Elise felt coiled and tense, her hands tight on the steering wheel. *Here it comes.*

"That cute young fireman with the tight ass." And Brenna peered at her face again, watching.

Elise relaxed, almost exhaling with utter relief. She hadn't guessed right. "I'll never say." She looked over at Brenna and smiled, full of relief.

A sly look crossed Brenna's face. "Uh huh."

"What?" Elise smiled.

"I texted Emily while you were inside the thrift shop. Wanna guess what she told me?"

Oh shit. Elise felt her face get hot immediately, and it was made worse by Brenna's gleeful laugh. "Oh my god, I was right! You're totally nailing Rome!"

Elise felt her shoulders hunch, and she wanted to hide under the seat of the car. Not a good idea, considering she was driving. "I'm not."

"You totally are. Look at your face. You look like you want to throw up!"

"Would I look like I wanted to throw up if we were talking about a guy I was dating?" Elise tried to divert.

"If we're talking about you? Yes! You always look like you want to puke when you get embarrassed, and you're embarrassed about dating Rome!" She turned in her seat and bounced.

"Emily said she wouldn't tell!"

"Well, she didn't, really." Brenna shot her a smug look. "I texted her and said 'How long have Elise and Rome been fucking?' and she spilled all the beans. It was a total guess on my part, but I'm awesome with guessing, looks like. Grant is totally going to shit a brick when he finds out."

"Brenna," Elise said, her voice sharper than she realized. "Please don't say anything."

"Why?"

"Because Grant's a little overprotective as it is. You know how he gets."

"Mmm, you might have a point." Brenna tapped her chin. "That might be bad."

"Please, Brenna. *Please*. Don't tell him."

Brenna sighed. "All right. It'll be our secret."

Elise gave a small whimper of relief.

At Rome's suggestion, they'd set up a large supply shed near the paintball course, and after the dry run this morning, they'd decided to go ahead and start moving over some of the equipment. Rome was responsible for setting up shelves and organizing things in an efficient way, but he didn't mind. Work was work, and he was glad for it. He'd just hung a large pegboard on the back wall of the shed and was using the power screwdriver to keep it in place when Grant came storming over the hill.

"Lozada," he called, his voice furious. "I need to talk to you."

Well, shit. Rome couldn't say that he hadn't been anticipating this day, but it had arrived a little sooner than he'd hoped for. With a sigh, he finished drilling in the screw, turned, and headed out of the shed.

Grant was there, dressed in his slacks and button-down shirt like he always wore, glasses perched on his nose. It was clear, Rome thought, who was the boss around here and who was the grunt, and Grant never let anyone forget that. The man's jaw was set so hard that he looked like he was going to break a tooth, though. He was furious about something.

Rome could guess what.

"Yeah?" Rome said, wiping his brow. Even though it was cool outside, the shed got stifling fast. They'd have to find a way to keep it cool in the summer, he thought idly. If he was still here at that time.

"You and I need to have a talk," Grant said, his voice tight.

Here we go. "Shoot."

"Brenna just texted me and tells me that you're seeing my sister."

Ah hell. Rome gave Grant a level gaze, saying nothing. "Well? Are you?"

Rome considered for a moment. "I don't know if that's anyone's business but mine and Elise's."

Grant's face darkened. "My sister is young, and impressionable, and very fragile—"

"She's an adult," Rome said bluntly. Hell, he made Elise sound like she was made of glass. She was human, not fine china. "She can make her own decisions."

"She doesn't have a lot of life experience—"

"I know. That's why she came to me."

His eyes narrowed. "What do you mean, she came to you?"

Damn it. That had been the wrong thing to say to her overprotective brother. "That's Elise's business, I'm sorry to say. Not yours."

"She's my sister."

"She's an adult."

"Elise has had a very sheltered upbringing. She's not very worldly. I don't want to see anyone take advantage of her."

"I'm not taking advantage of her," Rome said, but he knew the words were useless. Grant had already made up his mind about that, hadn't he?

"No?" Grant crossed his arms over his chest. "I know Brenna likes you because she thinks you're a rebel like her, but I don't see a rebel when I look at you. I see a drifter. I see someone who uses people to get ahead, and then when it's no longer profitable, he dumps them and leaves others to pick up the pieces. And I feel like I hand-delivered my sister into your lap. I hired you, so you must have been trustworthy, right? And instead I let you get close to a sweet, trusting, naive girl who happens to have an enormous bank account. That's exactly the kind of victim you're looking for, isn't it?"

Jesus Christ, the man made him sound like the worst kind of criminal. "I don't know anything about Elise's bank account, and I don't care about it. Your sister came on to me."

"Oh, stop with the bullshit," Grant said. "We both know that's not true."

"Whatever, man." Clearly Elise was sainted in his eyes.

"I want you to stay away from my sister from now on," Grant told him, stabbing a finger in Rome's direction. It made Rome want to reach over and break it off, he was so coldly furious. "It's only because we're shorthanded that I'm not firing you on the spot. Dane's out there busting his ass, handling double classes while Colt is out. I can't afford to lose a set of hands right now."

Rome's jaw tensed. "And when Dane gets back?"

"I don't know," Grant said, his smile tight and bitter. "I guess it depends on when Elise plans on heading back home. I'm tempted to run a background check on you, just to see what comes up. Would I like what I find?"

Rome thought about his four years in prison. His terrible credit. His juvie records that held a wealth of minor offenses. "Most likely not."

"That's what I thought. You want to tell me about it?"

"Depends. You gonna tell Elise?"

"Doesn't she deserve to know?"

He shrugged, feeling tense with anger. "It's not who I am anymore, so does it matter?"

"It does if it can hurt my sister," Grant snarled.

Rome said nothing. It wasn't any of Grant's damn business.

"That's what I thought. I'll leave you with this warning. Stay the hell away from my sister if you want to keep your job. One fuck-up and you're out of here, understand?"

Rome thought about the paycheck he got on a weekly basis. He'd been so hopeful to use that to start climbing out of the hole he found himself in. Get some repairs done on his old bike, put away for a nest egg. He thought about his cabin, how good it felt to have a home again that he could call his own. How he didn't have to sleep in shitty roadside motels with black mold on the ceiling, or crash on the couch of one of his parents' old friends. Or worse, sleep under a bridge. He'd done all of the above, and there was nothing quite like having his own place.

And he thought of Elise. Sweet, gorgeous, shy Elise, who responded to his touch like no one he'd ever met before. Who made him feel like he could do anything when she looked at him with those big, shining eyes.

And then he thought of his family. And how he never, ever wanted to be beholden to them again.

And he thought of prison.

So he sighed, defeated. "I understand. I won't speak to your sister anymore."

"Good." The hardness in Grant's jaw eased a little. "It's nothing against you personally, man. It's just . . ."

"I know," Rome said in a dead voice. "She's your sister. I get it. I won't even look at her. You have my word."

Grant nodded. "Thank you."

"Sure," he said flatly.

When Elise stopped by the ranch that afternoon, camera in hand, Rome took one of the ATVs out into the woods and headed to the supply cabin to chop wood. He made sure he was gone until sunset, long after Elise would have left.

He was going to have to break that girl's heart, wasn't he? She wouldn't understand why he'd suddenly blown so cold after their steamy sessions. He could tell her that her brother chased him off, but that would be unfair, wouldn't it? Family was family, and her brother was just looking out for her. Rome had known he was no good for Elise from the start. No sense in dragging down another person with him.

The thing that bothered him the most about the situation was that he knew Elise would blame herself. She was growing in confidence and in her sexuality, and he worried this might crush her.

Never mind what it would do to him to have to let her go. She was the best thing that had happened to him in a long, long time.

Maybe ever.

Elise stared at her silent phone and tried not to feel hopeless. She'd told Rome to text her when he wanted to get together again, leaving the ball in his court each time they went out. And each time, he always sent her a text message the next day and they'd get together. Every day, without fail, she heard from him. But now she was going onto day three and there was nothing but silence. She thought he might wait another day. Maybe two. And she'd hoped he'd pop up with the charming, funny text messages he often sent throughout the day to let her know he was thinking about her.

She'd never assumed that he'd just stop calling entirely.

It had been three days since she'd heard from him. She'd been hurt when she'd gone out to the paintball course to take action shots and he'd been deep in the woods. But that was his job, so she hadn't dwelled on it too much. Then she'd stopped by the Daughtry Ranch the next day to show the photos to her brother, hoping to catch a glimpse of Rome, but he never came through the lodge.

Her phone was utterly silent and the weekend was coming up. She knew Rome would have those days off. Did he not want to spend them with her? She'd . . . just assumed he would.

Was she an idiot for thinking he might want to? She didn't know what to do. Brenna had sworn up and down that she wouldn't tell Grant, and she believed her. Knowing Grant and his protective streak, he'd have gone nuts about the entire thing, but he'd been chipper and open the last few days, his mood great. He certainly didn't seem like something was wrong.

No, she had to conclude that Brenna hadn't said anything to Grant, and the fact that Rome was avoiding her was of his own doing.

And that hurt, a lot.

Was it her? Had he not enjoyed their time together? She thought he had. She had the box of condoms at the ready, and she'd decided that the next time she saw Rome, she'd have sex. Real, honest to goodness, sweaty, delicious sex.

Except she wasn't exactly sure there would be a next time.

So she moped around the Peppermint House and tried to keep busy. Emily had offered her one of the guest bathrooms to set up as a darkroom, but she hadn't bothered yet. The only pictures she had to develop were of Rome, and she didn't feel like looking at those at the moment.

She was at a loss.

Elise stared at her phone again, wondering. Should she just call? Ask what was wrong? Was he upset over something?

After a moment's indecision, she sent a tentative Hi to his phone.

No answer.

She waited an hour, then two. After five hours, she was pretty sure he was ignoring her text. Rome checked his phone more often than that.

She felt sick to her stomach.

TEN

Rome put the lock on the paintball shed and rubbed his lower back. It had been a long, hellish day. They were in full swing trying to get the paintball course ready to go for the big launch, which meant ordering extra supplies, testing out everything, and clearing any sort of debris that might trip someone up on the field. Grant wanted to make sure there were no "liabilities waiting to happen," so Rome and Pop had gone over the course repeatedly. Hell, Rome had spent an hour just jumping on the damn constructed castle to make sure it wouldn't fall apart due to a little roughhousing.

That had been hard work, of course, but that hadn't been the hellish part.

It was having to ignore his girl.

He'd stared at her text all day. Hi. He'd hoped that she'd send more. That she'd take the initiative and send him something even though he was ignoring her. He craved contact with her. His nights were filled with thoughts of her, and when he woke up and she wasn't beside him in his bed, it felt wrong. She haunted him, her sweet innocence and the spark of fire that showed when she was pushed too far. Over and over, he kept thinking of their session in the salon, when he'd parted her knees and licked her pussy until she'd come. She'd been blown away. Hell, he'd been blown away, too. She'd reached for him first. She'd wanted to touch him. He couldn't stop thinking about that.

He jerked off to it in the shower, daily, just thinking about her hands on him. She'd wanted *him*. Even now, his cock hardened at the thought of her. They'd never gone as far with each consecutive date, skirting around sex and just making out for what seemed like hours on end instead. That was good, too, but he was craving more of her with every waking moment.

Rome headed into his cabin. Pop was heading over to the main lodge to grab a few beers, but Rome needed time away from the others to cool off and unwind, to gather his thoughts. The last thing he wanted to do was sit around and try to act like everything was cool when he was all fucked-up inside.

Elise had to think this was her fault. Had to. And that was tearing him up. But all he needed was one wrong word said to her brother, and he'd be out on his ass, homeless. He was fucking stuck.

Frustrated, Rome opened the door to his cabin.

Elise sat there on the edge of his bed, her hands clasped on her lap. She stood up as he entered, her eyes widening. "Rome, there you are."

He glanced around to make sure no one had seen her when he opened the door, and then slid inside. "Elise, what the hell are you doing here?"

"I-I-I-I just thought . . . You weren't answering my texts . . ." She blinked rapidly, as if fighting tears, and her gaze dropped. "I just wanted to make sure you were okay."

Rome groaned. God, he was the biggest asshole in the world. He knew he should explain himself, kick her out so

her brother didn't see her, but he found himself moving forward instead and wrapping his arms around her. "Shhh,
please don't cry, Elise."

Her hand dashed over her face. "I'm n-n-not crying," she
said in a wobbly voice. "I just don't understand." Her voice
dropped to a whisper. "Did I do something wrong?"

Oh damn. "Stop, Elise. Shh. Please don't cry." He kissed
her brow a dozen times, pressing his mouth to every inch of
her face he could touch. His hand went to her long, silky
hair and he touched it, dragging his fingers through the delicious length. God, it felt so good to touch her again. He knew
he should resist, but seeing her here . . . "It's not you, okay?
It's me. I'm all fucked-up."

She gave him a skeptical, tear-filled look that told him
she clearly didn't believe him.

"It's true," he repeated. "It was nothing you did. God,
you've been nothing but great." He held her closer, enjoying
the feel of her body against his. "Don't you know I jerk off
to the thought of you every night? If you were here in my
bed, I'd fuck the hell out of you constantly, just so you'd
know how hot I find you."

"But . . . then why won't you talk to me? Or answer my
texts?" Her voice was small, wounded. Afraid of what she'd
find out.

"It's just . . . complicated." He stroked a hand down her
hair. "Trust me."

"You won't tell me why?" She pushed away from him,
suddenly frustrated. "I'm just supposed to accept that everything's fine and it's nothing I did and, oh yes, by the way,
you refuse to talk to me anymore? What am I supposed to
think, Rome?"

He raked a hand down his face. "I know it's crazy," he
muttered. Hell, it was crazy that she was still in here with
him. He should have politely but firmly booted her out
before her brother saw her in here and canned him.

"You won't talk to me, and you won't see me anymore.

You say it's not my fault, but . . . how can I not think it's me?" Her hands pressed to her chest and he watched her lower lip tremble again, her eyes full of tears.

Ah, shit. "Don't cry, okay? Tears from a girl just fuck up my head something awful." He rubbed his face again, thinking.

This was worse than not seeing her. All that pain in her eyes? It wasn't worth the paycheck and the cabin. He'd find another job, another place to stay.

But there was only one Elise.

And as he realized that, he came to a decision. He'd promised this sweet, innocent girl that he'd help her experience life. Seemed a shame to bail out on her now. So he grabbed her hand and pulled it to his mouth, kissing the palm. "It's been a hell of a week, and I've been an ass. I'm sorry. You want to get away?"

Confusion flashed in her eyes, followed by growing excitement. "Sure."

"Great."

He was going to give her a weekend to remember.

ELEVEN

Rome grabbed Elise and gave her a quick kiss, then grinned. "Let me grab a couple shirts and I'll be ready to go."

"A-all right," she said, a smile curving her mouth. "Where are we going?"

"We," he told her with a smug look, "are going to have an incredible weekend of life experiences."

"We are?"

"We are," he agreed. He was going to give her the best damn weekend of her life, and cram as much into it as she possibly wanted to experience. It was going to be all about Elise this weekend. Whatever she wanted to do, whatever she desired, he'd make it happen. He'd give her this incredible weekend, just like he'd promised.

And then he'd be gone. It would hurt, but at least she'd have memories. He'd move on to another town, another shit-ass job, another shitty motel, and his hand for company when things got too lonely.

He pulled his backpack out of the corner it had been flung

in and stuffed toiletries and his changes of clothing in there. It was a good thing he always packed light; hopefully she wouldn't realize he was packing up most of his stuff. After a moment's hesitation, he packed a strip of condoms. This wasn't about sex; it was about living . . . But if his girl wanted sex, he'd give her the best damn sex she'd ever had.

"So where are we going?" she asked, and he could hear excitement in her voice.

"I'm thinking either a beach or a casino. Which one strikes your fancy?"

"Oh, I love the beach," she told him. "I'm not really a fan of gambling, though. I don't see the point."

She wouldn't, would she? She'd never had to worry about money. Never hoped that the last ten in her pocket would magically turn into a hundred. "That's fine," he told her, and slung his bag over his shoulder. "How'd you get here?"

A hint of a flush colored her cheeks, but the excited look remained on her face. "I parked my rental out on the highway and walked in so Grant wouldn't see it. Are we taking your bike?"

He thought for a minute, then shook his head. If his bike was here all weekend, they'd see it and assume he was hiding out in his cabin. Sulking, probably. That was fine. If they thought he was sulking, they'd leave him alone and not come after him for dragging Elise away. "Why don't we take your car? So we can talk on the way down."

Her face shone. "I'd like that. You want me to drive?"

"I can drive if you'd rather."

She handed him the keys and grinned. "Shall we sneak out?"

"This another life experience?"

She giggled. "Running off to spend a wild weekend with my boyfriend? Definitely something I've never done before."

"Then let's go," he told her, and took her hand in his.

They turned off the lights in his cabin and shut the door quietly. Then, hand in hand, they tiptoed past the other cabins and headed out to the highway, avoiding the gravel parking lot, where every step was a loud crunch that might give them away. Rome felt for a moment like he was a teenager again, sneaking out to be with a girl. He was too old for this shit. But, looking back at Elise's glowing face, he realized that she'd never had a chance to experience anything like this.

And it was worth it just for her.

When they got out to the car, he went around to the passenger side and opened her door for her, a gesture that brought another giddy smile to her face. This, he realized, had been the right call. It was an adventure, and Elise's boring life was short on adventures. So she was heading off to the beach for a weekend of fun on a Friday night with a man she wasn't supposed to be seeing. That was all part of the thrill, right?

He got into the car on the driver's side and tossed his backpack into the back seat, then slid behind the steering wheel. The car wasn't exactly a hot rod; it was a champagne-colored sedan. For a moment, he wished they were taking his bike, just to give her the thrill of driving up to the beach on the back of a motorcycle, but he supposed the vehicle didn't matter. It was enough that they were doing this.

"Should we go back to the bed-and-breakfast and grab my clothes?" she asked him as he started the car.

"Nope," he told her. He worried that if she went back to her room, someone would see her with him and try to talk her out of going. "We'll buy you some clothes when we get to the beach. Or you can just go naked." He looked over and winked at her, and was rewarded with a lovely flush on her cheeks.

Then he tore down the highway.

The beach wasn't more than a couple of hours from Bluebonnet. He took the roads that led down to Galveston, one of the more scenic beach towns in Texas. He had vague childhood memories of a historic shopping strip there, chess on the beach, and other things that might appeal to a girl like Elise.

She seemed to be having a great time, though. She rolled down the window and sang along with the classic rock station he'd set the radio to, and he was entranced by her. The shy girl he'd first met who had been terrified to speak in front of him was nearly gone, replaced by this gorgeous smiling creature who let the wind ripple in her hair and kept flashing him excited looks as if he were the best thing on earth.

Damn, he loved this girl.

As soon as the thought flew thorough his head, Rome squashed it. It didn't matter if he loved her or not, because she was too good for him. Once she found out the truth about who he was, she'd look at him like he was dirt and that'd be the end of it. Best to hold any sort of emotion inside and take it with him when he left.

The air changed as they got closer to the ocean, the scent of salt water filling the night breeze. The land had flattened out, too, though it wasn't as easy to see that in the dark.

"Should we find a hotel to make sure we can get a room?" she asked him, finger-combing her hair. "I'm starving."

"Hotel coming up," he told her. "And then dinner."

He passed a large, expensive hotel and hesitated. Should he take her someplace like that? It'd wipe out his account in no time, and he hated the thought of having to cut their weekend short simply because he ran out of cash. But still, it was her weekend. "You want big hotel or want to see if we can find something more cozy?"

"Oh, cozy," she said, smiling. "My family always stays in the big hotels, and something different would be fun."

Thank god for that. He drove through the Galveston Strand and stopped at what looked like a quaint bed-and-breakfast. It was winter, so hopefully they wouldn't be too busy thanks to the off-season.

Sure enough, he was able to procure a room for the weekend, and he grabbed Elise's hand and they headed up to their room.

It was a girly room, clearly designed with honeymooners in mind. The tub was enormous, a triangle-shaped jacuzzi in the corner of the room with mirrors on both sides of it. The room was decorated in a Victorian style, and the large bed in the center of the room was a four-poster covered with an ornate purple quilt.

"Cute," Rome said. Elise was silent, so he looked over at her and was surprised to see her expression, her face bright red. He squeezed her hand. "What's wrong?"

"It's just . . . one bed." She brushed her hand against her cheek, almost automatically.

"One bed," he agreed. "And one shower." He touched her cheek. "And one guy that is perfectly fine with waiting on sex if you're not ready. This weekend is about you."

He could practically see her cheeks getting redder. She gave him another shy look, and then reached up and brushed her mouth against his. "I brought condoms in my purse," she murmured, and then licked his lip ring.

Rome groaned. "If you're not ready, we don't have to—"

"I'm ready," she told him, and she gave him a shaky smile. "Just a bit shy about admitting it."

He kissed her back, letting his mouth show all the appreciation and desire he had for her bravery. Then he pulled away and brushed her hair off of her face, touching the curve of her cheek with his fingers. "First, dinner, I think. Ravishment later."

She laughed at that, the tension on her face easing. "Ravishment later," she agreed. "Dinner first. Which is good, because I'm starving." She glanced over at the clock on the bed. It was ten thirty at night. "Don't you think it's a bit late, though?"

"Not for a Friday night," he told her. "Come on."

They walked the Strand, looking for a place to dine. At

one point, they stopped outside of a nightclub; the place was hopping with music and thriving bodies. He looked over at Elise. "You want to go in?"

The look she gave him was blankly terrified, and she shook her head. "I don't like dancing."

He wrapped an arm around her shoulders and hugged her closer as they walked. "Then we don't go." That was fine with him. Elise already felt edgy and tense—he could tell from her body language—and he guessed she was thinking about heading to bed with him later that night. No sense in putting her more on edge.

They found a restaurant that was open late, and got a table. Elise immediately ordered a longneck, and he did the same, but leaned in to whisper to her. "Just one tonight. I don't want you drunk."

Her blushing nod made his cock hard in his pants, and for a moment, he wished that they were getting food to go. But she was clearly enjoying being out with him, so he resolved to enjoy it, too.

They ate and chatted, the conversation full of flirty notes. He rubbed his foot along her calf idly as they waited for food, and enjoyed seeing her squirm in her chair . . . and the fact that she rubbed his leg with her own foot.

It was the longest damn dinner of his life. He couldn't wait to get back to their room so he could peel her clothes off and take his time fucking her. Tonight was going to be amazing.

But after they paid for the meal, Elise didn't look tired at all—she looked keyed up. Her hand automatically slipped into his and she gave him a teasing look. "Want to do a midnight walk on the beach?"

He wanted to go back to their room and make her scream out his name. But a walk on the beach would be fun, too. "I'm game if you are."

"Great," she said, and tugged his hand, dragging him in the direction of the beach.

It was a few blocks away from where they were, but the weather was mild for winter, and the night breeze was a light one. The dull roar of the waves was a soothing sound in the distance, and eventually they hiked over the sand dunes toward the beach.

Elise continued to drag him forward, like an excited puppy. "Let's go walk in the waves."

Rome chuckled, surprised by her enthusiasm. "All right. I hope we don't run into any nighttime jellyfish, though."

She looked back at him, a grin on her face. "I'll kiss all your boo-boos for you."

Damn. Just like that, his dick was hard all over again. "What if I get the boo-boos in some rather unfortunate places?"

"They'll get extra kissing," she teased.

"I've never wanted to be wounded so much," he murmured.

Elise laughed, the sound joyous to hear, and her long, dark hair whipped around her head in the night wind. She headed to the edge of the water, Rome's hand firmly locked in hers, and then leaned on him to take her shoes off. She grabbed them in her hand and stepped into the water, then shivered. "It's cold!"

"Of course it's cold," he said, amused.

"You going to take your shoes off?"

He glanced down at his heavy combat boots. They were his only shoes, and he didn't want to get them fucked-up with water. "Guess so. Give me a sec." He released her hand and knelt to undo his laces. When his shoes were off, she grabbed his hand again, and she dragged him into the water.

It *was* cold. It was also getting his jeans soaked, but he didn't complain. The sheer joy in Elise's face was lovely to see. She was gorgeous in the moonlight, letting the water run over her toes and gazing out at the open ocean. "This is beautiful," she murmured, then looked over at him and smiled.

"You're beautiful," he said, and it was the truth. He couldn't look away from her. She was so gorgeous and alive that it made his chest ache with want. She was better than he deserved. For a brief moment, he resented that he'd have to give her up after this weekend, but he pushed the thought away. At least he'd have her for this long.

Her face softened and she gave him another shy smile, then glanced out at the water. "It really hurt me, you know. When you didn't call me all week."

"I'm an asshole," he told her. It was the truth. "I never wanted you to think it was your fault, though. It's all me." *Me, and your brother warning me away.* But he wouldn't ruin her relationship with her brother. He was just doing what he thought was best for his sister. Rome couldn't hate that.

"Of course I thought it was me," she said, giving him a wounded look that let him realize just how deeply she'd been hurt. "What was I supposed to think? You said you'd call me and then you just started ignoring me. And since I don't have a lot of experience . . ." Her words trailed off.

He knew what she meant, though. *Since I'm the one no one's wanted up until now, of course I thought it was me.* Rome's heart ached. He hated that he'd caused her one minute of pain. "It wasn't you," he repeated again. "I wish I could make you understand it. I just had some stuff I had to sort through, and I wasn't sure I could bring you into it."

She gave him a soft, sympathetic look and squeezed his hand. "Do you want to talk about it?"

Your brother figured out that I'm trash and warned me off. "I can't. At least, not yet."

"Is that why we're running away this weekend?" She looked over at him, her hair whipping about her face. "You needed to get away?"

"Partially," he admitted. It was the truth. He did need to get away from everything. Suddenly being in Bluebonnet was too stressful. Being around her, wanting her, and having to avoid her without telling her why he couldn't talk to her anymore? It seemed too painful to fucking deal with anymore.

So he wouldn't. If he was the thing that kept messing up this equation, he'd simply take himself out of it. No more Rome in Bluebonnet, no more problems.

"You still shouldn't have shut me out," she said softly, and her hand squeezed his again as she waded in the ankle-deep waves. "You can talk to me. I'm a good listener."

She was a great listener, actually. He just couldn't tell her what was bothering him without losing her. "I know."

Elise paused. She looked at him patiently, clearly waiting for something.

Oh shit. She wanted an answer right now? Rome thought for a moment, scrambling to find something that wouldn't ruin the weekend and would satisfy her. He stared down at the waves rushing over his feet, the cold denim of his pants legs making the evening seem chillier than it actually was. He cast about . . . and then decided to go with the truth.

"I worry that you think that I'm just using you," he told her.

Elise's face relaxed into a smile. "What? That's ridiculous."

"It's not," he told her, easing into the topic. This was safe territory for him. "It's clear that you're used to money. I've never had more than a couple of nickels to rub together. Combine that with the fact that you want to have sex, and how can you not think a guy like me is just out to get some and then leave?"

He choked on the words, because wasn't that what this weekend was about? Showing Elise a good time in all ways, and then bailing out on Monday? Ah, fuck. He was a real asshole. But better him being the ass than her family.

Her face bloomed into a gorgeous smile and she moved forward until her hands clasped around the back of his neck, and she pressed her breasts up against his chest. "Do you really think that? When I'm the one that came on to you?"

Rome gave her a faint smile. "Well, yeah. If I was any kind of gentleman, I'd have turned you down."

"Then I'm glad you're not," she said in a light voice. "Because I'm really glad you didn't turn me down. And I think you're a gentleman after all."

She wouldn't think that if she realized how hard he was at the moment. "Mm-hmm."

"It's true. You could have just pulled out a condom, thrown me on the bed, and had sex with me as soon as I brought it up."

And if she'd been slightly more worldly? That wouldn't have been a bad idea. But doing that to shy, skittish Elise without a care for her feelings and the woman underneath? The thought repulsed him.

"And you wouldn't have had to go out with me. Or let me take your photo. You could have just nailed me and gone." One finger traced his jaw, rasping along the stubble there. "But you didn't. You're different. And you've always seen me for me, and not a freak."

He leaned into her touch, hypnotized by it. "That's what I don't get, Elise. You say you're a freak, but I've seen your cheek. It's not that bad—"

"It's not, now," she agreed. "But it was for a long, long time. And there were . . . other things. I've never had much confidence." Her fingers brushed over his chin, and then crept across his lips. "But when I'm with you, I feel bold. And pretty. And wanted."

"That's because you are," he told her. "You're all of those things."

The smile on her face was beautiful, even though she gave a little headshake. "I'll show you what I mean, but later."

"When we make love?" he guessed.

She nodded, ducking her head shyly again.

"Exactly how much later?" he asked in a low voice. His free hand went to her hips and he dragged her against his body, letting her feel his erection. "Because it's getting hard for me to walk."

Elise gave him a sultry look, and her hand went to the front of his pants. She glanced around at the beach, but it was empty. Then she gave him another wicked look. "Can I give you a hand job here on the beach?"

He groaned, prying her hand off his cock, even though it killed him to do so. "I would love to say yes, but tonight, we're going to do things right. Me, you, a bed, and all the time in the world."

She looked up at him, her eyes dark in the moonlight. Her fingers curled on his chest. "When do we get to do that?"

"As soon as we get off this damn beach."

She glanced around, then peeked up at him. "Can we go now?"

"I thought you'd never ask."

They grabbed their shoes and headed back toward the hotel.

TWELVE

If Elise's hand was a little sweaty and her fingers trembling as they walked back to the hotel, Rome didn't comment on it. She was anxious. Of course she was. Hell, he was nervous, too, and he'd had sex before. He just wanted to make it amazing for her. More than amazing. He wanted to leave her with such incredible memories that she'd get over her awful shyness and the next man she dated could benefit from her blossoming.

Then he thought about another man touching her and wanted to put his fist through a wall. Elise was fucking *his*. It wasn't fair. He didn't want her to look at anyone else but him the way she was right now.

They got back up to their room. Elise pulled her hand from his and wiggled her toes on the carpet. "My feet are a mess. They're all sandy."

She seemed nervous, too. He hated that. He didn't want her to be nervous around him, but he knew it was just the fact that they were going to have sex. At least, he hoped it was just that, and she wasn't scared of him for some reason. "You want to go clean off in the bathroom?"

"That'd be great," she agreed quickly, and disappeared inside. He figured it'd give her a chance to compose herself for a few moments and relax.

Which meant he could clean off his own sandy feet. He dropped his boots next to the front door, and grabbed a towel from the closet, then headed over to the hot tub–slash-bathtub in the corner of the room. He stripped off his wet jeans and adjusted his cock in his boxers, already throbbing and aching with need. Just the knowledge that he was about to have sex with Elise meant he'd been walking around with a hard-on all night. She fired him up in every way.

With a wet towel, he cleaned off his feet, stripped off his shirt, and got under the covers to wait for her. He could hear the shower going, and pictures of Elise, naked and wet and rubbing herself with soap, flew through his mind. Rome groaned at the thought and reached under the blanket to stroke his cock. He was already rock-hard and throbbing, and he could feel pre-cum beading the head of his cock. He'd have to pace himself tonight, or he wouldn't be showing her anything but a three-minute man. And that, he didn't want to do. He needed this to be special for her. Memorable.

Earth-shattering.

So he adjusted himself and tried to think of other things that would make his erection go away. Like prison. Yep, that always did it. Thoughts of the cells, and the beige uniforms, the endless days of lockup and monotony? The constant edge of worry that you were going to be jumped by someone with a grudge at chow line? He didn't ever want to go back. Never again.

When his desire was under control, Rome glanced back at the bathroom door. It was silent in there, the water off, but Elise hadn't emerged. He wondered if she was okay. Having second thoughts? Should he go in there and check on her? He started to get out of bed and then glanced down at his near naked body. Damn it. Should he get dressed first? Put on clothes so as not to make her think he was demanding sex?

He didn't want her to feel obligated to do anything. If she was having second thoughts, he understood that. Hell, maybe it'd be better if she did, considering he was abandoning her on Monday. Just thinking about that made his gut clench. Rome got out of bed and dragged out his bag, looking for a new pair of pants to put on. He'd dress, and then sit down and talk with Elise and ease her worries. He'd even get a second hotel room if it would make her more comfortable.

The bathroom door opened. He stopped, and got to his feet, dressed only in his boxers, and waited for her.

Elise came out of the bathroom dressed in nothing but a tiny white towel. Her hair was dry and pulled up into a loose bun atop her head. The towel was tucked under her arms, straining over her breasts, the fold of the fabric revealing a slender, pale leg. She was naked under the towel.

She also seemed really, really nervous.

Her gaze flicked to him, taking in his near nudity, and then moved back to his face. Then she dropped her gaze to the floor. "I wanted to show you," she murmured, her voice barely audible. "Why . . . why I'm shy."

His throat grew dry. He knew Elise, and he knew the courage this had to take for her to do. The light was on, and she was standing here before him in a towel, ready to bare to him whatever secrets she thought she had.

And in that moment, he was so damn proud of her for being so brave.

She turned her back to him, and she eased open the towel a bit. The fabric swept low, curving at her lower back, and he could see a faint scar, no wider than a pencil. It started at the base of her neck and ended at the dip of her lower back. On her hip, there was another scar, no more than six inches long.

He didn't understand what it meant. She had scars.

That . . . wasn't terrible. He'd seen the line going down her back before and hadn't asked. There had to be more to the story, so he waited.

He watched her shoulders raise as she took in a long breath, and then spoke. "When I was born, I had the birthmark on my cheek. I was very self-conscious about it, but my parents thought it made me special and unique, and they didn't like the idea of me getting rid of it. I guess they didn't realize how much it bothered me, because I've always been a little . . . withdrawn." She shrugged her shoulders. "Then when I was twelve, I developed scoliosis. It's a curvature of the spine, and instead of my back being a normal line, mine was an S shape. My rib cage was twisting around. I had to wear a back brace all day, every day, to try and correct it."

Her head drooped and she looked so forlorn that his heart ached.

"Overnight, I went from 'that weird kid with the cheek' to 'that weird kid with the brace *and* the cheek.' Kids made fun of me. A lot. I started hiding out from school, and nearly failed out. My parents got me a private tutor, and I finished my schooling at home. And eventually my back got so bad that I had surgery." She gestured at the slim column of her spine, marked with the scars. "They were able to fix most of it, but not all. I have the scars, of course. And my shoulders don't match up." She tapped her right shoulder. "This shoulder is lower than the other. My hips don't align, either. They're slightly . . . off, thanks to the surgery. They fixed everything they could, but it's not perfect. It'll never be perfect." She choked on the word.

His poor, sweet Elise. Rome moved forward to touch her, and at the brush of his fingers against her shoulder, she shuddered. "You look perfect to me," he told her. He didn't care that her hips weren't straight, or that she had a scar. Hell, he was covered in tattoos and piercings, all so he could look rough enough to fit in and not get his ass kicked in prison.

"That's just it, though. My back was fixed, and as soon as

I could convince my parents, I had my cheek taken care of. But every time I look in the mirror . . ." She swallowed hard.

He could guess. "You still see the girl with the back brace and the stain on your cheek?"

She nodded. "I just . . . it still bothers me, even though I know it shouldn't. And I guess that's why I'm shy. Because I don't think people see me, they see . . . you know." She swallowed. "The freak."

Rome's fingers touched the top of her scar at the base of her neck, and then trailed down, brushing the curve of her back. "Nope, I get it. You get told you're something often enough, and you start to believe it. It doesn't matter how much you change on the outside, you can't quite let go of what used to be. I get that. I really do."

She said nothing, but the breath she let go was shaky.

He touched her hip, the scar there. "I get the other one, but what's this for?"

"When they put the metal rods in your back, they take bone from your hip and graft it. You get two scars for the price of one." She looked at him over her shoulder and her mouth quirked in a half smile. "Lucky, right?"

"Maybe. Maybe not," he said. "If you ever wanted to get a tattoo over this, you just let me know. I'd hold your hand the entire time." He skimmed his fingers up her back again. "Not that you aren't pretty how you are."

She shivered under his touch, and the towel shifted a bit. "You don't think it's . . . weird? My shoulders aren't even. My clothes don't hang right."

"Baby," he said softly, leaning in to press a kiss at the base of her exposed neck. "The only thing I notice about your clothes is how fast I want to get you out of them."

Her breath shuddered again. "God, Rome. You're incredible for a girl's self-esteem, you know that?"

"I don't care about girls," he told her, brushing aside another tendril of hair so he could kiss her neck from behind once more. "I care about you. Only you, Elise."

She shuddered as he licked at the curve of her neck, and her hands trembled on the towel.

His hand moved to the front of it, pulling at her fingers where she held it closed, clutched to her. And she released it slowly.

The towel dropped to the ground at her feet, and Elise stood before him, naked.

She was beautiful. No matter how much she questioned it, there was never any doubt in his mind that seeing Elise gloriously naked would be memorable. He'd seen flashes of skin here and there, and he'd been intimately acquainted with the flesh between her thighs, but seeing the entire picture was different. Her eyes were wide, and her breathing rapid, her body clearly panicking despite his comforting words.

"Can I look at you?" he asked, brushing his knuckles over her cheek. "Or would you rather I turn the lights off?"

She took in a deep breath. "No, it's okay. You . . . can look."

He would. It was more important that she relax first. He brushed his fingers up and down her arms, trying to comfort her. She shivered at his touch, and her neck tilted, as if she were trying to get a better look at him. He leaned in and kissed her jaw. "Can I look while we lie down?"

She blinked, then nodded.

He took her hand and led her to the bed. He ignored her trembling. It'd go away soon enough, once she started feeling half as aroused as he was. Hell, he was so hard he was surprised his boxers hadn't flown apart.

Elise sat down on the edge of the bed, her body tense. Rome sat next to her and touched her jaw, moving her face toward his. Then he kissed her, ever so gently. Her mouth was tight under his, and he licked and coaxed at her mouth, trying to convince her to open up. Maybe he should have let her have a few more beers after all—Elise was locked down and tense as could be.

But after a few kisses, her mouth softened, her lips

parting under his ministrations, and he began to kiss her more deeply, licking at her mouth. His tongue slid slowly in and out of her lips, the motion a deliberate mimic of what he was going to do to her later, and she made a soft noise of pleasure in her throat. Her hand lifted, hesitated, and then landed on his shoulder.

Progress. Rome tried not to feel triumphant as she relaxed against him. His hands continued to touch and stroke her jaw and shoulders, his touch safe and soothing. He wanted her hair down, though, so he pulled it free of its bun and it slid around her shoulders like a silky, dark curtain that made him groan. "I love your hair," he murmured against her mouth.

She gave a soft sigh against his lips, her mouth opening just a bit wider in invitation of his kiss.

That's right, he thought encouragingly. *Open up for me.*

He made his kisses hungrier, more aggressive, until his tongue was openly fucking her mouth. Soft whimpers rose in her throat, whimpers of need, and she continued to kiss him passionately, responding to his touch. Elise wanted him; she was just nervous and not wanting to make a fool of herself. He suspected that part of her still waited for him to be disgusted with the way she looked, and somehow turn her away.

It was time to soothe that ridiculous fear of hers.

Between kisses, Rome buried his hands in her hair and began to speak slowly. "Been thinking about this for days now," he told her. "My tongue inside that pretty mouth of yours, licking that gorgeous skin, on your breasts, your belly, everywhere."

She moaned at his words, the look in her eyes soft.

"I remember your taste from the other day, in the studio," he told her, and stopped kissing her for a moment so he could see her reaction to his words. "Sometimes I close my eyes and think I can still taste you in my mouth, your thighs against my face. Fucking sweetest thing I've ever tasted."

Her eyelashes fluttered at his words, and she gasped. "Rome," she whispered.

"Yeah, baby?"

"Kiss me."

His finger trailed down her neck, brushed over her collarbone. Her skin was so pale, but she was beautiful. Everywhere, she was beautiful. He wanted to stare at those gorgeous, tight little breasts, but there'd be time enough for that. "Where do you want me to kiss you, baby?"

She gave a small mew in her throat. "Anywhere. Everywhere."

"Mmm." He kissed her face with small, pressing, tiny kisses. "Can I kiss your neck?"

She made a soft noise of assent.

He coaxed her head back, exposing the slim column of her neck. "This looks delicious," he told her, and pressed a kiss there.

She squirmed and laughed, surprising him.

He pulled back, a smile on his face. "What?"

"It just . . . made me think of vampires."

Rome chuckled. "Well, I wasn't thinking about the blood as much as I was thinking about all this lovely, smooth skin." His thumb rubbed her pulse point. "And how I wanted to lick every inch of it. But . . . I guess I could pretend to be a sparkly vampire if that's your thing—"

She giggled and punched him lightly in the arm. "Stop it. That's not my 'thing.'"

"What *is* your thing, Elise Markham?" he teased.

"I think . . . I like guys with tattoos," she said softly, her hands moving over his shoulders and then gliding over his pectorals. "And piercings. Nose piercings, lip piercings, you name it."

He groaned, his cock throbbing in his boxers. "God damn, I would love nothing more than to toss you down on this bed right now and fuck the hell out of you."

Her breathing became rapid with excitement, and her fingernails scratched at his chest. "Why don't you?"

"Because," he growled, dragging his arms around her waist and pulling her naked body into his lap. "I'm going to make this amazing for you."

"It's already amazing," she told him, her legs shifting on his lap in a way that made him ache all over again. "Just being here with you."

His chest ached at her sweet words. "Hey, I thought I was the one supposed to be doing the romancing here."

Elise gave him another sweet smile and leaned in to kiss him. She wasn't acting terrified any longer; that was a relief.

He kissed her back, his tongue playfully coaxing hers. His hand stroked up and down her arm, and her breast brushed against his fingertips more than once. He itched to touch her breasts, but he wasn't sure how skittish it would make her. He decided he'd talk her through it, instead.

"You have the sexiest little breasts, baby. Been dreaming about putting my mouth on those sweet nipples and tonguing them until you cry out."

She sucked in a breath, then draped her arms around his neck. "Touch me?"

"Love to," he murmured, and his hand slid up her stomach to cup one breast. "Mm, gorgeous."

She stiffened in his arms, her lips parting, but her gaze remained fixed on him.

He circled her breast with his fingers, hefting the weight in his grasp. "Small but full. My favorite kind of breast. And I love these beautiful pink nipples." His thumb brushed over one stiff peak, and he was rewarded with her soft intake of breath and subsequent moan. "You like it when I touch your breasts, Elise?"

She said nothing, only bit her lip, but her back arched and she pressed her breast further into his hand.

"I think that's a yes," he murmured, and his thumb

grazed over her nipple, over and over again. "They're nice and stiff, these little nipples. I think they're just aching to be sucked on, aren't they?"

She moaned aloud that time, her back arching again.

"Mm, that sounds like a definite yes to me." He dragged her backward on the bed, noticing with satisfaction the bounce of her breasts as she fell onto her back. His hand immediately went to cup one breast and he leaned over her, his mouth hovering above the other breast as he drew out her anticipation. "You ever had someone suck on your pretty nipples before, Elise?"

"N-no," she breathed. "Just you."

"Then I'm the luckiest man alive," he told her, and grazed his lips over the straining tip of one breast, his fingers carefully teasing and coaxing the tip of the other breast. He deliberately let his lip ring glide over her nipple, knowing she'd find that erotic, and was rewarded with another moan and a small flex of her hips in response.

He teased the tip with his tongue, circling and testing to see what she responded to. When he nipped at it with his lips, she gasped. When he flicked the underside of her nipple with his tongue, she moaned. When he teased it with his teeth, she nearly came off the bed.

"You like that?" he murmured, gazing up at her. His mouth continued to tease and play with her nipple as he waited for her response. His cock ached in his boxers; the head throbbed and he felt hard as iron at her timid responses.

She nodded again, but he wasn't satisfied with that. He wanted to hear the words coming from her own lips. "Tell me what you want me to do, Elise, and I'll do it."

Her mouth worked silently for a moment. He lifted his head, not touching her any longer, and she finally responded. "Put your mouth on me," she breathed, and pushed his head back toward her breasts.

"That's my girl," he murmured, and rewarded her with a delicious nip that made her shudder. His tongue flicked her sensitive nipples over and over again, and she moaned and wriggled under him with each touch. It was like she was starting to forget where she was, and the more she forgot, the more vocal she became. He loved that. He wanted her to lose utter control. He wanted to see her go wild underneath him.

His lips coaxed one nipple and then he took it into his mouth and sucked, hard. She moaned again, her hips flexing, and he released it with a pop, then moved over to her other, giving it the same attention. She had such pretty breasts, and thanks to his mouth, both peaks were upright, pointing and hard and cherry red. It was a gorgeous sight. "Look at how beautiful you are," he murmured, teasing her nipples with his fingers again. "Look at how flushed your nipples are. I bet your pussy's flushed, too."

She moaned at his words, her eyes closing. But her hips flexed again, indicating that she liked his words very much.

"Is it, Elise?" he asked, his voice low and soft. "If I touch you, am I going to find you wet for me? All juicy and pink and ready to be tasted?"

Elise whimpered at his words. "Please, Rome."

"Please what, baby?" He brushed a hand down her soft thigh, then rested it on her knee. It was her call as to what she wanted him to do. He'd do whatever she liked, as long as she gave the signal it was what she wanted.

"Please touch me," she begged, and her knee fell to the side, exposing her to him.

His beautiful, sweet Elise. Rome groaned, his cock nearly spurting. He reached down to his boxers and squeezed his dick to try and get his own raging desire under control. He wanted to make her scream with pleasure before he even thought of crawling between her legs.

"Touch you here?" He brushed his fingers over the curls of her pussy. She was wet, her curls dark with her juices. He wanted to bury his face there, but that might be too much, too soon. He'd let her drive for a bit instead.

"Yes," she said, her voice so soft it was practically

inaudible. But she followed it with a nod, and when his hand pressed on her thigh again, she let her legs fall open even wider.

Rome groaned. She made a beautiful picture, all soft and willing underneath him, her face flushed with excitement and a hint of shyness. He'd never seen anything as lovely as Elise Markham in that moment. He ran two fingers along the inside of her thigh, watching her tremble, and then he slid them down to her pussy. Using the same two fingers, he pressed into her folds, testing to see how wet she was.

Not quite as wet as he'd like, but getting there. He knew she was nervous; he'd make it even better for her, then. He wouldn't take her until she was dripping for him.

Using his fingers, he coaxed the moisture from her center and slicked it back and forth on her sex, wetting it. She moaned and pushed her hips against his hand, but he kept his rhythm slow, languid, and on pace. He wanted to drive her crazy, and keeping the pace too slow for her would soon have her wild with need. And as he moved his fingers back and forth, sliding over her pussy, he talked to her.

"I wanted you the very first time I saw you, Elise. When I walked into the lodge at the Daughtry Ranch and I saw you there, all sleep-tousled and gorgeous, my cock was hard for you. You remember what I called you?" He dragged his fingers around her clit, teasing it out of its hood and making it protrude for him. He couldn't resist giving it a quick lick, and was rewarded when a shuddering gasp escaped her.

"Bo Peep," she breathed. "You said I looked lost."

"You still feel lost, baby?"

"Not with you," she said, and he felt his chest ache again.

"That's a good answer," he told her in a husky voice. "Deserves a reward, don't you think?" And he put his mouth on her clit and sucked.

Her legs twitched and she gave a small cry of surprise. Then she moaned again, her legs falling open wider.

"Rome," she breathed, and he ground his cock into the bed at the sound of his name on her lips.

"I'm here, baby," he told her. "I've got you." And his mouth returned to her clit, sucking on the little nub and flicking his tongue over it.

Her hips worked again, the small, soft cries of pleasure erupting from her throat beautiful to hear. He slid a finger down to her core again, and she was slick, her juices coating his fingers.

"Now we're getting somewhere," he told her, and gave her clit a quick, teasing lick as he slid a finger inside her.

She whimpered, and he nearly did, too; she was incredibly fucking tight. If he was going to make this good for her, he needed to loosen her up. He went to work on her clit again, lapping and sucking at the small nub of flesh, and gently stroking his finger in and out of her core.

Her hands pressed on his head, and she was panting with excitement. "Rome, please," she begged. "I need—"

"I know you do," he murmured, and gave her clit another flick. "But I'm not letting up until you're ready for me." He pressed his lips to it again and sucked hard, enjoying her moan of response. Then he carefully added a second finger to the first.

She stiffened, as if not entirely sure she liked the change, and he dragged his fingers out of her viselike pussy, spreading her juices around. His mouth continued to work on her clit as he slowly eased both fingers in again. She relaxed, and her hands scratched at the short stubble on his head. "God, your tongue."

"You like that?" he murmured, renewing his efforts and flicking even faster against her clit.

"It makes me feel like I'm coming out of my skin," she told him.

"As long as you're coming," he teased, and pumped the two fingers in her faster, rougher. When she didn't flinch back from his touch, he spread his fingers inside her, scissoring them gently to widen her for his cock.

"Oh," she moaned suddenly. "I think I'm going to—"

He paused in his ministrations. "Not yet, baby."

She growled at him—actually growled—and tried to push his face back between her legs. "Rome, please," her voice was almost a sob. "I'm so close."

"I want you to wait for me," he told her. Maybe it was arrogance, but he wanted his girl to come around his cock tonight, to feel her squeezing him and sucking him even deeper into her as she shattered. He wanted to own that orgasm of hers.

Elise shuddered and pushed her hips at him again, but he withdrew his fingers from her and waited for her to calm down. She gave another frustrated whimper and panted, waiting.

He let a few moments pass before he leaned forward and kissed her pussy, right over her clit, and let his tongue flick over it. "You okay?"

She jerked in response, but her fingers scratched at his scalp. "Other than I want to choke you right about now? I'm great."

She sounded so annoyed; it was adorable. "Where's your orgasm at?"

"Long gone."

"Good."

"Not good. I—" She squeaked in surprise as his fingers pushed into her again, and his mouth returned to her pussy. "Oh . . ."

He chuckled at the sound of wonder in her voice. "You finding it again?"

"It's hanging on for dear life," she said in a dreamy voice, and her hips worked against his fingers. "Oh Rome, your hands. I can't . . ."

He pulled his fingers out again, and she whimpered. One hand went to her breast, toying with her nipple and dragging the peak up and down between his fingers. She moaned again, her hands pressing on his head with urgency, but he ignored her silent pleas for more. This was all about driving his girl crazy so when she came, she'd see stars.

She squirmed in his grip and he decided he needed a new tactic. Shifting his weight, he pushed her legs up until her thighs were on his shoulders. Elise moaned again, and her anticipation was so sharp he could practically feel it in the air. He couldn't stop the possessive smile curving his mouth, though. Poor Elise thought she was going to get relief; she had no idea he was just preparing her for the next phase.

Rome kissed the top of her mound again. "You taste sweet, Elise. I love your honey on my tongue."

"Mmm." She tossed her head on the blankets, her dark hair flying about. "Rome, please."

"In fact, I think I might need to stick my tongue into that little honeypot of yours and taste from the source."

He put his tongue over her core and circled her entrance. He felt her quiver against his tongue, heard the choked moan she gave. She was especially wet here, her core slick with her juices. Pointing his tongue, he stroked it into her depths, mimicking his fingers.

"Oh god!" Her fingernails dug into his skin, and her hips pumped, forcing his tongue even deeper. "Oh my god. That's so good."

The taste of her filled his senses, and he groaned with pleasure at being saturated in her juices. He thrust with his tongue again, then licked and teased at her opening, deliberately tormenting her.

She cried out, the sound wordless and full of need. "Please," she panted. "Please. Please."

His own cock ached so badly that every "please" she uttered made his pulse throb. He couldn't hold out for much longer. With another flick of his tongue, he sat up, and then carefully pushed three fingers into her, watching her reaction.

Elise moaned, her eyes closed with bliss.

His girl was as ready as she'd ever be. Rome grabbed a condom off of the bedside table and ripped it open, then rolled it down the length of his aching cock. "Just a moment, baby, and I'll make it good for you."

"Please," she begged again, her hips undulating on the bed. "Rome, I need you so bad. I ache inside."

He groaned. Her begging was doing crazy things to him. "I know, baby. I'm coming." He leaned forward and adjusted his weight over her body, then kissed her mouth, lightly sucking on her tongue.

She latched onto his mouth, kissing him with a ferocity that stunned him even as her legs went around his hips, pinning him against her. "Rome," she panted, her voice sweet with need, her hands cupping his face and keeping his lips to hers. "Rome, please. Now."

"Yes," he murmured against her mouth, his tongue flicking against hers. "I've got you."

He dragged his cock up and down the slick folds of her pussy, wetting it with her juices. Her moan of pleasure nearly made him forget all control and bury himself deep, but he held back. She was a virgin; the last thing he needed to do was rip into her. He could stand to be patient for a few moments longer.

With a deep, steadying breath, he fitted the head of his cock at her entrance. "Ready, baby?"

"Yes," she moaned. "Yes, yes, yes."

He began to push inside her. Inch by slow inch, he penetrated. She was tighter than a fist, her pussy clenching him so tight that it felt like a vise.

"No," she panted suddenly. "No, no, ow, that hurts."

"It's going to hurt the first time," he warned her, teeth gritted. Hell, he'd barely pushed into her and she was already protesting? This was torture for both of them. "It'll get better soon."

She made a wordless noise that he couldn't tell was a protest or assent.

Rome waited a moment, then pushed in a bit more. She sucked in a breath and winced.

He could feel her tensing around him, and that would only make things more difficult. Even now, she felt tighter and more constricted than before, and the pained look on her face wasn't helping. "That bad?" he asked.

"Maybe it's like one of those Band-Aid things," she told him, her breathing shallow. "You know, just rip it off and get it over with—"

She was right. They'd never get anywhere like this. He didn't need any more encouragement. Rome thrust forward, plunging to the hilt.

Elise gave a little shriek, and he pressed his mouth over hers in a kiss, silencing her. His lips worked hers, and despite the whimpers coming from her throat, she kissed him back, her legs trembling around his waist.

And oh god, his girl was tight around him. He was seated deep inside her, buried within her depths, and it was the best sensation in the world. Even now, he could feel his balls drawing up tight, ready to unload.

But he kissed her slowly, over and over again, licking at her soft, delicious mouth. She was tight under him for a moment, her lips rigid, but she eventually relaxed and began to respond to his kisses. He could feel her relaxing all the way through her body, too, the tension deep in her muscles not as taut as before.

Rome continued to press light kisses to her lips. "Better?"

"That," she breathed against his mouth, "did not feel like a Band-Aid."

He chuckled at that. She tweaked his ear for laughing, but then she smiled and kissed him again.

"Does this mean I can move now?" he asked, kissing along her jawline.

She gave a small sigh. "As long as you keep kissing me, you can do whatever you want."

"Mmm." He kissed her again, and his hand moved to her breast, teasing the nipple. She moaned in response, and he shifted his hips a little, testing. When she didn't flinch, he rocked slightly, drawing back and pushing into her again. "How's that?"

"Not bad," she said thoughtfully, and appeared to be considering it so studiously that it made him chuckle all over again.

"How about this, then?" He slid his hand between them and found her clit, rolling it between his fingers.

She moaned, her hips rising up on the bed, and he pushed into her again. When she only squirmed beneath him, he pulled back and thrust again.

"Oh god," she breathed.

He froze, worried he'd hurt her again. "What?"

"So full." Her eyes were wide, but blissed-out.

This time, he was the one who groaned. With another deep, sucking kiss, he pulled back and pumped into his girl.

She moaned, her hips raising up to meet his thrust.

"You like that?" he asked between thrusts. "Tell me if I'm hurting you."

"Not hurting," she murmured, voice tight. Her hands went to his neck, and then his shoulders, digging in, as if trying to find the right place to hold on to him. "Keep going."

"Yeah?" he breathed against her mouth. God, she was sexy. Her head was thrown back, her eyes closed, and her pretty tits jiggled with every thrust into her tight pussy. She was the most beautiful, sexiest thing he'd ever seen, and she was all his. "More?"

"More," she moaned in response. "Please,"

"No more Band-Aid?" he asked, pulling back and then slamming deep into her, loving the feeling when she took him. She was so tight, so fucking slick and tight that he'd never felt anything better.

"No," she said, and then gasped when he pushed into her again. "Opposite of Band-Aid. Promise. Keep. Going."

"And where's your orgasm?" he asked, pushing his thumb against her clit again.

She moaned, and her voice rose in volume as he sank deep again, finding a rhythm as he fucked her. "Closer," she mumbled, and when he thumbed her clit again, she sucked in a breath, her legs tensing around him. "Close! Close! It's . . . oh mercy, really close."

"Yeah?" He took his hand off her clit.

"Nooo," she whimpered, raising her hips. "Rome, please!"

He thrust harder, and was rewarded by her gasp of surprise. Her nails dug in and she clung to him.

"Good?" he asked, not stopping his steady rhythm of pumping into her.

"Yes," she cried, and he was surprised at how vocal his normally shy Elise was. Damn if it wasn't an intense turn-on, though. He fucked her faster, hammering into her sweet warmth, so hard that his skin slapped against hers. He waited for her to tell him that it was too much, but she only clung to him and began to moan. "Oh. Oh god! I can feel it. It's coming. Don't stop, Rome. Please. Don't stop."

He groaned. Her needy begging was making him crazy. It would take nothing for him to go over the crest, to come and come and come. But she wasn't there yet, and he wanted her there first. He palmed her breast as he fucked her, then reached between them again, searching for her clit.

When he touched it, she squealed, and he felt her pussy ripple around him in response. Ah, fuck, that felt amazing. Her hips bucked, as if she were trying to get away from his fingers, but he continued to play with the little button of her clit, and was rewarded with the clench of her pussy around him and another spasm clasping him deep. She was coming, his girl, and she was coming hard.

"That's right, baby," he groaned, pressing deep with every inch of his cock. "Come for me."

He felt her quiver all over again and she clutched at him. "Don't stop. Please. I'm so close."

It was fucking killing him, but he kept his pace just the way she wanted it, steady and fierce, pounding into her over and over again, his thumb bouncing on her clit with every motion of their bodies. He felt her pussy tugging on his cock, and her mouth opened, as if she wanted to say something, but nothing came out. Her head tilted back, and she sucked in a breath, her eyelashes fluttering, and he was fascinated by her face as she reached her peak.

Then, he felt it. An all-over body tremble, her legs locking around him, and a sudden burst of wetness from her pussy as she came. She cried out, the sound high-pitched and keening, her face frozen in pleasure as she clamped and clenched around his cock, over and over, milking him with her orgasm.

He growled low in his throat, hammering into her even harder, determined to make her orgasm last as long as possible. He wanted to shatter her and watch her rebuild, right before his eyes. He wanted her to fall to pieces. "That's right," he murmured. "Come for me, sweetheart." Her pussy was soaked with her juices, and every thrust was now met with a fierce little quake of her body.

When her legs relaxed against him, though, she gave a little moaning half sigh, indicating her orgasm was over. "Holy god."

Rome leaned in and kissed her one more time, a fierce claiming as he pushed deeper into her and began to thrust wildly, finally losing his own control. Now that he'd seen his girl come so sweetly, he could get his own. He hammered into her, his strokes rough and deep, and was rewarded by quivering aftershocks from her pussy. His balls slapped against her flesh, and then his own orgasm exploded deep, and he came so hard he nearly blacked out.

He collapsed on top of her, caging her under his sweaty arms. She clung to him, pressing kisses to his skin in a slow, languid caress.

"I love you," she murmured against his neck, softly.

And his own heart squeezed in response. He wanted to tell her the same thing back, but that would be just too cruel.

Because he knew he loved this girl. With all his heart. But leaving her was going to break his. Better to only have one broken heart instead of two, he told himself.

So he simply covered her mouth with his and gave her a kiss, distracting her from any confession he might have made.

He hoped.

THIRTEEN

Sleeping next to Rome, Elise decided, was quite possibly one of the best things in the world. Her hand lay on his flat, muscled stomach, and his skin was warm against hers. Her head was tucked against his shoulder, and she woke up with the scent of him in her nostrils and the feel of his arms around her. She was sore between her legs, and her hair was a snarl at the back of her head.

And she was happy. Blissfully, giddily happy.

She snuggled deeper against his chest, not quite ready to face the morning. Sunlight filtered in through a window, and she could barely see the alarm clock over his shoulder. It was past nine in the morning, but Rome was still asleep. Not an early riser, apparently. That was fine with her. She'd steal a few more minutes curled up in his arms, just enjoying the peace of being with him.

Somewhere on the far side of the room, her cell phone rang with the ring tone she'd assigned to her brother.

Shit. Grant. Was he checking up on her?

Elise flung herself out of bed, heading for her purse. She

heard Rome rouse behind her. "It's my brother calling," she told him as she grabbed her bag and fished her phone out. "Oh no. What does he want?"

"Don't tell him I'm here," Rome said quietly.

She wouldn't. The last thing on her mind was telling her brother that she just got laid. An embarrassed flush touched her cheeks as she realized she'd sprung out of bed totally naked. She couldn't let that worry her now—if Rome had a problem seeing her naked body, she supposed he would have said so last night. So if it didn't bother him, she was determined not to let it bother her.

Elise grabbed the phone and pressed the button to answer. "Hello?"

"Hey, sis, did I wake you?"

She rubbed her forehead, trying to think of an answer. "Um, yeah." She glanced over at the bed. Rome was sprawled in the sheets, all tattoos and tan, and her mouth went dry as she gazed at him.

"Sorry about that. Was just going to ask if you wanted to take some photos here at the ranch today? No business stuff. Thought it might be cute to have pics of me and Brenna for engagement announcements or something."

Today? Pictures? Seriously? She wanted nothing more than to crawl back into bed with Rome and lick his tattoos. Her mouth watered at the thought. "Uh . . . can it wait a few days?"

"Yeah, no problem. You okay?"

She blinked for a minute, thinking of an excuse. "Um. Just a migraine."

"You do sound kind of out of it," he said, sympathy in his voice. "You want me to bring some soup or something?"

"No, no," Elise said quickly, eyes widening at the thought. "Emily will take good care of me," she told him. "I'm just going to stay in bed and pull the covers over my head." She looked at Rome and crossed her fingers, hoping that her brother would take the bait on the lie.

"Okay," he told her. "Take it easy. You gotta take care of yourself."

Her annoyance softened at her brother's concern. "I know. Thanks, Grant. I'll call you if I need anything, okay?" She felt guilty at deceiving him—her brother thought she was ill and she was really just running off and having an irresponsible weekend with her lover.

Her lover. Elise glanced over at Rome again and felt a surge of excitement thrumming in her veins. God, he looked delicious right now.

This irresponsible weekend with her lover was pretty much a dream come true. She wanted to crawl back into bed with Rome. Heck, what was stopping her? "I'll talk to you later, Grant," she mumbled, doing her best to sound sick, and then hung up, tossing the phone back in her purse.

Rome sat up, a frown on his face. "Everything okay?"

"Yeah. He was just checking up on me." She crossed her arms over her naked breasts and shrugged her shoulders, trying to seem casual about the fact that she was totally naked. "Being a big brother and all."

"He hasn't guessed that we're here together, has he?" Rome's brow furrowed with concern.

Elise shook her head. "Nope. We're all clear."

A grin crossed his handsome face. "Good. You coming back to bed?" He patted the edge of the bed. "I'm keeping the blankets warm for you."

She bit her lip but was unable to contain the smile spreading across her face. She grabbed a corner of the blankets and slipped back under them again, tucking them around her body. It felt strange to be crawling back into bed with him. She wanted to put her head back on his chest but she felt suddenly a little shy about things. Would it bother him if she did?

He leaned in and kissed her gently. "How are you feeling this morning?"

Elise smiled. "Great."

"No regrets?"

"Not a single one."

His lips brushed over her cheek, sending shivers down her spine. "So, this is your day today. How do you want to spend it?"

"My day?"

"Yup. Today, everything we do is all about you."

She thought for a moment. Really, all she wanted to do was have him lie back in the bed so they could have sex again. But she couldn't resist teasing him, just a little. "Well, I hear there's a great yarn shop in the Strand."

He paused, and then nodded seriously. "Okay."

"And there's a quilting store a few blocks over that I'd love to spend a few hours in."

Bless the man, he was able to keep a straight face. "Whatever you want."

A giggle escaped her and she impulsively threw her arms around his neck, bearing him down onto the bed. "Or we could spend the rest of the day here in bed."

A look of relief crossed his face. "So the quilting and the yarn was a joke?"

She nodded, then leaned in and kissed his mouth, almost shyly.

"Thank god," he groaned, and then put his hands in her hair, dragging her face to his when she tried to pull away. His kiss was hard and fierce, and oh so possessive. "Not that I wouldn't look at yarn for you, but after seeing you prancing all over the room naked, the only thing I had in mind was more sex."

"I guess the yarn can wait," she teased, running her tongue along the stubble on his jaw. Really, stubble should not be that delicious on a man.

"I have unleashed an evil minx," he mock-growled, rolling over in the bed and pinning her naked body under him. "An evil minx with a cruel sense of humor."

She laughed wickedly, and her laughs were smothered

by his kisses. And then suddenly, she wasn't laughing anymore, because she loved being kissed by him. He made her feel so beautiful, so wanted.

When he reached for more condoms on the bedside table, she decided that staying in for the day would be a rather good thing after all.

At about two in the afternoon, Elise couldn't ignore her stomach's growl of protest any longer. She was exhausted from multiple rounds of sex and a subsequent nap, but she was loath to get out of the bed and leave their idyllic cocoon. "I think we might have burned too many calories to stay in bed," she murmured to Rome, her cheek pillowed on his sweaty chest. "My stomach's eating itself."

He dragged his fingers through her hair, and she tried not to wince at the tangles he ran into, since she knew how much he loved touching her hair. "You want to go out and grab a late lunch?"

"Or a really really late breakfast," she teased, sitting up and smiling at him. "We can carb-load and then come back."

He grinned at her. "I do believe I've created a monster."

She leaned in and nipped at his nipple in response. Mmm. "Nothing can possibly taste as good as you, though."

He groaned and dragged her away from him. "If you start that, we're never going to leave this room."

That honestly didn't sound so bad to Elise, but her stomach growled again, reminding her that they needed to eat. She dragged a hand through her tangled hair, wincing at the snarls. "Can I shower before we go out?"

"Only if you promise to save me some hot water."

She brightened. "You can join me in the shower."

He shook his head and pressed a kiss to the top of her head. "Not if we plan on getting anything done. I need to keep my hands off you to keep my sanity."

Elise gave him a mock pout, but she climbed out of bed

and headed for the bathroom, deliberately swaying her hips in case he was looking. Being with Rome made her feel so . . . pretty. So wanted. It was a heady, delicious feeling.

As she showered, Elise thought about the night they'd just spent together. Sex had been amazing. Okay, more than amazing. Mind-blowing. If sex was this good, she should have been having it years ago, shyness be damned. Then again, she suspected the partner had a lot to do with it, and there was no one more attractive to her than Rome. She loved his tattoos, his smile, his piercings, his gorgeous eyes, his laugh . . . everything about him. Even his personality seemed to hit her in all the right spots. He didn't mind when she was quiet, and didn't try to tease her about the things she was hung up on. He just accepted them, as if everyone had hang-ups and you just coped with them.

He was so patient and understanding. How on earth did she get so lucky?

True, she'd told him that she'd loved him last night and he hadn't said it back to her. But—and maybe this was naive of her—she didn't feel like he had to. He cared for her. It was in the tender way he held her when they first made love, waiting to see if he'd hurt her and looking down at her with agony in his eyes at the thought of causing her pain. It was in the way he touched her, his fingers dancing along her scar as if it were something that made her beautiful instead of strange. It was in the way he didn't see the port-wine stain still faintly outlined on her cheek, and always treated her like she was a goddess. It was in the way he tried to protect her from everything that might somehow hurt her feelings.

If he wasn't the type of guy to admit love and feelings, that was all right with her. He felt them. He didn't have to verbalize them for her to feel adored.

Just being with Rome made her feel wanted and special.

When she got out of the shower, she wrapped herself in one of the towels and made her way out, then gave him a fierce kiss when he headed in, to let him know she was thinking about him. He groaned and muttered something that sounded like "Lord have mercy" before heading in for his own shower.

By the time he came out, she was dressed in her clothes again, her wet hair pulled up into a loose bun at the back of her head. Rome dressed quickly, too, and then they linked hands and headed out for a walk on the Strand to find something to eat.

The air was crisp and smelled of the ocean, and Elise couldn't resist tugging Rome in that direction. "Can we grab something portable and walk on the beach?"

"You bet," he said, and steered her toward a burger stand in the distance.

They walked up and stared at the printed menu, trying to decide what to eat. Rome pulled out his wallet and began to count dollars, and Elise tilted her head, studying the sign on the burger stand when she felt an uncomfortable prickle on her neck. She glanced around and saw the guy at the counter was staring at her. Or rather, he wasn't trying to, but his gaze kept flicking to her face and then flicking away.

She touched her cheek, self-conscious. The sun was bright today, and she wasn't wearing any makeup to even out her skin. Given the fact that she'd been rubbing her face all over Rome's beard stubble for the past twelve hours, her face was probably flushed and the stain more noticeable than usual. Ill at ease, she stepped behind Rome, carefully using him as a shield from the man's gaze. She was sure he didn't mean to make her feel . . . small. But she did. He was probably wondering what a girl like her was doing with someone as gorgeous and confident as Rome. Her hand reached for her hair to pull it across her cheek, but it was in a bun.

"What do you want to eat?" Rome asked.

She shrugged, staring down. Her hand went to the band in her hair and she tugged it free, not caring that her hair was still wet, and began to drag it across her cheek in an

THE VIRGIN'S GUIDE TO MISBEHAVING   203

effort to conceal the stain. "Just order me something," she mumbled.

Rome's fingers touched her chin and he angled her face up, making her look at him. "Hey." His blue eyes searched her face. "What's wrong, Bo Peep?"

She shrugged. "That guy was staring at my face."

Rome leaned in and kissed her. "This beautiful face?"

A hot flush crept up her cheeks. "It's the only one I've got."

He grinned at her, and her heart thumped. "You want me to go growl at him and scare him?"

She shook her head, but she was smiling.

He winked at her. "You wait here and I'll take care of food, baby."

She nodded and sat down on a nearby bench, letting her wet hair flutter in the wind. She tried not to look over, but Rome seemed to be having a rather intense conversation with the man behind the counter, who looked terrified.

Rome returned a few minutes later with a paper tray, two burgers and fries, and a large drink. The guy behind the counter had disappeared. Rome set the tray down on the bench between the two of them.

"What did you say to him?" Elise asked.

Rome handed her one of the cardboard cups of fries. "I told him if I caught him checking out my girl again, I was going to make him sorry."

Her eyes went wide. "Rome . . . he wasn't checking me out."

"You said he was staring at your face."

"Yeah." She touched her cheek self-consciously. "Because it's . . . weird."

Rome shook his head and offered her one of his fries, as if she didn't have a cupful of her own at the moment. But she took it from his fingers with her lips, and tried not to feel absurdly pleased at the small gesture. "Baby, the only thing weird about me and you is why a sweet, classy girl like you got mixed up with a tatted-up loser like me."

She made a sound of protest, only to have him shove another fry at her mouth. This time she glared at him. "Are you trying to shut me up?"

"Maybe?" He gave her a mischievous look. "Maybe I just like shoving things into your mouth."

Her face went scarlet, a reminder of that morning.

They ate together, enjoying a quick bite on the bench, and then Rome gestured at their leftover fries. "Come on. Let's go feed these to the seagulls."

It seemed like such a mischievous little-boy thing to do, how could she refuse? Elise smiled and got to her feet. They linked hands again, Rome carrying the cup of leftover fries. They headed toward the beach and the water, and as soon as they got close, seagulls began to circle, crying out.

"Maybe this wasn't such a good idea," Elise said, shielding her face with a hand as the birds swooped overhead. Everywhere she turned, more and more seagulls were coming.

"Nah, it's all good," Rome said, and began to toss fries out onto the sand. He grinned when the birds dove for them, and looked back to her impishly. "They're hungry."

"I imagine they're always hungry."

"Yeah, I've been there myself," Rome mused, and tossed another fry out onto the sand. "Feels good to feed someone else's belly."

One cawing seagull got too close to her and she squealed, moving closer to him.

"It's okay, baby," he said with a laugh. "They're just birds."

"They're not just birds. They're scavengers," she protested, laughing and taking a few steps back. "They're filthy and nasty and all they do is wait for a handout. Normal birds don't do that. Normal birds get their own food."

For some reason, he looked at her for a long, long moment and she wondered if she'd said something wrong. Then he looked away and tossed the rest of the fries on the sand. "Come on."

Timidly, she slipped her hand in his, wondering if he was somehow mad at her. She didn't know what to think. What had she just missed here? Her free hand touched his arm. "Are you okay?"

"Yeah." He pulled her in close and kissed the top of her head again. "Just thinking."

"Want to share?"

"Nope." He grinned down at her and gestured down the Strand. "I think I saw a sex shop in that direction. You wanna go?"

"What?" she squealed, and she could feel her face turning beet red. "No!"

Rome laughed and wrapped his arms around her. "Come on. I'll buy you a nice dildo. Maybe a couple of plugs for when you're lonely."

She pounded on his arm with a playful fist. "I don't want anything but you."

His laughter died and a serious look crossed his face.

Elise held her breath, waiting in his arms. Had she said something wrong again? But Rome only cupped her face in his hands and tenderly, sweetly kissed her.

And he didn't need to say the words. Elise felt loved, regardless. She smiled up at him.

"Would I be a bad boyfriend," he murmured, lips brushing against hers, "if I dragged you back to our room and made love to you?"

Her entire body tingled with awareness, her nipples taut. "I think you'd be a bad boyfriend if you didn't."

FOURTEEN

Elise was a little sad to return to Bluebonnet on Sunday night. It had been so lovely in their cozy little nest all weekend. She'd fielded a few calls from her concerned brother, sure, and a text or two from Brenna, but she'd called and asked Emily to go along with her cover story, and Em was doing a great job of keeping everyone off of her trail. She'd had time to relax and enjoy just being with Rome.

And god, she loved being with Rome.

They'd spent most of Saturday alternating between bouts of lovemaking and a few more walks on the beach, just holding hands and enjoying each other's company. They talked about work; she talked about photo layouts and adding emotion to her pictures, and her old college roommate, Crissy, who had the job that Elise wanted. Or the job Elise *thought* she wanted. It occurred to her that Crissy was working long hours for low pay, hoping to get ahead at her job, and she hadn't dated anyone seriously in a long time because she was constantly at work. Elise glanced over at Rome, trying to picture him in New York City. He could probably make it, she reasoned, though jobs were probably hard to come by for a guy like Rome. He'd confessed that he had no college education and barely any high school, no degree. But Rome was charismatic enough; the question was, would someone like Elise be able to make it in a city like New York?

She used to think so. Now, she wasn't so sure. Being in Bluebonnet made her appreciate the slow lifestyle and the fact that she could get wherever she wanted with a rental car. In New York, she'd probably have to take the subway everywhere and live in a teeny tiny apartment with hundreds of other people in the same building, and eat out every night.

That . . . didn't sound like the way she wanted to live her life. Elise wondered if she needed to rethink her goals.

Rome was rather quiet when she talked about career and choices, and whenever she asked him something, he always turned the topic back onto her. It was like he loved hearing about her, but didn't want to talk about himself. There were still big gaps in her knowledge of Rome Lozada, but she resolved she'd fill them in with time.

And between conversations and walking on the beach, they made love over and over again. Elise waffled between sheer exhaustion and glorying in his body. She loved touching Rome, and discovered new parts of his body to admire every time. His belly button, for the sleek tautness of the muscles around it. His thighs, for their strength and the way they flexed when she put her mouth on his cock. She'd given him a blow job earlier that day—something she'd wanted to knock off her sexual bucket list—and had immensely enjoyed his reaction to it. Her mouth on him had made her feel sexy and powerful.

It was clearly something she'd have to do for him often.

But now they were driving back to Bluebonnet, with Elise behind the wheel, and Rome had gone from mostly silent to completely and utterly pensive. She glanced over at him as she drove. "Are you okay?"

He looked over at her and smiled, his hand touching her hair and then her cheek in a quick, affectionate gesture. "I'm fine. Just a little tired and thinking about work, that's all."

She smiled at him and lightly bit his thumb when it grazed her mouth. "We're almost back at the ranch. I could park the car out on the road again and go with you to your cabin and distract you for a bit."

He grinned at her mischievous smile but shook his head. "Actually, you should get back so Emily doesn't think I've carried you off into the wild."

"Emily wants me to get out there and date. I don't think she minds a bit."

Rome grew quiet again, and she chewed on her lip in frustration. It was like the closer they got to Bluebonnet, the more distant he got. She took the exit for the Daughtry Ranch, but pulled over instead of turning down the farm road that would lead to the parking lot of Wilderness Survival Expeditions.

She parked the car. Then she turned and looked at him. "You're not regretting this weekend, are you?"

He shook his head slowly, his blue eyes gleaming. Rome reached out and cupped her cheek again, his fingers infinitely tender on her face. "I can honestly say it was the best weekend of my life."

"Me too." Her hands covered his and she kissed his palm. "When can I see you again?"

He grimaced, considering it. "This week's going to be a little crazy with the opening of the paintball course. Brenna's already booked several groups, and I don't know what my hours will be, so don't get scared if I can't call you right away, okay? I'll text you and let you know what my schedule's going to be like once I have it figured out."

She smiled at him. "That's fine." Heck, she'd just swing by the ranch and hang out if nothing else. Just getting to watch him work would be a pleasure, and she could make up some excuse about photos and more action shots or something if Grant hassled her.

Rome glanced at the road and then back at her. "I guess I'd better get going. You should stay here so your brother doesn't catch you."

"At some point, he's going to have to find out about us," she said to him, and nipped at his fingers again. He had such sexy hands, she couldn't resist.

"I know, but I don't want anything to ruin my memories of this weekend," he told her.

Her smile faltered. That struck her as an odd thing to say. "We could always tell him tomorrow?"

"We'll talk about it," he said, and caressed her cheek again, his gaze roaming her face as he continued to cup her cheek in the dark interior of the car. "Have I ever told you how beautiful you are?"

She felt her cheeks heat with pleasure, even though he couldn't see her blush. "Repeatedly."

"Then it can stand for one more time," he murmured in a husky voice, leaning in. "Elise Markham, you are the most beautiful woman I have ever seen, and I'm going to remember this weekend—and you—forever."

Tears stung her eyes at the sweetness of his words. "I love you," she whispered hoarsely. "I'm so glad I found you, Rome."

He leaned in and kissed her mouth. "Me too, baby." His hands tightened on her cheeks. "And I miss you already."

She smiled at that. "I miss you already, too."

Rome dragged her closer. "I need to taste you one more time before I let you go." His hands wrapped around her waist and he pulled her closer to him. Her rented Impala had a bench seat for the front seat, and she slid right into his arms, her legs tangling with his.

His mouth possessed hers, hungry and erotic. She opened for him, her mouth seeking his tongue. She loved kissing

Rome, loved how his tongue and lips made her lose all sense of reality; when she kissed him, there was nothing but Rome's scent, Rome's taste, Rome's touch in her world, and she loved it. The kiss grew hungrier and more intense, Rome's mouth pressing so fervently on hers that she could feel the bite of his lip ring against her own mouth. His ferocity was surprising in its intensity, given that they'd spent all weekend making love, but she welcomed it. Her thighs clenched in response and she pushed her breasts against his chest, her nipples rubbing against his shirt.

"Need more than this," he told her roughly. His long-lashed eyes were already sleepy with desire. "Want to have all of you. Right now."

His hand went to the waist of her jeans, and she gasped when he undid the top button and slipped his hand inside, burrowing under her panties. She moaned a moment later when his fingers found her clit and he began to rub.

"Want to see you come for me," he murmured in her ear. "One last time for the weekend."

Her thighs gripped his hand as he began to rub in slow, sweet, maddening circles around her clit. In moments, she was wet with need, and he slicked a finger back and forth from her core to her clit, spreading the moisture.

"That's my sweet Elise," he murmured, and his mouth claimed hers again as he continued to rub her. "So damned delicious."

She moaned against his mouth, clinging to his neck as he kissed her and his fingers worked on her clit. Her hips began to jerk in response, and she rocked against his hand, encouraging the motion of his fingers. A soft whimper escaped her throat and he groaned.

"That's right," he told her. "God, that's so good. I love seeing you come." His mouth tore away from hers and she leaned her head on his shoulder, lost in sensation.

"Rome," she moaned. "You're going to make me . . ."

"Good," he said possessively, and he nipped at her ear. "Want you to look me in the eyes when you come, baby."

She whimpered again, caught off guard by his erotic fierceness, and opened her eyes. He was gazing down at her in the darkness, and she moaned anew as his fingers continued to stroke and pet her clit as he watched her face, drinking in her reactions to his touch.

"I'm . . . I'm going to . . ." she panted, then began to rock her hips fiercely against his hand, her own pressing down on his fingers. The friction suddenly became intense, and she gave a little scream that was just as quickly swallowed by his mouth as he kissed her again. She came with a familiar rush of wetness, soaking her jeans and his hand all over again.

He groaned as if in pain. "I love that so much."

Her heart skipped a beat for a moment, but then she gave a soft whimper, clinging to him as he tugged his fingers free of her now-wet panties and jeans. As she watched, he raised them to his mouth and licked them slowly, erotically. "Love your taste, Elise."

"And now my jeans are all damp," she chided him. But she couldn't be mad. How could she be mad when he'd just given her a quick, delicious orgasm?

"Sorry, baby," he said with another quick kiss. There was a pleased look on his face that told her he wasn't all that sorry. "Had to have you one more time before I let you go."

"You can have me all you want," she told him, dragging a finger along the curve of his ear. "You just tell me the place and time and I'll be there."

He smiled at her and nodded. "Of course." Then he gave her another fierce, quick kiss and grimaced. "I'd better go before someone investigates why this car is parked on the side of the road."

She quickly slid over to the driver's side again, squeezing her thighs together and enjoying the delicious aftershocks still reverberating through her legs. She looked over at him, and for a moment, her heart stuttered.

He looked so sad, so utterly lost in the darkness.

It surprised her, but she felt the same way. She didn't want to leave his side, and the thought of being separated again made her ache. Maybe she'd go to his cabin and surprise him.

She reached out and squeezed his hand. "Text me tomorrow?"

"I will." He gave her a brief smile and reached into the back seat, grabbing his backpack. Then he opened the car door, flashed her one last smile, and was gone.

Rome loped back to his cabin, half expecting to see his shit in a box on the porch. If Grant found out he'd stolen Elise away for the weekend, there'd be no saving his ass from the man's wrath. But his bike was parked next to his cabin and when he opened the door, everything was as he'd left it. Not that he'd left much behind, just in case he'd been cleaned out when he came back. But there was a small box under the bed, and he tossed his few remaining items into it. Some toiletries. A book. His DVD of *Lethal Weapon*. He picked it up, thinking of Elise. He could still smell her on his hand, and for a moment, longing and bitterness filled him.

Life had just dealt him one shit hand after another, hadn't it? The moment he found a girl he loved, he was being chased off all over again.

He tucked the DVD into the box and considered. He could go to Elise tonight. Tell her about his past. Confess that he'd done hard time and swear up and down that despite what the records said, he wasn't the one who was dealing drugs. That despite his bad rap and awful credit, he really wasn't using her for her money, and he loved her. That her brother was going to fire him from his stable job and he'd taken her away over the weekend despite her brother's warnings to him.

And then it could go two ways.

If she didn't believe him, he wouldn't blame her. Most people didn't. They took one look at his tattoos and piercings and his prison record and assumed he was guilty of whatever crime the paperwork said. She'd hate him for deceiving her and would assume he'd manipulated her and slept with her just to try and get to her money. Her self-esteem, always fragile, would be completely and utterly destroyed.

If she did believe him, no one else would. They'd assume that Elise was naive and with him because he was using her for her money. Grant would never believe otherwise, and he suspected Elise's overprotective parents would be the same. Staying with him would create a schism in her family. The people she loved the most in the world, the people she trusted, would think she was stupid and being used.

He either destroyed his girl or destroyed her relationship with her family.

He didn't want to do either. Family was important to him, oddly enough. Maybe it was because of how shitty his own was, but when he saw how much Grant cared for his sister, how much he looked out for her, he didn't want to trash that for his own selfish needs. How would his life have turned out if his brother Jericho hadn't up and left when he got old enough? How would Rome's story have been different if Jericho had stayed and looked out for *him*?

He probably wouldn't have gone to prison for his parents. J had always been able to see right through their lies, but Rome always fell for them. He'd always wanted to believe the best about family.

That had been beaten out of him in the four years in prison, though.

Rome shook his head and tucked the DVD into the box. Either way, if he stayed, he was fucking up Elise's life. Better to just make a clean break. It would hurt, but over time, it would get easier.

He hoped.

He rubbed his chest, wondering at the ache there. He'd never been in love before. Never really thought about it. There'd been a few women in his life, but most were just diversions instead of people.

Elise, though . . . Elise was everything to him.

He picked through the cabin, looking for any personal items he might have missed. He was lingering, he knew it. Hell, he didn't want to go. He wanted to turn around and call Elise and tell her to come back over. That he'd changed his mind. He picked up the small plastic plate she'd brought over when she'd showed up with the cookies and hit on him. He'd eaten the cookies, but he'd kept the plate. Stupid, really, but seeing it reminded him of her, and he packed it away carefully in his backpack, sandwiched between a few shirts. And suddenly, he wished that he had mementos from all of their get-togethers. That he'd stolen a candle from their sultry photo shoot, or taken a book of matches from their hotel this weekend.

That he'd pulled out his cell phone and snapped pictures of her gorgeous face and that shy smile so he could always carry them with him.

He put on his leather jacket, picked up his small box, and headed out of his cabin for the last time. He'd miss this place . . . but he'd miss one person in particular the most.

Rome texted her brother to let him know he was packing up and heading out, strapped the box on the back of his bike, and pulled out of the parking lot, heading onto the highway.

Heading for fuck knew where. He didn't care.

Elise rolled over in bed, feeling delicious and well-rested. It was nice to get a full night's rest after a weekend of too little sleep, she supposed, but it also felt weird to wake up in bed alone. She smiled into her pillows and reached for the nightstand to pick up her phone, hoping for a text from Rome.

The only texts on her phone were from family, though.

Having a good time in Bluebonnet, sweetie? When are you coming home? XOXO from her mother.

Your mother misses you. Expect her to start asking you to come home, but if you're not ready, stay a bit longer. Love you, bunny, from her father.

And from Grant, Hey, bit of a snag today. Can we put off the engagement photos for a week or two? Kinda have my head down with work.

Even as she was checking messages, one came in from Brenna. Your brother's being a dick and is all stressypants. If you come by, can you bring lunch or something? I'll take some cash out of his wallet and pay you back. We are totally slammed. :) I like my burger with no onions!!

Wow. It sounded like a crazy day over at the ranch. She immediately texted Rome. Hope you're hanging in there today. Want me to bring you lunch? :)

She hoped it wasn't too forward, but heck, they'd had sex all weekend and he'd dragged her into his arms in the car because he didn't want to leave her. She figured she could be a little needy in her texting.

But when there was no immediate response, she figured he was busy. Disappointed, she sat up in bed and started sending texts back.

Hi Mom, I am having a good time. Going to stay a bit longer.

Her mom immediately sent back How much longer? Be careful.

Not for the first time, Elise felt a little smothered by her mother's attention. Be careful of what? Farmers driving tractors two miles above the speed limit? Armadillos crossing the road? She was a grown woman, graduated from college and in her twenties. She could take care of herself, especially in a sleepy little town like Bluebonnet. She knew her mother meant well, but still.

So she thought for a moment and sent back, Thinking about opening up a photography studio here. Gonna wait until Beth Ann gets back from her honeymoon and discuss a joint business venture. :)

Oh, sweetie, that's great! Her mother sent back. I'm so proud of you! Let me know if you need anything from your daddy and me.

Will do. Love you!

As she sent back the message, she realized it wasn't a total lie. There was a place down on Main Street not too far from Beth Ann's hair salon that had recently come up for lease. It was a cute little cubby of a storefront, but she wouldn't need much for a studio, just some clients. And if Beth Ann was interested in doing the retro shoots, that'd be the perfect lead-in, along with weddings and parties. She began to get excited just thinking about it.

And if she stayed in Bluebonnet, she could stay close to Rome . . .

Not that he was the reason she was staying, of course. But having a sexy guy around certainly helped her lean in that direction. Even if things didn't work out with them, though, she rather thought she'd like to have a studio. Set up a little darkroom in the back, maybe. It'd be cozy and so much fun to have a place to call her own. And rent in Bluebonnet was a lot cheaper than most places.

It was a great plan, she had to admit. For the first time since she'd been rejected by Crissy's magazine, she felt excited about her career. She couldn't wait to pull out the photos of Rome and go through them.

Yawning, she texted her dad a happy note along the same lines, and then texted Brenna. Will bring lunch. Burgers it is. How many should I bring?

Five meals, Brenna sent back. You're the best!

Elise counted on her hand. There was Pop, Grant, Brenna, Dane, and Rome. And herself, of course. Which meant . . . six? Unless Dane was still out in the field today. Maybe

Brenna had counted wrong? She decided to pick up an extra meal, just in case.

She dressed in jeans and a pullover, and dragged her messy hair into a ponytail. Just as she was slipping on her shoes, her phone buzzed with an incoming message.

She clicked over and her heart stuttered. It was from Rome, and it was long. Excited, she began to read . . . and then her stomach sank as she continued.

> Elise, baby. I'm sorry. This is going to hurt your feelings, but I'm going to throw it all out there anyhow. I can't stay in Bluebonnet. It's nothing you did. Actually, god, you're pretty much perfect in every way. It's me and I'm the wrong kind of guy for you, and I feel like you'd regret being with me at some point. So I'm going to cut my losses now. I don't ever want you to think that it was you who drove me away, though. I meant it when I said you were the best thing that ever happened to me. You're way too good for someone like me, no matter what you think. That hasn't changed a bit, and I'm going to remember every detail of this weekend for the rest of my life, right down to that little shiver you do when I kiss your neck. You were utterly and completely perfect. It's me that's the problem, and so I'm going. And since I'm not into good-byes, this is it from me. I hope life treats you well.

Stunned, she stared at the screen of her phone, tears blurring her vision.

Maybe . . . maybe she'd read it wrong. She scanned the message again, slowing down and going over each word deliberately in case she'd misunderstood.

And then she read it a third time.

I hope life treats you well.

You're way too good for someone like me.

He was breaking up with her.

Now? After their beautiful weekend? After last night's

frantic petting session in the car when he'd held her and said he had to have her one last time?

Oh god. He'd been planning on breaking up with her even last night. That was what he'd meant!

Frantic, Elise tried calling his phone. There was no way he was breaking up with her over text, was he? She deserved at least a phone call, didn't she?

But it rang several times and then went to voice mail. Then it clicked over. *The caller you are dialing does not have a voice message box established—*

She hung up.

He was dumping her.

Elise lay back in the bed, stunned. She felt like she was breaking into a million pieces. Hurt tears gathered in her eyes, and she blinked them away. She didn't understand.

He'd nailed her and bailed on her. Should she be angry?

All she felt was . . . confused.

This past weekend had been wonderful. They'd had sex and he'd been so incredibly tender with her. He'd even offered to wait if she wasn't ready. That . . . didn't sound like a man that wanted to nail and bail. Moreover, they'd spent so much time together leading up to that first night of sex that she'd thought he genuinely enjoyed being around her. They'd dated. They'd flirted. They'd cuddled and slept together.

Why spend so much time enticing her into his bed if he planned on kicking her out of it afterward?

She frowned up at the ceiling. He hadn't even hit on her, actually. She'd come on to him.

It was yet another thing that didn't make sense. If he didn't want to be with her, why hadn't he just turned her down?

She read his message again, trying to decipher between the lines.

I can't stay in Bluebonnet.
I'm the wrong guy for you.

It almost sounded like he was apologizing for dumping her. But . . . he'd known ahead of time that he was leaving. So why be so incredibly, wonderfully attentive this weekend? He'd paid for everything, too. She'd tried to buy meals and the hotel room, but he'd insisted on "paying for his girl."

He'd made her feel like *his* girl.

Like he'd chosen her out of all the women in the world to be with.

Like she was special.

That was why this didn't make sense. Rome hadn't told her that he loved her, but it was in every touch, every gesture, every caress. The way he'd tenderly touched her scars when she felt self-conscious about them. The way he held her tight while they lay in bed in talked. The way he was so protective of her.

There had been real emotion there, she decided. She was naive in a lot of things, but she knew love when she saw it. It was in how Brenna did small things to irritate her brother out of constant, obsessive work mode. It was in how Grant picked up after Brenna's mess with an exasperated but loving smile on his face. How he touched her when he thought no one was looking. The way her parents shared a glance from time to time, each letting the other know just what they were thinking.

That was love. Even though she hadn't experienced it, she knew what it looked like.

And that was why Rome had never needed to say it to her.

She studied the text again. *I can't stay in Bluebonnet.* Not *I won't* but *I can't.*

Something was wrong here, and she was going to fix it, damn it. She was not about to let Rome give up on everything now that she'd finally found him.

Dashing the tears of self-pity out of her eyes, Elise got up from bed.

She was going to get to the bottom of this, and then she was going to get her man back.

FIFTEEN

Elise drove over to the Daughtry Ranch first thing. Screw burgers—she wanted answers. To her surprise, though, the parking lot was crammed full of cars and she'd had to circle twice before backing out and parking on the side of the service road that led to the ranch. If she got a ticket, damn it, she'd just deal with it.

Marching up to the main ranch, she passed Pop, the elderly handyman who did work at the ranch. He was rushing out the front door with a paintball jumper on, his chest splattered with yellow, and he held a paintball gun in his hands. He looked rather frazzled, too.

Normally, she would have just smiled in greeting as she passed by, too shy to start a conversation. But forget that. Today, she was getting answers from everyone, come hell or high water. "What's going on, Pop?"

He rubbed his sweating forehead and adjusted his trucker cap on his brow. "First day of the paintball course, Miss Elise. Your brother's running around like a chicken with his fool head cut off."

She forced a smile to her face at the thought, since he was smiling at her and it'd be expected. "Where's Rome?"

"Well, now," Pop said, adjusting his cap again. "I don't know. He didn't show up today."

She nodded, swallowing the ache in her throat. "I'll let you get back to work."

He turned and dashed up one of the paths to the woods, making a beeline for the course.

She turned and considered the lodge for a moment. Instead of heading in to confront her brother, though, she went around one of the side paths and up the hill to where the row of cabins was nestled nearby. She headed to Rome's first. His bike wasn't parked on the side of his cabin. She was expecting that, she supposed, given her cryptic message.

But she knocked at his door anyhow, and when he didn't answer, she opened it and went inside.

The tiny cabin had been cleaned out. The sheets and blankets were neatly folded on the bed, but all personal traces of Rome were gone. She looked at the empty coat hooks by the door, ran her hand over his pillow, and then peeked into his bathroom and even the mini fridge.

Nothing at all. It was like the place had never been inhabited.

Her heart felt heavy.

Sometime between when she'd seen him last night and this morning, her Rome had packed up and left. Not because he wanted to, but because he felt he had to. What was going on?

With determination in her step, she headed toward the main lodge of the Daughtry Ranch.

Inside it was chaos. Paintball guns and ammo were littered on every flat surface, and folding chairs were scattered throughout the lodge, along with a tray of sandwich remnants and a picked-over selection of drinks on a folding table. It looked as if she'd missed a party. In one corner of the room, at his desk, her brother was typing away, looking frazzled. Across from him, Brenna's desk was empty but strewn with stacks of messy paper.

Grant looked up as she entered. "Hey. Did you get my message? We have to cancel the shoot this week. I'm sorry." He rubbed his forehead and then ran a hand through his messy hair again. "The whole launch of this paintball course has been more of a mess than I hoped it would be."

She sat down in one of the chairs across from his desk, keeping her face calm. She didn't care about his problems, not really. Not right now. "Grant, I need to talk to you about something."

He gave a hard, unamused chuckle. "Can it wait? I'm serious when I say this week's gone to shit already and it's only Monday."

"Where's Rome?"

Her brother snorted and picked up the phone, punching buttons. "Wouldn't I like to know? He was supposed to be taking the lead on the paintball course and he's nowhere to be found. That's one reason why things have gone to hell."

She shook her head. "He's gone. His cabin is cleaned out. And this morning, he texted me and told me he couldn't stay in Bluebonnet. I'm trying to understand why."

Grant put down the phone and looked at her. He paused, thinking, then reached out and touched her hand. "Elise, I'm going to tell you this as your brother who is looking out for you, but maybe it's best that Rome left. He's not a good guy."

She pulled her hand out from under his. "That's where you're wrong. I think Rome is a great guy."

He gave her a look she'd come to realize was his "big brother" look. "No, he's not. I'm not going to argue about this right now, but all I want to say is that you need to stay away from him."

"Are you not listening to me? He's gone. He's left. He's not coming back."

"And like I said, maybe it's for the best."

Elise twitched in her chair. Normally she loved her brother, but he was being obstinate and a bit too stubborn at the moment. Her eyes narrowed at him. "You're an employee short and you're saying it's for the best?"

Grant shrugged.

"What did you do?"

He blustered, shaking his head and picking up a schedule off the corner of his desk. "I didn't do anything."

"Then why do you say he's not a good guy?" She crossed her arms over her chest. "Grant, if you chased him away, I'll . . ."

He gave her an exasperated look. "You'll what, Elise? Be mad at me for looking out for you? For warning a guy away from my little sister?"

She stiffened in her chair. "You what?"

Sighing, Grant rubbed his forehead again. "I told him to stay away from you or he was going to find himself unemployed."

Why on earth? She sputtered, an inkling of what had happened starting to creep through her mind. "Why would you tell Rome to stay away from me? He's done nothing wrong!"

"Oh please, Elise. Don't tell me you're that naive."

"Naive about what?" She was close to losing her temper, and she *never* lost her temper. But the fact that Rome had left a job and his life behind meant he knew he wasn't welcome, and it seemed like her well-meaning brother was a big part of the problem.

"It's clear he was just using you to get to your money."

She sucked in a breath. Her hands locked together in her lap. Her voice was low and deadly. "Why is that clear, Grant? Because I'm ugly?"

He blanched. "No, of course not. You know what I mean."

"No, I don't."

"It's just . . . Ah, hell, Elise. Don't look at me like that."

"Look at you like what?" Brenna came in the side door, an empty jug of paintball ammo balanced on her hip. She was splattered with pink and yellow, her face was flushed, and a wide grin was on her face. "Grant, baby, you should have seen the look on Pop's face when I nailed him right in the nut sack—" She broke off, giving them both puzzled looks. "Who died?"

"No one died," Grant said tightly. "My sister was just having a conversation with me."

"Yes," Elise said, letting sarcasm slide into her voice. It was either that or reach across the desk and strangle her brother. She looked over at Brenna. "My brother was just telling me that he ran off Rome because it was clear he was using me to get to my money."

"What?" Brenna gave Grant an incredulous look. "Are you the reason why he's gone? Seriously, babe? Why?"

"Elise has a trust fund," Grant said in a tight voice. His arms crossed over his chest and he glanced back between his fiancée and his sister. "It's obvious that he found out about it and was seducing her to get his hands on that money."

Brenna snorted. "Why? Because he has tattoos?"

"And because I'm so ugly?" Elise pointed out again.

"No! Jesus Christ." Grant got to his feet, clearly agitated. "You're ganging up on me and I can't think."

"You're kind of being a dick, baby." Brenna said, her hand on her hip. "Admit it. You never liked Rome because he's scary-looking."

"He's not scary looking," Elise protested. "He's beautiful."

Now both of them turned to stare at her.

"And I seduced him," Elise pointed out. "He didn't come after me. I approached him and asked him out. If there was any interest there, I instigated it."

"But Elise, you're so shy and trusting—"

"And clearly she must be *stuuuuupid*," Brenna added, fluttering her eyelashes at Grant. "Clearly that's why you're making all the decisions for her."

He gave Brenna a cross look. "You're not helping."

THE VIRGIN'S GUIDE TO MISBEHAVING   225

"I love you, honey, but I call a spade a spade, or a tool a tool. And if you ran Rome off, you're being a tool. That man needed this job. He didn't have two pennies to rub together and was desperate. I never saw a guy so happy to have a roof over his head."

Elise's stomach clenched at Brenna's words. Rome had been so pleased with that small cabin. She'd simply assumed that it was because he liked working there, but maybe it was because it was his first place to call his own. She needed answers and they weren't forthcoming.

Grant shook his head and pulled a piece of paper out of his desk drawer. "Look, I didn't want to talk about this, but I had a chat with Rome. He's a felon. Actually, he's an ex-con." He handed the sheet of paper to Elise. "I ran a background check on him after we hired him and pulled up a rap sheet a mile long. So if I seem a little overprotective, that's why."

Elise took the paper with trembling fingers. *John Lozada III*, the paper read.

Education—unavailable.

Criminal activity—Possession of narcotics with intent to distribute. Plea deal. Served time—Huntsville State Prison, six-year sentence, four years served. Charges of fraud—dismissed. Sealed juvenile record.

Credit—Extremely poor. This individual has outstanding bad debt in multiple states. Filed bankruptcy in 1997. Three vehicles repossessed in the last ten years.

She swallowed. On paper, it sounded horrible. She read the prison sentence over and over again. It didn't make sense. Rome had never even so much as smoked near her. Any time she drank to excess, he made sure she was safe. He didn't strike her as a drug dealer.

She was silent for a long moment, thinking of Rome. His ready smile and quick offers to pay for everything when he took his "girl" out. The protective way he looked after her when she was uncomfortable. The sad look he'd gotten in his eyes when they were feeding the seagulls. He'd commented that they were just hungry and trying to eat, and she'd gone on and on about how seagulls were scavengers and disgusting. And that had hurt Rome's feelings, and she hadn't understood why.

Oh god, she was such a privileged jerk, wasn't she?

Looking at the sheet, she wondered about his story. When had he gone hungry? When had he done without? There was more here that she wasn't getting.

After a moment, she handed the paper back to Grant. "I don't understand."

"What's not to understand? The man's a criminal. It's all on paper." He thumped it.

"Oh, come on," Brenna butted in. "Who doesn't have a police record in this day and age?"

Both Markhams turned and looked at her.

Brenna gave them a sunny smile. "Jaywalking. Lots and lots of jaywalking." And she sauntered over to her desk.

Grant looked as if he wanted to go over to her and quiz her, but he forced himself to look back at Elise. "You're asking me why I was concerned about you with that man? This is why." He shook the paper at her. "This is why I wanted my vulnerable baby sister staying away from a guy like him."

Elise considered the paper for a long moment, and then she looked up at Grant. "That's not him."

"What do you mean, that's not him? It's his social security number."

She shook her head. "That's not who he is, though. That's not Rome."

"You sure about that?"

"Has he ever tried to sell drugs to anyone while he was here?" Elise asked.

"No, but—"

"Borrowed money from anyone?"

"I think he borrowed five from me once," Brenna called out, then held up a hand. "Wait, never mind. I borrowed it from him. Carry on."

Elise turned back to her brother and arched an eyebrow. "Well?"

"He's never done anything," Brenna volunteered when Grant was silent. "Actually, he's a really good employee, considering we pay him shit."

Grant gave Brenna another warning look. "Please, love, you're not helping."

"She is, actually," Elise pointed out. "She's showing you how wrong you are."

"Zing!" Brenna called out merrily.

"The facts don't lie," Grant said. He picked up the piece of paper again. "This is on his official record."

"I know, and I'm sure there's a story behind it," Elise said calmly. "And I'm sure that's not the man he is today. You keep saying he was a bad man, but he treated me like a princess." Her voice wobbled a little as despair threatened to overcome her control. "He always said he wasn't good enough for me."

"He's not—" Grant began, and grew silent at the look Elise shot him.

"I don't care about who he was back then," she said calmly and got to her feet. "I care about who he is now. And who he is now is good, and kind, and used to being treated like shit by people like you and me."

Grant's jaw set mutinously but he said nothing.

"I'm sorry he didn't trust me enough to share this with me earlier," Elise said, gesturing at the paper. "Maybe if he had, this would have all blown over and you wouldn't have cared that I was in love with him."

"He's after your trust fund," Grant began again.

"That's funny," Elise snapped. "No one's ever mentioned the trust fund before you. Not me, not Rome, not anyone. So am I supposed to assume that you're after it, big brother?"

His face went red.

"Yeah, that's what I thought." She smoothed her pullover and tried to remain calm, when all she wanted to do was scream and fling some stuff at the wall to watch it break. "Look, Grant. I love you. You're my brother. But I am an adult. I can make my own decisions. And if I want to date an ex-con because he treats me like I'm a goddess, then I'm going to date an ex-con, understand?"

"You fucked up, baby," Brenna called out. "Admit it. I still love you."

"Brenna," Grant bit out. "Please."

"It's okay," Elise said to Brenna over her shoulder as she headed to the door. "We all know he fucked up. He can figure out how to fix it. I'm going to see how to get in touch with Rome again."

She texted him three times and tried calling him twice while driving back into Bluebonnet. He didn't answer, and she was starting to wonder if he was deliberately ignoring her. That hurt, but she felt like they needed to talk. If nothing else, they needed to clear the air.

She'd shown him all her scars, all her war wounds that had messed with her head and stolen her pride. Rome's scars were on the inside, and it was clear he hadn't trusted her enough to share them. That made her ache and question if she was so sure after all. Did he love her? Or was she just seeing it because she so desperately wanted to? Elise didn't know, and it was driving her crazy.

Numb, she parked her car and went into the Peppermint House. Should she stay? How could she possibly leave? She wanted to be where Rome was, though, and Rome wasn't here.

The house smelled delicious and homey, as always. Elise passed by the kitchen and saw Emily slicing a fresh-baked loaf of bread. At the sight of Elise, Emily smiled. "Hey, you're just in time for some fresh bread if you want to eat." Her smile faded when she saw the look on Elise's face. "Oh no. What's wrong?"

Elise's first thought was to hole up in her room. To internalize her pain and frustration and deal with it alone, like she always did.

But something about Emily's friendly demeanor and the warmth of her kitchen drew Elise toward her, and she found herself sitting at one of the barstools at the kitchen island. Emily never judged. She was sweet, friendly, supportive, and only a few years older than Elise. She was also divorced and lonely, which meant that she'd understand some of what Elise was going through more than Brenna, who was madly in love with Elise's brother . . . and, okay, also a little mad.

Emily put a cup of coffee in front of Elise and buttered a slice of warm bread, then put it on a plate and slid it toward Elise. "You need to talk?"

"Rome's gone," Elise said woodenly. "He just . . . left."

Emily frowned, pulling up a stool and sitting next to Elise. "But didn't you just spend the weekend together? Did something come up?"

Elise blinked rapidly, fighting back tears. Then, in a halting voice, she explained to Emily what was going on. Her shy, slow romance with Rome. Their weekend together. Returning and finding out that not only had he gone, but Grant had threatened him. The discovery of Rome's past. Everything.

Emily Allard-Smith was a great listener. She said nothing, only making sympathetic noises when appropriate, and she poured extra coffee when Elise gulped hers down.

"I . . . don't know what to do," Elise said, numb, the cup warm in her hands.

"How do you feel about Rome now that you know the truth about who he is?" Emily reached out and squeezed her hand. "Betrayed?"

Elise thought for a moment. "Actually, I don't feel any different about him. I love him. He's still the same person. It's just like . . . a few pieces of the puzzle have been filled in. Things that didn't make sense before now suddenly make a lot more sense." His loneliness that matched hers. His isolation. His constant commentary that he wasn't good enough for her.

"I have to ask, as your friend." Emily said, taking a bite of fresh bread and then setting it down. "This isn't some sort of martyr thing where you think you can save him and change him, right? Redeem the bad boy? I don't get that vibe from you, but I have to ask."

A wry smile twisted Elise's mouth. "He may look like a bad boy, but he's the nicest man I've ever met. And he treats me like I'm the most beautiful woman in the world to him." Her lower lip trembled. "And now he's gone."

Emily looked over at Elise. She exhaled slowly, and then pulled her phone out, thumbing through her contacts.

"What are you doing?" Elise asked, her heart racing with hope. Did . . . did Emily know Rome well enough that he'd answer her call? Could it really be that easy? She peeked over Emily's shoulder, watching her phone screen.

But Emily thumbed to a listing in her contacts labeled CARPENTER and dialed it. A moment later, she spoke. "Hey, Jericho? It's Emily over at the Peppermint House." She paused. "Yeah, that's the one. The big red Victorian." She looked over at Elise and rolled her eyes, amused. "I need you to come over for a bit, please. I want you to take a look at something." Pause. "Great, thanks."

She hung up and gave Elise a mysterious look.

"What was that all about?" Elise asked, a bit confounded by the change in topics. She'd been pouring her heart out to Emily and it made Emily decide to call her carpenter?

"Just someone you should meet," Emily said in an enigmatic voice. "He might have some info on your missing sweetheart."

Elise gave a sigh of relief. "Thank you, Em."

An hour later, the rumbling purr of a motorcycle came from the front of the Victorian, and Elise's heart pounded with excitement. Was it Rome? She dashed to the front of the house and peered through the curtain . . . and frowned. There was a bike there, but it wasn't the beat-up old Harley that Rome rode. This bike was sleek, shiny, and new, and the owner pulled off his helmet, revealing shaggy black hair that was entirely too long for Rome.

But his face looked remarkably familiar. So much so that her heart gave a little flip anyhow.

He flipped his hair back and began to saunter toward the door, and she was struck by how similar and yet different to Rome he looked. Whereas Rome was bulky with muscle, this man was extremely tall and lean. When he got to the door, though, she saw a stud under his lower lip. He didn't have the ring that Rome did.

She realized she was staring and hurried back to the kitchen to hide. A moment later, the doorbell rang and the front door opened. "Emily?" a deep voice called. "It's me."

Emily came down the stairs, and Elise realized she'd changed shirts and freshened her makeup. She beamed at the man just as Elise emerged from the kitchen. "Hey, Jericho! Thanks for coming by. I wanted you to meet Elise." Emily gestured at where Elise hovered in the doorway to the kitchen.

He stuck a big hand out for her to shake, and as she did, she realized he had the exact same, long-lashed blue eyes that Rome did.

"Elise is a friend of Rome's," Emily said, and then turned to Elise again. "This is Jericho Lozada. My carpenter."

She blinked in surprise. "You're Rome's brother?"

"One and the same." He gave her an assessing look. "You must be the reason he stuck around for so long."

Her face heated with a flush and she pulled her hand from his, then crossed her arms over her chest.

"Elise is upset that Rome left town," Emily said, heading toward Elise and putting an arm around her protectively. "They just spent the weekend together and then he up and left."

Jericho rubbed at his mouth. "He texted me last night and told me he was leaving."

"Where did he go?" Elise asked.

He shrugged. "Anywhere that he can avoid family, I imagine. He didn't tell me. I think he worried if he did it might somehow get back to our parents."

"I don't understand," Elise said.

Those familiar blue eyes narrowed at her. "How much did he tell you about his past?"

"I know he went to prison," she said. "Drugs. But I also know that's not who he is. I'm trying to make sense of it all."

"You seem very confident that you know just who Rome is," Jericho said, eyeing her.

"I do," she replied easily. "And he's not a drug dealer. Or if he was, that's not who he is now and I don't hold it against him."

A hint of a smile touched Jericho's hard mouth. He looked over at Emily. "This why you called me over?"

To Elise's surprise, Emily giggled like a schoolgirl. "Maybe. I also did some baking this morning. You're welcome to help yourself."

He grinned at Emily, and Elise suddenly felt like a third wheel. Was there something going on between the two of them . . . ?

"Come on into the kitchen," Emily told them. "I'll put on more coffee."

A few minutes later, they sat at the kitchen island again, plates of cookies in front of each of them and fresh coffee in their mugs.

"So," Jericho said, looking over at Elise. "You want to know about Rome's past."

"I do."

"You're right that Rome's not a dealer. Never was."

Elation flared in Elise's heart. "But then . . . why did he go to prison?"

"He went for Mom."

Elise's jaw dropped. "They were his mother's drugs?"

Jericho gave her a wry look. "Whatever picture you have in mind of motherly love, you might as well get it out of your head. Mama Lozada is a lot of things, but she's a shitty parent. Both my parents are, actually. The polite word to use to describe them is probably 'hippies' or 'bohemians,' but the reality is that they're just drifters. You move from place to place, following the party." He shrugged. "I spent my childhood crashing on couches and watching my parents spend their last few dollars to light up with friends. They've never stopped partying, not even for their kids. It was a shitty life. We barely went to school, and any time someone got concerned for our welfare, we'd skip on to the next town. It's hard to get a real job when you're homeless, so we panhandled, did odd chores, lived with friends, you name it. Mom and Dad sold drugs, too."

"It sounds awful," Elise whispered.

"It was," Jericho said flatly. "I hated every fucking minute of it. Always felt bad for Rome, too. I hated our parents, but he so desperately wanted to see them as real parents and not shitty human beings. As a result, they'd act up and get into some sort of trouble, and would throw Rome out there to take the rap. By the time I hit seventeen, the kid had a rap sheet a mile long, and a lot of it wasn't his."

Her mouth went dry at the thought. "But why did he—"

"Mom was great at figuring out what made Rome tick. He was always super responsible, even when they weren't. I remember she used to cry when she got in trouble, because she knew he couldn't stand to see a woman cry."

Her eyes widened. She remembered him saying that to her. *Don't cry, Elise. I can't stand it when girls cry.*

"She sounds manipulative," Emily commented.

"Oh yeah. She could teach a master class on manipulation, my mom." Jericho sipped his coffee and devoured another cookie. "That's why I got out of there as soon as I was old enough. Had to leave Rome behind, but didn't have a choice. Told my family I was running off to join an MC."

"MC?" Elise asked, puzzled.

"Motorcycle club. Actually I just joined the Army." He grinned, and for a moment, he wore the same mischievous little boy look that Rome had so often. "Spent four years in there. Came back and found out my brother was serving time for a drug deal sentence." He snorted. "Mama was real good with them tears."

"That's awful," Elise whispered.

"That's my parents. Here, let me show you something." He reached into his back pocket and pulled out a driver's license, then offered it to her.

She took it from him and studied it, trying to figure out what she was supposed to see on it. Then she realized his name was very familiar. "John Lozada," she murmured.

"Number two," he said with a laugh. "Dad is John Lozada number one. Rome is John Lozada number three. All the better to steal your identity with."

"What?" Emily sputtered, lifting her coffee cup to her lips. She took a sip and then shook her head. "You expect me to believe that your parents named you the same so they could steal your identity?"

"I'm sure it didn't start out that way. Maybe they just wanted me to be Junior. But by the time Rome arrived? No doubt in my mind that is what they were doing. We've had credit cards opened in our names for years."

"And bankruptcies," Elise said, thinking of the credit report for Rome. She'd wondered at the timing of his bankruptcy, since it would have happened when he was a very young teenager. It made sense now. "Your parents are awful people."

"Yes, yes, they are. That's why I left. I'm only sorry I didn't get Rome out before they fucked over his life." He shook his head. "So if he runs out the door at a whiff of family, that's why. We keep up with each other, but we're not close. He's been burned too many times. Now he doesn't let anyone close to him." Jericho gave her an up-and-down look and then smiled. "Before now."

"He must not have cared for me that much," Elise said softly, and hated how whiny she sounded. "He left me."

"Probably hated to, if I know my brother. You were the only reason why he stuck around so long in the first place."

An aching knot formed in her throat. "So how do I find him again?"

He shrugged. "Your guess is as good as mine. I doubt I'll hear from him again for months."

She didn't want to wait months. She wanted him back now. She wanted to pull him into her arms and comfort him for his awful life, and let him know that she loved him and things would be different from now on. But he wouldn't even return her calls.

She needed to find a way to get his attention. To make him come back to her. If she got him in front of her, she could let him know that she didn't care what Grant thought, or if his parents were awful people. If he'd gone to prison.

She just wanted to love him and be loved in return.

"By the way," Jericho said. "Don't tell him you talked to me or he'll think I betrayed him, and then I won't hear from him for years."

"I won't say a thing," Elise promised.

That night Elise took over one of the guest bathrooms on the second floor of Emily's bed-and-breakfast. She sealed the doorframe with painter's tape, set up a folding table over the toilet, and screwed a red lightbulb into the light socket. She set out her trays of processing chemicals and her tongs, and set up her enlarger on one end of the sink. She'd put her film into a developing tank overnight and was ready to process the negatives. As she pulled out the newly cut strips, she held them up to the red light, admiring her work.

Rome was stunning. She picked one negative in particular, slid it into the enlarger, and then flicked the light off so she could set up the photo paper. Using her hands in the dark, she set up everything, flicked the enlarger on to stamp the image onto the paper, and then flicked it off again. She turned the red light back on, then dropped her photo paper into the developer bath, waiting for the image to come up.

When it did, she sucked in a breath, watching Rome stare out at her from the photo. She quickly drained the developer off the photo and then dropped it into the stop bath, admiring it as she agitated the photo with her tongs.

It was one of the best pictures she'd ever done. It was a head shot of Rome, looking over his shoulder at her. Candlelight bounced off his gleaming skin, and his face was half hidden in shadow, but those blue eyes stared out at her from long lashes, and his lip ring curved over one full lip.

The look in his eyes was sultry and full of heat. Desire. Good lord, how had she ever been unsure that this man wanted her? He was practically making love to her camera. Just seeing the expression on his face made her sigh with pleasure.

She pulled the paper from the stop bath, gave it a dunk in the fixer, and then washed the print and hung it to dry on a small cord she'd strung from one end of the curtain rod to a nearby towel rack.

These pictures were incredible, and she'd never felt more proud of her work, or more in love with Rome. How could this beautiful, wonderful, sexy man think she didn't want him?

The next morning she retrieved her stack of dried photos from her makeshift darkroom and began to scan them into her computer. On a whim, she sent one to Crissy with just the email title of *What do you think?*

An email popped into her box a moment later.

YES YES YES!!! Crissy sent back. I love it! Look at that smoldering face! That is exactly what I wanted to see in your photos.

Good job, girl! They're not right for *City Girl*, but I know a friend who works at a tattoo magazine who would die for something like these. You interested?

Elise considered it. She considered it for a good long moment. These pictures were great, and not just in her own biased opinion. They oozed personality and lust. They could get her in the door for a couple of magazine spreads, and with a few professional pieces under her wing, she'd have her "in" for other magazines.

But when she wrote back, she said,

No, thank you. I just wanted to see if I was on the right track.

Actually, she'd known she was on the right track. She just wanted that validation from someone else. More than that, she wanted that other avenue open.

Because she wanted to know what she'd really, truly decide if she had all options open to her.

And she wanted to stay here. She liked the quiet lifestyle of the small town. She liked the idea of opening her own studio here, amongst family and friends. She liked the thought of taking photos of regular people and showing them a side they never saw. Elise knew herself pretty well, and she knew that she liked the idea of living in New York City and working for a magazine more than the reality of it. The reality would mean long hours, lots of travel, and low pay. It would mean living in a city that crawled with people who were used to a city that never really allowed anyone to be alone.

And that wasn't her.

Smiling, she hit "send" on the email, feeling good about her decision. Maybe she'd go walk a few blocks in the morning and check out the tiny storefront to see what she'd need to make it a real business.

It'd keep her distracted while she waited—and hoped—for Rome to answer her messages.

SIXTEEN

A week later, Elise was curled up on one of the couches in the main lodge, hugging a pillow and watching Brenna flick through one of Miranda's wedding magazines with an expression of horror on her face. "These are awful," she leaned over and whispered to Elise, pointing at a pink taffeta floor-length creation. "She looks like she's going to the world's gaudiest prom."

Elise grinned. "I thought you wanted your colors to be pink and orange?"

"I really don't want any colors," Brenna murmured, ripping the page out of the book and then crumpling it into a ball and tossing it into the fireplace nearby. "It's your brother who's making me go through this farce."

"Hey," Miranda protested from across the room. She came storming over. "You said you wanted to borrow a magazine, you doofus. You didn't say you'd be defacing them!"

"Trust me, I'm doing the world a favor with that one!"

"Bren," Miranda huffed, wrestling the thick magazine

out of her friend's arms. "I have to return that to the library. You can't tear pages out of it, you nut."

Grumbling, Brenna let Miranda have the magazine. She lay back on the couch and flopped dramatically, then looked over at Elise. "Why aren't you doing something exciting tonight? It's Saturday night. You should go out, get drunk, and get laid."

"Brenna, please," Grant called from his desk. He was still working, despite the fact that it was the weekend. "That's my sister you're talking to. Let's not encourage anything of the sort, all right?"

Elise smiled at the face Brenna made at Grant. "I thought I'd hang around and see how Beth Ann and Colt are." She looked over as Miranda curled up on one of the big leather couches opposite them, magazine in hand. Miranda's fiancé, Dane, had gone to pick up the couple from the airport. "Should we order food?"

"I'm picking up pizzas as soon as they get here," Grant called again, still listening in to their conversation. "Their plane was delayed, so we don't know what time they're getting back."

"Where's Pop?" Miranda asked, glancing up from the magazine.

"Um," Brenna said. "I might have left an ATV out in the woods with a flat. He went to go fix it."

"Brenna," Grant warned.

"What? Oh, come on, baby. You saw how anxious he was about Colt and Beth Ann getting back. The man needed something to do." She winked at Elise. "Plus, sabotage is fun."

Miranda cocked her head, listening. "I think they're here."

Brenna bounded up from the couch and went to the window, peering through the blinds. "Ooh, yup, they are! Yay!"

Everyone got to their feet, waiting for the newcomers to enter the lodge. Dane was first, grinning. "Guess who I found hanging out at the airport?"

He moved aside.

A smiling, rosy-faced Beth Ann entered the lodge, dressed in a heavy cable-knit sweater, jeans, and boots. Her long blond hair was pulled into two braids that hung over her shoulder, and she looked happy but exhausted. Behind her, Colt came in, a thick growth of hair on his chin and his normally short hair shaggy under his knit cap.

Brenna squealed. "Oh wow. You both went full mountain man!"

"Thanks, honey," Beth Ann drawled, but went forward to hug Brenna. "It's good to see you, too."

Hugs and handshakes were exchanged, and to Elise's surprise, she got a hug from Beth Ann as well. The woman was still beautiful, despite having dirty braids, a face devoid of makeup, and wind-chapped cheeks. They sat down on one of the couches and Brenna retrieved beers from the fridge while Grant went out to grab pizzas.

Colt's hand immediately went to Beth Ann's knee, possessive. "So." He glanced at Miranda and Dane, who took over the couch Elise had been sitting on. She moved to a nearby chair and took a beer from Brenna as she passed them out. "What'd we miss?" Colt asked.

"Nope," Miranda said. "We get to ask you guys about your trip first. How was Alaska?"

"Cold," Beth Ann said, putting her fingers on her cheeks. "This place feels like an oven right now. A warm, delicious oven. It was fun, though."

"Did you learn a lot about the outdoors?" Miranda asked.

Beth Ann's cheeks flamed even brighter. "Some."

"We spent our time well," Colt drawled. "Not much of it outdoors, though."

"Ew," said Miranda. "Tell me no more or I'm going to have all kinds of disturbing visuals."

Dane grinned and pulled his fiancée closer to him. "I keep telling Mir that we need to go up to the cabin for our honeymoon, but she keeps telling me no."

She poked Dane in the ribs. "If I want to rough it, all I have to do is go home, Mister I Don't Like Electricity."

He leaned over and kissed the top of her head. "True."

Colt gave Beth Ann another devouring look and then began to talk about their vacation, and Elise felt her heart squeeze. She was surrounded by all kinds of happy couples and here she was, alone.

Beth Ann and Colt chatted about Alaska for a while, and Pop eventually made it in to greet his son and daughter-in-law with bear hugs, and Grant came back with pizza, and they all ate and drank beer. It was a fun, cozy little impromptu party.

"I'm surprised you're still here," Beth Ann said to Elise with a smile. "Not that I'm not happy to see you."

"I'm actually going to rent a storefront on Main Street," Elise told her. "Set up my own photography studio nearby so we can do our pinup shoots."

Beth Ann gave a girlish squeal of excitement. "That's wonderful! I kept thinking about doing pinups as a business when we were on our honeymoon. I loved the shots we did and I think it'd be so fun to do more!"

Elise smiled. "Me too."

Colt glanced around. "So, am I missing something here? Where's the new guy?"

Miranda shot Elise an uncomfortable look.

Her face flushed hot. Rome. So even Colt had noticed he was missing. She got up and headed to the kitchen to avoid a painful conversation, even as she heard Brenna casually say, "Oh, he bailed on us. Grant was being a dick."

"Oh no," Beth Ann murmured.

Oh yes, Elise wanted to say, but she kept heading firmly toward the sanctuary of the kitchen. Once there, she began to clean up, throwing away paper plates and rinsing out beer bottles for recycling. Sadness threatened to overwhelm her. If it weren't for everyone thinking that she needed protecting from the world, Rome would be here. Why did everyone think she was so fragile that she couldn't make decisions on her own? Why did they have to run off a man who desperately needed a home and a place to call his own, and a family of his own?

Rome was lonely. She knew that now that she'd talked to Jericho and put all the pieces together. He'd had no one and nothing he could depend on, and Grant had made him leave it all behind again. Frustration at her brother welled up and she closed her eyes, willing herself to calm down.

The truth was, she was filled with envy.

Three couples were out in the living room, laughing and talking and leaning on each other, having a great time. They'd each go home tonight and cuddle in the other person's arms, content in their love and the fact that life was wonderful and secure.

Meanwhile, Elise would go home to an empty bed and Rome would be . . . she didn't know. Wherever he could find a roof over his head.

Heart aching, she pulled out her phone and checked it for the millionth time. No messages. Are you there? she sent. I miss you and I want to talk to you. It's so important. Please.

He didn't respond. He never did. It was like he'd taken his word to Grant at heart. After that wonderful weekend in Galveston, he'd cut all ties with her. She'd even tried calling him from Brenna's phone, just to see if he'd answer it. But he didn't. Rome had truly left everyone in Bluebonnet behind for good.

Elise had to think of a way to get him to respond. Somehow.

In the next week that passed, she kept herself busy so as not to feel the aching loneliness and hurt of Rome's abandonment. Did he miss her like she missed him? Sometimes she wondered. If it was so easy for him to cut her off and cease all communication with her, maybe she'd misread things entirely. She didn't know what to do.

So, she worked.

Upon Grant's suggestion, she moved temporarily into the extra cabin at the ranch. She'd have to vacate it in a month or so when they found a new instructor to take Rome's spot, but until then, Grant explained, she could live there rent-free and not have to worry about living quarters while she set up her business. She spent her time cashing out some money from her savings, purchasing equipment and furniture for her storefront, and renovating the inside of the small building. She had a sign made and purchased advertisements in local newspapers to run in a few weeks, and took photos. When she wasn't taking photos, she was printing them, framing them, and hanging them on the wall to display to customers. In the window, she'd put one of Brenna's playful pinup photos, and one of the engagement shots that she'd finally gotten done. Both Grant and Brenna were laughing in the picture and looked so incredibly adorable. She'd also done photos of Beth Ann and Colt and then Miranda and Dane, all free of charge as long as she got to hang them on her shop wall.

And she checked her phone every thirty seconds, hoping with each buzz that it was Rome. That he was looking for her because he was coming home and coming back to her.

But it was never him.

"I don't know what to do," she confessed to Beth Ann, Miranda, and Brenna over breakfast. They all sat at the big kitchen table at the Daughtry Ranch, ready to head out for a day of painting. Miranda had liked the new paint job on Elise's little studio so much that she wanted to paint the kids' books section of the library to make it more inviting, so the girls had volunteered to help out. It'd be fun with a few friends, and Elise had been looking forward to it . . .

Except she was getting desperate to hear back from Rome. She'd dreamed about him last night, terrible dreams of abandonment and prison, and she'd woken up with her heart pounding and tears in her eyes . . . and in a foul mood.

"And you tried calling?" Miranda asked. "What about email?"

"Daily calls," Elise said. "It sounds psychotic, I know. The longer he ignores me, the more I wonder if it *was* all in my head how things were between us."

"Nope," Brenna said, pointing a cereal spoon at Elise. "I saw the way he looked at you. It was like how Grant looks at me. Or like how Dane looks at, you know, anything vaguely muddy and camping related."

Miranda snorted. "Thanks."

"Honey, I don't know what happened, but maybe he doesn't want you to contact him because he wants to move on?" Beth Ann suggested in a gentle voice.

She'd thought about that, too, and discarded the idea. "But he wants to move on for the wrong reasons," Elise protested. "Doesn't he at least deserve to give 'us' another chance if he knows the truth?"

Miranda patted her hand sympathetically. "You would think so, wouldn't you?"

"Well, there's one way to make a man come running," Beth Ann mused. "The 'p' word."

The table was quiet for a moment.

"Perpes?" Brenna asked, all fake innocence. Miranda snorted another laugh.

Beth Ann gave Brenna a quelling look. "Pregnancy."

"Lie to him?" Elise choked on the words, thinking of Rome's reaction. "Won't he be furious?"

"He will be until you confess the truth and then give him a chance to correct the situation," Brenna said with a wink. "You know, tell him he can *really* make you pregnant."

"It sounds like a terrible plan," Elise murmured, wiping her mouth with a napkin, no longer hungry. She wasn't pregnant. She'd gotten her period just last week . . . but Rome wouldn't know that.

God, could she be that evil and lie to him just to flush him out? Would he forgive her?

Then again, what did she have to lose? If he grew mad and refused to talk to her again . . . she'd be exactly where she was.

Elise considered it all day. That night, lying in bed—Rome's bed, her mind noted—she picked up her phone, steeled herself, and texted him.

Rome nursed a bottle of beer in a shithole bar off the highway. He'd been at this shithole every night this week, mostly since the TV in his equally shitty motel room was broken, and the entire place smelled vaguely like musty sweat socks. Still, it was only twenty-two dollars a night, and since he was doing under-the-table construction for about forty dollars a day, he couldn't complain.

It was a living. Kind of.

A woman at the far end of the bar was giving him a few hot glances, but he ignored her. She looked nothing like Elise. He'd never had a type before, but now he could officially say that if he ever showed interest in another woman, she'd have to have long, silky brown hair that fell over one side of her face, and a shy gaze that made him feel like he was a fucking king instead of some asshole convict who couldn't get a real job outside of flipping burgers.

Then again, with the economy the way it was, he couldn't even get a job flipping burgers. Now he was having to compete with people with degrees and college students for that sort of thing. If you were going to hire someone to prep your fries, did you want the guy with the bachelors in liberal arts, or the guy who served four years in Huntsville? It was a no brainer, and he'd had no luck finding a job—any job—for days.

He'd driven his motorcycle aimlessly through a few towns, looking for a cheap motel and any place that seemed to be hiring . . . and ran across a bunch of guys standing around in front of a corner store early one morning. He recognized that kind of grouping. All the people who couldn't get hired at normal, decent-earning jobs? They stood in front of a corner store and waited for someone to come by and offer a low-paying, back-breaking crap job that would offer money under the table and off the records. It was horrible work and it paid shit.

But it was work.

The next morning, Rome had stood with the guys and they'd gotten work, all right. Some rich bigwig building himself a lake house wanted construction on the cheap, so Rome found himself hauling lumber across the site, moving stonework to lay a ridiculous quartz-stone walkway to the gazebo, and returning to his shit motel room every night, exhausted. He'd eat something off the dollar menu at the nearest drive-thru, shower, and then collapse into bed.

Rome had done this sort of lifestyle before. Hell, he'd done it for two years before passing through Bluebonnet. He told himself he could do it again, but for some reason . . . it was different now.

Now, it felt like torture.

He knew what he was missing now. He knew what it was like to have a job with decent friends (well, excepting Grant) and buddies who weren't looking at you wondering if you were going to somehow score them their next hit. To have his own roof over his head and a place where he belonged and could earn a decent wage.

He knew what it was like to wake up next to a woman you couldn't get enough of, a woman who adored you back, and hold her close. To kiss her and make love to her and think that maybe, just maybe, the world held a little hope after all.

Rome shook his head and took another long pull on his beer. Now he was just getting all maudlin.

His phone buzzed and he internally winced. The only person who texted him was Elise.

He'd thought—hoped, really—that once he left, she'd be hurt enough to internalize his leaving for a few weeks. That'd give him enough time to make the mental break, he hoped, and not feel every day like he was the world's biggest douche bag.

But she texted him every day, wanting to talk to him. Wanting to know if he was okay. Just wanting him, in general.

And part of him was upset that she didn't seem to be paying attention to his grand plan of "love her and leave her." She didn't seem to realize that he'd dumped her for her own good, because she constantly called, just trying to reach out to him.

The other part of him secretly liked that she hadn't given up on him. So many people often did. Even though he never answered her, it made him feel a little better inside to know that she was out there, waiting for him.

Which was shitty of him, of course. He'd set her free to find someone new. Someone better than him. Someone she deserved. His hand clenched tight on his beer bottle. Not that he wanted any asshole touching her . . . other than him.

Yeah, he was pretty messed up.

He didn't pick up his phone to read the message, though. He delayed checking it, so when he got back to his place— his decrepit motel room—he could savor it, mentally imagining her beautiful mouth forming the words. Just thinking about her, and knowing she was out there thinking about him, made his chest ache all over again. Damn it, he missed her.

For the first time in years, he hadn't felt lonely when he was with her. He hadn't felt completely, utterly adrift. She'd accepted him for being nothing more than a broke, tattooed and pierced guy that rode a beat-up Harley, and she'd loved him. For a moment, he was fiercely glad that he'd never given Grant Markham an excuse to tell Elise who he really was. He didn't want to see that love in her eyes flicker out and fade as soon as she realized he was an ex-con.

So Rome finished his beer, paid his tab, and headed out. He swung a leg over his bike, and hesitated. His phone pressed against him in his back pocket, reminding him of the text waiting for him. It called to him. Unable to wait, he pulled his phone out and clicked on the screen, her message lighting up.

I'm pregnant.

Fierce joy shot through him, followed by a gut-wrenching twist of horror. Oh god.

He'd ruined her life.

Shoving his phone into his jacket pocket, Rome turned his bike onto the highway, heading in the opposite direction of his hotel and straight toward the tiny town of Bluebonnet.

SEVENTEEN

A few hours later, Rome pulled into the parking lot of the bed-and-breakfast. It was past midnight, and the lights were off. He didn't care. He needed to talk to Elise, and she deserved more than a text. He'd been going over everything in his mind.

Somehow, some way, he'd make this right for her . . . no matter what she decided. He'd support her no matter what, even if her answer was just to slap him across the face.

The door to the bed-and-breakfast was locked, and for a moment, Rome was confounded. Why was he locked out? Emily never locked the damn place. He hammered on the door, then held his finger down on the doorbell. He was not waiting until morning to talk to Elise.

A minute later, a light came on. Rome heard footsteps coming up to the door, and his entire body tensed, waiting.

He wasn't prepared to see his brother Jericho standing there in the doorway with a sleepy look on his face, dressed in nothing but a pair of flannel boxers and a white T-shirt.

J gave him a tired smile. "Hey, man. You need a room?"

"Who is it?" A voice behind Jericho called, and a second later, a tousled Emily came to his side, pulling her robe closed. She looked surprised to see Rome, and then her face turned crimson as she touched a hand to her messy hair. "Oh, hi."

All right, clearly his brother was hooking up with cute Emily. He'd figure that out . . . later. Right now all that mattered was Elise. "I need to talk to Elise. Can you wake her up and let her know that I'm here?"

Emily gave him a confused look, yawning. "She's not here anymore."

His heart stopped for a second. Had she gone back home to her parents? Had he somehow missed that text? Was there no chance of seeing her tonight? "She's not?"

"Nope. Right now I'm guest-free." She looked up at Jericho and her cheeks pinked all over again. "Um. Sort of. Anyhow." Her eyes focused on Rome. "She's living out at the Daughtry Ranch right now. Something about a spare cabin."

A grin shot over his face. "Great. Thanks." He turned and hustled down the stairs.

"See ya, bro," Jericho drawled, a laugh in his voice. "Don't forget to write."

He shot his brother the finger as he hauled ass back onto his bike.

Elise was still in town.

Actually, she was sleeping in his old bed. The thought made him hard, and he quelled it, turning his bike onto the farm road that led to the Daughtry Ranch. Now was not the time to have a fucking boner. Now was the time to be thinking about babies and responsibilities and what the hell they were going to do.

His dick wasn't really listening, though. He stayed erect, picturing Elise, soft and sleepy and curled up in his blankets.

Rome turned his bike off before he pulled into the parking lot, rolling it just off the road and walking the rest of the way in. It was late, and if he roared in with it, the muffler would announce to everyone that he'd arrived, and he wanted to talk to Elise in private. One on one.

He walked to the line of cabins and headed toward his old one. For a moment, he wanted to peer into the window, but that would mark him as a perv, wouldn't it? Very carefully, he turned the doorknob, testing it.

Not locked. He carefully eased the door open and slipped in, then closed it behind him.

And gazed down at the woman sleeping in the bed.

She was wearing an old T-shirt to sleep in, her long hair spilling across the pillows. And she looked so achingly beautiful that his heart hurt. He moved to the bed, watching her sleep for a moment longer, and then crouched next to the side of the bed and brushed his fingers over her cheek. In the sliver of moonlight let in by the curtains, her cheek was perfect.

Hell, what was he saying? She was always perfect in his eyes. Always.

Elise started awake, her gaze automatically turning to him. Her eyes were unfocused, and then a smile blossomed across her face as she realized who he was.

"Hey, baby," he whispered, his voice aching with want. God, he wanted this woman. Not just for sex, but to be his, forever.

"Rome," she breathed, sitting up. To his surprise, she immediately reached for him and pulled his face toward hers. Her lips descended on his and she began to kiss him hungrily.

His shock abated a moment later and he kissed her back, his tongue sweeping into her mouth as if he'd never left her. As if the weeks of depression and self-loathing for ignoring her were forgotten. His Elise was kissing him, and the world was perfect in that moment.

His hands dug into her hair and he held her against him, his mouth working hers over as he gave her every ounce of his passion and longing. His tongue slicked against hers over and over again, and she made a soft mewing sound of appreciation that made his dick even harder. She was so very sexy, even freshly woken from sleep.

"Rome," she breathed between kisses. "Oh, Rome. You came back. I'm so glad."

He reluctantly pulled his mouth from hers, though he was unable to resist sucking on her lower lip one last time. Then he sighed. "God, I missed you."

"I missed you, too," she said softly. "Why'd you leave me like that?"

"I'm just . . . I'm wrong for you. It's a shit answer, I know. I thought it'd hurt less if I just up and left." He'd been wrong, though. He'd ached over it every hour of every day, even when trying to lose himself in mindless work.

"You really, really hurt me," she said, her hands covering his where they cupped her face. Tears spilled out of her eyes. "I didn't know if I was just imagining how things were between us, or if you really cared for me after all."

He felt like the lowest man on earth for making her cry. "Me leaving has nothing to do with how I feel about you. It was all me." He leaned in and kissed her mouth tenderly again. "I'm so sorry for hurting you, baby. But I'm here now, and we're going to make things right, okay?"

The look on her face became guarded, uneasy.

He hated that. He hated that she felt wary around him. Like she didn't know if she could trust him. He didn't blame her—he'd run off on her, hadn't he? Like a fucking dirtbag.

"Rome—"

"Shh," he told her, kissing her sweet mouth again. And again. He could kiss her for days and never get tired. "I just want you to know that whatever you decide, I support you. I'm here for you from now on." He didn't tell her that he wanted it, though he hoped she'd choose to have it with him. To have a family with him.

She closed her eyes as if in pain.

"I'll get a job somewhere. Anywhere. I'll make money for you and the kid. I promise. You can count on me. I know that sounds ridiculous, considering what just happened, but I want you to know that I'm serious about this."

She licked her lips, opened her eyes, and sighed.

"I'm not pregnant, Rome."

The breath whistled out of his lungs. He stared at her. "You . . . lost it? Already?" Was that why she looked so unhappy?

"No." Her fingers brushed his, trying to soothe him. "I was never pregnant. I said it so you would come back and we could talk. I'm sorry."

She *what*?

He jerked away from her, getting to his feet. Anger surged, mixed with relief and confusion. He ran a hand over his skullcap of hair, trying to get a handle on his mind, and paced.

"God damn it, Elise, that is a hell of a lie." The shock was beginning to settle in to him and he glared at her. "How could you do that to me? I've been in a panic all night, thinking I ruined your life!"

"I know," she said, pressing her palms to her forehead and looking just as distraught as him. "I know it was an awful thing to do, but I didn't know how else to get you back here so we could talk about you and me!"

"You and me?" Ah hell. If there was no baby, he had no excuse to be around her at all. "There can't be a you and me, Elise. You need to give up and find someone better than me."

She smacked a fist into the bedding. "Stop saying that, Rome! I'm so sick of hearing you talk down about yourself."

"This is a hell of a joke to play on a man, Elise." He shook his head and began to head for the door again.

"No!" she said in a panicked voice, and to his surprise, she barreled past him to press her body against the door of her cabin. "You're not leaving until we talk."

He looked down at her, at the tangles spilling over her shoulders, her breasts heaving under the thin material of the T-shirt, nipples pressing against the fabric. He could barely see a glimpse of bright pink panties. His cock reacted to her nearness again, and he forced himself to ignore it. "I don't want to talk to you if you're just going to try and manipulate me. I can't stand that."

"Because people do that to you all the time, don't they?" She gasped, a hand flying to her mouth. "Oh shit. I've made this worse, haven't I? God, I am so stupid!"

He shook his head. "Stop that. Elise, just let me leave, okay? Clearly this was a bad idea."

"No," she said, clinging to his shirt and blocking his way to the door. "I'm not going to be sorry, because it got you here with me, okay? You're just going to have to suck it up and deal."

He gave her a look of surprise. Tough love coming out of his sweet, giving Elise? That was a new one. "That was a shitty thing you did."

"And it was shitty of you to abandon me and ignore all my calls, so now we're even."

To his surprise, he found himself smiling down at her. His shy Elise was standing up to him and giving him lip? That was so . . . sexy.

She stared up at him, her gaze serious. "Rome . . . I know about your past."

Sickness churned in his gut, but he somehow managed a half-grimace that he hoped looked like a smile. "Guess it had to come out at some point."

She said nothing, simply watched him with shining eyes.

He jerked away, turning and pacing across the room.

Great. Just when he thought things couldn't get more fucked-up. "How did you find out? You run a background check on me or something?" So much for trust.

Elise leaned against the door. "Actually, my brother did. And he showed it to me."

"Figures," he murmured. Should have known. Grant had been waiting to nail him with the information after all. Rome paced, staring at the floor, at the wall, anywhere except at her. He couldn't look at her. Not right now.

God damn it, he felt embarrassed. Why had she called him back here? So she could rub it in his face?

"You should have told me."

He laughed at that, shaking his head. "It's not something you ease into a conversation. Hey, how are you doing? Did you know I served four years in Huntsville? Gee, hope this doesn't change your opinion of me." His voice was sarcastic, bitter.

"I wasn't trying to pry," she said quietly. "I only found out because I wasn't sure why you . . . abandoned me." He hated to hear the wobble in her voice. "Grant wanted me to understand . . . the bigger picture." She took a deep, shaky breath. "He's been trying to convince me that you're not right for me, and that you're dangerous, but I just keep telling him that I love you and your past doesn't matter to me."

He stilled. She still loved him? "Elise—"

"I know what you're going to say," she interrupted. "That you aren't good enough for me and that same old song and dance you constantly trot out all the time. I know you went to prison for four years. I know your credit's shit. I know you have a record. And I know on paper it looks really, really bad." She paused, and then added softly, "And I know none of that is you. Never has been. Never will be. You're not a dealer or a scam artist. You're just one person, very alone, trying to find a place in the world. And I know what that's like."

Rome stared at the wall, unable to turn around and look

at her. His eyes were burning rather suspiciously, but he blinked rapidly to quell any tears. He was a man, damn it. He didn't fucking cry.

Especially not when a girl told him that she believed in him. That the worst about him wasn't true.

No one ever believed in him. They just took one look at his appearance, at his record, and they assumed the worst. That Rome Lozada, aka John Lozada the third, was exactly the shitbird that showed on paper.

"Elise," he said, and hated how hoarse his voice was.

Her arms went around him from behind, locking around his torso, and he felt her cheek press against his back. "I never thought it was you. Not for an instant. And when I talked to Jericho—"

"God damn it, I knew it—" he began.

"Hush," she said with a light smack to his chest that surprised him and amused him at the same time. "I refused to take no for an answer. He can't be blamed. But he did tell me about . . . your family. And your childhood. And your mother, and that you took the fall for her. It just confirmed everything I knew about you. That you're a good guy who came from mixed-up people who tried to drag you down. And you're trying to rebuild yourself into someone new."

He swallowed hard.

Her hands continued to caress him, wrapped around him, her cheek pillowed on his upper back. "Just because I'm shy doesn't mean I don't know what I want, Rome. When I told you I loved you, I meant it. It's never changed."

His throat ached. "You deserve better than me."

"You and I both know that's not true," she murmured, her hands gliding up and down his chest, as if she couldn't get enough of touching him. It was strangely intimate to have her behind him, caressing him, when he couldn't see her face, couldn't know what she was thinking. "How could I possibly deserve better than a man who is sexy, kind, patient, wonderful, and makes a scarred virgin with lopsided shoulders feel like she's the most beautiful woman in the world when she's with him?"

Rome groaned and turned around in her grasp, cupping her face in his hands. He stared down into her shining eyes, so full of love and trust, and his heart ached all over again. Very slowly, very tenderly, he leaned in and kissed the tip of her nose. "How can I not think you're the most beautiful woman in the world when you are to me?"

She blinked rapidly, and he realized some of the shine in her eyes was tears. "You've always seen *me*, Rome. You don't know how rare that is. How can I *not* see you? How can I not love you with all my heart?"

"God, I love you so much," he said to her, and leaned in and gently kissed her mouth. "So, so much. I wanted to tell you how I felt, but that would have been so shitty of me when I was planning on leaving."

She kissed him back frantically, her mouth as urgent as his. "Why go, though? Why abandon me?"

"Grant wanted me to leave you alone," he said between hot, fierce kisses. Exultation poured through him as her mouth softened under his, welcoming his touch, and her hands dragged at his clothing, as if she wanted him naked. "It was either push you away or go. So I left."

"But you still pushed me away," she told him breathlessly, her hands moving to his belt buckle and undoing it. "Don't you understand? You still hurt me. Also, I'm going to kill my brother."

"You can't be mad at him," Rome said, burying his hands in her silky tangles—god, he loved her hair—and tilting her head so he could slick his tongue against her ear. "He was just looking out for you like a good brother. I'm not mad at him. If you were my sister, I'd have done the same."

"If I were your sister, I wouldn't be about to shove my hand down the front of your pants," she murmured breathlessly, and then did exactly that. "So let's not talk about family anymore."

Her hand wrapped around his dick and squeezed, and he groaned. That felt amazing.

"Come to bed," she told him softly. And she began to step backward, toward the bed.

Well, considering she had her hands around his cock, he'd follow her anywhere. He tore off his shirt as he headed toward bed with her, loving the soft little sound of pleasure she made as he bared his chest.

As they got to the bed, she gave his cock another squeeze and then moved her hands out of his pants and began to tug them down his legs. "I have condoms," she told him. "I bought them when I first asked you out." She gave him a shy little smile. "I'm so glad I did, too."

"I'm glad you did, too," he admitted. "I didn't bring any with me. I didn't picture . . . this. Not any of this." It was more than he'd dreamed of, to be honest. To know that Elise knew all of him and still loved him? He felt like the luckiest son of a bitch ever.

She grinned up at him and patted his leg. "Then you undress and I'll get the condoms."

"Yes, ma'am," he told her, shucking his pants and watching her walk to the bathroom. There was a sexy roll to her hips as she walked, and he wondered how he'd never seen it before.

Everything Elise Markham did was sexy. She even slept sexy. Damn, he was *lucky*.

She returned a moment later and held up the condoms, just as he slipped under the blankets, naked. "Found them."

"Then get over here," he told her, opening his arms.

A brilliant smile crossed her face and she looked so beautiful in the moonlight. She moved to his side of the bed and slid under the blankets next to him, her leg hitching around his naked hip.

He pulled her close and began to kiss her again, his mouth feverishly working hers with hot, nipping kisses. His hands tugged at her shirt, dragging it up and exposing her breasts.

Hot, delicious little whimpers escaped her throat as he kissed her, and her hands clawed at him, urgent in their need. Her mouth opened under his, hot, wet, and demanding.

Rome dragged her hips over his, his hands clasping her ass and spreading her legs so she straddled him. Then he pressed up against her sex with a push of his hips, and loved her moan of response. Her shirt was getting in the way, so he pushed it higher. He thumbed both tiny nipples, then took the closest one in his mouth, sucking on it.

She gasped and her hips bore down on his cock, and she gave a fluid little roll that rubbed her pussy down his length.

He groaned, teasing the nipple in his mouth even as he pulled at the waistband of her panties. He wanted her naked, wanted to feel that slick heat against his cock.

She rolled off to the side then, tugging her panties off with a speed that shocked him, and then dragged her shirt over her head. Then she was naked, all stretched out and glorious next to him, and he moved, pushing her down on the bed and covering her delectable body with his heavier one.

"Gimme that condom," he told her, then kissed her mouth again.

"I want to be inside you."

She moaned. "I want you inside me, too."

He took the condom from her and sat up, opening the package and quickly rolling the sheath down his cock. He tossed the wrapper on the ground and then fell over her again, kissing her hungrily. He had to make sure she was ready for him, though. His hand reached between her legs and he brushed his fingers over the folds of her pussy. She was already wet for him. "Damn, Elise. How do you get so wet so fast?"

"Your mouth," she said, pressing kisses to his jaw. "Your touch. Everything. You make me wet."

"I love you," he told her again, and pressed his length between her thighs. He dragged his cock up and down her slickness, lubricating it. "Love the way you're always so ready for me. Love the way you look up at me. Love the way you feel when you're around me."

"I love you, too," she said softly, and her fingertips danced over his mouth. "You make me so happy."

He kissed her again, even as he hitched her legs around his hips. Rome positioned his cock at her entrance, and then thrust deep.

She arched off the bed, her breath shuddering. "Oh, yes. Oh, I missed you, Rome."

He'd missed her, too. Missed her sweet body, her lovely smile, her shining eyes. He took her mouth again, even as he began to thrust into her, each stroke pounding into the tight clasp of her pussy. This wasn't going to be a long, tender seduction. This was a claiming, and he was staking his claim on Elise. She was his.

Her hips rose to meet his furiously, and she panted with each stroke. "Yes," she told him each time he pushed deep. "Yes, yes."

He reached between them and placed his thumb over her clit, her movements making friction in her most sensitive of places.

Her cries became louder, and his mouth covered hers, swallowing her shrill cries of "Yes, yes!" as he pumped into her fiercely, claiming her for his own. As soon as he felt her begin to spasm around him with her own orgasm, and felt her grow even wetter than before, he came, groaning her name and his love for her into her ear.

Some time later, they snuggled in bed together, fingers lacing as they talked. Her head rested on his chest, and Rome could honestly say he'd never been so content in his life.

"You should have told me," she murmured, tracing circles on his chest with her fingertip. "I showed you my scars. You should have showed me yours."

He sighed, holding her close. "It's just . . . hard for me to trust people."

"No, really?" she teased. "Tell me what that's like."

He tickled her sides and she squirmed, laughing. "I'm serious. I guess you get screwed over so many times, you just start expecting everyone to think you're garbage just because of who you are." He shrugged. "People hear 'ex-con' and their minds shut down. It doesn't matter who I am at that point, or even what I did. I'm a filthy animal who shouldn't be out on the streets."

She frowned. "So basically, people act like my brother."

"I still can't blame your brother," he said, stroking her soft skin. "He thought he was doing the best thing for his young, beautiful, incredibly naive little sister. I'd have hid you from me, too."

Elise made a face at him. "It doesn't mean he gets to try and take over both of our lives, you know. There's a difference between concerned and overbearing, and Grant needs to figure it out. He's way too protective, even when I don't need it. Part of it is his personal baggage, though. His ex-wife left him with a few issues." She kissed his skin. "We all have issues. It doesn't mean we get to use them as weapons."

"I don't care, as long as I have you and you want me."

"I always want you," Elise said, sliding a hand down his stomach to cup his now-at-rest cock. It stirred immediately at her touch, and she made a small noise of appreciation. "But don't you worry about my brother. I'll handle him."

"Why does that make me uneasy?"

Her hand stroked over his rapidly lengthening cock, teasing it to attention. "Because you've never seen me on the warpath?"

"I don't want to come between you and your brother,

baby," he told her. Actually, he didn't even want to think about her brother while she had her hand on his cock. "Let's just leave it alone, all right?"

"Nope. He was unfair to you and I'm going to make him see that," she said, and there was a stubborn note in her voice that made him sigh in frustration.

"And what if he gets your parents involved and they all come down against me? I don't want to get between you and your family."

Her fingertips traced the head of his cock in an absent motion that drove him absolutely wild. It took all of his control to not grab her hand, make a fist, and start fucking that tight warmth. "My parents?"

"Yeah. Aren't they going to mind that their sweet, innocent daughter is dating an ex-con?" Rome had had run-ins with parents before, and it always ended badly.

"They'll just be thrilled I'm dating someone. I don't know if you've noticed, but I've gone through a bit of a dry spell," she teased. "Anyhow, my mother is currently drowning her sorrows about me moving away in a shopping binge, but my father's ecstatic at my long-overdue independence. Most of all, they'll be happy that I'm happy. They love Brenna, after all, and she takes a bit of getting used to."

He rolled over in the bed, dragging her onto her back and pinning her underneath him. "You have an answer for everything, don't you?"

"I do," she said, her eyes shining as she looked up at him. "They'll see how happy you make me and they won't be able to help themselves. They'll adore you, just like I do."

He stilled. "Wait. Did you say you moved here permanently?"

She nodded up at him. "I bought a studio downtown. I'm going to do family photography and pinups."

"I thought you wanted to do magazine photos?" She'd talked about it a few times when they'd discussed her future.

Elise gave him a wry smile. "I thought so, too, until I sat

down and really thought about it. Then I realized I liked the dream more than the reality. Do you mind staying in Bluebonnet if I do?"

"I'll follow wherever you go," he vowed. "You just lead the way."

"I love you."

Rome leaned down and gently kissed her parted lips. "I love you, too. And . . . just to be clear. No baby?"

"No baby," she agreed. "Does that make you happy or sad?"

"A little bit of both, really. I'm relieved, but at the same time . . . I kind of didn't hate the idea." He pressed a kiss on her bow-shaped upper lip. "You?"

"I don't think I'm ready yet, but in a few years? I wouldn't mind starting a family. I think I'd like to have one with you."

He'd never given much thought to family, really. But little boys with her smile and little girls with that silky brown hair of hers? Ridiculous how pleasing the thought was. He'd never felt much for family in the past, but starting one with Elise?

Sounded pretty good to him.

The next morning, they showered together and, at Elise's urging, went to the main lodge to confront her brother. Rome was nervous, strangely enough. Once upon a time, it wouldn't have mattered what a guy like Grant thought of him. They'd rub along until things got too ugly, and Rome would leave.

Except . . . Rome was back. And Grant's opinion mattered because he was Elise's family. Even though Elise was full of positive words and affirmations that things would be fine, Rome wasn't so sure. He didn't see how someone like Grant could open up to someone like him and just be fine with the fact that his sister was dating Rome.

But Elise gave him another sweetly determined smile, and he found he couldn't refuse her anything.

When they entered the main lodge, Brenna was seated on the corner of Grant's desk, dressed in boxers and an old, ratty T-shirt. Grant was wearing what looked like an expensive sweater and leaning close to Brenna, and it was clear the two of them were whispering intently about something. They separated when he and Elise entered the lodge.

Grant stood.

Elise clasped Rome's hand in hers, squeezed it, and headed toward her brother. "Look who I found," she said casually.

"Welcome back," Grant said slowly, his face inscrutable.

Brenna launched herself off of Grant's desk, sprinting across the room with her arms wide. "Yay, it's Rome!" She flung herself onto him in a hug that surprised him. Rome gave Elise an amused look and awkwardly patted Brenna's back. "Hey, Bren."

She let him go and went to Elise's side, elbowing her. "Looks like the 'perpes' plan worked after all, huh?"

Elise flushed bright red.

"Perpes?" Rome asked.

"Yeah. Beth Ann suggested that Elise get your attention by telling you that she was pregnant. I suggested herpes, but that might have made you run in the other direction."

"Lovely," Grant said in a dry voice. "Why don't we all sit down and talk for a minute, okay?"

Brenna snapped her fingers. "I'll put on some coffee. Nobody move!" She bounded back to the kitchen.

Grant gave her retreating back a patient look and then gestured at the sofas by the massive lodge fireplace. "She's a little excited to see you again, Rome."

He'd bet she was the only one. He liked Brenna. She was offbeat, but incredibly friendly, and he suspected that he'd have never been hired if it weren't for her. "I'm happy to see her again, too."

"Rome and I wanted to talk to you this morning," Elise said in a firm voice. "About everything."

"Well, then." Grant headed toward the couches.

Elise gave his hand another little squeeze and followed her brother over to the sofas. She and Rome sat across from Grant, and they stared at each other uncomfortably.

"So," Grant said. He folded his hands in his lap and looked at them expectantly.

Rome had the odd feeling of a naughty child seated in front of a disapproving parent . . . which was rather ironic, given his upbringing.

But Elise sat forward on the sofa and gave Grant a direct look. "I want to ask you a few questions."

"Shoot."

"Before you found out about Rome's past, did you find him to be a bad worker?"

"Elise, honey," Rome began, reaching for her.

She shrugged him away. "No, I want to know the answer to this. Before you knew about Rome's past, did you find him to be a bad worker?"

Rome watched as Grant's jaw seemed to visibly clench. He relaxed when Brenna sashayed out of the kitchen holding a tray with four mugs of coffee on it, and began to place them in front of each person. "No, Rome wasn't a bad worker. He wasn't great, though."

Rome bit back his own frustration. Grant wasn't going to bend on his opinion of him. This was useless.

"Why is that?" Elise persisted.

"Well, you have to admit that he's not trained for the position," Grant began, taking a cup of coffee for himself. "I specifically told Brenna we needed someone with certifications and experience."

Elise waved a hand. "Ignoring that—was he a bad employee?"

Grant shot him a look. After a long moment, he answered. "No."

"Was he ever late? Rude? Demanding?"

"You mean other than when he totally abandoned his job on the day we opened the paintball course?"

"What Grant means to say is no," Brenna added help-fully, giving her fiancé a firm look. "And he knows that was his fault as much as anyone's." She leaned in, coffee cup in hand. "What my boo here isn't saying is that he was wrong."

"Brenna," Grant began.

"No, you were wrong," she continued. "Pop and Dane were just filling your ear yesterday about how much they missed having Rome around. They said he was a great worker, didn't they?"

Rome was surprised to hear that. He really liked both Pop and Dane. They were good guys. But he'd thought they'd turn against him like Grant had the moment they found out who he was. He began to relax a little. Maybe he'd made some friends here after all.

Elise looked over at him, beaming with pride and love.

"Anyhow, the others and I had a meeting and we agreed that if Rome came back, his job should be given back to him," Brenna announced, moving Grant's arm and sliding into his lap.

"What?" Grant asked. "When was this?"

"When you were busy, sweetie. We made a group busi-ness decision."

"A group decision? I'm the only one who works in this damn office," he grumbled.

She pinched his cheek. "You're so cute when you're grumpy." Brenna looked over at Rome. "He's sorry. He has control issues when it comes to people he cares about. We're working on the whole 'letting go' process, but he's still struggling."

Elise blinked and stifled a giggle, then put her hand on Rome's knee in a possessive gesture that he rather liked. "You mean he's finally acknowledging that he's an obses-sive control freak?"

"Hey now, when did this become about me?" Grant blus-tered, even as Brenna began to speak again.

"Oh, he's not really admitting it," Brenna continued. "But

he knows it's a problem. We're working on it. I took him skydiving. You should have seen his face—"

Grant clapped a hand over Brenna's mouth to silence her. He looked over at Rome and shook his head. "You sure you still want to work here? Nothing but a bunch of crazies around me."

Rome supposed that was pretty close to an apology. He smiled. "I'm good with crazies."

"Then . . ." Grant got an unfocused look on his face and he lowered his hand. "Brenna, quit licking me."

"I thought when you put things against my mouth, I was supposed to lick them," she said in a flirty voice.

Grant made a noise that could have been either embarrassment or frustration.

"Rome wants to tell you something about his incarceration," Elise said, looking at him with love in her eyes.

Grant and Brenna stopped playing around, and their attention swung back to him. "Oh?" Grant asked.

Rome shifted in his seat uncomfortably. He hadn't anticipated Elise bringing this up. "It's okay. They don't need to know."

"I want them to know the truth," she said steadily. She reached for his hand and squeezed it.

"It's going to sound like excuses."

"Not to anyone who knows you," she told him, and her love and support shone in her eyes. Damn. How could a man argue with that?

Rome sighed and began to unravel the story of his time in prison. His mother and father's penchant for drugs and illegal activity. His nomadic life. His mother's brush with the law and her request for Rome to take the hit. His time in prison.

When he finished, Grant said nothing, simply watched him.

Brenna gave him a sympathetic look. "God, reminds me of my mother. Don't you think?" She looked over at Grant.

He pulled Brenna close and hugged her, then rubbed her arm as if reassuring her. "Kinda does, yeah."

That surprised Rome. No judgment? No scoffing or accusations of lies? "You guys believe me?"

"Who *hasn't* been messed up by their parents?" Brenna said with a laugh. "Yours just sound shittier than most. I hope you wouldn't go to prison for her again, though."

Rome groaned and ducked his head, rubbing it. "Hell no. Learned my lesson, thanks."

Elise cleared her throat. "So Rome gets his job back with a raise?"

Grant's attention veered back to Elise. "What? Raise?"

"Baby, no, it's okay," Rome began.

"I think he gets a raise," Elise said in a firm voice. "You aren't paying him enough to live on. If you want him to make something of himself, how about you take a step in the right direction? You can't castigate a man for his past and then push him into a low-paying job that reinforces society's concept of who and what he is."

Rome was surprised at the ferocity in Elise's voice. Surprised . . . and proud. When she got her mind on something, there was no distracting her, was there? How had he ever walked away from her before?

"We could put it to a vote," Brenna singsonged.

Grant threw his hands up. "I give up. You two hash things out. Since Brenna hired him, she can re-hire him. I'm going to actually get some work done." He got to his feet, pressed a kiss on top of Brenna's head, and headed to his desk.

"And the cabin?" Elise pressed, unwilling to budge an inch.

"Aren't you in it at the moment?" Brenna asked.

"Yes, but it was his originally, and I want it to remain his," Elise said. "So he always has a place to call his own instead of being dependent on staying with me."

"In case you break up?" Brenna asked.

Rome leaned in and whispered against Elise's ear. "Not going to happen."

She smiled at him. "It's still yours."

Brenna shrugged. "Whatever you want."

"Good," Elise said. "He'll start again tomorrow, if that's what he wants." She looked over at Rome expectantly. "Are you okay with all of this?"

He rubbed his jaw. "Other than feeling a little awkward that my girlfriend got me my job back? Yeah."

"You're being run over roughshod by these two," Grant called from his desk. "Don't worry, though. You get used to the feeling eventually."

Elise just smiled.

Later that evening, when he was in bed with Elise, watching TV and thinking the world was sometimes a pretty perfect place, he got a text on his phone.

Rome pulled it off the nightstand as Elise yawned and snuggled closer. It was Jericho. So. Heard you were back for good.

Reaching an arm over Elise's head, Rome texted back. News travels fast around here.

Small towns.

True. Yeah, thought I'd set up shop long-term. Have a good thing here.

I met your girl.

So I heard.

She's cute. Determined little thing, too. Just wanted you to know that she had your back the entire time. She looked me right in the eye and told me she'd heard about your charges and knew it wasn't you, and wanted to know the real story. Kinda thought you should know so you can make sure that one doesn't get away.

Thanks, Rome texted back. She's pretty amazing.

Indeed. Later, bro. Lunch this week?

Sure.

Then he dropped the phone back on the nightstand and wrapped his arms around Elise.

She tucked her head against his shoulder sleepily, drowsy from their recent bout of lovemaking. "Everything okay?" she murmured.

"Everything's perfect," he whispered against her hair. "I love you."

She smiled, eyes closed. "Love you, too."

EPILOGUE

I just don't understand it," Pop said, scratching his head underneath his trucker cap. "Brenna's a smart girl. How the hell does she keep breaking so much stuff?"

"It's a mystery," Rome agreed, crossing his arms and leaning against the kitchen counter as Pop fiddled with the Keurig. "So . . . no coffee this morning?"

"Don't look like it," the elderly man said, and shook his head again. "Why that girl put a cup of sugar into the water reservoir, I don't know. She said she wanted her coffee sweetened when it comes out." He gave Rome an exasperated look. "If I didn't know better, I'd swear she was doing this on purpose to test me."

Or to keep you busy, Rome thought, but smiled to himself. It was the worst-kept secret at the Wilderness Survival Ranch that Pop wanted to feel needed, and the surest way for him to feel needed was for him to fix something. They were a small business, which meant that someone went around breaking things for him to fix. That was a task that normally fell to Brenna, and she relished the position.

Of course, that meant no coffee for anyone else this morning.

Rome glanced at his watch. "I've got an hour before the birthday party comes in for the paintball course. You want me to run into town and get some from the cafe?"

"Well, we ain't gonna be drinking out of this thing anytime soon," Pop said, pulling the top of the Keurig off. He snorted. "Sweetened coffee. Damn girl."

Grinning, Rome headed out of the kitchen and swung through the main lodge. Brenna was typing—however slowly—into a spreadsheet, and Grant was on the phone. Both Dane and Colt were out for overnight trips. "Making a coffee run. Anyone want anything?"

"Coffee would be fabulous," Brenna said with a mischievous look in his direction. "Get one for Grant, too."

He nodded, grabbed his keys off of the hook near the door, and headed out into the parking lot.

It was still early, but the day was misty and gray. Drizzle and fog seemed to be the order for the morning. On days like today, it made for shitty riding, so he kept his bike covered and borrowed Elise's new sport utility vehicle, which he'd been using to chauffeur her around town.

He'd driven her out to her studio earlier that morning—along with Beth Ann, since he was heading into town anyhow, and Colt would want his wife taken care of. Rome hopped into the car and texted Elise before he pulled out of the parking lot. Coffee run. Brenna broke the Keurig. You want one?

Yes, she sent back. Latte, extra shot of espresso! Thx! XOXO

XO, he sent back, then felt like a bit of a puss for doing so. Then didn't care.

Rome mused at how things had changed in the last two weeks. He'd returned to his job easily, and it hadn't been weird at all. Not even with Grant. Okay, it had been a little strange at first, waking up and crawling out of bed with Elise and then having to look her overprotective brother in the eye, but they were both moving past that. Dane and Colt had both been thrilled that Rome had returned, and Pop had taken him aside and hugged him. Pop, it seemed, had a son in prison and understood what Rome was going through.

He'd hugged the old man back, and tried not to cry like a fucking sissy.

Since coming back, life had been pretty much, well, perfect. His days were filled with work—good, honest work on the paintball course and helping Pop with odd jobs. He was more or less in charge of the paintball side of things, which meant making sure that everyone had paid before showing up on the course, checking safety equipment and waivers, fixing jammed guns in the middle of gameplay, refereeing battles when players wanted an arbitrator, and, of course, selling additional ammo on the spot when people ran out.

His nights were filled with Elise. Gorgeous, giving, smart, funny Elise. How he fucking loved that woman. He couldn't get enough of her. She was passionate in bed, and growing bolder every day. Out of bed she was just fun to be around, and incredibly thoughtful. There wasn't a moment when she didn't make him feel like the world's luckiest man, and now that they had declared to the world they were a couple, Elise was busy introducing him to everyone as her boyfriend. She'd dragged him over to have dinner with Emily—and Jericho, to his surprise. It seemed that his vagabond brother was also forming roots in Bluebonnet, and had his eye on the cheery divorcée who ran the bed-and-breakfast.

It was weird to have his brother around, but he was kinda getting used to it. They'd gone out for beers once after that. He'd gone out with Grant and the boys one night, too, and he'd felt like part of the crew.

He'd even met Elise's family. To his surprise, both Reggie and Justine Markham had met him with welcoming, open arms, and had doted on both him and Elise. They'd taken him out on the family boat and dragged them out for dinner at a white tablecloth kind of place once, which he'd endured only for Elise. But overall, they were pretty good people, and they hadn't made him feel like a filthy ex-con for touching their daughter. They seemed genuinely happy that Elise was happy.

Rome picked up a tray of coffees—and added an extra for Beth Ann, since he'd promised Colt to check up on her while he was out on a three-day survival run. He parked the car in front of the salon, dropped Beth Ann's coffee off, then headed down the street to bring Elise hers.

His steps slowed at the sight of two shiny, tricked-out Harleys parked in front of Elise's new studio. A tight sense of foreboding swept over him. *Oh no.*

His goddamn parents.

Rome peered into the storefront window, but he could see no one. God damn it. What were they saying to Elise? Were they trying to poison her mind against him? She wouldn't believe it, but she'd be distressed that they'd try. How had they found out he was seeing her?

Or worse, was this a shakedown? Were they demanding money from her? Rome never mentioned her money. He never wanted her to think he was with her because of it. He wouldn't care if she worked at a hot dog stand, as far as he was concerned. And he wanted to make his own money for a change. With the new wages that Grant was paying him, he had dreams of saving up. Maybe getting his own car in a year or so, and then they could start putting away and planning for the future.

Their future, together.

His parents weren't in his plans. Coffee in one hand, Rome carefully eased the door of Elise's shop open and stepped inside silently. No one had noticed him come in. He could hear voices talking in the back room that she'd converted to her office, and he edged closer so he could make out what they were saying.

"You must be doing really well for yourself," Rome heard his mother say in that disgusting, wheedling tone of hers.

He heard Elise murmur something polite, and he could picture her shy expression, hanging her head and letting her hair spill in front of her cheek like she did when she was nervous.

"Like we said," his father chimed in, "we're not trying to impose, but, well, times are hard. I'm sure if you talked to Rome, he'd agree to send us a bit of cash just to help out through the dry spell. Just a few thousand would really help get his mother back on her feet with her medical bills."

Rome stifled a groan. The "medical bills" excuse was one they'd trotted out to every relative who could be fleeced until they'd wised up to the Lozadas. He was pretty sure that between his parents, they'd "miraculously" recovered from cancer half a dozen times and pocketed every single dollar. He wanted to barge in before Elise could agree to anything. She had a soft heart where he was concerned.

"Yes," his mother was saying. "Rome would be terribly upset if anything were to happen to us. Just a few grand would go so far."

"I'm afraid I'd have to discuss it with Rome," Elise said in a kind, sweet voice. "We don't share finances."

"You don't?" His mother sounded surprised. "I'd have thought he'd want to share bank accounts with a lovely, well-to-do young thing like you."

As in, it was clear he was with her because she had money. Rage simmering, Rome nearly crushed the coffee cup in his hand.

"Actually," Elise said, and he heard a note of amusement in her voice. "I offered but he's very independent. He likes having his own money and I don't blame him."

"Perhaps you don't know about Rome's terrible, terrible past," his father said, and there was a hard note in his voice. "Be a shame if it got around in this town that there was an ex-con living here."

"It *would* be a shame," Elise said, her voice surprisingly emphatic. "You know what else would be a shame?"

"What's that, dear?" his mother said in her most saccharine voice.

"It would be a shame for me to file a restraining order against the two of you," Elise said. "And I'm sure Rome would file one as well. I'm very familiar with your role in his past, and unless he indicates to me that he wishes otherwise, you're not going to be in our lives. I'm good friends with the law officers in this town, and I'm sure they'd love to come down and ensure that you stay at least a hundred feet away from Rome at all times."

Rome was surprised—and proud—of the steel in Elise's voice.

"Don't you think that's a little extreme?"

"Actually, what would be extreme," Elise continued, ever so boldly, "would be me taking all that money you think I have and hiring the best lawyers I can find. Then, we could reopen Rome's old case and bring it back to court and have you somehow prove that it wasn't your drugs that sent your son to prison. That *would* be extreme. And that is precisely what I will be doing with all my money if you don't get out of my shop—and out of our lives—in the next two minutes."

Goddamn.

His baby was stone cold.

That was so fucking sexy.

Rome couldn't stop grinning as he heard the scrape of chairs when his parents stood up and rushed out of Elise's tiny office. A moment later, they were shocked to see him standing in the doorway of her shop, smiling his fool head off and clutching a cup of coffee.

"Mom, Dad," he drawled. "You were just leaving?"

His parents looked like they always did: a little rough around the edges, dressed in leather, and as if they'd spent the last twenty years partying hard. Which, they had. His mother scowled at him and his father looked as if he would spit nails.

"Hi, baby," Elise said. "Your parents are here. Did you want them to stay?"

"Nope," he told her. "The restraining order sounds pretty good to me."

"You piece of shit," his mother began.

Elise put her phone to her ear. "I'm calling the cops," she told them in a polite voice. "I suggest you leave."

They practically shoved him aside in their haste to leave. As soon as the two motorcycles roared away, Elise put her phone down and bit her lip. "How much of that did you hear?"

"Enough to make my dick hard with how ferocious you were," Rome said, grinning. He moved to her, handed her the coffee cup, and then gave her the longest, most possessive kiss he could. She was panting with need by the time his mouth lifted from hers. "I'm sorry you had to deal with that," he murmured to her, brushing his fingers over her beautiful face tenderly. God, he loved her.

"It was handled," she said breathlessly.

"I'll say. That was magnificent. I'm glad you weren't going to give them money."

She grinned. "Please. I recognize a shakedown when I see one. It was clear they weren't here to see you. They came in and started exclaiming over how nice everything was, and how expensive it must be to start my own business, and how well we must be doing." She rolled her eyes. "It wasn't hard to put two and two together."

"I'm sorry," he said again.

"I'm sorry, too," she told him. "I wasn't sure how you'd feel if I ran them off. I know they're your family."

He shook his head. "They stopped being my family the day I went to prison. I realized that they'd known exactly what was going to happen and hadn't cared." Rome wrapped his arms around Elise's waist. "All the family I need is right here in my arms."

"Well, eventually we might want to expand things," Elise said with a smile. "Eventually. I'm pretty happy with how things are right now, though. Just you and me."

"You and me," he agreed, kissing her again.

Yep. Things were pretty damn perfect, the way Rome saw things. Decent job, decent house, incredible, impressive woman who amazed him at every turn and loved him for all his flaws.

Things were pretty damn good, indeed.

Turn the page for a sneak peek at Jessica Clare's

next Billionaire Boys Club novel

ROMANCING THE BILLIONAIRE

Coming November 2014 from Berkley Books!

Violet DeWitt held the envelope marked 'To Be Opened By My Daughter Upon My Death' and carefully ran her fingers along the edges.

"Well?" The solicitor asked, clearly curious. "Aren't you going to open it?"

But Violet only eyed the calligraphic writing in her father's hand, reminiscent of medieval illuminations. She studied the ornate wax seal. Such an unnecessary thing on a modern envelope. So very much something her father would do.

She carefully placed the envelope in her lap and gave the man across the desk from her a polite smile. "No, I'm not."

The man's broad forehead wrinkled, and he looked disappointed. "But it's your father's last wishes, Ms. DeWitt. Don't you want to honor it?"

"I'm fairly certain I know what it says already, Mr. Penning," Violet said, keeping her voice brisk and cheerful as she tucked the envelope under her hands. "Now, is there anything else involved with my father's estate that you need me for?"

He cast her another puzzled look before turning to the stack of papers on his desk and flipping through them. She understood the look he was giving her. Most people that the solicitor saw were probably grieving or concerned about money they would inherit; Violet was not concerned with any of that.

"Your father was a great man," Mr. Penning commented as he pulled out another piece of paper and peered at it through his bifocals.

"Yes."

"His work was so very respected. I've read three of his books and even though I'm not much of an armchair enthusiast, I couldn't help but be fascinated. What an exciting life the man led. Really, just a great man."

"So I am told."

Now, Mr. Penning looked surprised. "Did you not know your father, Ms. DeWitt? I was under the impression—"

"I knew him," she corrected, wishing the conversation wasn't heading in this direction. Her father's estate solicitor probably didn't want to hear about her workaholic father's long absences, his abandonment of her mother, and his own callous treatment of Violet. Everyone just assumed that the legendary archaeologist Dr. Phineas DeWitt was as lovable and endearing to his family as he was to the documentary cameras. Not the case, Violet thought to herself. Not the case at all. But she put a patient smile on her face and leaned forward, as if interested in what the paper Mr. Penning was clutching read. "His estate?"

"Oh." He adjusted his glasses, refocusing back on the paperwork in front of him. "Yes, actually, I believe that is the last item outstanding. Your father, I'm sorry to say, racked up quite a bit of debt prior to his death. It seemed he was privately funding a few personal projects and ran up several mortgages on his house, which was taken by the bank three weeks prior to his death."

Violet made a sympathetic murmur in her throat. She didn't care about the money and she hadn't expected any. She just wanted to leave.

"Luckily, there was an anonymous third party donor who has paid off all of your father's outstanding debts."

"Very lucky," Violet agreed, her fist clenching. She had an idea who that donor was, curse the man. Now he'd expect her to be grateful and throw herself at him with gratitude. Not in this lifetime.

"I think that's everything, then." The solicitor gave her one last expectant look, his gaze sliding to the envelope in her lap. When she made no move to open it, he sighed and handed her a paper to sign. When she did, he stood and extended his hand.

"Thank you, Mr. Penning. Call me if I can be of any further assistance," she told him, shook his hand, and left the law office, unopened envelope clutched in hand.

When she got out to her car, Violet started the engine, tossed the envelope into the passenger seat, and then paused. She rubbed her forehead, willing the headache behind her eyes to go away. Envelopes were an old favorite of the late Phineas DeWitt. When she was eight, her father had given her an envelope for her birthday. Inside was a clue that, if followed, would lead her to a trail of additional clues. She'd been so excited at the time, and after a series of envelope clues, each one more complex than the last, she arrived at her present.

It was a copy of *The Encyclopedia on the Study of Ancient Hieroglyphics*. Used. The inscription inside said "To Phineas, thanks for being a great teacher."

Granted, it was an interesting book, but her eight-year-old self had wanted a Barbie.

Phineas paid no attention to Violet's other birthdays until she turned sixteen. She'd received another envelope in the mail and had been excited despite initial trepidation. At the end of the chase, however, her present had been a copy of one of her father's student's doctoral thesis on Minoan frescoes. He'd tacked a note onto it that read: *Pay attention, Violet. This is the sort of thing you'll need to write if you want to work for your father!*

Again, not something she'd particularly wanted. But Phineas DeWitt believed in two things—knowledge and adventure. All else was foolishness.

She'd tossed the photocopied thesis into the garbage and tried to forget about her father's terrible ideas of birthday gifts. When she was eighteen, she fell for it one more time, and was just as disappointed. The end of this envelope chase led to an ugly copper ring that turned her finger green and looked like something out of a tourist shop. That was after a week of frantic searching to find what her father had left her, hoping against hope that he'd remembered what she liked, her fears and hopes and dreams, and that he'd give her a present that showed he really, truly did understand his daughter.

Not so much. Phineas DeWitt gave presents, but in the end, it was still all about him. Just like everything else with her father's games, she knew that her initial excitement would lead to inevitable disappointment. The envelopes and the challenge were to mask the fact that Phineas put no thought or effort into her presents . . . just like he'd put no thought or effort into being her father.

And she knew what—and who—this last envelope game would lead to without even having to look.

Oh, Father. I know what you're up to. This is just one more little game, and I've no intention of playing this time. Nothing you say or do can make me want to talk to Jonathan Lyons ever again.

Violet didn't think she was a hard, unforgiving type. She was nice, darn it, and understanding. But when a guy gave you pretty words, got you pregnant, and abandoned you?

That wasn't so easy to forgive, or forget, no matter what her father wanted.

Some things you just couldn't let go.

"This is her classroom," Principal Esparza said to Jonathan, straightening her suit jacket. "You're sure Ms. DeWitt is expecting you? She didn't indicate to me that she was anticipating a visitor, and this is a closed campus." The principal sounded disapproving, but she hadn't kicked him out. It was amazing what you could do if you showed up in an expensive suit with your personal bodyguard. Of course, being famous—or infamous—in the right circles certainly helped.

"She's expecting me," Jonathan said, adjusting the front of his suit jacket. "Perhaps she simply forgot to notify you. Violet is an old family friend of the Lyons."

"Well," Esparza said with a happy smile. "I'm a big fan of your cars, though I certainly can't afford one!" She gave a girlish giggle at odds with her advanced age.

He gave her his best rakish grin, playing the part of the flirty playboy billionaire. "Shall I have one sent to you?"

"Oh no," Esparza giggled again, and tucked a gray-streaked lock of hair into her bun. "It's against school policy. But you're sweet to offer." She moved forward and knocked on the cheerfully lettered "Fifth Grade Social Studies" door.

Jonathan swallowed the knot in his throat and shifted on his feet. It was pathetic to be nervous. He'd rappelled off of cliffs in Nepal, snorkeled with sharks, been in god-knew how many cave-ins, and once ended up on a ship attacked by Somali pirates. He'd never been nervous in all those situations. Adrenaline-fueled? Absolutely. Nervous? Hell no.

But standing outside of a fifth-grade classroom, waiting for a woman that he hadn't seen in ten years? His palms were sweating.

What would Violet look like? His memories of her were

of certain things instead of the entire package. He remembered a short girl, no higher than his shoulder, with long, dark braids streaked with wild pink, a wicked smile, a lean figure, and a tramp stamp that said "Carpe Diem" across her lower back. He remembered the way she smelled when he sniffed her skin, the way she made soft little gasping cries when she came, and the tight suction of her mouth on his dick.

Just thinking about her brought a wealth of memories and regrets surging back to the forefront. There wasn't a day that went by that he didn't regret that last night, the last hour, last minute they'd spent together.

She'd wanted to get married. Wanted their little summer fling in Greece to turn into something real. She'd wanted to return to the States and settle down. And Jonathan had been nineteen, taking a semester off of college, and dazzled by the dynamic Dr. Phineas DeWitt, who seemed daily on the verge of yet another important archaeological discovery. They'd both been participating in DeWitt's latest dig for the summer, and it was the most exciting thing Jonathan had ever done.

But Violet didn't want a life of archaeological digs and adventure. She stressed that she wanted to return to the States and start a family, all at the tender age of nineteen. She'd suggested that last night that he give it all up and settle down with her.

Jonathan had laughed in her face, being a young asshole full of himself and full of life.

She'd slapped him, burst into tears, and stormed out of his life.

That was the night he'd lost her, and it didn't take long before he regretted his cruelty. Greece without Violet at his side just wasn't the same. In fact, nothing was the same. He began to miss her with the same intensity that he'd loved the archaeological expedition, and confessed to Professor DeWitt, whom he viewed as a mentor and friend, of his longing. He was thinking about going after Violet. Apologizing. Trying again.

But her father told him it was a mistake. Violet had been stateside for all of a week before she'd shacked up with an ex-boyfriend. And he'd handed Jonathan a stack of field notes. Devastated, Jonathan threw himself into work.

A few weeks later, Dr. DeWitt had told a moping, despondent Jonathan that Violet had married and it was time to move on. Did Jonathan want to accompany him to an unearthing of a new tomb in the Valley of the Kings?

He did. He had. And he'd sunk himself into adventuring, archaeology, extreme sports—whatever it took to distract himself from the fact that he'd fucked up and lost Violet.

It didn't work, of course. Ten years later, he was still mooning about Violet DeWitt and how different things would have been if he'd settled down with her after all.

Footsteps clicked on the linoleum flooring of the school, bringing him back to the present. An endless moment later, the door opened. Jonathan lifted his head.

There she was, standing next to the heavy wooden classroom door, a faint, disappointed frown on her face, as if she'd expected to see him but had hoped otherwise.

Just like that, his palms began to sweat again.

Violet was different than he remembered. That was to be expected—he wasn't the skinny nineteen-year-old boy with questionable skin and a lack of chest hair anymore. If anything, though, Violet had grown more beautiful than the last time he'd seen her . . . and more sedate. Gone was the wild, devilish look he'd loved so much, and the waist-length, streaked braids. This Violet was still tiny, but her lean figure had softened to lush curves, outlined by a demure black skirt and cream-colored blouse with a bow at the neck and long, billowing sleeves. She had plain black kitten heels on, no jewelry, and the long hair he remembered was cut into an asymmetrical black bob that was tucked behind one small ear and swung at her chin.

This was his wild Violet? It looked like her . . . and yet, not. Married life suited her, that was clear. She was as gorgeous as when he'd last seen her, and the thought of another man in her life made him ache inside. It should have been him at her side, but he'd been a selfish ass.

"Jonathan," she said in a flat, polite voice. "What a lovely surprise." Her voice indicated that it was neither a surprise nor lovely.

"Just a reminder, Ms. DeWitt, that visitors need to be checked in to the office in the future," Principal Esparza said, casting another friendly smile in Jonathan's direction.

"Of course. My apologies," Violet said, ever so polite. "Won't you come in, Jonathan?" She gestured at the classroom.

He gave a nod to his security guard, who turned to stand at the doorway in an alert pose. Not that Jonathan was expecting trouble at Neptune Middle School, of course, but Jonathan had found out a long time ago that looking important got you as many places (and sometimes more) than greasing palms did.

Violet's little heels clacked as she returned to sit at her oversized desk at the front of the room. He noticed she didn't offer him a seat, and eyed the ancient student desks lined up in neat rows. Her classroom was colorful and bold, pictures of exotic locations and maps of the world covering the walls, along with charts and flags. Despite the surroundings, the school was old and dark, the wood paneling warped with age, and he was pretty sure the tiles in the ceiling were going to fall in due to water damage."Nice place. Where are your students?"

"It's three thirty," she said in that too-smooth, too-controlled voice. "Class is over. This is detention."

He turned to look over at her, grinning in what he hoped was his best flirty smile that had never failed to melt her in the past. "Guess I've been naughty."

Violet clasped her hands on her desk. "Mr. Lyons, I think we both know why you're here."

"Jonathan."

"Mr. Lyons," she echoed, her even gaze almost daring him to contradict her. She stared him down for a moment longer, then reached into her desk drawer and pulled out an envelope and held it out to him.

He approached, taking the envelope from her, noting that the seal on the back was still intact. "You didn't open it?"

"I'm quite familiar with my father's little games. I don't need to open it to know I'm not going to play along. This is all a ploy of his for some purpose I haven't yet figured out, nor do I care to."

Jonathan wondered at her icy demeanor. Violet was being downright chilly to him, and he hadn't done a thing. "You still holding a grudge from the past?"

Her eyes narrowed.

That would be a yes. "Look, Violet. I was a kid, you were a kid. We were young. We did stupid things, made stupid mistakes. Can't we get past that and work together?"

"Work together? On what?"

He pulled his own envelope out of an inner pocket in his Fioravanti suit jacket and held it out to her.

She simply gazed at him, arching an eyebrow.

All right, he was going to have to do this the hard way. He flicked the envelope open, pulled out the paper inside, and read it to her. The first line was the middle school's address. The second line said "My daughter Violet holds the key." He looked over at her to see her reaction to the cryptic statement.

Violet rolled her eyes.

"Well? What do you think?"

"I think my late father missed his calling as a dramatic actor," Violet said. "If there's a key to be found, it's probably in my envelope. You can have it." She nudged it toward him and took a stack of papers off the corner of her desk and pulled them in front of her. Then, she bent over and picked up a red pen and began to grade, as if he wasn't there.

Jonathan stared at her for what seemed like forever. She truly wasn't curious? She didn't want to know? "Aren't you the slightest bit interested in what your father was hiding?"

"No." She didn't look up, just kept on grading.

"Would you be surprised to hear that upon his death, not only were all his journals missing, but there was rumor that he'd stolen something important from his latest dig?"

"I would not be surprised," Violet said, still not looking up. She scribbled a note in red on a test, flipped it over, and went on to the next one. "If it could create drama and tension for my father, he'd do it."

"That was my dig," Jonathan said. "Your father stole from me."

She ignored him.

"Don't you care?"

At that, Violet looked up and gave him another cool look. "I'm told that upon my father's death, an anonymous third party settled all of his debts and that they were not to be a concern of mine. I was also told to be thankful." Her mouth puckered on the last part, as if she'd bit down on a lemon.

So she knew he'd handled things and wasn't pleased. It didn't deter him. "I want that journal. More than that, I want what was at that dig site."

She looked back down at her test again, and nudged the envelope with her other hand, easing it toward him a bit more.

"Goddamn it, Violet. Talk to me, here."

"I am talking," she said in that same even voice.

"I want to work together on this. I need those journals and what he stole."

"I told you. You're free to take my envelope."

Irritated, he snatched it off her desk and tore it open.

There was nothing but a symbol inside, one completely unfamiliar to him. "I don't know what this means."

"That's really not my problem." She smiled faintly at him and pointed at the door, as if to suggest he should leave.

It was clear that she was done with him, just as it was clear to Jonathan that if he was going to get anywhere, he'd need Violet's help. Violet would have access to information about the late Dr. DeWitt that he wouldn't. Memories. Insider knowledge.

"I'll pay you a million dollars if you'll assist me with this."

She looked up from her paperwork, her eyes going wide with surprise. "You're serious?"

"I'm a billionaire now, or didn't you hear? I took over the Lyons empire."

"Hooray for you." Her face was impassive.

"So. One million dollars for you to agree to be my employee until we figure out whatever this means." He waved the letter in the air.

Violet thumped her pen on the papers, as if thinking. Then, she shook her head. "No."

"You're a schoolteacher. I'm sure you need the money."

"I am a schoolteacher," she agreed. "And it's the middle of the school year. I can't leave. That would put the school district under terrible distress."

"It's an adventure," he cajoled, remembering how her eyes used to light up at the thought of something like that. His Violet used to love a thrill as much as he did.

This time, the gaze she turned to him was steely. "No, Jonathan."

"Why?" He clenched his fist around the paper, dangerously close to losing his temper and storming out of the room.

"I just don't happen to care about my father's last little ploy to get the two of us together."

He inhaled sharply. So she thought her father was

deliberately throwing her at him? No wonder she thought he was the worst kind of scum, here to hit on a married woman. "Look, Violet, while it's great to see you—"

"I'm afraid I don't share the sentiment—"

"—I'm not here to fuck with your marriage," he continued, heart aching. He wasn't sure what he'd hoped for from her. Maybe a bit of affection? Wistfulness over old memories? Wishing over what once might have been between the two of them? It was clear that whatever had been was dead and buried, and Violet didn't want anything to do with him. She was married, anyhow. No sense in mooning after a happily married woman. "I just want an old friend to help me with something important to me, all right?"

She looked up. Tilted her head, frowning slightly, and tucked a lock of black hair behind her ear in a motion that brought back a wealth of memories. He remembered that thoughtful expression, and desire and longing came flooding back through Jonathan.

Ten years, and he was still insanely in love with Violet DeWitt, ice princess act and all. No wonder she wanted to scare him off.

"What did you say?"

He toyed with the button in the front of his suit jacket, thankful that it was buttoned up so it would hide any hint of an erection he'd just gotten at that small gesture of hers. "I said, I'm not here to mess up your life, all right?"

She got to her feet, smoothed her skirt, and then came around to his side. She extended her hand. "Let me see that letter."

Finally, he was getting somewhere. Eager, Jonathan held both of them out to her.

Violet skimmed them, and then cast him another puzzled look.

"What is it?" he asked.

"I'm not married."

Now it was his turn to be confused. "Excuse me?"

"I said, I'm not married. Wherever did you get that idea?"

The blood began to roar in Jonathan's ears. He watched, entranced, as she tucked a lock of hair behind her other ear. It made both of her ears stick out—which he remembered that she hated—but he found adorable. His Violet.

He'd given up on her so long ago because she'd married someone only days after she'd left his bed and regretted it ever since.

"You," he coughed, irritated at how hoarse his voice was. He felt like all the blood had rushed to his face . . . well, that and one other extremity. Clearing his throat, he tried again. "You called off the wedding?"

Again, she gave him a curious look. "What wedding?"

"Your father said that when you left . . . you married someone else. Right away."

She raised both eyebrows at him, as if to say 'really'? "And you believed him? Jonathan, your family was funding all of his digs at the time. He'd have told you cows flew on the moon if it was what it took to keep you at his side."

Well, goddamn it all. He'd known that Phineas was a sly old dog, but he'd had no idea he'd been taken for a ride on something so important. "You're . . . not married?"

"I don't see why it's any of your business—" She yelped as he grabbed her hand in his. It was just as soft as he remembered, her nails bitten short. It was a habit she'd never been able to break. There was no ring on any finger.

He'd been lied to.

He should have been furious. Filled with anger and hate and loathing that ten years had been wasted, ten years that had kept them apart.

But Jonathan didn't see any of that. All he saw was Violet—his Violet—standing so close to him that he could reach out and touch her again for the first time in so long that his entire being ached. Violet, with her hand in his. Never mind that she was trying to draw it out of his grasp.

His Violet was here, in front of him, and she'd never

married. He'd be damned if he'd let opportunity slip through his fingers again.

Grabbing her shoulders, Jonathan turned her toward him fully, leaned down, and pressed his mouth firmly to hers. He kissed her with all the fierce passion and longing of ten long, lonely years. She wasn't responding, but that was okay. He had enough need and love for both of them. She'd come around. He'd show her just how much he missed her. He'd never let her go again. He—

Violet's knee went between his legs, and connected with his groin.

Jessica Clare also writes as Jill Myles and Jessica Sims. As Jessica Clare, she writes sexy contemporary romances, including the Bluebonnet series and the Billionaire Boys Club series. You can contact her at jillmyles.com or at twitter.com/jillmyles, facebook.com/jillmyles, or pinterest .com/jillmyles.

She's pushing all the right buttons...

NEW YORK TIMES BESTSELLING AUTHOR
JESSSICA CLARE

THE *Expert's* GUIDE TO DRIVING A *Man Wild*

A Bluebonnet Novel

When Grant's marriage-minded mother comes to town, his free-spirited employee Brenna pretends to be his girlfriend. She's hoping to drive her strict boss crazy every chance she gets. But she wasn't counting on sharing a bed with Grant—or liking it.

Praise for the novels of Jessica Clare

"Not to be missed."
—*RT Book Reviews*

"Sexy and funny."
—*USA Today*

jessica-clare.com
penguin.com

M1415T0114